THE THEATRE OF

Nicholas Grene is Emeritus Professor of English Literature at Trinity College Dublin and a member of the Royal Irish Academy. He has published widely on Shakespeare and on Irish literature. His books include *The Politics of Irish Drama* (1999), *Shakespeare's Serial History Plays* (2002), *Yeats's Poetic Codes* (2008) and *Home on the Stage* (2014). With Chris Morash he is the co-editor of the *Oxford Handbook of Modern Irish Theatre* (2016).

THE THEATRE OF TOM MURPHY

PLAYWRIGHT ADVENTURER

Nicholas Grene

Series Editors: Patrick Lonergan and Kevin J. Wetmore, Jr.

methuen | drama

LONDON • NEW YORK • OXFORD • NEW DELHI • SYDNEY

METHUEN DRAMA
Bloomsbury Publishing Plc
50 Bedford Square, London, WC1B 3DP, UK
1385 Broadway, New York, NY 10018, USA

BLOOMSBURY, METHUEN DRAMA and the Methuen Drama logo are trademarks
of Bloomsbury Publishing Plc

First published in Great Britain 2017
This paperback edition first published 2019

Cover design: Adriana Brioso
Cover image: Catherine Walker and Declan Conlon in the 2012 Abbey Theatre
production of Tom Murphy's *The House*. (Photo by Anthony Woods)

A catalogue record for this book is available from the British Library.

A catalog record for this book is available from the Library of Congress.

ISBN: HB: 978-1-4725-6811-3
PB: 978-1-4725-6810-6
ePDF: 978-1-4725-6813-7
eBook: 978-1-4725-6812-0

Series: Critical Companions

Typeset by Deanta Global Publishing Services, Chennai, India
Printed and bound in Great Britain

To find out more about our authors and books visit www.bloomsbury.com.
Here you will find extracts, author interviews, details of forthcoming events
and the option to sign up for our newsletters.

For Gregory

CONTENTS

Contents

ACKNOWLEDGEMENTS

I wrote this book in 2015–16, the first year of my retirement from Trinity College Dublin. But before that I had several opportunities to teach Murphy's plays in the School of English, most recently in a specialist course on Friel and Murphy in 2014. I am grateful to the students of that course for help in forming the ideas expressed in this book. Some of the material used in Chapter 3 was previously published in *Hungry Words: Images of Famine in the Irish Canon*, George Cusack and Sarah Gross (eds) (Dublin; Portland, OR: Irish Academic Press, 2006). I benefited from the help of Barry Houlihan in the Special Collections of the Hardiman Library, NUI, Galway, Ireland, in accessing the digitized archives of the Abbey and Druid Theatre Company, and from all the staff of the Manuscripts Department of Trinity College Dublin Library, which holds the major collection of Murphy's papers. Patrick Lonergan, the co-editor of the series in which this book is published, was very supportive with an encouraging response to drafts of the early chapters. I appreciate also the positive attitude to the project of Mark Dudgeon and Susan Furber at Bloomsbury Methuen Drama, and the kindness and efficiency of Alexandra Cann, Murphy's literary agent, in arranging permissions.

All quotations from the published plays of Tom Murphy are reproduced by kind permission of the author and of the publisher, Bloomsbury Methuen Drama. All quotations from the unpublished material in the collection of the Murphy papers in the Library of Trinity College Dublin are by kind permission of the author.

I am very grateful to Lucy McDiarmid and Alexandra Poulain for contributing their fine essays to this book. My greatest debt of gratitude is to Tom Murphy himself not only for his generosity and patience in granting me an extended series of interviews but for creating the magnificent plays that are the book's subject.

The book is dedicated to my brother Gregory who shares a love of the theatre, which we both gained from our father before us.

Nicholas Grene
Trinity College Dublin
Ireland
January 2017 and June 2018

THE WORKS OF TOM MURPHY

Plays (dates given are those of first professional production)
A Whistle in the Dark (Theatre Royal, Stratford East, 1961)
Famine (Peacock Theatre, 1968)
The Orphans (Gate Theatre, 1968)
A Crucial Week in the Life of a Grocer's Assistant (Abbey Theatre, 1969)
The Morning After Optimism (Abbey Theatre, 1971)
The White House (Abbey Theatre, 1972)
On the Outside/On the Inside (Project Arts Centre/Abbey Theatre, 1974)
The Sanctuary Lamp (Abbey Theatre, 1975)
The J. Arthur Maginnis Story (Pavilion Theatre, Dun Laoghaire, 1976)
The Blue Macushla (Abbey Theatre, 1980)
The Gigli Concert (Abbey Theatre, 1983)
Conversations on a Homecoming (Druid Theatre, 1985)
Bailegangaire (Druid Theatre, 1985)
A Thief of a Christmas (Abbey Theatre, 1985)
Too Late for Logic (Abbey Theatre, 1989)
The Patriot Game (Peacock Theatre, 1991)
The Wake (Abbey Theatre, 1998)
The House (Abbey Theatre, 2000)
Alice Trilogy (Royal Court, 2005)
Brigit (Town Hall Theatre, Galway, 2014)

Adaptations
The Vicar of Wakefield (Abbey Theatre, 1974), subsequently revised as *She Stoops to Folly* (South Coast Repertory Theatre, California, 1995)
Epitaph under Ether (Abbey Theatre, 1979)
The Informer (Olympia Theatre, 1981)
She Stoops to Conquer (Abbey Theatre, 1982)
The Drunkard (Town Hall Theatre, Galway, 2003)
The Cherry Orchard (Abbey Theatre, 2004)
The Last Days of a Reluctant Tyrant (Abbey Theatre, 2009)

Television Plays

The Fly Sham (BBC Television, 1963)

Veronica (BBC Television, 1963)

A Crucial Week in the Life of a Grocer's Assistant (BBC Television, 1967)

Snakes and Reptiles (BBC 2, 1968)

A Young Man in Trouble (Thames Television, 1970)

Brigit (RTÉ, 1987)

Novel

The Seduction of Morality (Little Brown, 1994)

PREFACE

In April 1984 I went to the revival of *The Gigli Concert* in the Abbey, my first ever experience of Tom Murphy in the theatre. I had missed its premiere the previous autumn, and indeed all of his earlier work staged in Ireland, having been out of the country from 1969 to 1979. I had struggled with reading the texts of plays such as *The Morning after Optimism* and *The Sanctuary Lamp*. *Gigli* thus came as a complete revelation: the audacity of the conception of the man who wants to sing like Gigli, the astonishing performance of Godfrey Quigley in the part, the counterpointing of the music and the action, the miraculous tour de force when Tom Hickey as JPW King 'sang' at the end. It was for me one of those transformative nights in the theatre. And there were more of them to come shortly after: the pitch perfect ensemble playing of the Druid Theatre company in *Conversations on a Homecoming* in 1985, Siobhán McKenna's amazing Mommo in *Bailegangaire* when the Druid production came to Dublin in 1986. From then on, I made it my business to see all of Murphy's new plays and get to any revivals I could find. I wrote essays on his work, organized a small symposium to accompany the 2001 Abbey season of his plays and became a devoted acolyte.

What impressed me most about those 1980s plays and has held my admiration ever since is Murphy's daring theatrical imagination. He has often made the distinction between what he calls the 'formula' method of playmaking and the 'adventure' method.[1] The formula approach involves figuring the angles, thinking of the market and building a well-shaped vehicle for the stage with sure-fire dialogue and canny theatrical effects. The adventure method, which he himself favours, requires the playwright to follow wherever the initial notion takes him or her. It is a high-risk strategy and in Murphy's case the risks have not always paid off – there have been some disastrous failures – but such is the adventure of the theatre for Murphy.

Though there has been important critical work on Murphy's drama – Fintan O'Toole's pioneering 1987 study *The Politics of Magic* with its updated edition in 1994, Alexandra Poulain's fine monograph *Homo Famelicus: Le théâtre de Tom Murphy* (2008), which unfortunately has not yet been translated into English, Christopher Murray's 2010 edited collection of essays,

Alive in Time – his plays have been relatively understudied and undervalued. Having admired and enjoyed his work for so long, I was delighted to have the opportunity to devote a full book to him in this Bloomsbury series. A key resource in the project has been the rich archive of Murphy's papers in the Trinity College Dublin Library acquired in 2000. This enables one to track the genesis of individual plays, to see how they were received at first production and how often they have been changed in subsequent stagings, as well as understanding vital contexts from the many press interviews he has given over the years. The interpretations offered in this book are informed throughout by this archival material, and I acknowledge gratefully the help of the librarians in the Trinity College Dublin Department of Manuscripts in making it available to me.

Murphy had a career of over fifty-five years in the theatre; he produced some twenty original plays, half a dozen adaptations and a number of television scripts. He revised each play every time it was revived, often making quite radical changes, so that almost all his texts exist in multiple published versions. For *The Theatre of Tom Murphy*, I decided not to adopt a chronological approach, following through his development play by play. Instead, after a first chapter that offers an introductory overview, I have grouped the plays in two sequences: the first is concerned with those works that represent Irish history and society, the second with those that use less obviously mimetic forms of myth, fable and folklore. In each chapter, there is a major focus text, considered in the context of other comparable or associated works. Given the range of Murphy's original plays, I have decided reluctantly not to try to deal with his adaptations.

Chapter 1, starting from two major retrospective revivals of Murphy's work in 2001 and 2012, looks back over his career as a whole, his background, his period of working in London, his association with the Abbey and Druid Theatres and his major characteristics as a playwright. His first breakthrough success, *A Whistle in the Dark* is analysed in Chapter 2 in relation to the diptych, *On the Outside/On the Inside* and *A Crucial Week in the Life of a Grocer's Assistant*, all of them concerned with the crises of masculinity in an emigrant culture. Chapter 3 is centred on *Famine*, the epic dramatization of the most terrible event in Irish history, but compares the issues of staging history in that play to *The Patriot Game*, Murphy's representation of the Easter Rising. *Conversations on a Homecoming* is the main text in Chapter 4, a cut-back version of the earlier *The White House*, which had attempted less successfully to contrast the JFK-inspired optimism of 1960s Ireland with the deflated disillusionment of the 1970s; the theme of Irish imitations of America is considered also in this chapter as represented in *The Blue Macushla*, one of Murphy's most polemically political plays. The obsession with property and the associated idea of home are the concerns of Chapter 5, focused on *The House* but comparing it also with *The Wake*. Chapter 6 provides a reading of *The Sanctuary Lamp*, with its study of the extremes of alienation, and the comparable dystopic fairy tale *The Morning after Optimism*. Music has been crucially important throughout Murphy's work, and Chapter 7 is concentrated on the operatic tour de force *The Gigli Concert* set beside the similar *Too Late for Logic*. Chapter 8 looks at how Murphy developed techniques to represent the lives of women in the storytelling masterpiece *Bailegangaire*, its satellite texts *A Thief of a Christmas* and *Brigit*, as well as the desolate *Alice Trilogy*.

It is often alleged that Murphy's plays, so often revived and so acclaimed in Ireland, do not 'travel' well, are not easily accessible to non-Irish audiences. The two essays in Chapter 9 represent 'Critical Perspectives' by scholars from the United States and from France which may help to address that issue. Both essays concentrate on *Bailegangaire* and their very different approaches show just what a rich text it is and how little limited to its original Irish context: McDiarmid's analysis fruitfully applies the frame theory of the sociologist Ervin Goffman to *Bailegangaire* and *A Thief of a Christmas*, while Poulain shows how well *Bailegangaire* illustrates the philosopher Jean-François Lyotard's concept of 'survival'. I owe most of all to the dramatist himself who gave so generously of his time and patience, particularly in a series of extended interviews, an edited version of which also appears in Chapter 9. Tom Murphy died in May 2018, some eight months after this book was first published. I was delighted that he was able to read it and expressed his satisfaction with it. My hope is that, in the years to come, it will contribute to a deeper understanding and appreciation of a great playwright.

CHAPTER 1
RETROSPECTIVES

Tom Murphy has had two major theatrical retrospectives so far in the twenty-first century. In 2001 the Abbey staged a season of six of his plays: *A Whistle in the Dark* (1961), *The Morning After Optimism* (1971), *The Sanctuary Lamp* (1975), *The Gigli Concert* (1983) and *Bailegangaire* (1985) in full productions and *Famine* (1968) in a rehearsed reading.[1] In 2012 Druid mounted DruidMurphy, an ensemble production of three of his plays, *Conversations on a Homecoming* (1985), *Whistle* and *Famine*, conceived as a sequence which could be seen together in a single marathon sitting. It had originally been planned to include *The House* (2000) also in the programme.[2] That proved impracticable, but the play was in fact revived by the Abbey in June 2012 at the same time as DruidMurphy, and as a result, audiences were able to see all four plays within a single period. DruidMurphy was designed around the theme of emigration and was highly successful both in Ireland when it toured Britain and the United States, two of the countries with the largest populations of the diasporic Irish. Together with *The House*, the three DruidMurphy plays could be read as Murphy's deepest exploration of Irish social reality, the cultural and psychological deformations going back to the nineteenth-century trauma of famine. Local communities such as that dramatized in *Famine*, devastated by hunger and the enforced need to leave Ireland, had their successors in the alienated mentalities of the 1950s guest workers home for the annual debauch of the summer holidays in *The House*, the cult of violence of the 1960s displaced Irish in Britain so graphically staged in *Whistle* and in *Conversations* the disillusionment of the 1970s both for those who left and for those who stayed at home. The group of plays as a whole could be used to validate Fintan O'Toole's influential view of Murphy's drama constituting 'a kind of inner history of Ireland'.[3]

The 2001 Abbey season was not planned with any such thematic design in mind but simply as a tribute to the playwright showcasing the range of his work. It included, though, some of the visionary plays that reflected another aspect of Murphy. *The Morning After Optimism*, for instance, is a dystopian fairy tale that has no particular bearing on Ireland; the pairing of the two couples, James and Rosie, pimp and prostitute, against their wish-fulfilment counterparts, Edmund and Anastasia, figured an innocence and experience clash freed from the specificities of a local setting. *The Sanctuary Lamp*, no doubt, was expressive of an Irish anticlerical reaction voiced most violently and controversially by the juggler Francisco. But he is the one Irish character in a play set non-committally in a 'church in a city' and the other two characters who search for salvation in a Godless world are English.[4] *The Gigli Concert*, like *The Sanctuary Lamp*, is played out in a sealed-off space, in this case the consulting room cum living quarters of the quack pyschotherapist JPW King who must deal with the Irish Man's mad aspiration to sing like Gigli. And if the confined stage of *Bailegangaire* is the conventional rural cottage of so many previous Irish plays, the drama of the senile Mommo constantly retelling her never-finished tale of the laughing contest and her relationship with her adult granddaughters Mary and Dolly are in a theatrical mode remote from representational realism. Such plays use fantasy, myth and folklore to dramatize existential states that are only incidentally local and specific.

These two contrasting groups, the plays grounded in Irish social realities past and present, and those which transcend any such limits in their imaginative conceptions, do represent two main strands in Murphy's work. As such, they provide the structuring principle of the present book, dealing in turn with the principal plays in the two modes. However, no selective retrospect can do justice to the variety of Murphy's experimentation, the process of trial and error by which he has arrived at his realized drama. In a much-quoted 1980 tribute, Brian Friel said: 'The most distinctive, the most restless, the most obsessive imagination at work in the Irish theatre today is Tom Murphy's.'[5] It is a telling accolade from a writer who was so often paired with Murphy as the two outstanding Irish dramatists of their generation and whose work stands in a striking contrast with each other. Though Friel was innovative as a theatre maker, he never swung as wildly from one form and style to another as Murphy: naturalistic tragedy in *Whistle*, Brechtian history play in *Famine*, Dublin pastiche film noir in *The Blue Macushla* (1980) – a restless imagination indeed. Almost all Friel's plays are set in the one fictional Donegal small town, his hallmark Ballybeg. Murphy's work ranges from Ireland to England to nowhere in particular. Friel was an accomplished short story writer before he became a playwright, and his plays are finished literary texts which he insisted should be played exactly as he wrote them. With the exception of a single novel, *The Seduction of Morality* (1994), significantly soon adapted for the stage as *The Wake* (1998), Murphy has written dramatic work only for theatre, film or television.[6] His texts are constantly revised, often radically recast, in rehearsal and in revivals, as he searches for exactly the right theatrical realization. Friel had his failures as well as his successes, but his career had nothing equivalent to Murphy's sometimes spectacular oscillation between theatrical triumph and disaster. In the rest of this chapter, I want to take stock of Murphy's development over the more than fifty years he has been working in the theatre by way of analysing the character of his imagination and the complexity of his achievement.

Growing up in Tuam

The cathedral town of Tuam, second largest in County Galway, would have been relatively small with a population of less than 5,000 when Tom Murphy was born there in 1935, the youngest of ten children in his family. But it was big enough for the town dwellers to differentiate themselves sharply from the people of the neighbouring countryside. It is an important distinction dramatized in Murphy's first play, *On the Outside* (co-written with Noel O'Donoghue), in which two lads from the town unsuccessfully seek entry to the country dancehall. The playwright's carpenter father had to go to England during the war years in search of work and remained there for almost twenty years apart from annual holiday visits home. After ten children, Murphy discreetly implied, his mother would not have been unhappy to be without a husband. Over time, all of his older siblings left home and he found himself alone with his mother, who 'claimed' him, as he put it, as her own: 'It was a common enough thing, I would presume, the affection and the love, bypassing the husband onto a son' (Interview, p. 173).[7] It was a 'claustrophobic' relationship and one may guess that the anxious over-possessive Mother of the adult son John Joe in *A Crucial Week in the Life of a Grocer's Assistant* (1969) is a fictionalized version of Winifred Murphy, with the all but catatonic Father standing in for the absent Jack Murphy. Murphy recalled that his mother 'was constantly comparing me with other people – I grew up thinking I was a Martian or ET'.[8]

Many writers, growing up in working-class families that shared none of their interests, must have had this sense of anomalousness. What must be considered somewhat unusual in Murphy is the track he took towards a career as a writer. He has described graphically the brutality of the Christian Brothers regime under which he suffered at school: 'Out of a class of forty-two, thirty or thirty-five would be waiting around the room at ten o'clock – school started at half nine – waiting to be beaten!' (Interview, p. 174). As a relatively bright student, and a very pious one – an altar boy who managed to serve Mass every morning through a whole Lent, who had an early desire to be a mission priest – he escaped a good deal of the corporal punishment. But nonetheless, when he managed just about to pass his Intermediate Certificate, along with no more than four others from the class of forty, he chose to move to the lay Technical School.⁹ This was regarded as a decision to renounce the chance of further academic education and a move up into the professional classes in favour of vocational training. And indeed, after two years at the Tech, Murphy started an apprenticeship as a fitter-welder in the sugar factory, which was at that point one of the largest employers in Tuam.

He often referred to this as his university and remembered fondly the spirit of camaraderie with his factory workmates. But significantly in *The Fly Sham*, Murphy's first television play, screened by the BBC in 1963, the central character is an apprentice who has dropped down a class as the son of a bank manager father jailed for embezzlement, and who signally fails in his efforts to ingratiate himself with his resentful working-class fellows.¹⁰ During this time, Murphy began to study on his own and won a state scholarship to train as a metalwork teacher in Dublin. And therefore he found himself, after all, having moved that crucial class up to the position of teacher of religion, maths and metalwork in Mountbellew, a town some 30 miles from Tuam. It was a milieu which was to provide him with another of his television plays, *A Young Man in Trouble* (1970), reworked into *On the Inside* (1974), stage companion piece to *On the Outside*, in which the situation of the relatively affluent schoolteachers inside the dancehall is revealed to be not that much more enviable than those excluded without.¹¹

Murphy's real path to a career as a writer came through amateur drama. As an active member of the Tuam Theatre Guild, he was exposed to a wide range of plays that were to have a major impact on him as a dramatist. He had already joined the Guild as a teenager, playing Dan Burke, the crotchedy old sheep farmer in Synge's *The Shadow of the Glen*, at sixteen, and was involved again when teaching at Mountbellew. In the very active amateur drama movement in Ireland, Tuam Theatre Guild was one of the outstanding companies at the time, led by Father P. V. O'Brien. This was a period at which the Catholic Church was virtually all powerful in Irish society, and the bitterness of Murphy's disillusionment with it fed the rage that animates *Whistle in the Dark*, *A Crucial Week* and *The Sanctuary Lamp*.

But Murphy's memories of Father O'Brien are a reminder of the positive potential of individual priests' leadership as well. The Tuam Theatre Guild had a very adventurous repertoire for its time. Besides the more likely Synge and O'Casey, they staged plays by the then fashionable Italian playwright Ugo Betti, by Christopher Fry and John Drinkwater. Murphy remembers conversations with O'Brien about Tennessee Williams – *Camino Real, A Streetcar Named Desire* and *Cat on a Hot Tin Roof* – fairly remarkable given that this was exactly the time (1957) when the Pike Theatre in Dublin was shut down over its production of *The Rose Tattoo*.[12] *Streetcar*, in particular, was very important to him.

> We were greedy for some sort of breath of fresh air. I found this copy of *Streetcar Named Desire* and read it. … There seemed to be such energy in Williams' writing, that great sense of life force was there. One *had* Joxer and Captain Boyle and Christy Mahon and The Widow Quin. But Stanley was a modern man, a great ignorant modern man and one responded to him straight away.[13]

Murphy remembers reading Chekhov, Lorca (who brought him back to Synge) and Arthur Miller (whose moralizing he disliked) at this time, but the energy of Williams was that breath of fresh air he felt he wanted. And his earliest plays can be seen as attempts to render the ignorant modern men of his own time and place. Famously, in the often repeated story, *On the Outside* arose out of a Sunday morning conversation in 1959 with his close friend, Noel O'Donoghue, already a qualified solicitor, and a fellow amateur actor. 'Why don't we write a play?' suggested O'Donoghue. Murphy asked 'What shall we write about?' 'One thing is sure', O'Donoghue said, 'it's not going to be set in a kitchen.'[14] This was the time when 'kitchen-sink drama' represented the latest thing in radical British theatre, but for young Irish men like Murphy and O'Donoghue, the kitchen set belonged to the stereotyped Abbey play of the past. The 'quiet country road outside a dancehall' where Frank and Joe lurk without the price of admission in *On the Outside* was contemporary reality for the playwrights, even if, as working lawyer and quite well-paid schoolteacher, they themselves were by now on the inside of the society that excluded the young apprentices.

On the Outside, cheekily submitted under the pseudonym 'Aeschylus', won the 'fifteen guineas prize at the All-Ireland [amateur drama] manuscript competition'.[15] *A Whistle in the Dark*, under its original title of *The Iron Men*, Murphy's first solo-authored play – attributed this time to

'Dionysus' – was equally successful in the competition in 1961.[16] Rejected by the Abbey, promised production in the Dublin Theatre Festival by the Irish actor Godfrey Quigley, it was eventually staged by the Theatre Workshop company at the Theatre Royal, Stratford East in London and transferred to the West End, propelling Murphy into an international theatrical career. However, though he moved to London in 1962 and was never to live in his home town again, Tuam has remained all important in the formation of his work. It has not only provided the (always unnamed) setting for plays such as *Conversations* and *The House*, with memories of local individuals and incidents scattered throughout the plays. There is a substrate of unexplained Tuam slang that runs through his language, even though he never attempts to write a specifically Galway dialect: the 'shams', people of Tuam, whether 'buff shams' from the country or 'fly shams' from the town, have their own distinctive words, 'like "whid" (look at), "buffer" (country dweller), "choicer" (nothing), "a bull and a cow" (row)'.[17] Murphy as a playwright is a product of Tuam, of his peculiar position in a dispersed family of emigrés, his brutal Christian Brothers education, his time in the sugar factory and as a teacher, most of all, perhaps, as a writer exposed not to a conventional literary culture but to the range of modern drama he encountered in and around the Tuam Theatre Guild.

Living in London

There were multiple reasons for Murphy giving up his teaching position and moving to London as a full-time writer in 1962. There was the great success of *Whistle* with heady talk of very large sums to be paid for the film rights and the concomitant celebrity. He had met and fallen in love with the nineteen-year-old English woman Mary Hippisley, whom he was later to marry. Most strangely of all, there was a plan, mooted by the Head of Drama at BBC, for him to write a documentary play on the Congo where Irish soldiers were then posted as part of a UN peacekeeping mission. This advanced as far as a script conference before it was established that the Irish Defence Forces were not prepared to take responsibility for his safety. It was a big jump to go from a metalwork teacher in a school in Mountbellew to a freelance writer in London, but as Murphy remarked, 'I was a high jumper' (Interview, p. 177).

His time in London through the 1960s has been characterized as a wilderness period for Murphy because the three plays he wrote after *A*

Whistle were not staged.[18] This was not the way it appeared to him then, nor how he remembers it fifty years on. There was the excitement of a new social environment centred on the Queen's Elm pub on the Fulham Road in Chelsea. The publican was from Galway and there were other Irish there, but it was also a hangout for actors, writers and Chelsea footballers. He met television scriptwriters such as Alun Owen and Johnny Speight, the film producer Brian Desmond Hurst, actors Stanley Baker and Donald Houston, the playwright and director John McGrath, who directed *The Fly Sham* and was to become a lifelong friend of Murphy's. Television drama was a very important outlet for aspiring writers, directors and actors at this time, and a lucrative one. Murphy remembers being paid £925 for *The Patriot Game*, a script about the Easter Rising, commissioned to appear in 1966 for the fiftieth anniversary but which was never made because of budget overruns. This was good money for someone who had lived comfortably as a teacher on less than £500 a year.

Television plays, however, were not just potboilers; they were opportunities to try out ideas, work within the discipline of the form. As Murphy put it, it 'was part of my apprenticeship' (Interview, p. 178). There were commissions for two plays for the BBC in 1963, *The Fly Sham* and *Veronica*, Murphy's first work with an English setting. Starring a young and beautiful Billie Whitelaw, this centred on a successful actress, her back history as an illegitimate girl from a little town in the North of England, and the experiences in London that have made her 'bitter, cynical and distrusting'.[19] In some cases, television gave him a medium for unproduced stage work, such as *Crucial Week*.[20] That was an easy transition, however, because even the stage version of *Crucial Week* used cinematic–televisual techniques in its collages and fantasy sequences. More striking are the later plays that started life as television dramas. So, for instance, there was *A Young Man in Trouble*, recast as *On the Inside*, but also the half-hour *Snakes and Reptiles* (1968), the substance of what was to reappear expanded as *Conversations on a Homecoming*, both as the second half of *The White House* (1972) and later as the stand-alone play of 1985.[21] The television plays kept Murphy's name before the public and gave him the chance to work with some of the most talented actors of the day: T. P. McKenna and Fionnuala Flanagan in *Crucial Week*, Donal McCann in *A Young Man in Trouble* and Jim Norton in *Snakes and Reptiles*. In the career track that Murphy saw for himself in 1963, working in television in Britain was the way forward: 'I still regard Ireland as my home. But I can't afford to go back for good for another five years. Then I will go back for certain. I've first to establish myself in television and radio.'[22]

London was something totally new for Murphy, and for all his insouciance about being a 'high jumper', there was a sense of the remoteness from Tuam: 'The world I knew for twenty-seven years was suddenly gone' (Interview, p. 179). The social transition must have been a part of this. Mary Hippisley came from an upper-class family and Murphy remembers, early in their relationship, being 'vetted' by her uncle and aunt Sir Patrick and Lady Hamilton on a visit to a production of *The Good Person of Szechuan*. His mother-in-law lived in Spain but had a background in theatre and would come over to England for a month each year, when Murphy would join her and Mary at productions in Chichester, Guildford and the West End. Of the many plays that he saw at this time, four 'great evenings' stood out: 'one was Pirandello's "Six Characters" at the Mayfair, the second was Joan Littlewood's "Oh, What a Lovely War!" at Stratford East, the third was Durenmatt's "The Visit" with Alfred Lunt and Lynn Fontanne and the fourth was a production in Greek of "The Persians" at the Old Vic with a simultaneous translation in earphones'.[23] An eclectic selection indeed, but what he said about the production of *Six Characters*, starring Barbara Jefford and Michael Hordern, was probably true of all of these shows: it 'fed my spirit and let me know that all was not naturalism' (Interview, p. 179).

After the vivid realism of *Whistle*, Murphy sought other forms, other styles, but not any one specific idiom. 'The subject of every play', he has maintained, 'dictates the nature of its treatment.'[24] In the case of *Crucial Week*, for example, 'I had a principal character who was silent so I had to come up with a convention that allowed him to talk' (Interview, p. 178). This was the determining factor in the choice of the expressionist-seeming style. Brian Friel, when writing *Philadelphia Here I Come!*, solved the same problem, at almost the same time, with the split personality of Private and Public Gar.[25] *The Morning After Optimism* began with James's speech of disillusionment, written before any of the rest of the play: 'Once upon a time there was a boy, as there was always and as there always will be' (*Plays, 3*, 43). 'That dictated the style of the fairy tale' (Interview, p. 179). He is prepared to admit that Brecht had an impact on the writing of *Famine*, though the immediate occasion for the play was reading Cecil Woodham-Smith's popular history *The Great Hunger* when it was published in 1962. Brecht's alienation techniques provided Murphy with a means to distance himself from a subject that seemed too terrible, too vast to be staged.

There was no doubt disappointment for Murphy in the failure to get his plays staged in the aftermath of *Whistle*. At one point it seemed as if *Crucial Week* would be mounted for the 1963 Dublin Theatre Festival by the British producer Oscar Lewenstein, ironically the producer of Friel's breakthrough success, *Philadelphia*, in the following year's Festival. Michael Craig, a then very well-known film and theatre actor, took an option on *Morning After Optimism*, but it never reached production. Murphy's bitterest memory was entering *Famine* in 1967 for a playwriting competition sponsored by Irish Life, the insurance company, with a prize of £500: no prize was awarded that year because it was decided that no script came up to standard. It was only to be the following year that the play was produced with great success at the Peacock. But the years in London were of crucial importance in Murphy's formation as a playwright. He found expression then for the first time for some of his key themes: the claustrophobic sense of constriction in the small town of *Crucial Week*; the 'tyranny of the idealised self'[26] in the violent disillusionment of *Morning After Optimism*; the psychological legacy of historical deprivation in *Famine*. The sense of loss in being dislocated from the unquestioning faith of his childhood can also be detected in some of his less successful works of this time. *The Orphans* dramatizes the rootlessness of the central characters, one of them an ex-priest, in a secularized society; daringly, for a play staged in 1968, it featured a moon landing, still to come in 1969, as the emblem of technological advance that contrasted with moral and spiritual nullity – a motif Tom Stoppard was to take up in *Jumpers* (1972).[27] Return to Ireland in 1970, no more than two years later than he forecast in that 1963 interview, gave him a theatrical environment in which his backlist of plays could be produced.

Working with the Abbey

When *Whistle* was offered to the Abbey in 1961, it was returned with an angry letter of rejection by the manager Ernest Blythe. 'The characters, he said, were unreal, and its atmosphere was incredible. He did not believe that such people as were to appear in *A Whistle* existed in Ireland.'[28] At the time, Murphy says, he was not particularly upset by this rebuff; as an amateur writer he had no sense of entitlement. But after waiting seven years from the successful staging of *Whistle* without another play being produced, he was very grateful to Tomás Mac Anna for accepting *Famine* for the Abbey in 1968. Mac Anna was an appropriate director for the play because, having worked in Germany, he was heavily influenced by Brecht. Murphy was also fortunate in the casting of the heroic actor Niall Tóibín in the lead part of John Connor, when the play was first mounted in the Peacock, and was equally happy with Geoff Golden who replaced Tóibín in the part when the play transferred to the Abbey main stage. With the opening of the new theatre in 1966 and the retirement of Blythe the following year, the Abbey was moving into a more adventurous phase after the long semi-comatose years of exile in the Queen's Theatre, and Murphy's career benefited from the changed regime.

There was some resistance to the new style of play and production. Reviewers compared it to an older play on the subject, Gerard Healy's *The Black Stranger* (which Murphy himself had seen back in Tuam), and thought of it as 'less emotionally involving'. 'Mr Murphy undoubtedly creates a vivid impression of the human suffering of a starving people. He does it, however, on a rather detached and clinical level.'[29] For those who recognized the Brechtian technique, however, that was occasion for congratulation. 'At even the most harrowing moments, one never forgets one is watching actors representing an event that happened a hundred years ago. One is moved, deeply moved: but the experience provokes questions, not tears.'[30] There was excitement at the 'theatre in the round' staging by Mac Anna in the intimate space of the Peacock, still evidently avant-garde in Dublin. And the play itself was hailed as 'perhaps the most powerful and brilliant work the Dublin stage has had for years.'[31] There were no references to *Whistle*, even though it had been produced in Dublin in 1962; *Famine* was regarded as an unprecedented breakthrough. '"Famine," Thomas Murphy's new play at the Peacock, is the first real play to have come from an Irish author in years. Mr Murphy is not a new Synge or a new O'Casey. He is not a new anybody. He speaks with a voice that no Irish playwright has used before.'[32] Where in other theatrical environments Murphy continued to be associated with the hard-edged realism of *Whistle* and his experimentalism was deplored, from 1968 on he was treated as the standard-bearer for a radical *nouvelle vague* at the Abbey.

With *Crucial Week*, the following year, he achieved a real popular success, with an acclaimed performance by Donal McCann as the frustrated 'grocer's assistant' of the title. Here, too, though, the production by Alan Simpson (who had taken over from Mac Anna as the theatre's 'artistic adviser') was praised for its novelty:

> There is a refreshing lightness about Tom Murphy's new comedy. A picturesque fresco of small town life, acted and presented with dash and charm, it makes a welcome change from the usual stodgy three-act wedge of Abbey realism. Brian Collins' pretty toy-town set spread

out like a concertina is appropriate for this new treatment, as is the ingenious use of cinema organ music, acting as a sort of mock chorus to much of the dialogue.[33]

The much more difficult *Morning After Optimism* necessarily divided the critics. Though the performance of Colin Blakely as James was universally praised as a tour de force, there were complaints about the incomprehensibility of the play's fantastic form. 'I only wish [Murphy] would get back to the world he knows best, the world of dramatic realism.'[34] This was notably the view of non-Irish reviewers. 'After his success in London and New York with dramatic realism, it is sad to find Thomas Murphy wasting his time at the Abbey Theatre with the neo-symbolist whimsy of "The Morning After Optimism,"' wrote the *Daily Telegraph* reviewer,[35] and there was a still more savage dismissal from Mel Gussow in the *New York Times* when the play was staged at the Manhattan Theatre Club in 1974.[36] In Ireland, by contrast, most of the Irish reviewers, even those who did not claim fully to understand the play, responded with hyperbolic enthusiasm to the production by Hugh Hunt with its impressionistic set by Bronwen Casson. 'I still don't know it's a great play but one thing I'm sure of – it's great theatre.'[37] Others were less equivocal: 'the most interesting Irish play for years'; 'a play of immense power and beauty'; 'the most original and one of the most moving and impressive plays to have been presented by the Abbey in the past quarter century'.[38]

For an admiring reviewer of *Famine*, the play's staging at the Abbey was a signal justification of the National Theatre itself: 'It is inconceivable that this play should have been presented by any but a permanent company. Its production constitutes a triumphant vindication of the principle of subsidy.'[39] It certainly appears to have been the case that Murphy did not do as well under commercial management. The 1968 production of *The Orphans* by Phyllis Ryan's Gemini Productions at the Olympia may not be an altogether fair example because the playwright himself was very unhappy with the play. *The J. Arthur Maginnis Story*, planned as a spoof history of Guinness intended as a vehicle for The Dubliners, who had performed in Behan's *Richard's Cork Leg*, was an unmitigated disaster when produced in 1976.[40] In spite of an outstanding performance by Liam Neeson in the lead, *The Informer*, Murphy's adaptation of Liam O'Flaherty's novel, lost a great deal of money for the theatrical entrepreneur Noel Pearson who staged it in an expensive production in 1981. Murphy's position as something like a house dramatist at the Abbey gave him the security of a theatre committed to his work where he could stage his often experimental and not always successful plays. That commitment was strongly signalled when he was appointed to the Abbey Board in 1972.

Murphy needed such security because he works in a process of almost blind trial and error. So, for example, his play *The White House*, staged at the Abbey in 1972, had two parts separated by a ten-year gap in the action: 'Speeches on a Farewell' set in 1963, as the young people gathered in the White House pub run by J. J. Kilkelly, the supposed JFK lookalike, give Michael Ridge a send-off as he departs for an acting career in the United States; and 'Conversations on a Homecoming', later revised as the stand-alone play of that title, which shows his disconsolate return to the disillusioned group in the 1970s. It was originally played in reverse chronological order, with 'Conversations' before 'Speeches', the intention presumably being to have the ebullience of the second undercut by the irony of having seen the first. When the critical reaction to this was unfavourable, the playing order was reversed. *The White House* was completely realistic in style, unlike *Morning After Optimism* from the year before, and again unlike *The Sanctuary Lamp* in 1975, which aroused intense controversy because of its anticlericalism. However, against its most vociferous critics, came the remarkable endorsement of Cearbhall Ó Dálaigh, then President of Ireland, after attending the Abbey performance: 'I would think this play ranks with the first three of the great plays of this theatre. The Playboy of the Western World, Juno and the Paycock and The Sanctuary Lamp.'[41]

The pattern of fairly disastrous failures followed by major successes for Murphy at the Abbey continued throughout the 1980s and 1990s, without the theatre ever showing a loss of confidence in his work. *The Blue Macushla* in 1980, Murphy's daring attempt to write in a pastiche film noir style spliced with Dublin demotic, was such a flop that it had to be taken off after twenty-two performances. *The Gigli Concert*, three years later, came to be saluted as a major masterpiece, though critics initially complained of its inordinate length. In *Too Late for Logic* (1989), Murphy seemed to be making use of a similar technique as in *Gigli*, with operatic music underpinning the play's action, but without a similar effectiveness. Through the early part of the 1990s, Murphy devoted himself to writing his one novel *The Seduction of Morality* (1994). But it was the dramatization of this as *The Wake* (1998) which gave him his next triumph, critically acclaimed both when originally staged at the Abbey and when that production transferred to the Edinburgh Festival. The Abbey's recognition of the importance of Murphy's work has been repeatedly demonstrated in the twenty-first century, in the 2001 Murphy season, the staging of *Alice Trilogy* (2006, first produced Royal

Court 2005) and commissioned adaptations of *The Cherry Orchard* (2004) and of the Russian novel *The Golovlyovs* as *The Last Days of a Reluctant Tyrant* (2009). His plays have been staged by many other companies and in other places, but the relationship with the Abbey has been more significant than anything else in his career, except for the partnership with Druid and Garry Hynes.

Partnership with Druid

The appointment of Tom Murphy as Writer in Association with the Druid Theatre Company in 1983 was an arrangement with advantages on both sides.[42] For Druid, in the early 1980s a still young company set up in 1975 by Garry Hynes and Marie Mullen, just graduated from University College, Galway, along with the somewhat older actor Mick Lally, there was the prestige of working with the well-established playwright. Druid had made its name largely by its fresh and innovative revivals of classic Irish drama, most notably *Playboy of the Western World*, which they had produced many times and proved a major success on its transfer to London in 1985. But they felt the need to be working with new plays and playwrights.[43] For Murphy it represented a change from Dublin and the Abbey at a time when his personal life was in trouble, leading eventually to the breakup of his marriage and separation from his family. Though there was much emphasis in the press on the playwright's 'return to the west', he did not in fact move to live in Galway, but contented himself with visits for rehearsals as necessary.[44] However, it did obviously matter to him that this company of talented theatre professionals were fellow westerners, with a shared knowledge of the local language on which his plays were based. That sense of easy familiarity with West of Ireland speech, which had been an important dimension to Druid's revivals of Synge, was to work also in favour of Murphy's rhythmic dialogue.

As Writer in Association, the agreement was that Druid would produce one of Murphy's already established plays, give him the opportunity to return to a text that he felt had not worked properly and write them a new play. For the first of these, Murphy chose *Famine*, always a favourite play of his own which he had directed himself in 1978, because he wanted to showcase the range and scale of his work. For the 1984 production of that text, Hynes decided to use a ballroom in the seaside Galway resort of Seapoint, with the audience placed on tiered seating around three sides of the action, and a large-scale set built on the dance floor. However, it was the intimacy of their own theatre in Druid Lane, seating no more than a hundred, which worked so well for *Conversations on a Homecoming*, Murphy's reworking of the unsatisfactory *White House*, staged at the Abbey in 1972. The original play, which the playwright has never published because of his dissatisfaction with it, was a bulging piece which sought to conjure up the contrasting moods of the 1960s and 1970s, the 'Speeches at a Farewell', in particular, heavy with talk of art and ideas. In paring this back to the single act *Conversations on a Homecoming* with no interval, Murphy gave the play a classic unity of time and place, formed around the night's drinking of the group of friends in the White House pub. It was the sense of getting close in and personal that was picked out in the reviews as part of the effectiveness of the play's production in 1985: 'Garry Hynes brings her tactile sense of the physical reality of the things on stage, the slap of spilled porter on the bare floor and the rising miasma of cigarette smoke as the night descends towards revelation.'[45]

That original production transferred to the Dublin Theatre Festival in September 1985 and built expectation for Murphy's next play with Druid, *Bailegangaire*, which was to open in Galway in December of that year. As a three-hander set in a cottage kitchen, it was again especially well-suited to Druid's space and style. The great coup, however, was to cast Siobhán McKenna in the star role of the senile grandmother Mommo, sitting up in bed telling her never-finished story. McKenna had been for many years Ireland's most celebrated woman actor, but by this time she had come to seem old-fashioned and histrionic. Her performance as Mommo was seen as highly significant both for her and for the play:

> Siobhán McKenna emerges in *Bailegangaire*, as she has not done in Ireland in recent years, as a great actress. Her grand style and the amazing range of her voice work here not as mere display but as a superbly disciplined and well-aimed performance. The scale of her style, the fact that Mother Ireland hovers in the background of her stage persona, is exactly right here, precisely because she *is*, in one dimension of Mommo, Mother Ireland. But it is not the Mother Ireland of long and noble suffering, weeping and wailing. It is a Mother Ireland who spits and urinates.[46]

Mommo, like Murphy's other heroic character parts – Dada in *Whistle*, John Connor in *Famine*, the Irish Man in *The Gigli Concert* – challenges actors to play beyond their normal comfort zone, and McKenna's acting in this, her last stage part, was to be all the more vividly remembered because of her death the following year.

The great success of *Bailegangaire* was emphasized all the more because of the catastrophic failure of its companion play *A Thief of a Christmas*, produced within the same month at the Abbey. Druid had already been used as a stick to beat the Abbey with in relation to the production of *Conversations* earlier in the year, following the company's much acclaimed production of *Playboy* in London: 'A coalition between the best theatre company in the land and the most dynamic modern Irish playwright must produce something special. While the National Theatre crumbles quietly, Druid in Galway freshly triumphant from London, have returned to base to triumph yet again.'[47]

The Abbey's *Thief* in 'a flat, confused and messy production which tries, and fails to make up in spectacle what it lacks in imagination' served only to underline the contrast between it and *Bailegangaire*.

> It is ironic that one of Tom Murphy's great successes of 1985, *Conversations on a Homecoming*, came from rewriting the 'actuality' of parts of *The White House* as a story remembered by the characters of days gone by. In *A Thief of a Christmas* he has tried to do the opposite, rewriting a story from *Bailegangaire* as actuality. On the evidence of this production, the attempt hasn't worked and *Bailegangaire* stands as the definite and triumphant use of this material.[48]

Druid were invited to bring *Bailegangaire* to the Sydney Festival but due to the death of Siobhán McKenna, they had to substitute *Conversations*, giving the theatre a new sort of international prominence: 'The Druid's selection for the festival was a coup for the company. Just about every theatre group in the world would love to play Sydney at festival time.'[49] They had already taken the play to the United States, where their production at the PepsiCo Summerfare Festival in Purchase, New York, had been saluted by Mel Gussow in the *New York Times*: '"Conversations on a Homecoming" is a welcome introduction to the Druid company, which, in the last decade, has made a reputation as one of Ireland's most valuable alternative theatres.'[50] Both in the United States and in Australia, it was the ensemble playing of the company that was considered a key part of the success of the play. 'Murphy has the benefit of a fine company of actors, the Druid Theater Company of Galway, Ireland, which performs as a flawless ensemble. Undoubtedly, as a repertory company, they have grown together, and it pays off in a production that is as effectively choreographed as a ballet.'[51] An Australian reviewer made the same point with a different metaphor: 'This is some of the finest ensemble acting I have seen, each member a vital strand in a tapestry that succeeds in creating a picture full of highlights and relief.'[52]

In spite of such successes, Murphy ended his formal association with Druid in 1986, taking up a position as Writer in Association at the Abbey instead. But Druid effectively came with him. The Abbey hired Garry Hynes to direct *Whistle* in 1986, *Crucial Week* in 1988, and in both cases she cast many of the actors of the Druid company to play the key roles, a practice she continued in her revivals of Murphy when appointed as Artistic Director of the Abbey in 1990. The transposition of Hynes's vision and the Druid style to the larger space of the National Theatre produced new versions of the plays. So, for example, she contrived a 'claustrophic set' for *Whistle*: she 'dispensed with that institution of the big stage and … moved the play out on a platform into the audience'.[53]

> Earlier productions of the play opted for its domestic realism, allowing the intensely dramatic and incoherently concise writing to provide the theatricality. Garry Hynes has opted to impose theatricality – a stylishly theatrical grey set on a thrust stage in white lights – on the piece and has, incidentally, succeeded in rendering the Abbey space a much more intimate arena than any before her.[54]

A greater degree of stylization with her production of *Crucial Week*, with Monica Frawley's 'surrealistic, claustrophobic setting of dark, faceless, forbidding houses', gave it 'a fresh dimension, to make it a more important play that it seemed in its first presentation at the Abbey in 1969'.[55]

Hynes's prolonged relationship with Murphy's work, initially with Druid in the 1980s, then in the Abbey in the period of her artistic directorship 1990–3, and more recently with DruidMurphy in 2012, has allowed for a continuing reimagination of the plays. Anthony Roche has evoked vividly the difference between her original 1985 production of *Conversations* and the Abbey revival in 1991.

> The first drew on the intimacy and in-the-round qualities of Galway's Druid Theatre to stress the representational dimensions of the play; the effect was like being in a pub with the five main characters, eavesdropping on a series of conversations in the course of an evening's drinking. When she restaged the play in Dublin as the

Abbey's Artistic Director in 1992, Hynes did not seek to bring the audience closer to the play in this proscenium setting, by taking out seats and thrusting the stage into the auditorium, as she had done in her production of *A Whistle in the Dark*. Rather, she emphasised the distance and stressed the play's symbolic aspects, this bar of lost souls along Eugene O'Neill lines, with Frank Conway's hyper-real bar stretching the length of the stage and the characters isolated in pools of light as they turned outwards to face the audience – and themselves.[56]

This example highlights the production choices that exist for a director of Murphy plays – between realism and stylization, small-scale intimacy and larger effects – and Hynes coming back to texts repeatedly has had the opportunity to explore the range of possibilities.

So, for instance, in her 1984 staging of *Famine*, a 'huge set' was constructed on the floor of the Seapoint Ballroom; 'to the rear was the cabin of John Connor and bisecting the set was a stony road traversed by most of the action of the play'.[57] She returned to the play for her last production as Artistic Director of the Abbey in 1993. The playwright himself very much admired this version, with its set of broken stones shipped up from Galway for the purpose, its mixed period costuming and overtly Brechtian-projected signboards, but it provoked a mixed reaction from reviewers. Some complained of the play's 'schematic form'[58] and its lack of individual characterization: 'It amounts to an impressive, comfortless experience, but one which I found oddly unmoving, perhaps because all the people who die have never (in dramatic terms) been sufficiently alive first.'[59] For others, on the other hand, it was 'a starkly eloquent production', 'a taxing, but unmissable event'.[60] Whereas in 1984, there had been a more or less representational vision of the epic event with its specific Irish associations of the infamous famine roads that led nowhere, for both the 1993 production and for the 2012 staging of *Famine* that was the culminating play in the daylong experience of DruidMurphy, the attempt was to find a theatrical idiom that would bring out the transhistorical dimensions to the play. In 1993, it was a symbolic assembly of bare stones, suggestive of the grim essentials of the action. In 2012, instead, Hynes and her designer Francis O'Connor came up with an imposing backdrop of rusting corrugated iron, reminiscent of shanty-town building materials across the world.[61] The box sets used for *Conversations* and *Whistle*, which were insets for the first two plays of DruidMurphy, had always been lurking behind them this massive construction representing the epic scale of the tragedy that underlay the events of the latter-day dramas of the twentieth century.

Hynes tends to work with a single pool of preferred actors. In the 1980s this was the Druid group, many of whom had been with her almost from the beginning of the company: her co-founders Marie Mullen and Mick Lally, followed by Maeliosa Stafford, Jane Brennan, Sean McGinley and Ray McBride. As the reviews of *Conversations* suggested, their experience of years of playing together gave their ensemble work the quality of formal choreography that the play demands. For DruidMurphy Hynes was able to gather a company of seventeen actors to work intensively on the project over a period of months. Cross-casting was a key feature binding the plays together, showcasing both the virtuosity of the performers and the range of Murphy's work. So, for example, Marty Rea played both the Michael of *Conversations*, the failed actor clinging to his romantic dream of the past, and the weak older brother Michael of *Whistle* struggling to resist reassimilation into the brutal ethos of his family. Aaron Monaghan appeared in all three plays, as the vulgarly successful Liam in *Conversations*, the dominant Carney brother Harry in *Whistle* and most strikingly as the crippled malcontent Mickeleen in *Famine*. The continuity of Druid's longstanding engagement with Murphy could be illustrated in the case of Marie Mullen. In 1985 Mullen had played Peggy, the long-suffering fiancée of Tom in the original production of *Conversations*; in 2012 she moved up to Missus, the downtrodden, shuffling landlady of the White House pub. It was even more striking in 2014, when she took on the role of Mommo in *Bailegangaire*, having played Mary opposite Siobhán McKenna in the premiere of the play. For those of us who saw both productions, the two performances of Mullen spoke to each other across the thirty-year gap in time, with memories of McKenna haunting Mullen's no less effective but very different Mommo.

For Garry Hynes, 'The point and purpose of [DruidMurphy] was to restore Tom's place in the world of international theatre, and it did that.'[62] Indeed it did. The touring of the show first to London and then to the Lincoln Centre in New York produced ecstatic reviews and proper respect for Murphy's work: 'The scope of Mr Murphy's achievement is not possible to accommodate even in an undertaking as ambitious as "DruidMurphy."'[63] Hynes's track record in New York (where she won a Tony Award for Best Director in 1998), and even more the precedent set by the marathon production of DruidSynge in New York in 2006 prepared the ground for the reception of DruidMurphy. Yet the puzzle for some New York reviewers was the previous obscurity of the playwright. 'Thanks to 26 plays over the last 50-plus years, Tom Murphy is one of Ireland's best-known and influential dramatists. Who? That's apt to be the reaction in New York, where the 77-year-old writer's works are rarely performed. The superbly acted and staged "DruidMurphy" changes that – in triplicate.'[64] This remains a conundrum for all admirers of Murphy's work who include so many of the current generation of Irish playwrights who see him as a major influence.[65] Murphy's plays have been seen in successful productions in Britain, in Australia and in the United States, but why have they not built an international reputation like that of his contemporary Brian Friel? The answer must lie in the sort of writer he is.

Writing, rewriting, recycling

Murphy does not find writing easy. Some dramatists can apparently write a play in a couple of weeks – Martin McDonagh claims to have drafted *The Beauty Queen of Leenane* in ten days – but with Murphy it generally takes two years, and sometimes more. For plays such as *Famine* and *The White House*, there was painstaking research on the historical context of nineteenth-century Ireland and the Kennedy era before writing even began. He always writes in longhand, has fair copies typed professionally, and then returns to the pen for subsequent revised drafts. He begins without any fixed concept of the shape the play is to take. In some cases, this involves him creating a great deal of extra material which never reaches the final script. So, for example, in the case of what became *The Sanctuary Lamp*, a play of four characters in a single location over the one night, there were early sketches of the circus environment out of which the strong man Harry and the juggler Francisco emerged, a pub scene providing a backstory of the orphan waif Maisie and her relationship with her abusive grandparents.[66] The process of change and revision goes on even after the play reaches the theatre. A dress rehearsal for *Bailegangaire* at which it became apparent that the play was going to run well overlength resulted in Murphy cutting some thirty-five minutes out of the text. For each revival of one of the plays, whether Murphy is directing himself or not, there are further revisions, often involving the excision of passages that are felt to be irrelevant or slow down the pace of the drama. And such cutting is often necessary because his scripts tend to be overloaded, full of wayward turns and diversions that can lose an audience.

Looking back at *Whistle* from the distance of forty years, Murphy commented: 'I'm astonished at how extraordinarily well structured the play is.'[67] *Whistle* is indeed an admirably crafted play, building the tension steadily and inevitably through its three acts to the terrible tragic catastrophe of its ending. It is not surprising that it transferred to the West End and has continued to be Murphy's most revived play. But it is the only such 'well-made' play he has ever written. He made the reasons clear in an interview with Colm Tóibín in 1986. 'There is a decision you make, he says, when you are writing a play between 'playmaking' or 'saying what you want to say'. Playmaking means compromise, leaving the play to the actors and director as a well-made script.'[68]

Murphy has never been a 'playmaker' in this sense. He is conscious that the results of 'saying what you want to say' instead of giving his work a more conventional dramatic shape leaves him open to criticism. For example, it has often been felt that in *Gigli* the figure of Mona is underdeveloped, dominated as the play is by the two male figures; and in fact Murphy did write a radio version of the play in 1986 which reduced it to a two-hander. In response to the charge that 'giving Mona cancer was a bit of an easy trick', Murphy responded: 'Well, it does appear heavy-handed, but what could I do with her?. ... I felt that I needed Mona because you have two other characters walking a fine line between sanity and insanity, and eventually you have JPW walking a fine line between life and death, and I felt I needed to anchor them.'[69]

Again and again in Murphy there is this sense of his need to struggle with his imaginative conception of the work rather than going with what might seem more obvious dramaturgical decisions. There is an integrity in this commitment, an aesthetic satisfaction for those who appreciate the depth and resonance of the drama produced, but it makes the plays hard to place with standard theatre managements.

In Ireland Murphy would long have been regarded as one of our two greatest contemporary dramatists along with Brian Friel. Outside the country his reputation remains much more uncertain, with nothing like the visibility of Friel. One explanation might be that his plays are too 'Irish', limited by their local themes and idiom. However, it may be rather that his work does not conform to what international audiences expect from Irish drama. This is particularly true of his language. From the time of Synge with his dictum, 'In a good play every speech should be as fully flavoured as a nut or apple,'[70] there has been an expectation that Irish dramatic language should be eloquent, lyrical, with a high colloquial colour. Friel, with his lively yet always accessible dialogue, his mellifluous narrative voices, more than answered such an expectation. In this and in other things, Murphy has worked against the grain. Some of his central characters, JPW in *Gigli*, or Mommo in *Bailegangaire*, are gifted with cascades of language, spoken arias, rich in sound and meaning. But typically he works with the expressiveness of the inarticulate. The frustrated reaction of Harry to his more educated brother Michael in *Whistle*, his refusal to allow Dada to put words in his mouth, may be taken as representative:

Harry He doesn't think we can think straight. The things that's behind him. The things – where does he stand? Getting fed two sides, like. The sort of – the – the –
Dada Implications.
Harry *Things!* (*He kicks a chair.*)
Dada I understand –
Harry No.
Dada I --
Harry No.
Dada Actions have roots, I can explain.
Harry No! Not to me. No explaining to me. Things are clear enough to me. There's so many intelligent blokes for so long explaining things to thick lads.

(*Plays*, 4, 79)

Murphy's aspiration as a playwright is to 'make the inarticulate sing with feeling' and his characters do find their own raw and rhythmic language of real theatrical power, but it is certainly not as fully flavoured as a nut or apple.[71]

If Murphy's drama is written in a rebarbitively fragmented language, it does not open itself readily to an interpretative scheme of things either. As he disliked the moralizing of Miller, the playwright is impatient with the passages in his own work that seem most obviously to yield a key to its meaning. One of the most often quoted speeches in *On the Outside* is Frank's impassioned denunciation of the dispossessed situation of people like himself:

You know, it's like a big tank. The whole town is like a tank. At home is like a tank. A huge tank with walls running up, straight up. And we're at the bottom, splashing around all week in their Friday night

vomit, clawing at the sides all around. And the bosses – and the
big-shots – are up around the top, looking in, looking down.

(*Plays*, 4, 180)

Murphy himself dismissed this as 'the worst speech in "On the Outside"
… it's obviously myself preaching'.[72] He has equally little time for efforts
to relate his plays to the topical contexts of the time of their production.
'There are still an awful lot of stupid fucking people around who think that
you must be writing about current affairs, when in fact the badness and
the awfulness and so on in people continues whether there's trouble in the
North or not.'[73] Murphy's plays demand to be taken on their own terms,
not as parables of social dispossession or coded representations of the
Northern Troubles. Insofar as they are *sui generis*, that makes it difficult to
place them in one or another order of critical understanding and audience
perception.

As a writer, Murphy is both spendthrift and frugal. He is uneconomical
in the amount of text that ends up on the cutting-room floor during
composition, in the extravagance of his theatrical conceptions where the
practical cost is never counted. But he is thrifty in adapting and recycling
earlier material for later purposes. His 1960s television play, *Young
Man in Trouble*, focused on Frank, '23, a schoolteacher, a self-pitier, a
boy, an innocent', and Margaret, his 18-year-old telephonist girlfriend,
whom he thinks he has got pregnant.[74] The title puns on 'getting a girl
into trouble', a standard euphemism of the time, because the trouble
is Frank's, feeling as he does that he is being trapped into marriage.
The happy ending comes when it is revealed that she is not pregnant
after all, but the couple mutually commit themselves to spending the
night in unrestrained lovemaking and presumably marriage thereafter.
That central situation and much of the original dialogue was reframed
in the 1974 *On the Inside*, which as a staged counterpart to *On the
Outside* became a much broader study in the furtive repressions of
Irish sexuality, as well as a summer-bird-cage like representation of the
frustrations of the socially excluded matched by the stifling oppression
of those within.

The recycling of the 1968 TV play *Snakes and Reptiles* is an even more
striking case. Most of the cast of characters that were to reappear in *The
White House* and then in *Conversations* – Tom, Michael, Peggy, Junior,
Anne – were already in place, as was much of the dialogue all but word

for word. The main difference is that Michael has left his home town for England and not for the United States, and has been away much less long, three years and not ten. The title comes from a bitter comment by Michael, as he prepares to leave for good in his disillusionment. The drunken Junior gestures towards a statue of St Patrick over the door of the pub:

> **Junior** Look at St. Patrick up there taking all in. How yeh, St. Patrick! Did you know that after his forty days' fast, he banished all the snakes and reptiles from Ireland?
> **Michael** (*Quietly; humourless*) And, I suppose he called them emigrants.[75]

As one such emigrant, Michael has realized by the end of the play that there is no longer any place for him at home: 'That's settled then, isn't it? Mission is accomplished, isn't it? I know where I stand here. I can forget this place, can't I?'[76] In spite of the interrogatives, in *Snakes and Reptiles* Michael's is a definite decision to opt for England and an assimilated life there. *The White House* opened up the whole relationship between Irish and American culture, establishing the gap between the euphoria of the Kennedy era and the 1970s morning after optimism. The 1985 *Conversations*, a further decade on, was less a period study and more a theatrical realization of the psychodynamics of the group in the rituals of the occasion. The original script, confined within its BBC slot of 'Thirty Minute Theatre', through its extended gestation had become an extraordinarily accomplished, subtle and resonant stage play.

Characters, lines and situations lodge within Murphy's imagination, are tried out in one form and transmute into others until they find their proper place. The not-altogether-achieved novel *The Seduction of Morality* was dramatized as *The Wake*. What was originally planned as a screenplay, at various times entitled 'The Golondrina', and 'A Little Love, a Little Kiss', eventually took shape as the play *The House*.[77] Most remarkable of all is the series of works that have been created around the story of the laughing contest. Fintan O'Toole has shown the trilogy that Murphy originally planned: *Brigit*, a television play, screened by RTÉ in 1988, concerned with the woodcarver Seamus, commissioned to make a statue of St Brigit, his relationship with his wife and the three grandchildren they care for; 'The Challenge' also planned as a television script but which became the full dramatization of the laughing contest in *A Thief of a Christmas*, in which Seamus and his wife are the protagonists; and a never written play about a religious gathering at Glenamaddy near Tuam witnessed by Murphy in the 1950s where the Virgin was supposed to have appeared, only indirectly related to the other two.[78] What emerged from this, apparently unplanned, was *Bailegangaire*, the laughing contest as remembered long after by Seamus's wife, the by-then senile Mommo, told as a never-finished bedtime tale to her now grown-up granddaughters Mary and Dolly. In *Bailegangaire* there are glancing references to the events of *Brigit*, the dispute with the church over the statue and the fraught relationship between the long-married couple. These, however, emerged with a new clarity when, in 2014, Murphy rewrote *Brigit* as a stage play and it was produced by Druid in tandem with *Bailegangaire*. Echoes and references, verbal and visual, crossed between the two works. There was a terrible poignance in seeing the young children Mary, Dolly and Tom in the new play, as we learn of Tom's accidental death, his sisters' afterlives in *Bailegangaire*. Published with a revised text of *A Thief of a Christmas*, as *The Mommo Plays*, they represent a remarkable trilogy, even if it is different from the one Murphy originally planned.[79]

The West End success of *Whistle* turned out to be a one-off. Murphy has never become a mainstream commercial playwright and it seems unlikely that he ever will. His plays demand too much of directors, actors and audiences in their idiosyncratic form, their experimental use of language, rhythm and music. They need and deserve the kind of commitment given to them in dedicated productions by the Abbey and Druid, and indeed many other companies inside and outside Ireland that have mounted the plays at different times.[80] They benefit from and reward the actors who can rise to the challenge of playing Murphy's often exacting parts, making use of his elliptical, subtextual stage directions. The integrity and tenacity of his theatrical imagination, the sheer range of his work, is the more manifest in large-scale events such as the Abbey retrospective of 2001 and DruidMurphy in 2012. But the individual plays come startlingly alive again in magnificent revivals such as *The Gigli Concert* staged by Dublin's Gate Theatre in 2015. They are bold enough in imaginative conception, rich enough in texture to repay careful and detailed rereading. This is certainly the conviction that underpins the book that follows, in which I hope to analyse the key texts of Murphy's *oeuvre* on the page and in performance to help to illuminate the greatness of his achievement.

CHAPTER 2
PREDICAMENTS OF IRISHMEN: *ON THE INSIDE/ON THE OUTSIDE, A CRUCIAL WEEK IN THE LIFE OF A GROCER'S ASSISTANT, A WHISTLE IN THE DARK*

'If you don't mind my saying so', someone told Murphy at the West End opening of *A Whistle in the* Dark, 'you know nothing about women.' It was a remark he still remembered more than twenty years on when writing *Bailegangaire* with its all-female cast.[1] Whatever its general validity, it is certainly true that Murphy's early plays are male dominated, seeking to make sense of what's wrong with Irish men. One part of the diagnosis had to do with the dominance of the Catholic Church. 'The men have a celibate education which influences their personality; they never consider Christian marriage as high an ideal as celibacy.'[2] Malachy in *On the Inside* expands upon his author's views: 'From birth to the grave, Baptism to Extreme Unction there's always a celibate there somewhere, i.e., that is, a priest, a coonic. Teaching us in the schools, showing us how to play football, taking money at the ballroom doors, not to speak of preaching and officiating at the seven deadly sacraments' (*Plays*, 4, 207).

Though priests appear relatively rarely in Murphy's first plays – the shrewdly manipulative Father Daly in *A Crucial Week in the Life of a Grocer's Assistant* is the exception – their influence is as ubiquitous as Malachy suggests, particularly in the conditioning of male attitudes to sexuality: the furtive longing and groping of *On the Outside/On the Inside*, the Mother/ Whore projections of John Joe in *Crucial Week*, the aggressive misogyny of *A Whistle in the Dark*. These men are located in a quite particular period and place. The time of *On the Outside*, we are told in the prefatory stage direction, 'is 1958' (*Plays*, 4, 166). As many commentators have pointed out, this was the date of T. K. Whitaker's Government white paper, *Economic Development*, implemented in 1959, the year when *On the Outside* was actually written. This was the beginning of the modernization of Ireland, the death of the nationalist ideal, which Fintan O'Toole saw as the fundamental context for Murphy's work. 'Where nationalism proclaimed the unity of the classes in the common name of Irishman and the unity of city and country in the common land of Ireland, *On the Outside* creates its extraordinary impact by showing the division of the classes and the antagonism between city and country.'[3] Aidan Arrowsmith extends the analysis of the impact of the new economic dispensation to *A Whistle in the Dark*. 'In *A Whistle*, Murphy presents the Carneys as the inevitable product of Lemass's post-nationalist, capitalist modernity and the embodiment of its contradictions. Once, perhaps, these Mayo men might have qualified as the lifeblood of "authentic" Western Irishness. Now, however, the Carneys of Co. Mayo are an embarrassment to the "new" Ireland.'[4]

Claire Gleitman comments on what she calls the 'homosociopathic' world of the Carney men in *Whistle*, their violent hypermasculinity overcompensation for actual powerlessness.[5] Throughout these early plays of Murphy, Lionel Pilkington argues, 'What causes the sense of seemingly hopeless claustrophobia is the universality and apparent intractability of Ireland's class hierarchy at a time in which the ideology of the state is re-oriented to a language of egalitarianism and democracy.'[6]

In *On the Outside/On the Inside*, *Crucial Week* and *Whistle*, the states of being of the men can be read as products of their church-conditioned attitude towards gender, the changing economic and cultural climate of the time, the oppressions of class or the legacies of colonization. O'Toole sees these plays as part of a 'rough trilogy' (*Plays*, 4, x), and they are certainly linked by cognate themes and preoccupations. However, to call them a trilogy is to make them seem more homogeneous than they actually are. The predicaments of Irish masculinity are different in each text, and for each Murphy finds his way to a different mode and style. The aim of this chapter is to analyse the distinctive dramatic forms given to the men's situations in *On the Outside/On the Inside*, *Crucial Week* and *Whistle*.

Shut out, shut in

'Physically locked out, Joe and Frank are mentally locked in,' writes O'Toole of the central characters of *On the Outside*, Murphy's first play (*Plays*, 4, xi).[7] With the addition of the complementary one-act *On the Inside* in 1974, Murphy created a diptych in which this combination of exclusion and claustration is expressed theatrically as well as psychologically. In deciding that whatever the subject of their play, it was not going to be 'set in a kitchen', Murphy and O'Donoghue were rejecting not only the by-then clichéd 'Abbey play' but also the ideological baggage it brought with it.[8] The box set representing the country cottage kitchen, which figured in so many plays staged in the Abbey in the first half of the twentieth century, had come to stand in for the family that inhabited it and by extension the whole society of which it was a metonym. It was this mould that Murphy sought to break with his play set on a 'quiet country road outside a dancehall' (*Plays*, 4, 167). Just six years before the play was written, one of the revolutionary features of *Waiting for Godot* (1953) was its use of an exterior rather than an interior setting, and 'Beckettian elements' have been identified in *On the Outside*: 'two men waiting; a determined effort by one to keep up the spirits of the other; a belief that, if they get inside, all their troubles will be over'.[9] Attractive as this alignment is, Murphy's play depends precisely on those details of social specificity that Beckett suppresses. Frank and Joe are apprentices of twenty-two who have to give most of their limited wages to their parents, retaining only a meagre allowance as pocket money. They must ingratiate themselves to their overseer for a hand-out of cigarettes – 'The fags we get out of him – just from soft-soaping an imbecile' (*Plays*, 4, 180) – and husband what supply they have, each furtively smoking in the other's absence in order not to have to share. And of course what prevents them entering the dancehall outside which they wait is the lack of the six shillings price of admission. Their position on that quiet road represents their limbo situation: too old to be part of their families yet dependent on them, 'townies' ('buff-shams' in the Tuam argot) as against the 'fly-shams' who control the country dancehall, working-class trainees excluded from the dance organized by the professional Irish National Teachers Organisation.

That exclusion is a part of a class system registered from the very beginning of the play. Frank has made a date with Anne to take her to the dance, but as the action starts is in hiding because he has not the money to pay for her – he does not yet know that he has not even enough to get in himself. Anne's more experienced companion Kathleen has a cautionary tale for her about going out with the wrong sort of man:

I was going with a fella last year in Dublin. Not bad looking either. And, of course, fool here was real struck. I liked him. Richard Egan. And then one night we met – yeh know Mary O'Brien nursing in the

Mater? And later she took me aside. 'Do you know who he is?' she said. 'No.' 'He's the porter at the hospital.' The shagging porter. *And* his name wasn't Richard.

(*Plays*, 4, 168)

The superior sounding alias Richard Egan was intended to mask the totally ineligible job of hospital porter. The starry-eyed Anne has romantic ideas about Frank, whom she has only just met, but when she discovers the truth about his pennilessness – or at least sixshillinglessness – in her bitter disillusionment she walks off with the loutish but car-owning Mickey Ford.

The dancehall itself is a significant feature of its time and place. The opening stage direction describes it with wry irony: 'an austere building suggesting, at first glance, a place of compulsory confinement more than one of entertainment' (*Plays*, 4, 167). There may even be a hint here of those state-sanctioned places of compulsory confinement that were to become notorious, the 'industrial schools' for socially disruptive children. Dancehalls themselves, licensed under the 1935 Public Dancehalls Act, were established in order to monitor and control potentially promiscuous sexual activity.[10] For Frank and Joe, however, this grim building is imagined as a place of erotic fulfilment in which they might 'square' girls. In fact, as we see, any sexual activity that goes on will happen outside the building and is only available to men with access to cars. Joe is hopeful that they may get 'pass-outs', readmission tickets for paying customers who are going out temporarily: 'There's bound to be someone leaving soon: jiggy-jiggy in the passion wagons' (*Plays*, 4, 175).

The apprentices are on the outside, shut out of what feels to them like the place of privilege, of class status and masculine success. The action of the play dramatizes the twists and turns by which they seek to gain admittance, and their rising frustration at their continued exclusion. But the image of the town as a tank quoted in the previous chapter (which Murphy himself came so to dislike for its moralizing tone) is one of enclosure and surveillance.

You know, it's like a big tank. The whole town is like a tank. At home is like a tank. A huge tank with walls running up, straight up. And we're at the bottom, splashing around all week in their Friday night vomit, clawing at the sides all around. And the bosses – and the big-shots – are up around the top, looking in, looking down.

(*Plays*, 4, 180)

This is the locked-in mentality that is the psychological counterpart to the physical and social alienation. Brief and simple as it is, the little one-act play contrives to sketch in simultaneously a situation and a state of mind.

In the television play, *Young Man in Trouble*, to be rewritten as *On the Inside*, the running motif is of the troubled young schoolteacher (at this stage also called Frank) driving between Tuam and Ballinasloe, to see his girlfriend Margaret whom he thinks he has got pregnant.[11] As he drives, now desperate to find a way out of the relationship, there are flashbacks to the stages in the development of the affair, being introduced to Margaret's parents, Margaret's moving to a flat so they can meet alone, pub scenes with Joe, an older layabout who pretends to be knowledgeable about sex, staffroom scenes with the uptight headmaster Mr Collins. The images of the young man in the car figure Frank's sense of entrapment. The denouement comes when it is revealed that after all Margaret is not pregnant; the couple are relieved, yet at the same time disappointed, and we see them take their clothes off to make love unashamedly. The coda has a shot of a thoroughly happy Frank driving back to Tuam.

The story line, and much of the dialogue, was retained when Murphy decided to turn the TV script into a stage play as matching counterpart to *On the Outside* showing the inside of the dancehall which Frank and Joe so desperately wanted to enter.[12] We see the same poster advertising the INTO dance, the band and the admission price, which Mr Collins the headmaster in charge ironically decides was too high at six shillings. Inevitably the scene within is nothing like the place of fulfilment imagined by the thwarted young men without. In fact, it is a continuation of just that system of closely observed class distinctions so resented by the outsiders. In the wary mating game that is the dance, the key questions are 'Who are you, where do you come from, what do you do,' only in this middle-class environment you are not supposed to ask straight out: 'The cheek', complains the older teacher Miss D'Arcy, of Willie, the eager ladykiller who does just that, 'no finesse' (*Plays*, 4, 196).[13] Mr and Mrs Collins preside over the soft drinks bar – no alcohol is allowed in the state-licensed dancehall though bootlegged whisky is available for purchase on the sly – and monitor the interchanges between the sexes. The headmaster who is prepared to lend his junior teacher his car, however grumblingly, is no tyrant, but he oversees everything that goes on.

It is symptomatic that it is only in the headmaster's car that Kieran (as he is now called so as not to confuse him with the outside Frank) and Margaret are able to make love, insofar as they can. It is this sordid constricted sex which for Kieran has led to the death of real feeling. By contrast, he romanticizes earlier innocence: 'Out in the open with it … you'd get maybe half a dozen kisses of an evening and you're in love. But then, when the rest of it starts … . Fronts of cars, backs of cars, doorways, steering wheels, gear-levers, and love starts to fade, and we've had our chips.' His sense of entrapment is expressed in the key exclamation, 'how does a fella get out?' (*Plays*, 4, 200). The cynical Malachy, supposed Lothario, is there to offer worldly advice and diagnose the difficulty in the oppressions of the celibate church mentality: 'Holy medals and genitalia in mortal combat with each other is not sex at all' (*Plays*, 4, 213–14). Yet ironically he is a perfect illustration of his own theory, funking sex when it is on offer from Bridie, the local woman home on holiday from Birmingham, and it is in his vacant house that Kieran and Margaret go off to 'do it right this time' (*Plays*, 4, 221).

It appears to be an upbeat ending, suggesting that it is possible to escape from the claustrophobic inside of the social panopticon and the introjected guilt that accompanies it. Yet the play concludes with Malachy's ironic singing of a famous line from Cole Porter, 'What is this thing called love?' (*Plays*, 4, 222) – the subtitle of *Young Man in Trouble*. Kieran's urge to a rapprochement with Margaret, when he discovers that she is not in fact pregnant, is in part drink-fuelled: he has been in the pub with Malachy before arriving at the dance and has put away his share of a quarter bottle of whiskey while in the hall. The popular songs that are interspersed through the play, the 1958 hit 'Let's Go To the Hop,' and the Elvis number 'Tonight's So Right So Right for Love' provide a conducive atmosphere. *On the Inside* dramatizes a rite of passage, by which a couple come together, Irish country style, just as *On the Outside* figures a rite of impasse for the shut-out young men. But in both cases, as Murphy noted to himself about *On the Inside*, 'these characters are ordinary people – no great heights, no great depths. They go thro' life dealing with their problems', as against 'extremes' who 'react in extreme ways'.[14] The same is in some sense true of *Crucial Week*, but it is certainly not true of *Whistle* in which Murphy moves into the territory of dysfunctional masculinity, which is indeed extreme.

Staying or going

With *Crucial Week*, Murphy explained in the statement quoted in the previous chapter, form was determined by subject: 'I had a principal character who was silent so I had to come up with a convention that allowed him to talk' (Interview, p. 178). It was not actually quite as simple as that makes it seem. The first draft of the play was in a relatively standard mode of realism, and in it John Joe has plenty to say for himself, in long anguished apologias to his girlfriend Mona.[15] This early version is much more obviously autobiographical. Apparently written in Tuam early in 1962 before Murphy moved to London, John Joe's dilemma as to whether to stay or leave may well have been the playwright's own, different as their situations were.[16] This John Joe has a bedroom full of books, reads Shaw – 'A bit wordy at times', he comments to Father Daly – and writes bad poetry. The play is overcrowded with characters as Murphy tries to get in the whole small town atmosphere that is so stifling to John Joe, including the national schoolteacher who lodges with his parents, plays the tin whistle and lectures on patriotism, and an electioneering politician making capital out of his service in the War of Independence, along with an enlarged cast of gossiping neighbours. The subject is summed up in a covering note by Murphy: the play 'covers a week in the life of young man, a shop-boy, who can neither live in nor leave his home town; who can neither marry his bank-clerk girl nor end the romance'.[17] This version begins with John Joe's return from an aborted attempt to emigrate, having lost his nerve at the station at the last moment, and ends with a matching failure, as Father Daly once again persuades him not to leave, and we see him exit in his working clothes: 'All the neighbours beam at him as good neighbours should.'[18]

This initial version of *Crucial Week* was in some sense closer to Friel's *Philadelphia Here I Come!*, the play which it so superficially resembles, written at much the same time. John Joe, alone in his room, listens to Liszt's Hungarian Rhapsody, as Gar O'Donnell plays Mendelsohn's Violin Concerto. John Joe's father, in this early draft, is much more characterized than the cypher-like figure he becomes in *Crucial Week* and John Joe has a real feeling for him, which, however, like Gar, he can never bring himself to express. Friel, by solving the problem of the inarticulate protagonist with the introduction of Private Gar, the fast-talking alter ego to Public, allows not only more sympathy for his central figure, but an aura of warmth and affection that plays about the small town Ballybeg itself. In recasting the action of *Crucial Week* in semi-expressionist style, in moving his characters towards caricature, Murphy created a harsher, more satiric vision of John Joe and his cramping environment.

In the first drafts of what was then called *The Fooleen*, there was just one dream sequence, John Joe's nightmare imagination of the characters who loom up in his consciousness: the sexually alluring Mona, Father Daly denouncing him from the pulpit, his family whom he denies out of social shame, the neighbours who turn into a lynch mob.[19] What changed the play radically was the decision to separate out the erotic, wish-fulfilment element of this paranoid phantasmagoria, and open the play with Mona's appearance in John's Joe's bedroom in a 'pool of unreal light' (*Plays*, 4, 91). Significantly, she climbs in through a window, to the amazement of the dreaming John Joe: 'That poor window has always been stuck' (*Plays*, 4, 92). Adding to the pressure is the sound of the train as Mona urges him to escape with her through that miraculously unstuck window: 'This is your chance' (*Plays*, 4, 91). But at the very moment of union and flight, as she leans over him, 'the medals on the chain about her neck brush (or drop into) his mouth' (*Plays*, 4, 92), all but literalizing the image of bad Irish sex from *On the Inside*: 'Holy medals and genitalia in mortal combat with each other.' Soon it is the threatening figure of Mother, censor of John Joe's dreams, who appears and anathematizes the siren Mona. And presently she metamorphoses into the actual Monday morning Mother, trying to wake John Joe to get up for work.

Yet the actual character of Mother has some of the distorted features of the dream too. This is how Murphy describes her:

> **Mother** is about fifty-five, big lined face, given much to grimacing to emphasize what she says; appearance is slovenly – she wears too many clothes, and these are drab and old; harsh in expression and bitter; a product of Irish history – poverty and ignorance; but something great about her – one could say 'heroic' if it were the nineteenth century we were dealing with.
>
> (*Plays*, 4, 94)

This is the hard-working, long-suffering Juno of O'Casey's *Juno and the Paycock*, supporting the family as washerwoman to the town, aided by whatever income Father brings in as occasional gravedigger and John Joe's wages as lowly grocer's assistant. It is, however, not the nineteenth century we are dealing with, and Mother, for all there is 'something great about her', in her own day is an adept emotional blackmailer. Father is reduced to a virtual nonentity, staring vacantly into space, tunelessly singing snatches from doleful ballads, 'The Ship that Never Returned', or 'The Shores of Americae', only animated by sudden inexplicable bursts of violent temper.

In rewriting his earlier version of the play, Murphy excised many of his supporting characters – the national schoolteacher, the politician – and reduced his gossiping neighbours to just two, the appalling Peteen Mullins, always lurking in the shadows, alert for 'newses', and Mrs Smith, 'her voice … a crying, whining, poverty-stricken tremolo' (*Plays*, 4, 97), who never appears without her infantilized 28-year-old daughter Agnes, female counterpart to John Joe. John Joe himself was stripped of the features that originally made him something like an autobiographical stand-in: no more writing poetry, reading Shaw or listening to Liszt. The final John Joe is almost the fooleen that the town takes him for, his retardation made all the more prominent in successive iterations of the play as his age was moved from twenty-nine to thirty-three.[20] This is a figure whom the stultifying atmosphere of the town has really stultified.

Escape from the locked-in local mentality was imagined in *On the Outside* and *On the Inside*: Frank in his frustration and disappointment at losing Anne declares he will go to England; Kieran dreams of a new life in Canada. But it is only in *Crucial Week* that emigration becomes the central issue. To illustrate the inadequacy of that solution to the problem, and add another dimension to the satiric exposé of the town, Murphy wrote in a new scene with the returned migrant Pakey Garvey, John Joe's predecessor as grocer's assistant, coming in to pay Mr Brown for his father's coffin: as in so many Irish small towns, the 'grocer' doubles as undertaker. Pakey subverts Mr Brown's attempts to go through with the mandatory eulogy of the deceased by insisting on the realities of the life of his drunken father, 'Rags' Garvey:

Mr Brown   … he had a good life.
Pakey   He had, half-starved. Fond of the bottle too, Mr Brown?
Mr Brown   He was, he w– Aw! No, now Patrick. Ah-haa, you were always the joker, always the –
 Pakey   Not a great sodality man, Mr Brown?
Mr Brown   Always the joker.
Pakey   But maybe he was ashamed of his suit.
Mr Brown   Well, you never changed. (*Solemn again.*) No, Patrick, your father, Bartley Garvey, could take a drink, and he could carry it. And that was no flaw in Bartley Garvey's character.
 Pakey (*solemnly*)   Musha, poor auld 'Rags'.
Mr Brown   Ah – well – yes.

(*Plays*, 4, 102–3)

This is followed by a parodic version of the successful emigrant's return:

Mr Brown   ... But you're doing well?
Pakey   Oh, yes, Mr Brown
Mr Brown   Saving your money, Patrick?
Pakey   Oh yes. And when I have enough saved –
Mr Brown   You'll come home.
Pakey   I will.
Mr Brown   And you'll be welcome.
Pakey   And I'll buy out this town, Mr Brown.
Mr Brown   You will, sir.
Pakey   And then I'll burn it to the ground.

(Plays, 4, 103)

Getting away, doing well materially, does not necessarily allow you to escape. As John Joe reflects to himself on Pakey's boasts of his well-paid English position, 'Well, if it's that good, what are you so bitter about?' (*Plays*, 4, 104).

Crucial Week realized Murphy's ambitions, articulated in his note on the earlier version: 'The play does not aim at a typical week or at realism in the sense of showing how the characters continually live. Its main concern is to recreate the feelings of a young man and *his* attitude towards, and his vision of, the environment he lives in.'[21] It is this expressionist, subjective point-of-view perspective on the town that makes possible more comic or more darkly satiric scenic realizations, from 'Brian Collins' pretty toy-town set spread out like a concertina' in the Abbey premiere through to Monica Frawley's 'surrealistic, claustrophobic setting of dark, faceless, forbidding houses' in the 1988 revival.[22] However it is imagined theatrically, the town so hedges in John Joe that he makes Mona walk out miles to a hayshed for their romantic encounters and even then, as she puts it to him ingenuously, 'You're an awful bad court.' Wherever he goes, the eyes of the town are upon him, and he is haunted by guilt about his mother: 'If I was rich, the first thing I'd do is give a million pounds to my mother. Pay her off' (*Plays*, 4, 114). The only elsewhere he can conceive of for erotic fulfilment with Mona is a purely fantastic hut on a desert island.

The scene in which John Joe, driven to despair by the breakup of his relationship with Mona and one more row with his mother, stands out in the street and indulges in his own one-man doomsday, shouting out all the carefully kept secrets of the town, is the climax of the play and was always intended as such. It is his attempt to crash through the walls of silence that close him in, his protest against the asphyxiating atmosphere he associates with his mother: 'The house is filled with your bitterness and venom. A person can hardly breathe in that street. I don't know what started it. Whether it's just badness or whether it came from a hundred years ago' (*Plays*, 4, 159). All the humiliating privacies of poverty and pretence are made public:

> We have flour-bags sewn together for sheets. … Oh, but we know Mrs Smith doesn't use a sheet at all. Did you know that Mrs Smith? We know that from the day Peter Mullins climbed in your back-room window, because it was the only room in your house he hadn't seen. But he said it was clean, but he wouldn't give you two-pence for the furniture. And what else? The rig-out Mrs Mullins had on last Wednesday wasn't new at all; a cast-off, bought by her sister in Seattle off one of them cheap-jacks they have over there, for thirty-eight cents. And that she doesn't sleep with Peter; and hasn't for a number of years.

And the Moran family itself is not spared, their most shaming story exposed: 'My brother Frank done jail in America. Fourteen months, drunk and fighting a policeman. Say a prayer for him' (*Plays*, 4, 160).

The case of Frank, along with the embittered Pakey Garvey, helps to illustrate the issueless dilemma of emigration or remaining at home, as John Joe voices it at the conclusion of this scene: 'It isn't a case of staying or going. Forced to stay or forced to go. Never the freedom to decide and make the choice for ourselves. And then we're half-men here, or half-men away, and how can we hope ever to do anything' (*Plays*, 4, 162).

The first draft of the play ended grimly underlining this message as a defeated John Joe, thwarted a second time in his attempt at escape, returns to the imprisonment of his working life. Murphy was clearly unhappy with such a glum conclusion and, in recasting the play, contrived an alternative upbeat last scene. One of the incidental examples of the townspeople's spite in the original version had been the information given to the pension authorities against Uncle Alec – a more important and evidently homosexual figure in this draft; he has not declared the all but non-existent income from his small shop and will lose his long anticipated pension as a result. In *Crucial Week* it is Mother who informs on her own brother to induce him to give the shop to John Joe and thus keep her cherished son with her. The plot apparently succeeds and in the final scene, we see John Joe entering with a new signboard for the shop. However, when the signboard is turned over at the last moment, it reads ALEC F. BRADY: John Joe has given his uncle back the property as a gesture of contempt for the spirit of his mother's machinations.

This is just one sign of a new confident spirit of independence in John Joe. He declares that 'I'm going up town to get a job for myself' – the emphasis being on 'for myself', because his last two jobs have been arranged by the priest. 'And I'm going to open a bank-account with a girl I know' (*Plays*, 4, 164) he adds, implying a renewal of his relationship with Mona. It is clear what Murphy wants here. John Joe has achieved the 'freedom to decide', is no longer locked in to that impossible choice of staying or going. He will stay and make a life for himself. It's admirable in spirit but it is doubtful if it can be made convincing theatrically. Will John Joe be able to get a job in the town whose meanest secrets he has betrayed? What money will he have with which to open a bank account? And what are the chances of a renconciliation with Mona whom he has earlier insulted in the most brutal possible terms? 'You mean nothing to me. You are a silly, stupid bitch. Whore if you could be' (*Plays*, 4, 153). Apart from these literalist questions of plausibility, the surprise return of the shop to Alec does not make a large enough theatrical impact to effect the desired reversal. What is significant in this early play is Murphy's felt need to work through the emotional stasis represented by the John Joes of small town Ireland, to take them beyond the impossibility of staying or going.

Whistling in the dark

Fintan O'Toole claims that Pinter used *Whistle* as 'a direct model for *The Homecoming*' (*Plays*, 4, xiii), a view that Murphy seemed to support when asked about it by Michael Billington.[23] Bernard F. Dukore has shown that it is unlikely Pinter would have known *Whistle*, but the resemblances are striking.[24] Both represent violent families of fathers and male siblings, with a single female character in each. Lenny and Harry, the dominant sons in the two plays, are both pimps, aggressively contemptuous of women. Iggy, Murphy's 'iron man', is matched by the boxer Joey in Pinter's play. By contrast, Teddy in Pinter and Michael in Murphy are the ones with a measure of superior education and are both resented and despised for it within the family group. Yet the differences are as striking as the similarities.

As in the case of *Waiting for Godot* and *On the Outside*, Murphy supplies just the sort of detailed information that Pinter deliberately withholds. So, for example, in early versions of *The Homecoming*, the family was clearly Jewish, but in the final text the indications of their ethnicity were removed.[25] It seems probable that Lenny is a pimp, given the ease with which he comes up with the plan for Ruth working as a prostitute for the family, but we are not explicitly told that. The sudden outbursts of violence in *The Homecoming* come out of nowhere and are completely unmotivated at least on the surface. There may be explanations for all the bizarre things that happen in Pinter but, if there are, the audience has to try to piece them together for themselves. In Murphy, we know precisely who is who, where they come from, why they behave as they do, and can follow each stage of the action as it moves inexorably to its terrible conclusion.

The Carneys are from Mayo, in the remote north-west of Ireland, a county poorer than Murphy's own neighbouring Galway. Frank and Joe as apprentices in *On the Outside* and John Joe as shop assistant in *Crucial Week* are working class, near the bottom of the social food chain. But the Carneys belong in an underclass lower than that again. None of the sons, except Michael, will have had more than primary education, and Michael had only two years at secondary school. The term of abuse that is hurled at them is 'tinker', the derogatory name for the Irish Travellers: 'Go home, you tinker! Go back to your tent, Carney' (*Plays*, 4, 42) Michael remembers having yelled at him as a boy back in Ireland, and when the sycophantic hanger-on of the family Mush falls out with them in the last act, his parting insult is 'Tinkers! Carneys! Tinkers! Tinkers!' (*Plays*, 4, 70). The name of Carney is all but synonymous with the marginalized outcasts of Irish society.

Harry remembers vividly the prejudice this brought him at school, when the teacher asked the boys what they wanted to be when they grew up:

> Some said engine drivers, and things. And Dada was then sort of selling things about the countryside. Suits and coats and ties and things. Well, just when he came to my turn, and I was ready to say what I was going to be, he said first, 'I suppose, Carney, you'll be a Jewman.' (*pedlar*)
>
> (*Plays*, 4, 43)

Murphy remembers this as a real incident that happened in his school in Tuam when he was nine, though significantly not to himself but to another boy in the class. 'And I saw what it did to that child, the connotations, even the insult to the Jews.'[26] Harry's actual ambition was to be a priest, regarded by the teacher as laughable because no one from Harry's family was ever going to make it to priesthood, the most venerated caste of all. Murphy makes us aware of the vicious class prejudice suffered by the Carneys, while not justifying what they have become as a result. Harry lives off the work of underage prostitutes – 'little girls … Kids' (*Plays*, 4, 35); Iggy as foreman on a building site runs an extortion racket hiring Harry's clients, 'mostly darkies and men that find it hard to get work' (*Plays*, 4, 34), and taking a cut of their wages. Even Michael, the supposed success story among the brothers, is no more than a labourer, not averse to petty thieving – 'a can of paint, a bit of timber, a few bricks' (*Plays*, 4, 35) – provided it is not enough to get him in trouble with the police.

In the classic definition, the working classes are those who have nothing to sell but their labour power. The Carneys belong to a group that has nothing to sustain them but their capacity for violence. Their peculiar form of machismo is supported by a virulent disdain for women. Betty, as Michael's English wife, is subject to an exaggerated measure of this hostility. 'Person'lly, my 'pinion, English women is no good, 'cept for readin' real true love stories,' comments Harry, apparently à propos of the fact that one of his socks has a hole in it – presumably Betty should have darned it. And as Betty fails to rise to the bait, the insults become grosser: 'Don't mind selling but person'lly wouldn't be wasting good money on no English charver' (*Plays*, 4, 5). The slang word 'charver', used both in British and Irish English, is defined by the *OED* as 'a promiscuous woman; a prostitute. Hence: women considered sexually'. Harry equates his sister-in-law with the female flesh he trades in but himself regards as poor value for money. It is to be noted, however, that earlier Harry has tried to sleep with Betty, an assault brushed aside by her husband Michael: 'Don't make a big thing out of it. Harry was drunk that night' (*Plays*, 4, 8).

The men's misogyny is extended from women to the home and domesticity associated with them. The play's opening scene shows the Carney brothers taking over the house of Michael and Betty in which they are notionally guests.[27] There is a cacophony of male voices as each of them, preparing to meet their father Dada and younger brother Des, occupies his own private space, Harry searching for a missing sock – 'Sock-sock-sock-sock-sock? Hah? Where is it?' the hair-oiled Hugo 'singing snatches of a pop song', Iggy, tense with waiting for the others, stammering, 'Are we r-r-ready?' All Betty gets in response to her questions is a passing dig in the ribs from Harry. She is not even allowed to answer the doorbell,

'HUGO beats her to it' (*Plays*, 4, 3). The horseplay between the men develops to the point where they are throwing dirty socks, smashing cups against the wall. When Michael comes back from work, they hold the handle against him to prevent him getting in. The scene represents not just the appallingly boorish behaviour of the Carneys but a more or less deliberate trashing of the house as it stands for marriage, feminine principles of order and manners. The Carneys, who are identified with the Travellers, stigmatized in the prejudiced view of the settled community, take their revenge on the home.

The violence of the men is all the stronger because it can identify no adequate object for its anger. It is an unnameable 'them' that is the enemy. Harry declares an open war against all comers: 'I'll fight anyone that wants to, that don't want to. I'm not afraid of nobody!' But when Des innocently asks who 'they' are, the only reply is an emphatic, 'Oh, they – they – they – they – THEM!' (*Plays*, 4, 44). Similarly, Dada in his cups interrupts a rambling, sentimental monologue with a sudden outburst: 'I hate! I hate the world! It all! … But I'll get them! I'll get them! By the sweet, living, and holy Virgin Mary, I'll shatter them' (*Plays*, 4, 60). And if Harry and Dada can imagine no specific people on which to vent their frustrated fury, Michael cannot imagine what it is he aspires to for himself and his cherished younger brother Des. 'I want to get out of this kind of life. I want Des – I want us all to be – I don't want to be what I am' (*Plays*, 4, 57). The iron laws of social and psychological determinism bind all the Carneys into a space of hatred and self-hatred.

In this, Harry is the central figure. As Murphy declared, 'Michael may be the principal character in the play, but in certain ways Harry is like the hidden hero who is articulating for the thick people of the world.'[28] In fact, articulating is what he finds very difficult to do, and resents all the more those who try to explain to him, voice his meaning: 'No explaining to me. Things are clear enough to me. There's been so many intelligent blokes for so long explaining things to thick lads' (*Plays*, 4, 79). Harry is the strongest personality in the family, but we see that blocked strength twist now one way, now another, as he takes pleasure in shifting the object of his attack. So, he uses the parasite Mush in support of his view of a community ranged in conspiracy against them: 'Everyone has a motive these days, even for a smile.' But then Harry rounds on his yes-man: 'Okay. What's your motive for going 'round with me?' (*Plays*, 4, 15). Michael is Harry's main antagonist, Betty comes in for his worst abuse as Michael's English wife. Yet at a key moment in Act 3, Harry unexpectedly challenges his father by echoing

Betty's question as to where he was at the time of the fight with the rival Mulryan gang: 'Like she said, where were you?' (*Plays*, 4, 64).

The extraordinary power of the play derives from Murphy's capacity to make us understand fully the mentality of the Carneys – and even feel for them. This is the culmination of Harry's denunciation of the 'intelligent blokes', mainly directed against Michael: 'The preacher. Family. Home. (**Harry** *is suppressing tears.*) But I'm thick. Thick lads don't feel, they can't be offended' (*Plays*, 4, 79). Dada is an even more remarkable case. Imagine a Falstaff with a family, with an inner life, in a tragedy and not a subversive comic-sideshow within a history play: that's Dada. Murphy took Falstaff's evidently fictitious account of his single-handed fight against ever proliferating opponents in the Eastcheap scene of *Henry IV, Part 1* (2.4) as model for Dada's just as made-up story of his run-in with the one, two, three men who attacked him and prevented him from joining his sons for their clash against the Mulryans.[29] But Dada, unlike Falstaff, deceives himself and his delusions have disastrous consequences. This is how Murphy summed up his character in notes to himself at an early stage of drafting the play: 'a man whose life is mostly a dream. Obsessed with violence though a coward. Light-headed and senseless who builds up his family with wrong ideals and continues to *live on* in his stupid state of unreality'.[30]

Dada has come down in the world. He was a Guard, a policeman, no doubt dismissed for incompetence or corruption or both. He still likes to make himself out to be the companion of John Quinlan the doctor and Anthony Heneghan the architect, chatting fluently in Irish with them in the golf club. That illusion, however, came to an end when the reality of his class position was brought home to him, as he reveals in the final act: 'They accepted me. They drank with me. I made good conversation. Then, at their whim, a little pip-squeak of an architect can come along and offer me the job as caretaker' (*Plays*, 4, 60–1). In a meaningless act of revenge, he stole Heneghan's coat and can no longer return to the club. But Dada at least makes an effort to observe the proprieties. He addresses each of his sons by their full names, Henry, Hubert, Ignatius, Desmond as though lifting them out of their casual selves as Harry, Hugo, Iggy and Des. Unlike the others, he is initially polite to Betty: 'How do you do, ma'am! … I hope we aren't too much trouble, inconvenience' (*Plays*, 4, 20). Dada has a notion of the grammatical distinction between an adjective and an adverb, even if his self-correction sounds funny coming at the end of a sentence so full of other mistakes: 'If the Mulryans is bragging about what they'd do to sons of mine, then they have to be learned different. Differently' (*Plays*, 4, 29). He attempts to convince Betty of his high level of literacy in a drunken tête-à-tête at the start of Act 3: 'Did you ever read *True Men As We Need Them*? ... No. ... I bet you never read *Ulysses*? Hah? – Wha? – Did you? No. A Dublin lad and all wrote *Ulysses*. Great book. Famous book' (*Plays*, 4, 60). The juxtaposition of a nineteenth-century Catholic 'book of instruction for men in the world'[31] with Joyce's modernist masterpiece could not be more grotesque, but Dada has heard of *Ulysses* and does know its reputation as a 'great book'.

Dada is a monster, a bully who mistreats his wife and has turned his sons into the thugs they are. Yet in subtextual stage directions, Murphy allows us to see the inner emotional weather of such a man. In Act 1, hardly a few minutes in the house, Dada has worked himself up into a confrontation with Michael and takes off his belt to administer the beating with which he cowed his son in childhood. At that moment Betty comes in with a tray of food. '**Dada** sees **Betty**: he hesitates for a moment – embarrassed – then he lashes the table with his belt savagely; he feels he has let himself down; it drives him to excess' (*Plays*, 4, 31). At the beginning of Act 2, '**Dada** is viewing himself from different angles in the mirror. But eventually he is standing motionless, his face hopeless, looking at himself in the mirror' (*Plays*, 4, 33). The mixed medley of inchoate feelings is most evident in the culmination of his harangue to Betty in Act 3.

> Oh, I wish to God I was out of it all. I wish I had something, anything. Away, away, some place. ... No. No! I'm proud. I did all right by my family. Didn't I? ... Yaas! (*Passionately to himself.*) On my solemn oath I did my best. ... My best, my best, my best. I'm proud of them. Yah – yah – hah? I hate!
>
> (*Plays*, 4, 61)

Significantly, in response to this, Betty comments, 'Michael talks like that sometimes' (*Plays*, 4, 61). In fact we have already heard Michael voice a similar desire for some unimaginable other world, other self: 'I want to get out of this kind of life. I want Des – I want us all to be – I don't want to be what I am' (*Plays*, 4, 57). On the face of it, this might seem a strange resemblance between the braggart father and his oldest weakling son, whom he has beaten to bed as a child. Through the first two acts, Michael speaks for an alternative ethic of peaceable accommodation rather than fighting, seeking assimilation as Irish emigrants instead of the aggressive defiance of his brothers. But then, late in Act 2, the truth comes out of the encounter with the 'Muslims' at which Harry has hinted so often. Under attack, he tells Betty, 'I kept shouting for help. And then I saw my three *thug* brothers running down the road to help me. … That was the only time in my life I knew my brothers were for me. I could have been near them that night' (*Plays*, 4, 56). Instead he ran away, leaving Harry to be badly beaten up. This urges even Betty to tell him to go out and join the Carneys in their combat with the Mulryans: 'Fight! They'll think more of you. Respect you. I'll think more of you' (*Plays*, 4, 58). Though he does dash out at this point, he will not be able to overcome his cowardice any more than his father can. His doctrine of avoiding conflict, as much as Dada's braggadocio, is no more than a whistling in the dark.

One of the most painful things about the play is the failure of Michael to uphold the principles of decency for which he appears to stand; it was what the initial reviewers found hardest to take. 'One wanted to see Michael turn on his tormentors and gain their easily-granted respect. One wanted to see the father, a gas-bag and boaster, deflated.'[32] This is just the sort of conventionally moral turn that Murphy will not allow his audience. The catch-as-catch-can logic of power in the play sees the weak Michael forced by the goading of his family to turn on his wife, hit her and effectively break up his marriage: she leaves shortly afterwards. It is not that he is degraded to the level of misogynist prejudice of the others but that he has to deflect the aggression directed at himself on to someone still less capable of defence. And it is of course the culmination of that same principle that has Michael finally take up the broken bottle that he failed to wield in the fight with the Mulryans and kill Des, the youngest brother whom he has throughout regarded as an innocent to be protected from the world in which the rest of them live.

Michael, unlikely tragic hero that he is, has the presentiments of catastrophe that you might expect. 'Thou wouldst not think how ill all's here about my heart,' Hamlet tells Horatio (5.2.208–9). 'I've this awful feeling that something terrible is going to happen,' says Michael (*Plays*, 4, 35). However, Murphy builds towards his tragic conclusion with one of the funniest scenes in the play, in which the Carneys celebrate their victory over the Mulryans. This is the first of many such climactic party pieces in Murphy's work. The drunkenly swaggering men have a cup presented to them by Dada as 'Champions of England! Great Irishmen!' (*Plays*, 4, 67), followed by recitations and songs. Mush seeks to ingratiate himself as always by delivering a poem in honour of Iggy, the Iron Man, a marvellous parody of the heroic ballad style, in which the sense of geography is as shaky as the verse form:

When Iggy crossed the Atlantic foam
To England's foggy dew,

His name had swam before him
And all the tough-uns drew;
They tried to take his crown from him
But in the end they ran,
The hair oil scalding their cut-up heads,
Away from the Iron Man.

(*Plays*, 4, 68)

(The hair oil is the one authentic detail here.) This is followed by Dada's singing of 'The Boys from the County Mayo', with its chorus resoundingly ironic in the context: 'So, boys, stick together in all kinds of weather, / Don't show the white feather wherever you go' (*Plays*, 4, 69). To read this as a post-nationalist declaration of regional identity, from which 'declarations of loyalty to the nation state are significantly missing' seems a touch over solemn.[33] This is just drunken Irish bull, and recognizable as such. It is no surprise to find the self-congratulatory camaraderie quickly degenerating into a scrimmage in which Mush is put to flight by the Carneys. These are men strutting their stuff, whether in ludicrously sentimental heroic posturing or in tinderbox aggression.

In the initial staging of the play at Stratford East, Dada was left as the unequivocal villain of the piece: after the death of Des, he went out only to return with the police to finger Michael as the murderer. Revising the play for the West End transfer, Murphy removed this clangingly melodramatic conclusion, and replaced it with a tableau in which Dada is isolated, while all of the others join Michael standing around the body of their dead brother. Dada is left to babble the clichéd disclaimers of responsibility that have been his hallmark:

Brought up family, proper. Properly. No man can do more than his best. I tried. Must have some kind of pride. Wha? I tried, I did my best …I tried, I did my best … Tried … Did my best … Tried …

(*Plays*, 4, 87)

It is a really telling ending, the best possible indictment of the 'man whose life is mostly a dream', but who 'continues to live on in his stupid state of unreality'.

It was the level of violence that was the talking point of all the play's reviewers when it was staged in London. In the English press, it provided confirmation of standard stereotypes and produced striking levels of racist abuse. 'Mr Murphy has undoubtedly invented the Most Anthropoidal Family of the year. The only thing that separates his characters from a collection of wild gorillas is their ability to speak with an Irish accent.'[34] The Home Secretary was called upon to deport all Irishmen, as *Whistle* showed 'just what bog vipers we are nursing in our bosom – savage kerns like the five Carney brothers'.[35] Even those who admired the play emphasized its violence. Kenneth Tynan called it 'arguably the most uninhibited display of brutality that the London theatre has ever witnessed';[36] 'Mr Murphy', wrote Alan Brien, 'can throw a word like a stone and wield a sentence like a bicycle chain.'[37] Of course, the controversy was good publicity and when, after a run in the West End, a new production was mounted in Dublin in March 1962, it was advertised as 'the Irish Play that Shocked London'.[38] But from an Irish point of view that was just what was so deplorable: 'No blacker picture of the Irish has been painted for the stage. … It is a mournful thought that this was the picture of the Irish race that was paraded for three months last year to the wondering gaze of London theatregoers.'[39]

Murphy defended himself against this sort of nonsense, arguing that the violence could be that of any country and the men were only Irish because that was the background he happened to know.[40] The defence is understandable but a bit disingenuous. *Whistle* is certainly not 'a picture of the Irish race', but the Carneys are more than merely incidentally Irish. They have been formed by a historical context, social conditions and attitudes towards gender that is specifically Irish. John Lahr, in a long and thoughtful review of the play's New York premiere, made a detailed comparison between *Whistle* and *The Homecoming*. 'In "Whistle in the Dark," Murphy has found a metaphor for social violence within the breakdown of the family unit. His literary instincts are sociological; Pinter's are metaphysical.'[41] While one might disagree with the general accuracy of this opposition, it does pinpoint usefully the level of social and psychological embeddedness of Murphy's early work. It may help us to be more aware of the differences between the 'homosociopathic' behaviour of the Carneys – to borrow Gleitman's term again – and the predicaments of the Irish men in *On the Outside/On the Inside* and *Crucial Week*. The critical tendency has been to collapse these differences and view all these works as similar condition of Ireland plays. Murphy is from the beginning more imaginatively nuanced than this makes him appear. He was writing at this stage about the social world he knew, in its range from the shut-out apprentices and the shut in schoolteachers, the young men caught between staying in the small towns or leaving, through to the outcast emigrés who went from the margins of their own community to the urban underworld of England. His own extended time as a full-time London-based writer enabled him to stand back from such experiences and dramatize their historical origins.

CHAPTER 3
STAGING HISTORY: *THE PATRIOT GAME, FAMINE*

The J. Arthur Maginnis Story, one of Murphy's least successful plays, was staged in 1976 to disastrous reviews.[1] Originally intended as a vehicle for the popular singing group The Dubliners, it was eventually produced and toured by the Irish Theatre Company, directed by Joe Dowling, and billed as a 'musical extravaganza'. This was how Murphy himself described the style of the show: 'Songs, tunes, dances punctuate as well as become inherent episodes which go to make up the story. The story is a history … of an Irish drink called "Maginnis"; its evolution from a crude pot-boiled beverage in a mud cabin to a multi-million pound product which is sold the world over.'[2] The absurd names of the characters in this spoof version of the history of Guinness and the brewing family suggest the facetiousness of the tone. The 'J' in 'J. Arthur Maginnis' stands for 'Jaysus', the exclamation of appreciation of those sampling their first pint. The lecherous first son of the patriarch is Dan Wan na mBan, Don Juan of the Women, punning across Spanish, English and Irish – Mozart's *Don Giovanni* is one of the parodic intertexts right through the play; the two younger sons have names that mock the heroes of Padraig Pearse's pious tales in Irish, 'Eoghainín na nÉan', and 'Iosagan', that figured so largely in the school Irish syllabus.[3] The play was clearly intended as an arch and knowing send-up of Irish story-making and its sacred cows.

Yet among the drafts of *The J. Arthur Maginnis Story*, there are no less than forty pages of detailed notes on the history of brewing.[4] Murphy has carefully copied out information about the various members of the Guinness family, statistics on the growth in beer consumption, a glossary of technical terms used in brewing, with page numbers for each citation. It is exactly the same technique that he used in preparing to write *Famine* and indeed *The White House*, with its background in the Kennedy era. While it is obvious that the playwright would have felt the need for historical research for a representation of an event such as the Famine, and perhaps important, given the mimicking of J. F. Kennedy in *The White House*, to know just what was being mimicked, it seems odd to have invested so much time and effort in establishing the facts of the Guinness brewing empire if the only design was to create a ludicrous farce. Murphy's dictum that subject dictates style has already been quoted, but with his plays based on history, however loosely, the struggle has been how to find a style appropriate to the subject, how to mediate theatrically between the fact-based narrative and the fiction of the play.

This has not only been a matter of staging the pastness of history in the live form of theatre. It has also involved bringing home the realities of the past as they are manifested in the present of the author and audience. In the pantomime-like *Maginnis*, this needed to be no more than a few laughing allusions to well-known members of the Guinness family of the time, Desmond Guinness, founder of the Georgian Society, 'Dr Doric Dessie, the gorgeous Georgian', or the long-haired Garech Browne, founder of Claddagh Records – 'Oh, take that ribbon from your hair, Gareth.'[5] Much more seriously, the research into the Famine triggered by the publication of Cecil Woodham-Smith's *The Great Hunger* in 1962 led him to see its consequences still affecting his own period, his own life. 'Was I', he asked himself, 'in what I shall call my times, the mid-twentieth century, a student or a victim of the Famine? It was that thought/feeling, I believe, that made me want to write the play, the need to write about the moody self and my times' (*Plays*, 1, xi).

In that same Introduction, Murphy writes about how important it was that he was out of Ireland when researching and writing the play. 'I was living in London at the time and I believe that the geographical distancing from my roots both objectified and personalised what might otherwise have been a purely emotional, racial response' (*Plays*, 1, x). The history of Ireland as a long colonized country has always been a controversial one. Murphy would most likely have been taught in school from James Carty's very nationalistic *A Class-book of Irish History*.[6] Already by the 1960s there were alternative versions which were to become known as 'revisionist' Irish history.[7] The issue of commemoration has tended to be particularly divisive, as landmark moments in the narrative are remembered very differently depending on who is doing the remembering. The dramatization of Irish history, therefore, is not just a matter of finding the right theatrical idiom but of the political loading carried by one degree of distanced perspective or another. This chapter is concerned with such issues as they are played out in *The Patriot Game*, first conceived as an (unproduced) television script in 1966 but eventually staged by the Abbey in 1991, and in the major play *Famine*.

Commemoration

Anniversaries are occasions for commemoration – in modern Ireland none more than the Easter Rising of 1916. At the time of writing, 2016, the state is celebrating the centenary as the centrepiece in what is planned as a Decade of Centenaries from the apparent coming of Home Rule in 1912 to the establishment of the Free State in 1922.[8] The objective of the ten-year programme has been to recognize the vicissitudes of this crucial period of Irish history in all its complexity: the struggle of organized labour against the collective power of capital in the 1913 Lockout; the participation, so long occluded, of so many Irishmen in the British forces in the First World War; the dramatic event of the Rising and its aftermath in the decisive electoral victory of Sinn Féin in 1918; the setting up of Dáil Eireann, the War of Independence and the Anglo-Irish Treaty. Among many official commemorative events, there have been several Rising-themed plays and shows. Some have been site-specific, in the GPO, the central battleground of the rebellion, in Moore Street where the rebels made their last stand, and in Kilmainham Jail where the leaders were shot.[9] One play represented the 2016 commemorative campaign itself with satiric emphasis; a children's show dramatized the costs for non-participant businesses and people caught up in the event.[10] The challenge of such commemorative plays has been at once dramaturgical and political: how to represent the action of a hundred years ago so as to engage audiences in the present time of theatre, and how to balance the desire for celebration with an awareness of the multifaceted nature of the historical moment, and its implications for the contemporary Irish society that has inherited the consequences.

Tom Murphy's *The Patriot Game* was revived by the Lyric Theatre, Belfast, for a week's run in April 2016 staged by a (mostly Belfast) youth group of aspiring actors aged between 18 and 25. Some of these had so little idea of the Rising, that they thought initially it was a play about the Resurrection. To give the sense of the distance in time from the historical events, the director Philip Crawford chose to set the play in a museum, with the seven signatories of the Proclamation and Eoin McNeill, the Chief of Staff of the Irish Volunteers, as costumed exhibits, while the rest of the cast of twenty-two in contemporary dress acted out the show after museum closing time.[11] From the beginning, however, *The Patriot Game* was a commemorative text, written originally as a television script for the fiftieth anniversary in 1966, and then recast as a play for the seventy-fifth anniversary in 1991. Both television drama and stage play illustrate not only the issues for Murphy himself in staging the Rising but of the audiences and times for which they were written.

The Patriot Game was commissioned by the BBC to be broadcast in 1966, though in the end it proved too costly to produce. Murphy was evidently very conscious of the need to fill in the story for a British public who might know little or nothing about the historical context. He chose, therefore, to use a narrator as a demotic filter for the necessary information. On the backstory of the relationship between England and Ireland, the Narrator begins: 'You wouldn't know rightly where to start or how far to go.' There is a wry self-consciousness about the long parade of the colonial connection, the arbitrariness of choosing a single point of origin: 'You could start on the day seven hundred years ago and more when England first put her foot in Ireland and has it there still. … Or you could begin with Home Rule.'[12] The Narrator is there to identify the various figures involved and the interests they represented: among the rebels, as well as the principals, we are introduced to Bulmer Hobson, along with Eoin McNeill, one of the leaders of the mass movement Irish Volunteers, Constance Markievicz and Michael Mallin from the Irish Citizen Army, the small labour militia; on the other side, we meet the Lord Lieutenant Lord Wimborne, Chief Secretary Augustine Birrell, Under-Secretary Sir Matthew Nathan and Sir Lovick Friend, the Commander in Chief, Ireland.

Murphy's technique is to intercut sequences of dialogue and scenes of action with speeches, songs and poems of the period, often supplemented by commentary from the Narrator. So, for instance, the lines on Markieviecz from Yeats's 'Easter 1916' – 'That woman's days were spent / In ignorant good will, / Her nights in argument / Until her voice grew shrill.'[13] – are followed by a sardonic summary of the previous life of the Countess: 'Tired of the social circles, tired of the court, of the woman's suffragette movement, of art, of her attempts to master Gaelic … Now in her forties, this must be *the* cause.'[14] Other poems are recited in part or in full, including that of the rebels themselves, notably repeated lines from Padraig Pearse's famous 'A Mother', written as if from the point of view of his own mother after the death of himself and his brother.

It was an overloaded script calling for filmed action scenes such as the bloody Battle of Mount Street, and it is hardly surprising that it overshot its budget and had to be shelved. The script was framed by a choric group of Dubliners who appear at the start abusing and jeering at the captured rebels. By the end the same group has changed their attitude as the leaders are executed. Murphy was here representing the historical reality by which the people of Dublin and Ireland generally, initially hostile to the Rising, were moved to sympathy by the death of the executed men. The script thus ended on a fully upbeat note with the recitation of the positive last lines of 'Easter 1916'. This would have accorded with the overall celebratory mood of the 1966 commemoration in which, though there was anxiety to avoid triumphalism and a need to emphasize the modernity of contemporary Ireland as well as the achievement of the past, no doubts were expressed about the heroic nature of the Rising.[15]

By 1991 it was very different. Twenty-three years of the political violence in the North in which the ideals of 1916 were constantly invoked to justify the Republican cause had left the authorities in the south very reluctant to play up the seventy-fifth anniversary of the Rising. Indeed some committed intellectuals complained bitterly at what was referred to as 'the elephant of revolutionary forgetfulness' in the lack of official celebration.[16] Murphy's recasting of his television script as a play for performance in the Peacock, the Abbey's studio space, was effectively a way of revising the Rising in tune with the 1990s. Although much of the original text was retained, it was radically altered in spirit and style, and all the more so in the production directed by Alan Gilsenan in May 1991.

The play was explicitly metatheatrical, beginning with '**Pearse**, a young actor' coming in and dancing to a 'distorted version of "God Save the King"' on a wind-up gramophone. The Narrator is 'a young actress' in leather jacket and white dress and 'the narration appears to her to belong to another age'. She introduces it as 'The Disgraceful Story of 1916, by Tomás Macamadán (son of the Idiot)' (*Plays*, 1, 93); in a draft Murphy had explicitly identified himself as this idiotic author.[17] Instead of 1916 mediated by a neutrally offhand figure designed for the BBC audience of 1966, this is the Rising as seen by a latter-day generation of young Irish people for whom it means nothing, indeed who are actively hostile to it, at least in the case of the Narrator. It is significant that it was Nell Murphy, the playwright's own daughter, born in 1969, who was cast for the part. We are told that the actress 'doesn't like the emotion of nationalism' (*Plays*, 1, 93). Throughout the play there is a much greater degree of irony than in the television script. So, for instance, Murphy points out in the stage direction, a propos of Pearse's 'A Mother', that the 'poem was written by Pearse for his mother; the sentiments in it, therefore, are his – male. ... The actor playing **Mother** is free in interpretation to question the sentiments' (*Plays*, 1, 115).

Alan Gilsenan's direction of *The Patriot Game* certainly highlighted the distanced alienated style of the piece.[18] He dispensed altogether with Pearse playing to the distorted version of 'God Save the King', and substituted a stage rehearsal opening, the darkened set swathed in coverings, a male actor and then female actor wandering about before the coverings were removed, the group of performers bursting upon the stage playing violent games among themselves. Nell Murphy as Narrator had to reassemble a loose-leaf script, which had been battered around like a football, before she could start to read out her part, only gradually moving into performance mode. The playing style was completely non-representational. The actors wearing casual contemporary dress took on roles when necessary, with only minimal concessions to mimesis; for instance, Michael McMonagle, playing Eoin McNeill, had a slight Northern accent to indicate McNeill's origins. But the acting was very low relief; Brecht would have been pleased with it. Seven of the thirteen actors were women and they took on male or female parts indifferently. Pearse's big set speeches, the oration at the graveside of O'Donovan Rossa, the reading of the Proclamation, were delivered with sincere feeling but with no attempt to give them rhetorical afflatus. Props were minimal and used metonymically, red-upholstered armchairs for the British presence (or absence), bentwood chairs for the meetings of the IRB or hoisted as barricades. The staging was strikingly inventive as a sketched in story, with the Narrator's periodic interjection 'Yeh?' somewhere between a gesture to the Irish audience familiar with the material and snorting disbelief.

And yet the trajectory of the play, both in Murphy's text and in the production, was to bring the Narrator, however reluctantly, towards sympathy with the Rising. She struggles initially to appear in control, to neutralize her detestation of nationalism, which breaks out recurrently. At the defiant singing of 'The Soldiers' Song' by the rebels as they prepare to surrender, 'she does a little dance in celebration of their defeat, her victory' (*Plays*, I, 146). For this generation of young people in the 1990s, the clanging militarism of the National Anthem might well have seemed ludicrous along with the quixotry of the Rising itself. She recites with a sort of vicious satisfaction, the facts and figures of the duration of the rebellion and its cost: 'Five days, three hours, forty-five minutes. Five hundred dead, three hundred of them civilians; two-and-a-half thousand wounded, two thousand of them civilians' (*Plays*, 1, 147). Yet there are signs from earlier on of her conflicted emotions: 'I hate nationalism! (*To herself.*) England has no right to be here. I hate the English. No. I am honest and in control. I hate nationalism. It doesn't exist. I love life. Heigh-ho! And I'm not getting involved' (*Plays*, 1, 129).

With the final sequence in which the several leaders make their last statement before they are shot – the shots made by one of the actors hitting a mallet on the floor – she is forced to admit that nationalism does exist and she cannot stay uninvolved, as she shouts out 'UP THE REPUBLIC!' (*Plays*, 1, 149). Where in the television script Murphy had shown the historical change of attitude towards the Rising of a representative group of Dubliners, in the play this shift is transferred to a late twentieth-century Irishwoman resistant to the canonization of the event.

The play was staged in the Peacock simultaneously with a production of *The Plough and the Stars* in the Abbey main house, and Alexandra Poulain has argued that *The Patriot Game* was intended to write back to O'Casey with a more upbeat version of the Rising.[19] That certainly seems to have been the effect, to judge by the reviews, but it is remarkable that it should have been so. In context, it might have been felt that both productions were expressive of a new iconoclastic dispensation. Garry Hynes had just moved to the Abbey as Artistic Director, and her provocative production of *Plough* was a stripping back of the by this stage much loved O'Casey classic. It was played in expressionist style, the actors with shaved heads, the speaker, who in O'Casey's text mouths the words of Padraig Pearse as a mere Figure in the Window, played in Hynes's version as a modern costumed actor who stood up from among the audience. It was inevitably highly controversial, producing protests at what many regarded as a travesty. *The Patriot Game*, too, uses expressionist techniques; the British authorities, so carefully identified and named in the television script, appear only as the Lord Lieutenant, the Chief Secretary, stereotyped functionaries. With Murphy already a close associate of the young female Artistic Director newly in charge of the Abbey, *The Patriot Game* might well have appeared not at odds but at one with the radical *Plough* as a twin assault on the received orthodoxies of Irish historical and theatrical tradition.

One reviewer, intensely hostile to Hynes's *Plough*, was in fact surprised to have 'admired and enjoyed Tom Murphy's *The Patriot Game*, for it had a heart-stopping resemblance to a deconstructed version of its odious big brother next door in the Abbey'. However, in the end, she was reassured that Murphy's 'was the revolutionary view, in the context of all the criticism of 1916 leaders that has surfaced'.[20] Another critic agreed that 'Tom Murphy is not a revisionist'.[21] Indeed the play was saluted for its unequivocal attitude: 'The author does not sit upon the fence about what happened – he has come to vindicate the heroism of that era in full celebratory trottle [*sic*].[22] When the play was staged with a reduced cast of nine in Glasgow later in the year, there was an equally enthusiastic but more nuanced response. The play was produced at the Tramway Theatre as part of a Theatres and Nations series. Joyce McMillan commented on the emotional impact of the ending: 'Some in the Tramway audience wept with emotion when the pull of old Ireland became too strong for Nel's [*sic*] commonsense cynicism; but whether in joy or grief, elation or foreboding, I should not like to say.'[23] This seems a well-judged response. *The Patriot Game* releases the theatrical power of the Rising, even when staged in such a strategically alienated style, and dramatizes its continuing political impact for better or worse.

Trauma

Murphy tells about how he first read the history of the Famine in Cecil Woodham-Smith's popular history. '*The Great Hunger* was a major event in the publishing world (1962) and I expected it to inspire a half-dozen plays on the subject of the Irish Famine. I'm still surprised that they did not materialise' (*Plays*, 1, x). Chris Morash has commented, in fact, on how few Irish dramatizations of the event there have been. As against the outpouring of novels and poems about the Famine from the time of the event itself, it was not until 1886 that the first play appeared, and across the span of the twentieth century only five playwrights took it as their setting.[24] Margaret Kelleher has highlighted the general problem of representation that recurs in so much famine literature: 'Can the experience of famine be expressed; is language adequate to a description of famine's horrors?'[25] This problem is all the more acute in the theatre because of the immediacy of representation and the palpable limitations of the medium. These are live actors before us, in a restricted stage space that cannot possibly reproduce the extent of country-wide desolation. It is perhaps suggestive that, in what appears to have been the first draft of the play, Murphy began in discursive form as though starting on a nineteenth-century style novel before breaking into dialogue.[26]

A prolonged period of historical research had preceded the writing of the play. It was Woodham-Smith's 1962 book that made the first impact, but he diligently read and took detailed notes on a whole series of other historical sources: the major scholarly volume, *The Great Famine*, edited by R. Dudley Edwards and T. Desmond Williams from 1956; James

Connolly's *Labour in Ireland* (1916); the nineteenth-century histories of John O'Rourke, *The History of the Great Irish Famine of 1847* (1875) and Sir Charles Gavan Duffy, *Four Years of Irish History, 1845-1849* (1883) as well as Sir Charles Trevelyan's contemporary account, *The Irish Crisis*, originally published in 1848.[27] His initial struggle was to find a means to incorporate this historical information into the play itself. At one point, he considered intercutting, as ironic counterpoint to the dramatic action, spoken excerpts from Trevelyan's *The Irish Crisis*; one notebook was filled with extensive quotations keyed to the scenes in which they were to be used.[28] A number of scenarios for the play involved an alternation between scenes in the starving village and vignettes of the public debates elsewhere, Lord John Russell, prime minister at the outbreak of the Famine, in the House of Commons, or the disputes between Young Ireland and followers of Daniel O'Connell.[29] But in the end Murphy felt he had to narrow the focus down to the single situation and mediate all the history through the voices of the people themselves.

Literary and oral sources were vital to the development of a style for *Famine*. Murphy read no less than three novels of William Carleton, *Valentine McClutchy*, *The Emigrants of Ahadarra* and *The Black Prophet*, in each case noting passages of dialogue and colloquial phrases. One line from *The Black Prophet* that he jotted down, evidently struck him as especially significant: 'This world has nothing good or kind in it for me – and now I'll be equal to it.'[30] A version of this line appeared already in a very early scenario for the play[31] and becomes the crucial concluding statement of Maeve, the one surviving daughter of the Connor family, in the last scene of the play: 'There's nothing of goodness or kindness in this world for anyone, but we'll be equal to it yet' (*Plays*, 1, 89). Even more important were Murphy's researches in the collections of the Irish Folklore Commission.[32] It was there he found the words of the 'Colleen Rua', the fantastical ballad that Liam and Maeve sing exultantly in Scene Four, ironically titled 'The Love Scene', one of the brief moments of exhilarated happiness in the play (*Plays*, 1, 47), just before they see the corpses of a dead family. And it was from the same source that he transcribed the words of a traditional keen that was to provide the play's opening.

This is how the original text begins:

Cold and silent is thy bed. Damp is the blessed dew of night; but the sun will bring warmth and heat in the morning, and dry up the dew. But thy heart cannot feel heat from the morning sun: no more will the print of your footsteps be seen in the morning dew, on the mountains of Ivera, where you have so often hunted the fox and the hare, ever foremost among young men. [33]

In Scene One of *Famine*, this is distributed between two speakers, the mother of the dead Connor daughter and a neighbour, identified only as Dan's Wife, with a chorus of mourners providing antiphonal responses:

> **Dan's Wife**   Cold and silent is now her bed.
> **Others**   Yes
> **Dan's Wife**   Damp is the blessed dew of night,
> But the sun will bring warmth and heat in the morning and dry up the dew
> **Others**   Yes
> **Mother**   But her heart will feel no heat from the sun
> **Others**   No!
> **Dan's Wife**   Nor no more the track of her feet in the dew
> **Others**   No!
> **Dan's Wife**   Nor the sound of her step in the village of Connor,
> Where she was ever foremost among young women
>
> (*Plays*, 1, 5–6)

With the keen for John Connor's dead daughter, Murphy brings us into the community of Glanconor in August 1846. Mourning is still expressed through the ritual forms of the keen, giving a collective voice to grief, a dignity and solidarity to the experience of death. But already at the edges of this scene there is a very different kind of language, the broken exchanges of the men, desperately anxious about the potatoes:

> **Mark**   (*nervous staccato voice*) But – but – but, ye see, last year the first crop failed but the main crop was good, and this year the first crop failed, but the main crop will be – will be – will be.
> **Dan**   Hah?
> **Brian**   Oh, you could be right
>
> (*Plays*, 1, 8)

By the end of the play, Dan will be left alone to repeat the keen over his dead wife Cáit, who had led the original lament, without the support of other mourners. And overlaying Dan's intoned words are the last violent confrontation between Mother and her daughter Maeve, Mother and her husband John Connor, the final breakdown of the family. Murphy's play dramatizes, enacts, what the economic historian Cormac Ó Gráda sums up as the general effect of large-scale famines on the poor: 'Kinship and neighbourhood ties eventually loosen or dissolve, theft becomes endemic, collective resistance yields to apathy, and group integrity is shattered.'[34]

Murphy had originally planned to make Malachy O'Leary the central character in tracing this collapse of communal values, the young man who returns from England to find both his parents dead from starvation and is driven to violence by despair. But he chose instead to focus on the figure of John Connor, as the unelected leader of the village. Connor, baffled and beaten down by suffering, places his faith in a dogged unwavering adherence to the laws of God and man. When the assembled villagers demand 'what are we going to do?' his answer comes as if an inspiration:

John   What's right!
The statement seems to surprise himself as much as it does the others.
What's right. And maybe, that way, we'll make no mistakes.

> (*Plays*, 1, 22)

Throughout the action John acts on this self-validating principle of righteous action, restraining violence, stopping the men from attacking the convoy of corn-carts leaving the village, insisting on providing hospitality even when his own family is starving. And it gets him nowhere. Mother is the articulate voice of the contrary point of view: 'What's right? What's right in a country when the land goes sour? Where is a woman with childre when nature lets her down?' (*Plays*, 1, 32). The play's drama consists in the clash between her desperate pragmatics and his monolithic, blind idealism.

Vivian Mercier has written on the resonance of the Book of Job for Murphy's work, but John Connor is a Job whom God has forgotten.[35] In the face of his afflictions, John affirms his belief: 'Welcome be the holy will of God. No matter what He sends 'tis our duty to submit. And blessed be His name, even for this, and for anything else that's to come. He'll grace us to withstand it' (*Plays*, 1, 16). But he is not given that grace. Instead the violence that he has barely restrained in others and repressed in himself is used as his 'sacred strength' in the terrible act of killing his own wife and young son. For this Job there will be no second set of sheep and camels, sons and daughters to replace the first. By any normal standard of judgement, Mother is right, John is wrong throughout the play, but his deluded mistakenness has an element of the heroic in it. It is this that makes him a convincingly tragic figure. He is an Oedipus or a Lear, central to his community yet distinct from it in the individuality of his conviction, a conviction that we in the audience know to be disastrously misplaced yet have to respect for its massive integrity.

Famine, however, is no *Oedipus Rex* or *King Lear*; Murphy gives his play none of the grand afflatus of tragedy. Even though John Connor may be considered a descendant of Ireland's high kings, he is a bewildered, reluctant leader, inarticulate in his anguished struggle to deal with the situation. Fintan O'Toole, reacting to Garry Hynes's 1993 Abbey revival of the play, commented on the political implications of what he saw as Connor's obtuseness. The production, he claimed, 'demolishes the idea that John Connor … is any kind of hero':

> He is, from the start, incapable of grasping, much less altering, what is happening to his society. To take action, he would need to be able to get his bearings, but this world of famine is a world without reference points. Culture, all the accumulated associations by which people understand themselves, has been wiped away by hunger. By showing us its absence, Murphy shows us its importance.[36]

This is to read John Connor as Mother Courage, Mother Courage as Brecht himself saw her, an object lesson in failed understanding. Scene Five, 'The Relief Committee', certainly does give a powerful representation of the political forces at work in the famine: the landlords keen to offer assisted emigration as a means of clearing the land for more profitable purposes, the silently collusive merchant who has been benefiting from high grain prices, the parish priest, seeing the ulterior purposes of the others but powerless to stop them or help the suffering people.[37] This is the one scene in the play that takes place outside the village community itself, in Brechtian style putting before the audience what John Connor and the villagers so signally fail to comprehend. Yet the play is hardly as politically tendentious, nor its vision as alienated, as O'Toole makes it appear. The experience of *Famine* is the experience of the people themselves; it is expressed in their own language and we are drawn in to their suffering. Its terrible climax, with the killing of Mother and Donaill by John Connor, is some sort of dreadful act of defiance, an affirmation of the only freedom left to them, as Mother herself says in urging her husband on to the murder: 'They gave me nothing but dependence: I've shed that lie. And in this moment of freedom you will look after my right and your children's right, *as you promised*, lest they choose the time and have the victory' (*Plays*, 1, 88). To choose the time and manner of one's death is no more than a profoundly tragic consolation. Yet it represents the urge within the play to render the inalienable human dignity of the people, not to allow them to appear merely the unknowing victims of a historical calamity beyond all human scale or imagining.

As a young boy, Murphy was taken by his mother to a performance by a local amateur group in Tuam of Gerard Healy's Famine play *The Black Stranger*. It made a big impression on him.[38] Although he deliberately avoided reading the play as an adult, fearing it might interfere with his own imaginative project, some features of Healy's work may have stayed with him when writing *Famine*. The choric figure of Sean the Fool, for example, who announces the 'black stranger on the roads' whose 'first name is Hunger',[39] has some sort of equivalent in Murphy's grotesque truth-teller, the hunchback Mickeleen. The contrasts between the two plays, however, are more striking than the similarities. *The Black Stranger*, first performed in 1945, the centenary of the start of the Famine, is trapped within the traditional mode of the well-made Abbey play: the realistically rendered family cottage, crossed love affairs, standard naturalistic dialogue, all worlds away from Murphy's radically innovative theatrical style. What is more significant is the legacy of the Famine as the two playwrights render it. The hero of *The Black Stranger* is Michael Corcoran, political militant and trade union activist before his time, who is driven by the extremity of Famine to a suicidal one-man attack upon the British soldiers: 'I've strength in me yet – strength enough to send a few of the red-coats ahead of me before I go.'[40] Bridie, who was in love with Michael, at the end of the play will marry his less radical brother Bart: 'He has Michael's blood in him an' a son be Bart could be taught to take the place of the son that Michael'll never have.'[41] The political implications are clear. The descendants of the victims of Famine will be the freedom fighters who are to liberate Ireland from its colonial yoke.

Malachy O'Leary is Murphy's version of Michael Corcoran, the figure who rejects John Connor's doctrine of passive resistance. There is an early notebook sketch of Malachy, when he was still envisaged as the play's central character: '28, tall, well-built, a good deal of cunning, a survivor, lucky, violent'.[42] We see these characteristics in the play as the wordless violence of his reaction to famine is turned into action: he lures two policemen to a quarry, kills them and takes their gun, with which he then kills the relatively fair-minded Justice of the Peace supervising the relief works. At the end of the play, he has disappeared. Liam remarks, 'Some say Malachy is dead. … I don't know. Some say he's in America, a gang to him. Whichever, this country will never see him again.' To which Maeve replies darkly, 'It'll see his likes' (*Plays*, 1, 89). Murphy supplies a gloss on this open ending to Malachy's story as the 'violent *consequence* of famine. … I saw Malachy as a foretaste of the atrocities that were to follow in the Land Wars; I saw him, also, as a precursor in a direct line that led to Michael Collins, the great, decisive, guerilla leader who came seventy-or-so years later' (*Plays*, 1, xvii). But in this vision of the militant there is none of Healy's unqualified political celebration. Malachy may just as well have ended up as one of the Irish gangsters who warred on the New York streets in the 1850s, a lawless violence ethically undifferentiated from the guerilla action of a Michael Collins.

Murphy's treatment of Malachy O'Leary is closer to his counterparts in Brian Friel's *Translations*, the ever unseen Donnelly twins, and the comparison, as so often with the two playwrights, is significant. In the encounters between the 1830s Irish-speaking community of Baile Beag and the British soldiers making the Ordnance Survey map, the Donnelly twins are always somewhere offstage as the threat of violence. Just as Malachy in *Famine* kills the well-intentioned JP, so in Friel it is the innocent Hibernophile Yolland who is missing, presumed killed by the Donnellys for his cross-community relationship with Maire. *Translations*, as the inaugural production of the Field Day Theatre Company in 1980, placed the Donnelly twins as the forerunners of the Republican paramilitaries, the figures of violence who fill the vacuum when efforts at political understanding break down. And even if Murphy, by his own 1992 account, had not planned to expound the message 'that the result of a shameful present is a violent future', 'the play keeps coming up with it. (Even – though undesignedly – anticipating the outbreak of hostilities in Northern Ireland.)' (*Plays*, 1, xvii).

Friel and Murphy are at one in regarding troubled twentieth-century Irish politics as the outcome of the disasters of nineteenth-century history. But they see the pre-Famine period differently. Though *Translations* is set a decade before the Famine, it is repeatedly trailed as the catastrophe waiting to happen, with talk of the 'sweet smell' that is the first sign of blight. Maire's spirited defiance of such anxieties – 'Did the potatoes ever fail in Baile Beag? Well, did they ever – ever? Never!'[43] – we know will be overtaken by events. Friel links the coming Famine in the play to the Anglicization of the Ordinance Survey map-making and the institution of the National Schools as the factors that destroyed the Irish language and the precolonial society it expressed. In his comparison of *Translations* and *Famine*, Fintan O'Toole points out that Friel's play 'depends on a notion of history as a fall from a Golden Age, a time when people spoke Irish and were happier'.[44] By contrast, Murphy's view of pre-Famine Ireland is anything but Edenic.

In Scene One, already, we get glimpses of earlier famines, like Dan's grotesque reminiscence: 'Well, I remember in '17 – and the comical-est thing – I seen the youngsters and the hair falling out of their heads and then starting growing on their faces.' This starts off a competition in horror stories, with each of the men trying to outshout the others in their testimony to the bad years of the past: 1822, 1836, 1840, 1841. Once again it is Dan who tops all his competitors in ghastly memory: 'In '22 – In '22 – In '22! I counted eleven dead by the roadside and my own father one of them. Near the water, Clogher bridge, and the rats. I'm afeard of them since' (*Plays*, 1, 13). It is Dan, the oldest character in the play, who provides a long-term retrospective on the course of Irish history before the Famine, in his rambling speech through the penultimate Scene Eleven: 'What year was I born in? 1782 they tell me, boys. There's changes since, Brian? There is, a mac. And Henry Grattan and Henry The Other and prosperity for every damned one. Hah? Yis – Whatever that is. (*Laughs*.)' (*Plays*, 1, 84). The Volunteer Parliament, in which the leading figures were Henry Grattan and Henry Flood, meant little liberation for the likes of Dan. It is the same with the later landmark events of his time: the 1798 Rebellion – 'we had the sport, 1798 yis, out all hours under the bushes' – or Catholic Emancipation in 1829. 'Emancy-mancy – what's that, Nancy? – Freedom, boys! Twenty-nine was the year and it didn't take us long putting up the new church. The bonfires lit, and cheering with his reverence. Father Daly, yis. And I gave Delia Hogan the beck behind his back. I had the drop in and the urge on me' (*Plays*, 1, 84, 88). The official narrative of Irish history with its epoch-making dates is transformed into a series of carnival occasions for drink and otherwise illicit sex. Murphy's play encourages few illusions about the situation of the people before the Famine, demystifying any view of Irish history as a long march towards freedom.

There can be no doubt about the transformative effect of the Famine on Ireland, however it is interpreted. For Murphy, in particular, it is seen as a trauma with long-term psychological consequences. His statement on this in the Introduction to *Plays*, 1 needs to be quoted in full:

The absence of food, the cause of famine, is only one aspect of famine. What about the other 'poverties' that attend famine? A hungry and demoralised people becomes silent. People emigrate in great numbers and leave spaces that cannot be filled. Intelligence become cunning. There is a poverty of thought and expression. Womanhood becomes harsh. Love, tenderness, loyalty, generosity go out the door in the struggle for survival. Men fester in vicarious dreams of destruction. The natural exuberance and extravagance of youth is repressed … . The dream of food can become a reality – as it did in the Irish experience – and people's bodies are nourished back to health. What can similarly restore mentalities that have become distorted, spirits that have become mean and broken?

(*Plays*, 1, xi)

Famine itself dramatizes the immediate effect of starvation on the family, the community and the nation beyond, in the stand-off between John Connor and Mother, the emotional costs to Maeve and Liam of survival, the symptomatic fates of Mickeleen – a corpse in the final scene – and his violent brother Malachy, those like Mark who are forced to emigrate and are regarded as deserters and those who are doomed to stay. But in other plays Murphy explores the continuing impact of that trauma, as he sees it, in his own period. It was this interconnectedness that the three-play staging of DruidMurphy was designed to highlight with its regressive sequence from *Conversations on a Homecoming*, with its 1970s setting, through the 1950s of *Whistle* to the originating tragedy of *Famine*. The psychopathologies of masculinity looked at in the previous chapter were one sort of consequence, the boastful coward Dada of *Whistle* a travesty version of the patriarch John Connor. In *Conversations*, the main focus of the next chapter, it is the loss of any sort of self-belief, the fantasy of success expressed in the imitation of others, which shapes the descendants of the famine victims.

CHAPTER 4
BEYOND MIMICRY: *THE BLUE MACUSHLA*, *THE WHITE HOUSE*, *CONVERSATIONS ON A HOMECOMING*

'We are such a ridiculous race', says Tom in *Conversations*, 'that even our choice of assumed images is quite arbitrary' (*Plays*, 2, 54). The self-contempt for the Irish as a 'ridiculous race' is significant; in Tom's rancorous vocabulary 'ridiculous' is a favourite word. But the play does indeed illustrate the arbitrariness of those assumed images he attacks, like the American country and western music so wonderfully exemplified in Liam's singing of 'There's a Bridle Hanging on the Wall', or indeed calling the small-town pub The White House in tribute to the presidency of John F. Kennedy. As a key part of the campaign for cultural nationalism in the late nineteenth century, Douglas Hyde urged 'the necessity for de-Anglicising Ireland'. That campaign, a century and a quarter later, must be judged to have failed in that English remains the mother tongue of almost all Irish people, in spite of the state's insistence on Irish as our first national language. The cultivation of American styles of behaviour, however, could be considered a postcolonial flight from British imperial culture. To act and sound like the English was to be a 'shoneen', a 'West Briton', the worst insult that the nationalist Molly Ivors can throw at the would-be cosmopolitan Gabriel Conroy in Joyce's 'The Dead'.[1] But to identify with the United States was to associate ourselves with the greatest country in the world, which had long ago managed to liberate itself from British rule, the country whose diasporic Irish population fed those remaining at home with an imagination of expansive success.

Of such success, the election of JFK to the White House was of course the ultimate token. This was our man, the first ever Catholic to be elected to the office of president, a Kennedy who was proud to claim descent from his emigrant ancestors in New Ross. Kennedy's visit to Ireland in June 1963 was a high point in this sense of vicarious self-fulfilment, still nearly fifty years after, considered sufficiently marketable to rate a whole popular history devoted to it.[2] The assassination, coming just five months later, was

accordingly felt as a peculiarly intimate loss in Ireland. The afflatus of the
Kennedy presidency and its aftermath Murphy used in his play *The White
House* as a figure for an imagined buoyancy of the 1960s – Camelot comes to
Tuam – and the backwash of disillusionment that was to follow. What in the
United States and a wider world was the mushrooming disaster of Vietnam,
in such dreadful contrast to the hopeful mood of the 'We Shall Overcome'
generation, in Murphy's Ireland is represented as merely a sinking back into
small-town stagnation, feeling all the smaller and the more stagnant for its
temporary escape into fantasy.

One of the signs of the narrowing back of the enlightened pluralism of
the early 1960s in *The White House* and again in *Conversations* is the return
to a knee-jerk nationalism leading to pub talk of a crusading march on the
North. After the recrudescence of political violence in 1969, the decade of
the 1970s was to prove a terrible time for Ireland. In 1972 alone, nearly 500
people were killed.[3] With the introduction of internment in the North in
1971 and the establishment of the Special Criminal Court in the Republic
with its juryless trials, it appeared as though normal processes of law and
order had been suspended in both jurisdictions. What is more, the 1970
Arms Trial, when two government ministers were accused of collusion with
the IRA to import arms, even though they were acquitted, left a widespread
suspicion of corruption at the highest levels. The proliferation of breakaway
groups from within the Republican paramilitary organization, the bank
raids and kidnappings in which they were involved, heightened the sense
of a country spiralling out of control. Murphy has always denied that he
is a political writer;[4] he claims that he started to write *The Blue Macushla*
because he 'wanted to have fun', putting 'a live gangster movie on the stage'.
But he admits that in doing so he found he had discovered 'an apt metaphor
for a play about Ireland in the 1970s' (*Plays*, 1, xxi).

The Blue Macushla had its admirers, including Brian Friel who wrote
an eloquent programme note for the 1980 Abbey production, but it was a
box-office disaster, having to be taken off after three weeks of its five-week
scheduled run, something almost unprecedented for the theatre at the time.
The White House in 1972 was also problematic. Originally, its two acts,
'Speeches on a Farewell' showing the White House pub in its 1960s heyday,
and the disillusioned 1970s 'Conversations on a Homecoming', had been
played in reverse chronological order, the audience knowledge of what was to
happen ten years later intended to make more deeply ironic their experience
of the Kennedy era optimism. When this appeared not to work, the acts were
switched with 'Speeches' coming before 'Conversations'. However, Murphy

remained unhappy with the play and did not allow it to be published. It was only when he returned to the text in the 1980s as Writer in Association with Druid that he conceived of the stand-alone *Conversations*, which was to be one of his outstanding achievements, a play that is much more than merely a representation of post-1960s let-down. These plays, which are so centrally concerned with issues of success and failure, illustrate as well as anything else in Murphy's work the continuing experimentation with dramatic form by which he has managed to turn failure into success.

Borrowing a style

It was in watching American gangster movies of the 1930s and 1940s during a two-year break from writing that Murphy discovered the inspiration for *The Blue Macushla*. The title itself evidently derives from the 1946 film noir *The Blue Dahlia*. As in Murphy's play, The Blue Dahlia is a nightclub and its criminal owner is called Eddie. The habit Eddie has of tossing coins in Murphy was caught from George Raft whose motif this was in the 1932 film *Scarface*. Billy Wilders's great film *Double Indemnity* (1944) used a deceptive opening sequence leading into a flashback, as Murphy's play also does. In *Double Indemnity*, too, the dying Fred McMurray has a last cigarette lit for him by his antagonist Edward G. Robinson, a grace afforded Eddie by Danny Mountjoy in *The Blue Macushla*. Eddie's position as the little would-be big man, at the mercy of the forces of the paramilitaries and the state, parallels many of the 1930s gangster heroes played by Robinson and James Cagney caught between the law and the mob.[5] Roscommon, Murphy's good time girl with the heart of gold, is another standard Hollywood figure, reminding several reviewers of Jean Harlow, and singing in the style of Marlene Dietrich.

For *The Blue Macushla*, Murphy invented a plotline of true gangster movie complexity. Eddie O'Hara, the backstreets boy who has created in the nightclub his dream of glamorous success, has two sorts of problem on his hands. To fund the club he has robbed a bank, attributing the raid to a Republican splinter group Erin Go Brath. This organization comes after him, insisting on pain of torture or death, that he join them and allow them to use the club as a safe house. At the time of the action, this involves the brutal interrogation of someone they take to be a British Intelligence defector but who turns out to be a young priest who has self-sacrificingly taken the defector's place. The machinations of the plot demand that Eddie shoot the priest, which he appears to do in the opening sequence. Eddie's second problem comes from his old friend, Danny Mountjoy, who has served five years in jail taking the rap for a crime in which the two of them were involved, and who returns at the start of the play demanding his share in the club established originally on the money they had jointly made.

Through the narrative of blackmail, extortion and double-crossing, no-one is what they appear to be. The very inauthentic seeming 'Countess' turns out to be a Northern Irish agent of Erin Go Brath. No 1, the head of the Republican terrorists, who plays a suave Sydney Greenstreet role, is eventually revealed to be an upper-class English woman. The hooded figure whom Eddie shoots at the start of the play is not the young priest but the substituted Countess. In the melée to which the action builds, where most of the characters, including Eddie and No 1, are killed, the camp club pianist Pete moves in to control the situation as the undercover Special Branch agent he actually is. We hear Pete on the phone to a government minister reassuring him that the elusive 'black book' which everyone has been chasing is back in safe hands, the book with its incriminating list of the prominent public figures (including the minister) who have contributed to the cause of Erin Go Brath. Only the (relatively) innocent Danny and Roscommon go free.

It's a play that mimics in detail the style and form of the Hollywood movies from which it derives. And yet, of course, the very title of the club speaks its own absurdity. The Blue Dahlia nightclub has the dahlia as its emblem and it becomes a key image right through the film. But 'macushla', an Irish term of endearment, literally meaning 'my pulse' (*mo chuisle*), as in 'pulse of my heart' (*a chuisle mo chroí*); with the English word 'blue' stuck in front of it is an evident nonsense. 'Macushla', which Roscommon sings early in the play, is by way of being the club's signature tune. The 1909 song, with its treacly lyrics – 'Macushla, Macushla, your sweet voice is calling / Calling me softly, again and again / Macushla, Macushla, I hear its dear pleading / My blue-eyed Macushla I hear it in vain' (*Plays*, 1, 155) – had become enormously popular in a version sung by John McCormack. In a notebook used while drafting the play, Murphy noted, 'The songs – Macushla, Where the River Shannon flows, Off to Philadelphia, Cathleen Mavourneen, Ireland, Mother Ireland etc – are off [*sic*] the Irish-American genre.'[6] In one early version, Roscommon's first song, 'Sure'n the shamrocks were growin'' on old Broadway', is sung specifically to 'a party of Americans'.[7] The Blue Macushla is the sort of ersatz Ireland imagined by and for Irish-America, corny and wholly unreal.

Beyond Mimicry

At the same time, that artificial creation is expressive of Irish adulatory imitation of all things American. Eddie, in his white tuxedo, affects the style of a Hollywood nightclub owner. He boasts to Danny of the position he occupies. 'People come in my door up there, Kid, the classiest: that's the boss they say an' he just smiled my way. They know who's runnin' things. An' those guys I got workin' out there – Okay, so I'm vain, so what? – but it's "Sure, Boss, yeah, Boss, you're the boss, Boss"' (*Plays*, 1, 167).

The main action is set on St Patrick's Day and Mike, the enormous, dumb but loyal doorman – another Hollywood type – is properly impressed by 'Them 'Merican girls', the drum majorettes marching in the parade (*Plays*, 1, 160). St Patrick's Day in its most florid manifestation, green beer and the rest, can be seen largely as an Irish-American invention, but it has been reimported back into Ireland along with the marching bands. Besides aping American icons of success, glitzy nightclubs and movie manners, we imitate the American imagination of ourselves.

The satire in *The Blue Macushla* thus works two ways, mocking the spurious Irish-American idea of Ireland, fed by the songs of John McCormack, and at the same time the provincial need of the Irish to act out a synthetically glamorized Americanism. Yet there is also the local, specific political application of the play. Erin Go Brath is a 'splinter o' a splinter group' (*Plays*, 1, 189), a dissident Republican organization of which there were several active in the 1970s. So, for instance, Saor Eire, was a left-wing group that broke away from the IRA in 1969 and robbed banks to raise funds for the political cause, killing a policeman in the course of one such robbery.[8] Another offshoot of the IRA, which lasted much longer, was the Irish National Liberation Army (INLA), set up in 1974, which was to be responsible for the assassination of the British MP Airey Neave in 1979 along with many other deaths.[9] The activities of such paramilitaries, much given to internal feuding, were often hard to distinguish from ordinary crime, a twilight zone Eddie O'Hara exploits when he tries to pin his bank robbery on Erin Go Brath. It is clearly just a clever plot device to have the sinister No 1 turn out to be an English woman, but audiences in 1980 would be very aware of the high-profile real-life parallel of Rose Dugdale. Dugdale, like No 1, came from a very wealthy upper-class English family before being converted to militant Irish nationalism. This sort of adopted Anglophobia is voiced by No 1 in her markedly English accent at the start of Act 2: 'No material motives prompt me to do what I do! And though I too am English, I am proud of Ahland, my chosen native land, and I have no desire to do aught but frustrate the schemes of my chosen country's enemy – *England!*' (*Plays*, 1, 199).

In *The Blue Macushla* Murphy hits off his various targets – the manufactured images of Irish-America, the Irish mimicry of Americanism, the gangster-like state of 1970s Ireland – with his invented form of a Hollywood movie on stage. Though an early draft of the play was written like a screenplay, the arrival of Danny, for instance, headed '*Scene 2 Interior, Taxi-cab*',[10] from the beginning Murphy seems to have had in mind ways of reproducing such cinematic effects theatrically. For exteriors he suggests the use of a series of cardboard cutout models of cars to suggest the road that winds down to the club, while 'profile lighting is used to create the illusion of "Interior Car"'.[11] And for this hybrid movie-on-the-stage, Murphy invented a new language. A note on one draft states that 'the play is played in a Dublin (or Irish) accent with an American intonation superimposed'.[12] But there is more to it than that. The characters in *The Blue Macushla* use a whole vocabulary and set of speech traits borrowed from Hollywood movies, however Irish the accent may be. Eddie introducing Roscommon's nightclub act might be taken simply to be mimicking the appropriate style: 'An' now, folks, prepare to be transported, star of our li'l show, star of the galaxy, is gonna sing li'l number has kinda special meanin' for us here at The Blue Macushla!' (*Plays*, 1, 154). But Roscommon herself can speak this language too: 'You're a nice guy, Mr Mountjoy, stay that way. Thanks for the drink.' She resists his advances at this point because, as she says, with the disillusioned air of the too often betrayed torch singer, 'There's always been a guy with slow-movin' eyes for me to end the night with, learnin' a new trick on the tamborine' (*Plays*, 1, 172–3). Even Mike the doorman can produce the hard man style of the movies, as he responds to the men from Erin Go Brath trying to get in to the night club out of hours: 'I said the place don't open till six-thirty! What they bangin' the staff door for? Don't yiz got ears out there an' don't yiz wanta keep them?!' (*Plays*, 1, 161). All the characters in the play share a common language, Irish English heavily overlaid with gangster speak.

That is in fact one of the difficulties of the play, as identified by the largely hostile reviewers of the original Abbey production. 'The characters affected an accent which was an uneasy marriage between Chicago or Brooklyn and downtown Dublin. This was confusing and awkward to the ear, making the characters half-farcical and half real.'[13] It probably did not help that so much had been invested in a scenic design and costumes that suggested the style and period of the films it mimicked rather than the contemporary Dublin where it was supposedly set.[14] The hybrid form of the play was judged a failure: 'Treated differently it might work as a send-up of the old gangster movies or as a satire of modern Ireland,' but the effort to combine the two resulted in a superficial unreality.[15]

Those who defend *The Blue Macushla* claim that the gangster movie form distracted its audience and reviewers from the essential seriousness of its critique. '*The Blue Macushla* like *Conversations on a Homecoming* is an examination of the Irish consciousness and the starvation, the "famine" of the Irish spirit.'[16] Alexandra Poulain argues persuasively that in *The Blue Macushla*, as in Behan's *The Hostage*, 'individual and national identities are shown to be theatrical constructs, a matter of performance rather than substance'. It is specifically a postcolonial phenomenon: 'Awakening from the colonial nightmare, a stranger to itself, Ireland constructs its Blue Macushla, its American dream or Utopia.'[17] Murphy himself maintained at the time of the play's first production that 'it isn't pastiche, it isn't spoof either'.[18] But it is difficult to get past the impression of pastiche, given the language used. 'I just wantedta become a person …' pleads Eddie at the end of his long opening monologue in which he tells of his deprived background (*Plays*, 1, 154). Kathy McArdle sees here 'the essence of Murphy's work … the struggle of the self to express itself'.[19] However, the sense of the ventiloquized adoption of a borrowed idiom inhibits conviction. It is similar with his bravura final line 'clutching crucifix': 'Oh God, don't let me die, I got a few more parties to throw' (*Plays*, 1, 229). It's the quintessential Hollywood heroic anti-hero, true to his false ideals to the last. The later revival of the play by Red Rex in 1983, for which Murphy substantially rewrote the text, seems to have come closer to realizing the playwright's design for the play than the unhappy Abbey premiere.[20] But boldly ambitious as *The Blue Macushla* was, Murphy had to find other means effectively to dramatize the Irish-American dependency and its social consequences.

Images

The play that was to become *Conversations* in 1985 had an unusually extended genesis. As was mentioned in Chapter 1, it began as *Snakes and Reptiles*, a 'Thirty Minute Theatre' television play for the BBC broadcast in 1968. Though most of the characters and much of the dialogue that formed the basis for the final *Conversations* were already in place in that version of the emigrant's unsatisfactory return home, there was no equivalent to the once charismatic J. J. Kilkelly. The bar owner in *Snakes and Reptiles* was the near catatonic Benny whose only relationship was with his cat, and who, as a returned emigrant from Britain from many years before, represented a terrible warning to Michael of the long-term consequences of coming back. In *The White House*, Murphy conceived the idea of marrying this existing play with a new piece set back in 1963 when the group in the bar, stultified and distorted by small-town living in *Snakes and Reptiles*, were young and fired up with enthusiasm by the Kennedy look-alike publican Kilkelly. The reverse chronological order of playing was planned from the start: the disenchanted pub scene, set in 1971, was to come before its hopeful 1963 prequel, which ended abruptly with the assassination of JFK. In fact, at one stage Murphy seems to have had the idea of a three-part work going back in time, from 1971, through a never written 1967 episode to the 1963 beginning of the story.[21] Unhappy with *The White House* as it was staged in the Abbey in 1972, Murphy returned to work on it again in the early 1980s, and a revival was planned as part of his period as Writer in Association with Druid. It was only at quite a late stage that he decided to cut it back to the single-act reworked *Conversations*.

Through many of the drafts of the second part of *The White House*, the title given to it was 'Images', though it was eventually to become 'Speeches of Farewell' as symmetrical counterpart to 'Conversations on a Homecoming'. Murphy has talked about how taken he was with seeing David Storey's *The Contractor* in London in 1970, with its theatrical action of the building and dismantling of a wedding marquee on stage. What we see in 'Speeches' is something comparable, the redecoration of the bar of The White House prior to its grand opening, which is due the following day. Under JJ's supervision, everyone is busy at the work: Larry O'Kelly, a local architect and painter, finishing the signboard, the aspiring actor Michael and the schoolteacher Tom painting walls, the dressmaker Helen finishing off the curtains with the assistance of the shy young Peggy, the still more youthful Junior helping out where he can. We see Larry's controversial nude, 'Bridget Reclining' being hung in spite of the opposition of the local parish priest, who is outmanoeuvred by JJ, and the picture of J. F. Kennedy given a place of honour. At a late stage, all the décor is rearranged on a diffident suggestion from Peggy that it needs to be less 'formal'.[22] What is being created is something between a bar and a cultural centre. We are shown it in the process of construction but fully conscious of its fragility. It is the night of 22 November 1963; rumours are coming through of the events in Dallas well before the news breaks at the end of the play. And for the original audience, there would have been a huge overhang of irony watching The White House bar being put together in all its glory, given that they had already seen it in its shabby later version in 'Conversations'. The second act of *The Contractor* shows the disassembly of the marquee. The White House is theatrically pre-disassembled.

Fintan O'Toole identifies a possible model for JJ Kilkelly in the businessman who ran the Coca Cola bottling plant in Tuam. 'People said that Tom Naughton looked like John F. Kennedy, and, in fact, he modelled himself more than a little on the young, apparently heroic President.'[23] Certainly Kilkelly, who is at the centre of the conception of *The White House*, gives the impression of having been drawn from a real-life model. An old diary used for drafts of the play begins with an extended account of a figure then called Tom: 'A man who looks like J.F. Kennedy running a business in a small town.'[24] There is suggestive physical detail in the sketch of the character in draft stage directions: 'He is adept at mimicing [*sic*] and imitating Kennedy; remembering to effect [*sic*] the Kennedy hunched shoulders and Kennedy poses when he is being watched. ... But a nervousness about him, the way he smokes, the loping stride that can quickly change to a dance-like shuffle, when moving away after a joke, or turning back to make some point.'[25]

Another draft gives the psychological profile: 'Life has dealt him a few hard knocks and, privately, he doubts his ability to overcome a further one. A suggestion from him of sadness; insecurity that makes him require a double assent from others; a need for people to be on his side and on Kennedy's side. One suspects that his weakness is his source of strength: John F. Kennedy.'[26]

In order to provide himself with material for the imitation Kennedy, Murphy undertook an extended reading course on the historical JFK, taking detailed notes in particular on James McGregor Burns's *John Kennedy: a Political Profile*, which covered his career before the presidency, and *A Thousand Days*, Arthur M. Schlesinger Jr's memoir of his time as Kennedy's special assistant in the White House.[27] Throughout the text, Kilkelly quotes repeatedly from Kennedy's speeches, specifically some of the most famous passages from the inaugural. They ring out grandiloquently, as the great idealistic programme for the future set out by the President is applied to the refurbishment of a small-town Irish pub: 'All this will not be finished in the first one hundred days. Nor will it be finished in the first one thousand days, nor in the life of this Administration, nor even perhaps in our lifetime on this planet. But let us begin.'

Some of the quotations have a more pointed application than others: 'So let us begin anew – remembering on both sides that civility is not a sign of weakness, and sincerity is always subject to proof.' This final phrase is especially significant in a play where the sincerity and authenticity of JJ himself is so much the issue. Above all, repeated again and again, is Kennedy's appeal to the young: 'Let the word go forth from this time and place, to friend and foe alike, that the torch has been passed to a new generation.'[28] The thirty-fifth president, a notably youthful Democrat, coming after the elderly Republican ex-general Eisenhower, was marking the change in dispensation and all it represented. JJ, in gathering together his group of young people to create his imagined pub-cum-cultural centre, borrows the afflatus of that call.

Tom is sceptical at the start of the play, seeing the posturing in JJ's Kennedy airs. Asked to write a speech for the opening of The White House, JJ's inaugural, he composes a spoof praise of drink, as an obvious exposure of JJ's commercial interest in the enterprise. They argue back and forth about the merits of Kennedy, his handling of the Bay of Pigs fiasco and the Cuba missile crisis, and though Tom maintains his negative position, it is clear that he half wants to be convinced, by both JJ and Kennedy, to believe in the possibility of political and cultural transformation. (Another of the Kennedy quotations used in the play reaffirms the interrelation of the two: 'Art and the encouragement of art is political in the most profound sense, not as a weapon in the struggle, but as an instrument of understanding of the futility of struggle between those who share man's faith.'[29]) Late in the play, JJ produces a speech of his own, as though an address he might make when standing for election to the County Council, attacking all the abuses of the Ireland of his time – familiar targets for Murphy: the backward-looking politics left over from the War of Independence; the vicious education system founded on corporal punishment; the repressively puritanical attitudes towards sex; the complacent philistinism. This speech draws significant praise from Tom:

Tom   You're nearly there, J.J.
J.J.   What, Tom? (*Almost childishly flattered.*)
Tom   You're nearly yourself.
J.J.   What, Tomeen?
Tom   You don't need him.[30]

The image of Kennedy is a crutch for JJ, which, Tom suggests, he should not need if he can come to trust himself.

Of course, the whole point of the play is that JJ never can reach that point of self-reliance, any more than provincial Ireland can release itself from the provinciality that needs to look elsewhere for sustaining fantasies of success. Yet there is some sympathy, even admiration, in the characterization of JJ in Murphy's draft stage direction: 'He is inclined to patronise and to flatter, but not in an offensive way; he has a great deal of charm, boyish, but not undignified; he has the ability to inspire; he is magnanimous, generous; he loves to talk and to perform.'[31] In this sense, he is to be seen as the tragic figure of 'Speeches of Farewell', collapsing completely when his idol is killed. A small intimation of disaster comes when in the course of the redecoration, an ornamental vase is broken. JJ tries to put a good face on the matter: 'I never liked it anyway.' This then provides the cue for the play's last line. When the news of the assassination finally breaks, the other characters drift off, leaving JJ in tears, his head cradled in the arms of his wife Missus: 'I never liked him anyway,' he sobs repeatedly.[32]

The White House was premiered at the Abbey in March 1972, and because it was staged as part of the Dublin Theatre Festival, it attracted reviews in the international as well as the national press. There was a good deal of admiration for the playwright and the play, though qualified with reservations about the dramatic structure. John Barber declared: 'I doubt Ireland has a more talented dramatist than Thomas Murphy,' praising the Act 1 'Conversations' in particular as 'a comic, claustrophobic portrait-in-depth of vegetating and lethargic lives'.[33] This was the part of the play that was most appreciated by other reviewers also: 'The first act is a beautifully sustained poem of small-town life, the effect of it on J.J. and his eclipse.'[34] 'Speeches' drew a more mixed response, with a feeling that it was anti-climactic and that it badly needed cutting. The most acute criticism came in an otherwise positive review from Garry O'Connor:

> Overall the main structural flaw is that Mr Murphy has written two interesting first acts, but neither really completes the other. … But in the flaw clearly lay Mr Murphy's main ambition, to marry the two parts into significance, relating the small-town mentality, the death of Kennedy and the death of idealism at large. This ambition seems not to be at the heart of the piece.[35]

That is indeed the design of *The White House*. In the year after the dystopic fairy tale *The Morning after Optimism* had been produced, Murphy wanted to localize historically the sense of early 1970s Irish disenchantment in relation to the brief euphoria of the Kennedy presidency, which ended with the assassination. There was, however, too much of a mismatch between the theatrical styles of 'Conversations' and 'Speeches' to give full dramatic effect to the study in image-based illusion and disillusion. That was to come at last in the final realization of the project in the 1985 *Conversations*.

Orchestrating the ordinary

In response to the criticism of the structure of *The White House*, Murphy responded by authorizing a rearrangement of the acts during the initial run of the play at the Abbey, playing them in chronological order, 'Speeches' before 'Conversations'. But in spite of an RTÉ television version of the two parts that he thought 'almost' succeeded, he remained dissatisfied with it (Interview, p. 182).[36] He did not publish the text and in the early 1980s set about reworking it. He experimented with a different conclusion to 'Speeches', removing the news of the assassination, and having JJ ironically ask, 'What is the worst thing that can happen? No-one will show up on Sunday night? So what am I worried about?'[37] A number of songs were introduced early on, designed to resonate through the text: Junior sings 'There's a Bridle Hanging on the Wall', Michael gives a tuneless line or two from 'The Gay Bachelor' – 'And he loved her as he's never loved before' – and there is a duet of 'All in the April Evening' sung by JJ and Larry. In his programme for his period as Writer in Association with Druid, a revival of the revised *The White House* was one of the planned productions. In the event, what the company played in April 1985 was the new rewritten *Conversations* played on its own. Working with the 'Conversations' that had provided the first part of *The White House*, Murphy cut some characters, spliced in passages from 'Speeches', and gave a special theatrical prominence to songs.

The earlier 'Conversations' had parts for Johnny Quinn, the handyman who appeared also in 'Speeches', and the sexy bank-clerk Josephine, who lodges in the White House (which was originally a hotel, not merely a pub). Apart from the economy in personnel, Murphy obviously saw the benefits in making these offstage figures. We hear the exchange between Junior and the unseen Johnny, the only customer in the public bar behind the partition, early on: 'How yeh, Johnny! (*Exaggerated nasal brogue.*) We'll have fhrost! *Chuckling voice off, in reaction*: We will, a dhiabhail' (*Plays*, 2, 3). The ritual repetition of what is evidently Johnny's standard phrase, half mockingly imitated by Junior, serves as an establishing shot for the situation in the White House. Josephine is all the more effective as the absent object of the local men's prurient projections, as they plan to fix Michael up with her:

> **Junior**   She stays here and all: a quick nip up the stairs on your way out tonight and 'wham, bang, alikazam!'[38]
> **Tom**   The most ridiculous whore of all times.
> **Junior**   No bra.
> **Liam**   Dirty aul' thing.
>
> (*Plays*, 2, 17).

It is symptomatic of the draining away of custom from the White House to the rival pub that Anne eventually reports Josephine's message to Missus, who has been keeping an evening meal waiting for her: 'She's up in Daly's lounge. She said she had a sandwich and not to bother with her tea' (*Plays*, 2, 61).

JJ is of course the all-important offstage figure in *Conversations* as he was in the earlier version of the text; he is the alcoholic wreck who has given up even trying to run the pub, leaving Missus to cope as best she can. In *The White House*, the contrast was between the charismatic if flawed JJ the audience saw in 'Speeches' and this latter-day degenerate who never even appeared. In *Conversations* all that is there to be judged are the alternative constructions of JJ by the 'twins', Tom and Michael. For Tom, 'JJ is a slob. ... Is, was, always will be A slob' (*Plays*, 2, 51-2). Tom, sunk deep into disillusionment, denies any sort of reality at all to the past. Michael badly needs to believe in an earlier, better time and insists on the significance of JJ in it: 'He had his own idealism. ... He re-energised this whole town' (*Plays*, 2, 52). As Murphy said in an interview at the time of the first production, 'It is through the way that you analyse the past and how you look at the present situation that you're in that you reveal your character. ... So that is part of the fabric and make-up of the play.'[39] *Conversations* is built around the clash between Tom and Michael, the professional cynic against the incorrigible romantic: the past character of JJ, over which they battle, becomes one of the play's dramatic undecidables.

In *Conversations* JJ no longer channels JFK; instead Tom and Michael replay JJ's imitation of the President, adding another dimension to the ventriloquized voices of the past. The group in the White House re-enact the remembered scenes with the gusto – and the disputatiousness as to the exact script – of actors in some long-ago production. So, for example, the argument between JJ and Father Connolly on the hanging of the nude is written into *Conversations* now as recalled by Tom, Michael and Junior. In 'Speeches' it was a fairly straightforward stand-off between the progressive publican and the reactionary priest. In its recycled form it becomes a multilayered comedy of the past and the present. Michael quotes JJ, paraphrasing Kennedy: 'When long-held power leads men towards arrogance, art reminds them of their limitations' (*Plays*, 2, 20).[40] Michael and Junior remember together JJ's next retort to the priest's charge that the nude was a 'dirty picture':

> **Michael**   As far as you're concerned then, Father –
> **Junior]**   'Art galleries –'
> **Michael]**   'Art galleries – '
> **Michael** *and* **Junior** *laugh*
> **Michael**   'As far as you are concerned then, Father, art galleries all over the world are filled with dirty pictures?'

Tom is happy to play along, mimicking the prissy tones of Father Connolly, whose nickname was 'Benny Diction':

> **Tom**   (*playing Fr. Connolly*) Please, please – Boys! – please don't talk to me about art galleries. Holy Moses, I've visited hundreds of them.
>
> (*Plays*, 2, 20)

The little play within the play is expressive of the recreated joy and companionship of the men. Yet the final lines of Connolly's speech performed by Tom are equally significant. He denies that he is threatening JJ, known to his friends as John-John: 'Holy Moses, Michael – John-John – we don't have to threaten anyone. We don't have to. We, the poor conservatives – troglodytes, if you will – have seen these little phases come and go. All we have to do is wait' (*Plays*, 2, 23).

The play's action indeed illustrates the truth of the priest's remarks, mocked as they are here: in small-town Ireland the conservative forces of inertia have overcome whatever liberal impulses were represented by the 1960s White House.

One of the most significant changes Murphy made in recasting his earlier play as *Conversations* was in Michael's country of emigration. In *The White House*, as in the original *Snakes and Reptiles*, Michael had tried to become an actor in England; in *Conversations*, he is based in New York. Much of the dialogue remained unchanged, even when it made the odd line implausible. Liam, taking in the implications of Junior having lent Michael his car, comments: 'He didn't bring a bus home with him then?' (*Plays*, 2, 5). A successful emigrant to England might well have brought a car home with him; someone returning from the United States on a brief visit would be very unlikely to have done so. The issues of success and failure, of going away or staying at home, remain the same whichever the destination of those who leave. But Michael's return from New York gives a new emphasis to the Irish-American nexus in the play. Liam is the main specimen here, described in the introductory stage direction: 'He is a farmer, an estate agent, a travel agent, he owns property … he affects a slight American accent; a bit stupid and insensitive – seemingly the requisites of success' (*Plays*, 2, 4). Junior later mocks him for the affected speech, picking up on Liam's 'gals'. '"Gals". Jasus, you have more of an American accent than him!' (*Plays*, 2, 17).

Liam, who habitually addresses his companions as 'fellas', combines his fake Americanisms and his crass materialism with an unreconstructed pietistic nationalism, wonderfully illustrated in his drunken reproof to Michael:

> And there's a thing called Truth, fella – you may not have heard of it. And Faith, fella. And Truth and Faith and Faith and Truth inex – inextricably – inextricably bound. And-And! – cultural heritage – you may not (have) heard of it – No border, boy! And cultural heritage inex-inextricably bound with our Faith and Hope and Hope and Faith and *Truth!*
>
> (*Plays*, 2, 49)

And that's telling him. This extraordinary eructation is linked to Liam's other comic set piece, his country and western song: 'There's a bridle hanging on the wall / There's a saddle in a lonely stall / You ask me why my tear drops fall / It's that bridle hanging on the wall' (*Plays*, 2, 69). This sort of barroom rendition was sufficiently familiar to an Irish audience even in 2012 that, when Aaron Monaghan as Liam sang it in the DruidMurphy production in the Galway Town Hall Theatre, he could not be heard for the laughter. The Irish devotion to country and western music illustrates perfectly Tom's infuriated comment on JJ's imitation of Kennedy, quoted at the beginning of this chapter: 'He could just as easily have thought he was John McCormack or Pope John. He had so little going for him and we are such a ridiculous race that even our choice of assumed images is quite arbitrary' (*Plays*, 2, 54).

In a later speech, Tom links the absurd Irish cult of country and western to the reactionary politics of the country: 'The real enemy – the big one! – that we shall overcome, is the county-and-western system itself. Unyielding, uncompromising, in its drive for total sentimentality. A sentimentality I say that would have us all an unholy herd of Sierra Sues, sad-eyed inquisitors, sentimental Nazis, fascists, sectarianists, black-and-blue shirted nationalists, with spurs a-jinglin', all ridin' down the trail to Oranmore' (*Plays*, 2, 67). The borrowed images of American popular culture are not merely ludicrous but the symptom of a deeply dysfunctional social and political order.

The White House set up an elaborate theatrical structure to contrast 'after' with 'before', the let-down of the 1970s with the ebullience of the 1960s that came to a tragic end with Kennedy's assassination. The single-act *Conversations* seems to offer something much simpler, a low key naturalistic representation of the reunion of a group of friends for a night's drinking in the pub. The extraordinary success of the play derives from the skill with which this is shaped into a subtle and resonant dramatic structure. This is a play that happens in something like real time; at least we are very conscious of the two clocks ringing out the hours from 8 to 11, the town clock always chiming a little ahead of the church clock. (It is typical that for the conventional believer Liam this is proof that the town clock is fast, whereas for Tom it is the occasion for a wry joke: 'Another discrepancy between Church and State' (*Plays*, 2, 5).) Periodic visits to the Gents by the men in the pub punctuate the otherwise continuous action, allowing for different configurations of characters on stage while one of them is absent.

Later on in the evening, the garage mechanic Junior, the best-tempered member of the group who really is there just for the drink and the 'news', points up the generic nature of the drinking bout and its several phases: 'We've had the complimenting stage, let that be an end to the insulting stage, and we'll get on to the singing stage' (*Plays*, 2, 68). Even the early 'complimenting stage' has elements of wary suspicion in it, as the old friends eye up the homecoming emigrant – 'What brought you back? … At this time of year' (*Plays*, 2, 10) – while Michael is prickly and defensive:

Tom That's a fancy-lookin' suit you have on. –
Michael What's fancy about it? –
Tom Nothing.

(Plays, 2, 7)

But there are sequences in which memory allows the group atmosphere to be rekindled in dialogue which is almost without content, a matter of shared gestures:

Junior Jasus, you weren't home for …
Tom Must be ten years.
Junior That race week. (*He starts to laugh.*)
Tom Aw Jay, that Galway race week!
They start to laugh
Junior Aw Jasus, d'yeh remember your man?
Tom Aw God, yes, your man!
Junior Aw Jasus, Jasus! (**Junior**'s *laugh usually incorporates 'Jasus'.*)
Tom The cut of him!
Junior Aw Jasus, Jasus!
Liam Who?
Junior D'yeh remember?
Michael I do
Junior But do yeh? – Jasus, Jasus!
Liam Who was this?
Junior Do yeh, do yeh, remember him?
Michael (*laughing*) I do!
Junior Jasus, Jasus!

(Plays, 2, 10)

For all the observation about Junior's favourite profanity (repeated ten times in this one passage) and the contrast with Tom's more euphemistic 'Jay', this is not an attempt to differentiate character through speech. It is something more like a linguistic ballet. It does not matter that we do not know who 'your man' was, nor what he did that occasioned all the laughter. What is important is that Liam does not share this memory and his questions, 'Who?' 'Who was this?' mark his position as the outsider being denied admission.[41] The very expression 'your man', standard in Irish English, suggests a nudge-and-wink common knowledge. At Junior's instigation he and Tom work up the hilarity to draw Michael back into a self-consciously recreated companionship, which he has to reaffirm with his repeated 'I do'. It is the rhythm of the interchanges and the dynamic it enacts which make this compelling theatre.

The insulting stage is much more prolonged than the complimenting stage, which is hardly more than *pro forma*. Tom and Michael are old adversaries, the 'twins' not just because they were always together but because they always argued. As Junior remarks, 'The two of ye together might make up one decent man' (*Plays*, 2, 68). But there is a bitterness to their fight on this occasion that is different; at one stage, Murphy considered calling the play 'The Death of the Twins'.[42] In insisting on destroying Michael's illusions about JJ, Tom is actually bent on destroying Michael himself: 'I'm marking your card. You've come home to stay, die, whatever – and you're welcome – but save us the bullshit' (*Plays*, 2, 59). Michael in turn insinuates that Tom's belligerent attitude towards JJ comes from the depth of his disappointment: 'Did you believe too much in him?' (*Plays*, 2, 58). But the rancour between the twins is only one part of the aggression released by the alcohol. Tom launches a sustained attack on Liam, also, the successful auctioneer and businessman who is still anxious about whether he will inherit the eight-acre family farm. The tirade against Liam ends in the culminating insult 'You're only a fuckin' bunch of keys!' (*Plays*, 2, 72). Even Junior comes in for a sideswipe of Tom's malice: 'And your father won't leave you the garage. One of the young brothers will have that' (*Plays*, 2, 68).

It is Peggy who suffers most from Tom's dyspeptic bad temper, and their relationship is the most telling illustration of the crippling effects of small-town stagnation. Ten years engaged, their engagement has become like a very bad marriage. Everything Peggy does irritates Tom, and nothing more than her anxious attempts to appease and cajole him. 'Will you sit down and don't be making a show of yourself!' (*Plays*, 2, 31) is typical of the way he addresses his fiancée. Nonetheless, his final attack on her is unprecedented in its brutality:

Peggy   I'd like to go home, love.
Tom   What?

Peggy   I don't feel well, love.

Tom   Well, go! Who's stopping yeh? My God, you walk up and down from your own house twenty times a day with your short little legs! No one will molest you!

(*Plays*, 2, 79)

The pathos of Peggy's plight is caught in the stage direction that follows: 'She hurries from the room, stops in the front doorway, can't leave, her life invested in Tom – and hangs in the doorway crying' (*Plays*, 2, 80). The insulting stage of the drinking session is male dominated, and it brings out just how marginal to this group the women actually are. When Peggy suggests to Junior that his wife Gloria should join the party, he replies 'Won't I be seeing her later!' (*Plays*, 2, 73). The offstage Josephine is lusted after and despised, and Peggy is isolated, ignored and humiliated. Michael, who has proposed an innocent walk in the woods with Anne, is warned off her as 'Liam's territory' (*Plays*, 2, 85). This is a different sort of sexism from that exposed in the earlier plays, *Whistle* and *Crucial Week*, but no less damning.

What lifts the play into another dimension is the 'singing stage', which the night's drinking does finally reach. Music is important in many of Murphy's plays, and he works with a very varied repertory from classical opera through Catholic hymns remembered from his childhood to a range of popular music from different periods and of diverse styles. So, for example, in the original *The White House* JJ's particular theme tune was the jaunty musical-hall song 'Any Umbrellas'. This, however, was changed to 'All in the April Evening', a popular setting of Katharine Tynan's nineteenth-century devotional poem 'Sheep and Lambs', when the 'Speeches' section of *The White House* was being revised. A number of other songs that were to make their way into *Conversations* were in Murphy's mind at this time, such as 'The Gay Bachelor' and 'The Bridle Hanging on the Wall', but he still had to decide who was to sing them and when. It was only by experimenting with the placing of these songs that he came to achieve the complex modulations of mood in the final version of *Conversations*.

Assigning the country and western song to Liam made structural and thematic sense. It creates a comic climax some two-thirds of the way through the action and marks the beginning of the 'singing stage'. Beside the sheer ludicrousness of the small-town gombeen man playing the cowboy lamenting his dead horse, it skewers precisely that 'total sentimentality' which Tom diagnoses as the Americanized hallmark of reactionary Irish culture. When Michael starts to sing 'The Gay Bachelor' – 'At seventeen he falls in love quite madly with eyes of tender blue' – it is still in mimic mode: 'Michael has started singing/performing – perhaps Rex Harrison/ James Cagney style – for Anne' (*Plays*, 2, 75). And the lyrics have an obvious application to Michael: 'When he fancies he is past love. … It is then he meets his last love. … And he loves her as he's never loved before' (*Plays*, 2, 75–6). The romantic Michael, well gone in drink, imagines that Anne, JJ's own daughter, will provide him with a renewal of his younger self.[43] The 'Hymn to Mary', sung initially by Junior and Michael as a duet, with Anne then joining in, changes the mood (*Plays*, 2, 78–9). As a hymn that they would all have learnt in childhood, it represents a shared emotion rather than the competitive male displays that have gone before.

This quiet trio continues 'until it is stopped by **Tom**'s attack on **Peggy**' (*Plays*, 2, 79). Tom's vicious dismissal of Peggy that forces her to the doorway of the pub is in part an effusion of his own self-hatred, prefaced by an exclamation of general disgust: 'Ugliness, ugliness, ugliness' (*Plays*, 2, 79). It leads into a bitter recitation of Hal's speech from *Henry IV, Part 1*, 'I know you all, and will awhile uphold the unyoked humour of your idleness' (*Plays*, 2, 80). Hal's soliloquy, which in the original play promises the audience the discarding of his Eastcheap companions and the glorious transformation of the madcap prince into the warrior king Henry V, has a pointedly bathetic irony declaimed by the provincial schoolteacher in his thirties, who is never going to become the writer he had once dreamt of being. At one point, Murphy had planned for Tom himself to sing at the end of this speech, having brought Peggy back into the pub: '(*Still with his eyes tightly shut, he starts [to] sing, quietly, doggedly and essentially to himself*) "Tantum ergo sacra mentum [*sic*] …"'[44] This snatch from 'Pange lingua', St Thomas Aquinas's medieval Latin hymn was probably meant to express Tom's sense of his lost capacity for feeling: 'I cannot feel anything about anything anymore,' he confesses to Michael (*Plays*, 2, 76).

Relatively later on in the process of revising *Conversations*, Murphy decided to give the solo at this point to Peggy, and to have her sing 'All in the April Evening'.[45] This had been trailed from early in the play by Junior – who has any number of songs in his head generally jumbled up – trying to remember the opening lines (*Plays*, 2, 39, 57). He prompts Peggy to sing it, and there is a false start in which she begins and then turns her performance to parody, 'fixing herself into the pose of the amateur contralto at the wedding' (*Plays*, 2, 69). When the song comes therefore, it is expected by the audience and yet, in the middle of the men's drunken bull session, completely unexpected. And it grows into the dramatic climax of the whole play:

> She starts to sing – at first tentatively, like someone making noises to attract attention to herself. Then progressively, going into herself, singing essentially for herself; quietly, looking out at the night, her back to us, the sound representing her loneliness, the gentle desperation of her situation, and the memory of a decade ago. Her song creates a stillness over them all.
>
> (*Plays 2*, 81)

'All in the April Evening', which has been identified as 'JJ's song', sung by the woman whom he encouraged in her ambition to become a professional singer, has a special poignance as a marker of the lost past. But sung by the female voice that has been so continuously drowned out by the men talk of the pub, sung from the literal margin of the stage, it is powerfully expressive of all that those loud 'conversations' have been unable to articulate. The Victorian lyrics and the lushly sentimental tune may be maudlin, yet in the theatrical context the singing creates a moment of transcendent beauty in striking contrast to the ugliness Tom decries and represents.

For the audience in the theatre, the action of *Conversations* reveals dramatic truths over the course of the night's drinking. For the characters themselves it is just one more evening in the pub, all vituperation and insults forgotten at lights out with the semi-sobering return to normality. 'Give us a shout tomorrow,' says Tom to Michael, unaware that anything decisive has happened to their relationship: 'We didn't get a chance to have a right talk' (*Plays*, 2, 86). It is a fairly depressing conclusion. The *Irish Times* reviewer of the first production of *The White House* called it 'the bleakest dramatic statement ever made in, or about, this country'[46] and *Conversations* could be seen as an equally damning indictment of 1970s Ireland. There is not only the post-1960s deflation of mood, the national morning after optimism, sunk back into festering inertia. The very generic nature of the occasion, the 'conversations' that go nowhere and bring no change to the talkers, underlines the irrecoverable deadness of these lives. Tom, for all the animus he has vented against Liam, backs him up in warning Michael off any sort of relationship with Anne. She is part of the town 'territory' and a rootless returned emigré has no business with her; he is welcome only to the 'gammy one', the blow-in Josephine who has no stake in the place. If Michael leaves, 'not as confused as I was', it is only because he has come to see that he too is an outsider in what used to be his community (*Plays*, 2, 86).

And yet Murphy was unwilling to let this sour conclusion be the final impression left by the play. The parting between Michael and Anne is low key. The date to go down for a rural stroll to Woodlawn the following day was a casual one, and it is casually cancelled:

> **Michael** (*whispers*)　I have to go in the morning. … They've probably cut down the rest of the wood by now, anyway.
> **Anne**　There's still the stream.

The possibility of romance is gently blanked out. It is Michael's final message to JJ that represents a last affirmation of belief: 'Tell JJ I'm sorry I didn't see him. Tell him … (*He wants to add something but cannot find the words yet.*) Tell him I love him' (*Plays*, 2, 87). This is a bigger dramatic statement than it might appear on the surface. Earlier in the play, when still trying to defend JJ from the ravening scepticism of Tom, Michael declares 'I like him', only to be shot down in flames: 'A-a-a-w! Back to the flowers. How nice, how fey, how easy for you! "I like him"' (*Plays*, 2, 56-7). It takes courage at the end to push this up to 'I love him', in a deeply inhibited culture where the word 'love' is nearly unspeakable, all the more by one man about another. For all JJ's current bombed-out life, Michael pays tribute to the reality of his past self. Anne's role in the final tableau adds another dimension to the muted upturn in mood. In response to Michael's declaration of love for her father, 'she nods, she smiles, she knows'. After his exit, '**Anne** continues in the window as at the beginning of the play, smiling her gentle hope out at the night' (*Plays*, 2, 87). In the light of the threat of a marriage with the egregious Liam that is planned for Anne, this could be read ironically. But Anne's smiling silence and 'gentle hope', like Michael's declaration of love for JJ, and the singing of Peggy, work against the otherwise comprehensively satiric vision of the representative pub life of the Irish small town.

'Jesus, images: fuckin' neon shadows!', exclaims Tom about JJ's JFK imitation (*Plays*, 2, 57). The cultural dependency on an imagined America is for Murphy one of the outstanding symptoms of the poverty of contemporary Irish culture, a sort of neocolonial cringe. In revulsion against the corrupt politics of the 1970s, he conceived the idea of a Dublin gangster movie on stage, where the Irish underworld characters talked like James Cagney or Edward G. Robinson, and the theatre itself created pretend Hollywood cinema with cardboard cutouts. *The Blue Macushla*, however, technically and imaginatively ambitious as it was, became a prisoner of its own idea, the central metaphor inhibiting an independent dramatic reality. *The White House* used a quite different strategy. The pub in the process of creation in 'Speeches', preceded by its dilapidated latter-day version, was designed as an 'after and before' illustration of 1970s and 1960s Ireland. Calling the pub the White House as part of the publican's Kennedy act was an inflated gesture of cultural deference. The short-lived nature of that illusion was enacted in the theatrical construction and deconstruction of the pub itself. Again, as with *The Blue Macushla*, the concept weighed too heavily on the dramatic execution for *The White House* fully to work on stage.

Conversations acts as an echo chamber of the 'Speeches' section of *The White House* which is no longer there. The Kennedy lines mouthed by JJ are replayed in mockery or reverence by Tom and Michael in their contests over the past. The glamorous Camelot that fired up the imagination of the young people of 1963 has long gone. The neon shadows of the 1970s centre on the American affectations of a Liam with his twanging cowboy songs. The play works more tellingly as the dramatization of a culturally impoverished society than the blatantly satiric *Blue Macushla* or the elaborately designed *White House*. However, derivative mimicry is only one element within *Conversations* and that not the dominant one. The play uses for its basic structure the snapshot of a group on a night out, the ebbs and flows of drink and talk providing its only arc of development. There is a simple mimetic pleasure in recognizing the dynamics of the situation, from the initial wary greetings and self-conscious bonhomie through the drink-fuelled truculence to the final confessional camaraderie. It is also extremely funny. But in the talk, the sounds, the songs, *Conversations* builds to something other, something more than a study of 1970s Ireland and its discontents, a less specific drama of language and gender, of the experience of loss in time.

.

CHAPTER 5
THE PURSUIT OF PROPERTY:
THE WAKE, THE HOUSE

In the Introduction to *Plays, 6*, the Methuen Drama collection of his theatrical adaptations, Murphy tells of a meeting with the theatre director Anthony Page in London in 1998, where without explanation he was given a copy of Mikhail Saltykov-Shchedrin's *The Golovlyov Family* (*Plays*, 6, xv). It is likely that Page had seen the novel as one that Murphy might find a suitable subject for adaptation, and so it proved when *The Last Days of a Reluctant Tyrant* was staged by the Abbey in 2009. Improbable as it might have seemed, Saltykov-Shchedrin's book provided a Russian imaginative field for the working out of some of Murphy's characteristic Irish preoccupations with property and family dynamics.

The Golovlyov Family (1880), Saltykov's 300-page rambling narrative, written as a serial over five years and not originally planned as a novel, could not have seemed a very obvious case for dramatization. The author summed up the clan whose story he relates close to the end of the book: 'This family's history, over several generations, is characterised by three distinctive features: idleness, unfitness for any kind of work and drunkenness.' They are a Russian equivalent of the irreversibly dissolute Rackrents in Maria Edgeworth's novel *Castle Rackrent* (1800). The only figure temporarily to halt the family decline was the forceful matriarch Arina: 'Thanks to her personal energy', Saltykov tells us, 'this woman had raised the family to its highest-ever level of prosperity.' But all to no avail; failing to pass her qualities on to her children, she 'died entangled in a web of lethargy, idle talk and pettiness.'[1]

Murphy's cue for his theatrical conception came from a late paragraph where Porphiry, Arina's spectacularly hypocritical, evil and predatory son begins to suffer belatedly from remorse. 'From everywhere, from all corners of that loathsome house, ghosts of the wronged seemed to be creeping. Whichever way he went, in whatever direction he turned, grey spectres were moving. There was his father, Vladimir Golovlyov, in white nightcap, mocking everyone and quoting Barkov. There was brother Stepan-Blockhead, together with the quiet and priggish Pavel.'[2]

The playwright made Arina rather than Porphiry the protagonist and had her, the reluctant tyrant of his play's title, haunted by an ever increasing train of ghosts on stage as one after another of her family members die. What is more, the casual mention of Barkov here – Vladimir the father 'mocking everyone and quoting Barkov' – inspired Murphy to introduce a whole series of poems deriving from the scandalously obscene verse of the eighteenth-century Russian poet Ivan Semenovitch Barkov. Victor, Murphy's Irish equivalent of Vladimir, shares a bawdy Barkov duet with his good-for-nothing son Steven (Stepan-Blockhead), and recites his own Barkov-like address to his penis:

> O glorious member mine,
> Patient in abstinence,
> Come, now arisen, unto your reward.
>
> (*Plays*, 6, 278)

Later Steven continues in the same vein with the delivery of an equally explicit poem by the seventeenth-century English poet Rochester. The anarchic sexual energies of the men in life, reprised as onstage ghosts, represent all that the tyrannically controlling Arina has to repress in her acquisitive drive to build the Golovlyov property empire.

What Murphy seized out of the long messy story of the Golovlyov misadventures was a mutant version of *King Lear*. Arina is a female Lear who disastrously divides her property between her three sons. Peter, Murphy's counterpart to Porphiry, is Goneril and Regan rolled into one, the 'little Judas', endlessly professing love and duty to his 'dearest Mama', unceasing in his pursuit of complete power. Neither of the other two sons, the 'blockhead' Steven, nor the silent and withdrawn Paul, have the makings of a Cordelia. But Arina is like Lear in needing their love and being hurt by its denial. Murphy ends the play with a final tour de force, Arina's impassioned defence of her role as a reluctant tyrant: 'What was she to do? Things were out of hand. Let things go from bad to worse? – To nothing? Someone had to take over, full control. … I showed you as much love as was safe!' (*Plays*, 6, 351–2). Out of Saltykov's satiric novel of the decadent Russian gentry, Murphy creates an Irish family tragedy of land hunger and its psychological deformations.

On the face of it, nothing could be less like the Golovlyovs than the ultra-respectable petit bourgeois O'Tooles in *The Wake*. Murphy, however, saw an affinity between the self-deceiving hypocrisy of Saltykov's Porfiry and that of Tom O'Toole in *The Wake* 'who believes utterly everything he himself says' (*Plays*, 6, xvi). And Henry Locke-Browne, the last dissolute descendant of the Protestant landed gentry who has married into the O'Tooles, has a family likeness to the useless Golovlyov men. The O'Tooles are townspeople, the property they pursue for the most part takes the form of real estate, local business premises, rather than the land empire which Arina builds up. But the acquisitive urge is the same, with everything – love, loyalty, family feeling – subordinated to that one compulsion. The family itself becomes a war of all against all in which every move has a material objective however it may be masked. Within this context, also, repressed or marginalized sexuality goes rogue, not as the rampant masturbatory bawdry of *Reluctant Tyrant* but in the exhibitionist self-degradation of Vera the call girl.

For most of the characters in *The House*, there is no prospect of acquiring property. The guest workers returning from England for their annual two weeks holiday have no stake in their home town and no means of acquiring one. They have nothing but the savings from their year's wages and these will be splurged in a fortnight-long drinking bout that will once again leave them with nothing. The one exception is the central character Christy, with his fetishistic attachment to 'the house' of the title, the home of the de Burcas, which symbolizes for him the ideal family life which he himself has been denied. Christy is prepared to go to violent lengths to preserve, or in the end to take possession of, this house so freighted with his imagined projections of it, destroying the adored family in the process. His relationships with the de Burca daughters and their mother illustrate his inability to achieve a normally mature sexual development; it is significant that he is a pimp as Vera in *The Wake* is a prostitute. In the two plays Murphy anatomizes the disjunctions in Irish family and society between love, sex and material acquisitiveness, in which the pursuit of happiness becomes the pursuit of property.

Grasping and letting go

The Seduction of Morality (1994), Murphy's one novel, tells the story which he subsequently dramatized as *The Wake*. It is a story of multigenerational family inheritance intrigues worthy of Balzac in its byzantine complexity. Mrs O'Toole, mother of Vera, Tom, Marcia and Mary Jane, following the sudden death of her husband, persuaded her brother-in-law Brendan – he becomes Stephen in *The Wake* – to come to live with her in the family home which is also the central town hotel, and to divide up his property between the four children during his lifetime. Tom was given his uncle's house, Marcia the Shamrock Ballroom, Mary Jane the Odeon Cinema and a little shop. The Wool Stores was intended for Vera, but when she hung back from this sharing of the spoils of a still living relative, Tom acquired this too.[3] However, the intention was that, when they had the money, the children should recompense their mother for having endowed them with such a portfolio, and this unspoken contract they failed to honour. In revenge, as a 'last harsh laugh' from the grave, she transferred ownership of the hotel, the jewel in the crown of the family inheritance, to Vera.[4] With the death of the mother where the action of the novel begins, the O'Tooles are aghast to learn that the hotel now belongs to Vera, absent in the United States, where she works as a high-class prostitute. Tom and Mary Jane hatch a scheme by which he will acquire the hotel at a knock-down price through a rigged auction, and Mary Jane will be given the vacant Wool Stores, which she needs to expand her business. However, Vera returns unexpectedly, to attend her grandmother's funeral as she imagines, and upsets all their plans.

Vera has had a special relationship with her grandmother, but that too was part of another legacy-hunting scheme. When she was three, Vera had been sent to live out in the country with Mom, her widowed maternal grandmother, in the hope of having her made the heir to the farm and farmhouse. Mom and Vera got on very well, but the old woman stubbornly refused to transfer the property into her granddaughter's name. And as a punishment to Mom, Vera was recalled to live with her family. The same jealous eye to the grandmother's estate led Tom to warn the Conneeleys, Mom's kindly neighbours, against visiting her – 'he thought we were after the farm'.[5] And so she died in a tragically preventable accident. It is the discovery of this horror, and the fact that her grandmother died months before and she was never told, that leads to Vera's revolt against her family, and the scandalous display she puts on in town in defiance of them. However, in the novel, but not in the play, there is one further twist to the property story. Tom thought that he had succeeded in inveigling his grandmother into leaving the farm to him: 'He has it stocked these two months,' as Mrs Conneeley tells Vera bitterly.[6] But Mom has outwitted him, going to a solicitor in another town and making a second will, leaving the farm and house to Vera. And the novel ends with Vera, the hotel having been sold at last – and not to Tom – returning from America, having got herself deliberately pregnant, to take up occupation as a single mother in her grandmother's old house where she herself had lived as a child.

Inevitably when Murphy began to adapt the novel for the stage – which he was doing already in the year *Seduction* was published[7] – he had to compress much of the action, cutting Vera's return for her mother's funeral, updating letters from the family, the auction of the hotel and the like. The concentration was on the predatory O'Tooles, their motivation and character, and the situation of Vera coming to terms with them. The working title for the play was *Whoresplay*, an unhappy pun which was intended to point up a deliberate ambiguity. Rather like Wilde's subtitle for *Lady Windermere's Fan*, 'A Play about a Good Woman', it forced the question as to who was the whore. It is the whore's play of Vera, who flaunts her profession by shacking up initially with the thoroughly disreputable Finbar and then engaging in a days-long threesome with him and her own brother-in-law Henry in the uncurtained upper room of the town's central hotel. But the O'Tooles, who sacrifice anything and anybody to their greed for gain, are just as meretricious: 'Whores, every single one of them!', the grandmother shouted out in one of the drafts where Vera's childhood memories were played out in flashback.[8]

The play is a study of the O'Toole family collectively, and the 'culture that produces these people: A people starved of "nature" being withered by greed and materialism'.[9] But it also gives detailed attention to the individual family members. Marcia is, as her husband Henry says, only 'a bit-player in the plot' (*Plays*, 5, 121). She is appalled by the disgrace Vera brings on the family name by her antics, but the only property she really cares about is her husband when her sister has lured him away: 'I could roast her, I could scald her … I'd stick a knife in her' (*Plays*, 5, 148–9). It is her vindictive suggestion 'I'd lock her up' (*Plays*, 5, 151) that leads to the family having Vera committed to a mental hospital. Tom is invulnerable because he is so completely insulated from self-awareness by his assumed persona: 'It is difficult to insult him. … Almost invariably he is professionally jolly or professionally sad/concerned/angry' (*Plays*, 5, 102). He has driven his wife Caitriona, whom he calls Little Treasure, into mental illness. (In an epilogue to *Seduction*, she tries to kill herself and her children and eventually leaves Tom, returning to her parents' home.)

Mary Jane, the youngest sibling and Tom's partner in conspiracy, is a more interesting case. She is much cleverer than he is, and is often impatient with his obtuse insistence on masking the reality of what they are doing with his habitual moral posturing. When she is first introduced, Murphy comments in a stage direction: 'Something she has lost or betrayed has made her hard, cynical, impatient – and innocent' (*Plays*, 5, 101–2). The last epithet seems puzzling. Some light may be thrown on it by a note on the character in one of the drafts: 'There is an innocence about her also, something "lost": perhaps it is her sexuality which she has "betrayed" (sublimated) herself.'[10] Mary Jane may be seen as 'innocent' in the unawakened sexual dimension to her life, which she has lost or sublimated. Certainly there is a degree of resentment and jealousy in the attitude she shows to Vera and her freedom of behaviour. It may be that, while Vera feels outcast by being fostered with her grandmother, Mary Jane regards it as an instance of the special treatment her sibling was given.[11] She scornfully rejects the idea that Vera is 'shy'. 'For a shy person, Vera has always managed to get an extraordinary amount of attention and managed extraordinarily to do anything she liked' (*Plays*, 5, 107).

Whatever the difference in individual characterization between Tom and Mary Jane, they represent a formidably acquisitive combination, summed up graphically by Henry: 'It is a clanship between night-runners. One containing the usual, concessional understanding: when he tumbles the sheep she will get the hindquarters … '. And Henry goes on to extend the metaphor: 'These marauding family expeditions happen on a national scale' (*Plays*, 5, 124). *The Wake* is not just a study in small-town provincial acquisitiveness; it has implications for Irish society as a whole. In many ways, it could be described as Murphy's angriest play. In writing *Seduction* and in most of the early drafts of the stage version, the action was set specifically in the 1970s. But he evidently felt that it was still applicable enough to the 1990s, at the time of the big boom in the Irish economy, to move the date up to the contemporary period when it was being written.[12] The three dissidents, Vera, Finbar and Henry, who come together to shock and provoke the proper burghers of the town, in what they say and what they are, constitute an assault on twentieth-century Irish principles and practice.

Murphy sketches in Fintan's character, when he first appears in Scene Three:

> **Finbar** is forty-one, lives alone in squalor, a bachelor. A mess of hang-ups to do with class and sex. He is a product of a culture. (Lifted as a boy by the 'authorities' and put into care, brutalised there and sexually abused by the Christian Brothers.) He sells second-hand furniture and holy medals. 'Fuckin'!': a squeak, a nervous, vocal tic. Quick flash-point. A frightened scavenger.
>
> (*Plays*, 5, 85)

The indictment of the 'culture' that has produced Finbar is all the more effective for the laconic way his backstory of brutalization and abuse is filled in, as though this is – as it was – only one of hundreds of such lives. It is an added irony that holy medals should be among the pickings on which this scavenger lives. He does not know what to make of the unexpected appearance of Vera at his door in the middle of the night, Vera with whom he had a brief boy-and-girl romance many years ago abruptly terminated by her relations. His first reaction, when she suggests staying with him, is 'What would your family think, your brother say, your sisters?' (*Plays*, 5, 92). He goes on to explain his position in relation to people like the O'Tooles:

> The authorities in this town can be very serious people. *I'm* the one they say is the danger, an enemy to their order? I'll tell you. Because, unlike my colleague in the antique business up the road there, John-John McNulty, who can say fuck them *and mean it*, the reason why I say fuck them is because I'm frightened of every single one of them.
>
> (*Plays*, 5, 93)

The 'authorities' for Finbar are the middle-class property owners, the church and the state, and he has very good reason to be frightened of them.

More details of Finbar's childhood emerge in a later scene. He reacts touchily when Henry identifies the school he was sent to as 'Letterfrack, the borstal?' 'Letterfrack, Connemara, borstal, Industrial School – all right? Establishment' (*Plays*, 5, 131–2). The school, which had been set up by the nineteenth-century Quaker estate owners of Letterfrack, was to become notorious as the institution run by the Christian Brothers in which so many boys were incarcerated and abused. From 1954, it was only juvenile delinquents who were sent there – hence Henry's casual reference to it as a borstal – but earlier it had functioned as an Industrial School, supposedly training homeless or antisocial boys in a trade. Finbar goes on to remark, almost by the way, 'there's a graveyard there with one hundred children' (*Plays*, 5, 132). It was not until 2002, four years after *The Wake* was produced, that the Christian Brothers confirmed that this was indeed the exact number of children who were buried in Letterfrack in unmarked graves.[13] The full details of the treatment of boys in institutions such as Letterfrack were only to emerge finally in the Ryan Report published in 2009.[14] While it was not Murphy's principal purpose in *The Wake* to expose the abuses of church-run institutions that were only coming to light in the 1990s, Finbar is given a powerful moment of angry expostulation at one point: 'Beating the children, Henry, then buggering them: I was "in care," Henry' (*Plays*, 5, 140).

Henry, Finbar's interlocutor at this point, is Vera's other ally in her deliberately provocative defiance of her respectably conformist family. As a Locke-Browne, he is a product of a mixed marriage; though raised as a

Catholic, he has, he declares, 'Protestant and protesting genes: my mother's side, the Lockes' (*Plays*, 5, 132). As a briefless barrister, given to periodic drinking binges, however, his protest against the O'Toole family ethos into which he has married seems to follow the example of his father, the colonel, who developed a 'taste for Bushmills whiskey and young women – women all-sorts' and died scandalously in the arms of one such woman in the 'Punjab', the town no-go area where Finbar lives (*Plays*, 5, 132). He is attracted to the sheer bravado of Vera's suggestion that she burn down the hotel: 'The generosity of it! … Put it to the torch, leave it in ashes and I'll purify myself in the flames with you bejesus!' (*Plays*, 5, 125). But there is no realistic prospect of him escaping his predicament, as the self-despising marginal member of the family clan. The draft suicide note he reads out with such a flourish at the end of the play elicits only the confident reassurance from Father Billy that 'he'll be grand now for another six months' (*Plays*, 5, 176). Happy as Finbar and Henry may be to join Vera for drink and sex in the antimasque with which she shocks and titillates the town, she can rely on neither of them to stand with her at the last. Resolution in her stand-off with her family, insofar as resolution is possible, can only come by means of the wake.

There was a party scene of sorts in *Seduction* but only as an incidental coda in the final chapter entitled 'The Future'.[15] In recasting the novel for the stage, Murphy had planned from the beginning that the get-together with singing and recitations would be the theatrical climax of the play. It was, however, relatively late in the process of redrafting that Murphy came to place this as the belated wake for the dead grandmother, retitling the play *The Wake* rather than *Whoresplay* to accentuate the point.[16] In *Famine* the ritualized forms of collective mourning that constituted the wake, which we see in the play's opening scene, are not possible by the end with the breakdown of community that starvation has produced. For Vera's grandmother's death, as Mrs Conneeley notes grimly, 'There was no wake. There was an inquest' (*Plays*, 5, 85). When Vera declares that she came back, imagining her grandmother was recently dead, to pay her respects at what she assumed would be the wake, 'the reason for **Vera**'s coming home is news to **Mary Jane** and **Tom**' (*Plays*, 5, 162). The absence of a wake, the lack of an opportunity of Vera to join in mourning her much loved grandmother, had simply not occurred to them. When they assemble somewhat sheepishly, after Vera has been released from the mental hospital to which they have committed her, they adjust as best they can to her determination to have a party rather than discuss the business which is uppermost in their minds. 'I want to finalise, bury everything and mark the occasion with – a wake. Now is that not possible?' (*Plays*, 5, 163). At the request of Vera who still owns the hotel they all so want, anything is possible.

The party that follows is of course nothing like a formal wake, not least because there is no corpse: the person mourned is long dead and buried, and is never mentioned as the occasion of mourning. And it does not resemble a traditional wake, as each of the participants performs his or her party piece: a snatch of the lyrical Gershwin 'Summertime'; the languorous jazz of 'Misty'; nineteenth-century Irish favourites like 'The Moon hath Raised her Lamp' from Jules Benedict's operetta *The Lily of Killarney* or the treacly 'Little Grey Home in the West'; and as a culmination, the recitation of James Clarence Mangan's 'A Vision of Connaught in the Thirteenth Century'. It is possible to treat the whole scene as grotesque parody, as was the style of the 2016 Abbey production. Though Tina Kellegher, playing Marcia, sang 'Misty' straight, all the other songs were guyed, 'The Moon Hath Raised Her Lamp', sung in duet by Lorcan Cranitch as Tom and Pat Nolan as Father Billy, being milked for every possible laugh. But this is to miss the ambiguity of the scene's tone, as Murphy designed it, which can be traced in successive draft stage directions. In one version, he noted the change it brings in the O'Tooles: 'This scene of "musical interlude," while it lasts, has a noticeable softening effect on them. It's as if they forget their aquisitive [*sic*] selves, they forget the hotel and Vera. … (The scene is meant to be moving Hopefully!)'[17] In a somewhat later draft, he goes further: 'In what follows, while it lasts – favourite songs, party pieces – it's as if they redeem the innocence of their better selves. All rather beautiful.'[18] In the final text, this is more equivocal: 'In what follows (and though there is an element of prostitution in what they are doing) they succumb to their own songs and show/redeem something of their innocence' (*Plays*, 5, 167). In the 'element of prostitution' it is clear that these are still the 'whores' of 'whoresplay' – they are playing up to Vera for the property they crave – and the redemption of innocence is only partial, but that change of feeling needs to be registered for the wake (and *The Wake*) to achieve its full emotional trajectory.

The recitation of 'A Vision of Connaught' is of key importance here. It is led by Mary Jane, who at one point, breaks off in her declamation, dismissing it as 'rubbish' (*Plays*, 5, 172), but the others urge her on to continue with what ends up as a choric performance. This is a poem that all of them would have learnt off by heart at school, so reciting it together becomes a part of the bonding of the scene.[19] We can see why the tough-minded Mary Jane might well react against the overripe rhetoric of Mangan with its clanging refrain: 'it was the time, 'twas in the reign of Cathal Mor of the Wine Red

Hand' (*Plays*, 5, 171–2). The reign of Cathal O'Connor, King of Connacht in the immediate wake of the Norman invasion, is rendered in the poem as a time of precolonial peace and prosperity: 'seas of corn / And lustrous gardens a-left and right' (*Plays*, 5, 171). This idyllic vision, however, is to be violently contrasted with the present when 'the sky showed fleckt with blood / And an alien sun glared from the north'. This is in 'Teuton's land', and the poem as a whole is a powerful expression of nationalist protest against England's blighting colonial presence (*Plays*, 5, 173–4). It is significant that the figure that dominates this latter-day desolation is a skeleton. The poem was written at the time of the Famine and that appalling contemporary reality inflects the anti-colonial protest. Within the context of the play, Mangan's rhetorical afflatus, now recycled as a group party piece, reads back into Murphy's vision of Connacht in the late twentieth century, by this time a land of relative plenty but with its own desolation in the hunger for land and property, which is in some sort a consequence of the nineteenth century famine.

For Vera the party represents not only the wake for her grandmother that never happened, but for herself an American wake, the final parting for emigrants leaving for the United States. The nature of her response to the sing-song matches the ambivalence of the event itself.

> **Vera**'s recurring 'Ah-haa!' is a complex of emotions: the sound of an afternoon girl in an afternoon bar pretending to be having a good time; at another level there is harshness in it as having been betrayed, while at the same time there is a cry in it for the thing that has done the betraying; a modern olagon at a wake … .
>
> (*Plays*, 5, 167)

The development of Vera's emotions and the changes of feeling that take place within her constitute the central dramatic arc of the play. Being fostered by her grandmother and then abruptly withdrawn from that foster home have left her with a double feeling of insecurity. 'I used to – wonder – what had I done wrong for them to send me out here to live with grandma,' she confessed to Mrs Conneeley (*Plays*, 5, 81). What unworthiness had prompted her initial banishment from her family, but then what inadequacy occasioned her recall? In a draft note on the character, Murphy commented on the emotional neediness that resulted: 'Inwardly, privately, she is scarred, her being fostered out in childhood has left its mark. The "flaw" in her character is in her need to belong, and there is nothing to belong to except her family. Her belief in her family is her secret refuge.'[20] What the events of the play do is to destroy that secret refuge.

A sequence of shocks precipitates this change. There is the initial discovery of the date of her grandmother's death, which she assumes has just happened – she has flown the Atlantic to pay her last respects. When Mrs Conneeley reveals that it took place months before in February, 'a dream is about to turn into a nightmare' (*Plays*, 5, 82). This is then followed by the much more terrible disclosure of how the old woman had died. Living alone, with failing eyesight, she had fallen into the fire and been left to die unaided, her body only discovered days later. And this can be attributed to Tom O'Toole having warned the well-meaning Conneeleys against visiting their neighbour, believing as he does that they were looking to inherit her property. Still Vera clings to her illusions. Even after Finbar has told her how Tom is trying to cheat her of the real value of her inheritance with a rigged auction of the hotel, she resists: 'You're making statements about my family: I want you to stop. ... They mean an awful lot to me. So they do. They keep me going. Lifelong fear that I might be on my own' (*Plays*, 5, 117). When Henry finally manages to convince her of the family conspiracy against her, it precipitates a volte-face, renouncing her previous delusion: 'All my life the feeling of belonging has eluded me. Why should I go on thinking I'll find it? The thought of here *hasn't* kept me going: the thought of here cripples me' (*Plays*, 5, 124).

The mistaken attachment to home and family of which she is unworthy is indeed what has distorted Vera's sense of self and has turned her into the prostitute she is. As she puts it simply to Finbar in a discarded draft line: 'I'm a call-girl. I never liked myself.'[21] There is a kinship here with Murphy's other sex workers, Harry in *Whistle*, James and Rosie in *The Morning after Optimism* – Christy in *The House* is the most complex study of the type, as we shall see. Vera's lack of confidence in a grounded identity prompts her to treat her body instrumentally as an act of self-abnegation. At the same time she flaunts her sexuality in protest against the stifling Puritanism of the Catholic bourgeois ethos in which she grew up. There was a measure of rebellion in her taking up with the lower-class Finbar even as a teenage romance. Her revenge on her family takes the spectacular form of an orgy played out for the benefit of the townspeople. In a culture of respectability, repression and net-curtains, what could be a greater affront than publicly staged sex with the 'knacker' from the Punjab and her own brother-in-law?

It is no wonder that the family contrives to have Vera committed to a mental hospital; the wonder is that the psychiatrist releases her after a mere three-and-a-half days of examination.

Vera's psychological deformation, attached to an idea of home that continues to cripple her abroad, is a familiar trope in Murphy's work, given resonant expression already in John Joe's much-quoted exclamation in *Crucial Week*: 'It isn't a case of staying or going. Forced to stay or forced to go. Never the freedom to decide and make the choice for ourselves. And then we're half-men here, or half-men away, and how can we hope ever to do anything' (*Plays*, 4, 162). In different plays, different endings dramatized alternative means of escape from this predicament. Michael in *Conversations* aborts his 'homecoming', finally convinced of the unreality of his utopian memories of the White House community. John Joe, having defied the town with his public broadcast of their secret sins, resolves to stay and make himself an independent life. In *The Wake* Murphy makes use again of the plot twist that ended *Crucial Week*. Where John Joe hands back to Uncle Alec the ownership of the sweet shop that Mother has conspired to get for him, Vera prepares to give over as a free gift the hotel that her siblings so covet. In both cases it is a gesture of contempt for the mean-minded spirit of acquisitiveness. But whereas in the case of John Joe it seems a bit theatrically contrived, it has been prepared for in *The Wake*: 'Why didn't they ask me for it?' asks Vera early in the play, as she muses bewildered at her family's scheming to get the hotel for her; 'that's all they had to do' (*Plays*, 5, 123). And in her case, the gifting of the hotel to her siblings is an act of severance before she leaves forever.

This is the significance of her breakdown in the graveyard in the play's final scene where she once again meets Mrs Conneeley. She has been reflecting on a comment made by Mrs Conneeley at their earlier encounter: 'It's a strange thing, isn't it? Loneliness. … Sometimes, d'you know, I think about it and I have to laugh. What? Married or single or widowed or as children … it's all the same, that's the way we are' (*Plays*, 5, 81). When Vera recalls this in the last scene, Mrs Conneeley laughs:

> And **Vera** starts to laugh too. But now she is crying. Tears that she cannot stop, that she has been suppressing throughout. She begins to sob. Her sobbing continues, becoming dry and rhythmical: Grief for her grandmother, for the family that she perhaps never had, and for herself and her fear for this, her first acceptance of her isolation.
>
> (*Plays*, 5, 180)

It is impossible to tell what this might mean for Vera's future life. The position to which she goes back in New York, as a call girl who has failed to show up for a date for which she has received an advance payment, sounds a pretty desperate one. Maybe it will be possible for her, as she wishes, 'to begin again in a clean elsewhere' (*Plays*, 5, 179). What is important is that she has come through her grieving to the point where she can leave. It is a bleaker, if more convincing outcome, than the rather implausible 'happy ending' of *Seduction*.

'Ritual is part of all drama,' Brian Friel once declared: 'Drama is a RITE, and always religious in the purest sense.'[22] Murphy, like Friel and any number of other modern playwrights, seeks forms of theatrical ritual in an almost wholly secular society. Liminal situations of parting or returning, a night's drinking in the pub, can be shaped up to that end. The wake as it is staged in Murphy's play, however, only underscores the fact that it is not the collective act of mourning that in traditional Irish culture it once was, where grieving for the dead was supported by a ceremony in which the whole community could express its solidarity. The grandmother's death was not followed by a wake but the judicial process of an inquest. What Vera stages is a travesty of a wake, insofar as there is no body present, and the family is being uneasily re-assembled after a spectacular falling out over property. For the characters – and for the audience – it does produce something of a wake-like release in the shared occasion of singing and recitation. But in the end this produces not a reaffirmation of community but the acceptance of irredeemable isolation.

House and home

The House, like *The Wake*, had a textual prehistory before it was premiered by the Abbey in 2000. Ten years before, Murphy wrote a film script with a number of working titles including *The Swallow* and *La Golondrina*. 'La Golondrina' is a popular nineteenth-century Mexican song in which the swallow is used as emblem for the longing of the exile for his homeland. In an early outline of the film, Murphy summed up the story of Christy, the central character: 'A man's childhood dream is activated into an obsession which leads to murder, corruption and the destruction of himself.'[23] In the film script there are many generic scenes filling in the small town background – people in the central square, Mass-going, the dancehall, some nuns and novices – but the focus remains on Christy and his fixation on the house and the family who were his childhood images of perfect grace. When recasting the film as a play, Murphy had to get rid of many of the cinematic features, which he had initially included in the theatrical drafts: flashback scenes of Christy's life as a little boy intercut through the action, his robbing to get the money to buy the house – stealing from the London brothel where he works in one version, robbing the local publican in another – a melodramatic ending where Marie, the sister who has long been in love with Christy, discovering that he murdered Susanne, drives the two of them to a double suicide.[24] Eventually, Murphy realized the greater effectiveness of leaving more to the imagination of the audience, including the murder scene, itself dramatized on stage in many of the earlier versions. But he also juxtaposed the exceptional, psychopathological case of Christy with more representative examples of guest workers returning to their home town from England or America for their annual two weeks of holidays, giving the play its distinctive double focus.

This latter is of course familiar territory for Murphy. Indeed, *The House*, coming some forty years after the start of his playwriting career, could be seen as the complementary counterpart to *Whistle*, his first solo-authored play. In *Whistle* the emigrant Carneys from Mayo are seen abroad in Coventry; in *The House* the men from the East Galway town – transparently Tuam, though never named as such[25] – are back with the community that no longer recognizes them as its own. The characters in both plays are displaced and alienated: 'half-men here, or half-men away'. Formally, however, Murphy attempted something very different in *The House* from the tightly plotted action of *Whistle*. In *Conversations* he had built his dramatic structure around the rhythms of a night out in the pub from the first congratulatory round to the last drunken farewells. In this later play, he extended the time period to the full fortnight of the men's home holidays, but it is a similar effect as we watch the phases of the emigrants' behaviour and spirits as the main dramatic focus. The tradition by which the publican Bunty supplies one free round of drinks on arrival, another on departure, marks out the beginning and end of the process, as they move from flush and exhilarated celebration to penniless pre-parting dejection.

The House is set in the 1950s, the period of Murphy's own adolescence and young manhood. In his group portrait of the returning migrants, he is drawing on his personal memories of people like his carpenter father who only came back from his work in England on brief annual holidays. But he added to these first-hand memories with research for the play. So, for example, he read and took notes on the government report of the

Commission on Emigration and other Population Problems 1948-1954 published in 1956. He drew also on Tony Farmar's popular social history, *Ordinary Lives*. This is the source for the police inspector Tarpey's comment on the rowdy behaviour of the men in the pub: 'They go to England and America to hone their criminal skills there' (*Plays*, 5, 250).[26] There was prejudice against the men who went away among those who stayed at home. John McGahern put it in a programme note for *The House*: 'Strangely, these emigrants were looked down on by the new elite that had done well out of Independence. Somehow it was all their own sin and fault that they had to go into unholy exile.'[27] Living abroad, in the viewpoint of those remaining at home, could and did lead to a betrayal of Irish Catholic values. Murphy remembers how an elder brother who got divorced in England was not only excommunicated by the church but also written out of the family record: 'One of my sisters rooted out the photographs of him and burned them!' (Interview, p. 174)

When we first meet the men in the pub, the argument as to the relative merits of England and Ireland is already under way between the stay-at-home Jimmy and the emigrant Peter. The material benefits of high wages, the National Health Service, the Welfare State, according to Jimmy, is just evidence of 'the spreading of communism' (*Plays*, 5, 196). Peter as an expatriate is accused of a lack of commitment to his homeland: 'Do you love your country? … or you have an anchor at all, at all?' (*Plays*, 5, 196-7). This is no more than drunken pub-talk, but as the scene goes on we are made aware that violence in this group is always a possibility. These are labourers, at the peak of their physical strength and, without anything to do for their two weeks' lay-off, there is a great deal of surplus energy. One notices, for instance, that Christy has no difficulty recruiting them to help him rebuild the de Burcas' wall in Scene Four; they evidently take pleasure in the exercise. An incident in the first pub scene illustrates the potential of this unused force: '**Jimmy** … moving to go out to the Gents, has staggered and a heavy drunken hand on **Goldfish** to steady himself. Big violence potential: for a moment it looks as if **Goldfish** is going to head-butt or hit **Jimmy**, but he contains himself' (*Plays*, 5, 203).

This is a trailer for the later moment in Scene Five when, without any apparent reason, Christy does suddenly attack Jimmy, violently banging the back of his head against the wall. In the earlier scene, Christy has declared 'No provoke!' (*Plays*, 5, 203), a phrase glossed in one of the drafts of the play: 'Smiling; Spanish accent; a line from a film: I don't provoke anyone, don't provoke me.'[28] Christy has in fact had quite a lot of provocation from

Jimmy's leering hints about Louise and Christy's affair with her – 'a good night's lodgings there, boys' (*Plays*, 5, 203). But it may be that the source of Christy's assault is a delayed response to Jimmy's declaration of the emigrants' rootlessness: 'Lads, ye belong nowhere, ye belong to nobody' (*Plays*, 5, 203). As he savagely batters Jimmy, he shouts out, 'Where d'*you* belong? I'd kill for here! Would you kill for here? I'd kill! Know what I mean?' (*Plays*, 5, 226).

Christy, with his obsessive attachment to the house, is marked off as the exceptional case. His two friends, Peter and Goldfish, are presented as more representative examples of the type of the returning migrant worker. Peter is back from England where he works in construction as a steel-fixer, based in Birmingham but travelling wherever the job takes him. As Britain rebuilt after the war and began laying down the M1 as the first of its motorways, there was plenty of employment for Irish labourers like Peter, Birmingham having a particular large diasporic settlement. Peter has come home with his English wife and two 'kiddies', and they are staying with his mother. But it is typical of the distrust of those living abroad that his mother should suspect that her daughter-in-law is not a real convert to Catholicism, as Peter claims, and that he has only pretended to have a Catholic Church wedding. This is like Jimmy's claim that the emigrants do not love their country, have no anchor. And it is as though in defensive affirmation that Peter ends Scene Two with the singing of the particularly sentimental Irish-American song 'That's how I spell Ireland!' (*Plays*, 5, 204).

Peter insists both on the material advantages of England and on his continuing commitment to the values of Irish Catholicism. 'I do love my country!', he responds to Jimmy's challenge. 'And I do dream about it and all' (*Plays*, 5, 197). However, his long and desolate speech shows just how little he finds his home town corresponding to the dream:

> I wakes up this morning. Was it early? Was and all, mate, was and all. And I'm lying there like I'm drowning. Like it happens (at) times, the other side, but does you expect it at home – ay? But my eyes is so open, like you'd see in a man doesn't want to cry.
>
> (*Plays*, 5, 224)

The description that follows of walking round the empty town, standing in the square with nothing to observe beyond a dog scratching himself, is an extraordinary evocation of alienated vacancy, a high point of the play as delivered by Andrew Bennett playing the part of Peter in the 2000 Abbey premiere.[29] Attendance at early Mass does not help. 'What d'yeh pray for?' asks Goldfish. Peter is at a loss: 'For? … Some of God's grace like … So that I'd understand' (*Plays*, 5, 228). It is only when very drunk in a later scene that Peter gets to mumble what is in fact a version of an old Irish monastic prayer: 'Oh Christ … Sweet Christ … grant me the grace, to find a small hut, in a lonesome place … and make it my abode' (*Plays*, 5, 251).[30] The irony of the lost migrant worker, far gone in drink, mouthing the phrases of a seventh-century monk is obvious, but Peter too can feel the need for grace, the unsatisfied desire for a place of abode.

Though the drunken Peter can turn belligerent and denounce 'the poxy pack of fuckers in this town. Watching me. Talking about me' (*Plays*, 5, 248), he is a peaceable soul by temperament, and contrasted in this with Goldfish. Goldfish, who is normally based in the United States and who speaks his own special dialect compounded of American film lingo and pidgin Spanish, is a very different case. His aggression is noticeable from the start, as Murphy describes him at first appearance in the pub: 'A lot of energy – he moves like a boxer – and he is given to drumming violent rhythms on counter' (*Plays*, 5, 194). With Christy's brutal and unprovoked assault on Jimmy, which shocks the others – and the audience – Goldfish 'is delighted' and 'beats a silent drum roll' in applause (*Plays*, 5, 226). Where Peter is still trying to fit in with the Catholic ethos of the town, Goldfish has no doubts about the pious churchgoing townspeople signalled by the offstage bell-ringing for Sunday Mass: 'Holy Joes: they hate us. But with cunning. We is varmint, man, outcasts, white trash. … And I hate them' (*Plays*, 5, 220). It is Goldfish's explicit antagonism, his willingness to talk back to the judge who is sentencing the rowdy returned emigrants for their breaches of the peace, which results in him being much more heavily fined than the others. While Peter can return to his default state of illusion – 'Finest little fuckin' town in the world this' (*Plays*, 5, 285), he exclaims as he leaves for the train – Bunty can tell that 'we won't see Goldfish again' (*Plays*, 5, 286).

In a couple of the drafts, Murphy noted that Goldfish 'may be homosexual'.[31] Stage directions in Murphy are often put in this tentative form, and it is not clear whether in excluding this reference from the final text he had decided against this suggestion of the character's sexual orientation or merely left it as a subtext to be explored (or not) in rehearsal. It may be that some of the aggressiveness of the character may be accounted for as the result of repression. There is evidently a special relationship between Goldfish and Christy, the only character who consistently addresses him as

Martin, his real name. Whether as mere homosocial companionship or gay love, Goldfish at the point of leaving, offers Christy an escape from the town and his obsessive focus on the de Burca house:

> Fuck that aul fuckin' house, fuck here! We're bigger than here, we're
> – the energy! They're all old – even the young ones! Fuckin' place is
> dyin' – Dead! … Fuck them and their prayers for emigrants. Hop on
> a train with me, *now*, take ourselves away out of here, we'll spend a
> few days round Dublin, work out a plan for the two of us – Yeh! –
> something really interesting! Yeh? Yeh, Chris, yeh! … I'd die for yeh!'
> (*Plays*, 5, 285)

This speech, in which it is noticeable Goldfish does not use his normal affected idiolect, could be interpreted as a romantic proposition, and there was at least a hint of that in the way Don Wycherley played the part in the original production in 2000. But, if so, Christy is too far gone in his fixation on the house to be able to respond.

Christy is one of the lads in the pub, greeted with enthusiasm when he arrives, sufficiently familiar with the running of the bar that he can actually help Bunty out as assistant on the crowded night of the dance. But from the beginning it is evident that he is different from them. Though he comes back to the town at the same time as the rest, he stays beyond their regulation of two weeks. He does not work as a builder's labourer; as Susanne maliciously points out, 'you have lovely hands. … What do you do on the building sites to have lovely things like those?' (*Plays*, 5, 242). His main difference from the other returning 'swallows', however, is his attachment to the de Burcas and their house. This is not a Big House, of which there are so many in Irish literature, the eighteenth-century Palladian mansion so familiar in various stages of decay from Maria Edgeworth to Somerville and Ross and Jennifer Johnston. Murphy notes: 'The house is a four/five bedroom affair, early Victorian' (*Plays*, 5, 228), with only some three acres of land attached, as we learn at the auction. According to Riana O'Dwyer, who herself comes from the town, 'Woodlawn is Murphy's name for Gardenfield, an area with a big house on the outskirts of Tuam. … The family name was Kirwan.'[32] In the first film version, the family was called Cavanagh, the daughters Mary, Susan and Margaret.[33] In changing these to de Burca, Marie, Susanne and Louise, he moved the family upmarket, so to speak, de Burca being the Irish version of the Norman name de Burgh. As Christy's friend, the lawyer Kerrigan comments reflectively: 'They're an odd bunch. … Normans!

Norman blood sure from way back: it never left them. D'you know what I mean? They're – different' (*Plays*, 5, 209). Christy knows all too well what Kerrigan means and it is the de Burcas' 'difference' that makes them so important to him.

A reviewer of the first production of *The House* noted the Chekhovian substrate to the play: 'Tom Murphy … knows and loves his Chekhov. [In *The House*] The Cherry Orchard meets Three Sisters.'[34] Though there are three sisters in Murphy's play and they do all have variously frustrated lives, it is *The Cherry Orchard* which is the really significant intertext – a play which Murphy in fact went on adapt for the Abbey in 2004. Though Murphy claims that the germ of the play's plot derived from the story of the faked alibi which he heard from someone on a plane and adopted for Christy's cover-up of his murder,[35] the imaginative starting point for *The House* is the *Cherry Orchard* situation, specifically the relationship between Lopakhin and Ranevskaya.

In the first scene of *The Cherry Orchard*, as Lopakhin waits for the return of the owners, he remembers his first encounter with Ranevskaya, quoted here in Murphy's own version.

> The eyes, you know: the kindness in them. Always … I'll never forget it for her: I was fifteen, and my father – oh he'd 'progressed' to having the little shop over in the village then. And we'd come here, to the yard out there, for something or other, and he hit me. Drunk, of course, what else. Smack, here in the face with his fist, and the blood started to pour. And Lyubov Andreyevna, so young then, *so* – slender – took me in. I mean into here, the house, to this room, the washbasin that was over there. 'Do not cry, little peasant, it will get better before you are married.'[36]

Like Raneyskaya for Lopakhin, Mrs de Burca represented for Christy a childhood glimpse of an alternative to drunken brutalism. Christy's mother used to work for the de Burcas as a cleaning woman and he would come along with her; after she died, when he was still just a child, he ran away from his father, and showed up at the house: 'I'd like to be this family please' (*Plays*, 5, 185), he is remembered as saying. Mrs de Burca wanted in fact to take him in and have him educated, but his obstinate father would have none of it. In a childhood where he knew nothing but being beaten until he was old enough to beat his father back, Mrs de Burca stands for maternal tenderness: in the play's stage prefixes she is referred to only as 'Mother'. That motherliness for Christy is associated with the shelter of the house, its superior graciousness of living, its grounds and gardens. And that is the reason why he is so desperate to preserve it.

This is the major twist that Murphy gives to the *Cherry Orchard* situation. Ranevskaya dreads the idea of having to sell the cherry orchard but will do nothing practical to save it. Lopakhin, the friend of the family and go-ahead businessman, has the solution: clear the land of cherry orchard and house and let the property for the building of holiday homes. In Murphy's *The House*, it is Mrs de Burca who is determined to sell – she is old and ill and, since the death of her husband, she cannot manage such a large place. It is Christy who passionately wants her to stay, for everything to stay the same. He gives up much of his holiday time to cutting the grass, repairing the walls. The key exchange between the two of them comes in Scene Four when he tries to persuade her not to sell the house:

> **Mother**   It's too big. Now. It isn't working out. And – Christy! – the past is the past.
> **Christy**   Aw, I don't know so much about that!
>
> *(Plays, 5, 217–18)*

Where Lopakhin with his plans for urban summer holiday makers represents the future, Christy needs to retain the past as his only vision of an alternative to his own life, the violent product of a violent upbringing, someone who has worked as a pimp in London to make the money he uses to buy the house.[37] Christy, like Lopakhin (and again like him reluctantly), becomes the purchaser of the estate when it comes to auction. But Lopakhin's great speech when he makes the announcement in Act 3 of *The Cherry Orchard* is a brilliant study in mixed feelings, awed amazement at being the owner of 'the most beautiful estate in the world', with class triumph in the prospect of destroying it, seeing 'the trees come "tumbelling" down to the tune of Yermolay Lopakhin's axe'.[38] By contrast, for Christy there is nothing but joy at having saved the house with all it means to him.

In exploring the psychology of Christy's obsession, Murphy turned – perhaps rather unexpectedly – to Lacanian psychoanalysis. He took notes, in particular, from Jacques Lacan's 'Desire and the Interpretation of Desire in Hamlet'. So, for example, Lacan states: 'The object of the fantasy, image and pathos, is that other element that takes the place of what the subject is symbolically deprived of.'[39] Quoting this in part, Murphy applies it in his notes to the death of Christy's mother, with the transference to the de Burca family and the house of all that he has lost. The ungrammatical 'I'd like to be this family please,' not 'I'd like to be a part of this family,' is significant as it suggests how necessarily impracticable this aspiration is. Lacan comments on 'the impossible as object of desire. What characterises the obsessional neurotic in particular is that he emphasises the confrontation with this impossibility. In other words, he sets everything up so that the object of his desire becomes the signifier of this impossibility.'[40] Picking out this last sentence in his notes, Murphy evidently saw the de Burcas' house as such an impossible object of desire for Christy. His other source here was the psychoanalytic critic Elizabeth Wright's interpretation of Lacan. 'The Real turns up in relation to man's desired objects. It makes its appearance because the signifying system is revealed as inadequate: the desired object is never what one thinks one desires. What one imagines, according to psychoanalysis, is always the primordial lost object, the union with the mother.'[41] This chimera of an impossible union with the mother lies behind the peculiar psycho-sexual difficulties of Christy.

Christy is a sex worker – a pimp, if we are to believe Susanne, though in earlier drafts he had been a pornographic photo model or someone who engaged in sex for the benefit of peephole voyeurs.[42] For him, as for Vera in *The Wake*, the work he does abroad represents a self-betrayal that does not matter because of an attachment to home and family that sustains another, better idea of self. In the case of Christy, however, it is not his own family but a composite ideal of the house which includes the nurturing mother Mrs de Burca and her three lovely daughters. He desperately needs that ideal to stay stably in place – hence his unhappiness with the dilapidated state of the Woodlawn grounds, and his horror at the fact that the house is for sale. Equally, something like an incest taboo demands that sexual relationships should be kept out of this fantasy. He has had an affair with the unhappily married Louise, at her instigation much more than his, but wants out of it. He tries to enlist Susanne as an ally in his plan to buy the house in order to keep it as an unchanged haven for the de Burcas. She, however, mocks his idea of the house as 'heaven on earth' (*Plays*, 5, 245), and makes taunting sexual advances to him instead, leading directly to her murder.

Through many drafts of the play, Murphy dramatized the actual murder before realizing how much more effective it was theatrically to leave it as a key gap in the narrative, re-distributing much of the dialogue from the scene into the earlier exchange between Christy and Susanne in the pub where they make the assignation to meet in the woods. The draft scenes, however, make the psychological motivation of Christy's reaction more explicit. Susanne derides his notion of buying and preserving the house, urging him to make love to her instead: 'Do unto me what you do to Louise – only better. What Marie would like you do to do to her. You can screw that next. She's there for you. For what maybe you've done to "Mrs de Burca"?!'

It is at this point he attacks her and when she goes on, 'Fuck away your fantasy', he hits her.[43] Susanne herself is a damaged person, exploiting her sexuality in London if not as a professional prostitute, at least as someone accepting 'presents' of goods and money from a variety of men. Christy, however, has continued to idealize her along with the rest of the family, even against the evidence of his own senses. He tells Mrs de Burca in the opening scene: 'I was in a place over there [London] one night and I'd nearly have sworn it was her I saw. … But hardly: it was hardly Susanne's kind of place, if you know what I mean' (*Plays*, 5, 188–9). It is thus completely intolerable when Susanne crudely, brutally sexualizes the bodies of all the de Burca women culminating in that of the mother herself, breaching the most closely guarded taboo. And it is typical of Christy's infantilism that he should make a gapped, censored confession of this to Mrs de Burca herself, expecting some sort of forgiveness, precipitating her death instead.

The gentle, all but asexual, Marie, who has long been in love with Christy, is the daughter that would have suited him, if he had not imagined she disapproved of him. He realizes this only too late. In the play's final scene, there are hints of a possible relationship between them: Christy has taken possession of the vacant house, and Marie is going to spend her first night in her new flat.

> **Christy**   You don't have to. (*She looks at him.*) If – Yeh know?
> **Marie**   Stay? Here?
> **Christy**   Well. (*Shrugs:*) Yeh. (*Then:*) Yeh.
>
> (*Plays*, 5, 288)

But that is as far as it goes, as far as it can go. This after all is the man who killed Marie's sister, was responsible for the death of her mother; though she does not know that, he does. The contrast with *The Cherry Orchard* is again significant. Lopakhin tries and dismally fails to organize a celebratory send-off for the family, tries and fails to propose to Vera as everyone wants him to, and takes himself off to his next business deal in Kharkov, while the first blows of the axe are heard that will bring down the cherry orchard. Murphy's house remains, with Christy its owner in sole occupation, but he has destroyed everything that gave it meaning for him. He is trapped in the shell of his own fantasy.

'It initially appears to be a natural successor to Murphy's *The Wake*,' wrote one reviewer of the premiere of *The House*. 'But it delves much deeper.'[44] The two plays are indeed obviously related, Christy some sort of male counterpart to Vera, as the returned emigrant trying to work through illusions or obsessions about house and home. But *The House* does indeed delve deeper in the psychology of Christy and in the dramatization of the group dynamics of the other returning workers. It is in many ways a grim enough play. As another reviewer commented, 'in Murphy's bleak world both Nietzsche and Schopenhauer cast long shadows and there is no redemption from isolation and loneliness.'[45] Yet by comparison with the fierce indictment of the greed-driven society of *The Wake*, *The House* appears a warmer play, with a kind of empathy rather than mere understanding for all its characters: the tragic case of Christy, the frustrations of Peter and Goldfish, the plight of Kerrigan the lawyer who feels contaminated by having been made an involuntary accomplice to murder in helping Christy fake his alibi. Above all, the kindly decency of Mrs de Burca, realized in her tender relationship with her daughters and Christy her surrogate son, serves as a moral centre all the more luminous for the inevitability with which it is destroyed.

At the time of the production of *The House*, Fintan O'Toole, always Murphy's most persuasive advocate, commented: 'Lesser playwrights have to choose whether to be realists or poets, excavators of a given patch of ground or wide-ranging explorers. Murphy is always both at the same time.'[46] *The House* and *The Wake*, like the other plays considered so far in this book, might be considered characteristic of Murphy in his realist mode, excavating the specific patch of ground which is Irish provincial society, from what he sees as its nineteenth-century shaping conditions in the trauma of the famine to the deformations of its modern conditions. If in *Famine* he reached back imaginatively to historical origins, in most of these plays he writes from what he himself knows, the small town ethos in which he grew up, the comings and goings of diasporic workers, the distortions and disabilities such a community produced. His characteristic style, well described as 'a fragmented vernacular rubble of Irish and English,'[47] vividly realizes the speech habits of a particular time and place. Yet none of this is limited to documentary realism nor yet to a merely diagnostic social anatomy. Murphy's plays are certainly political in spite of his repeated disavowals: there is real political edge to *Crucial Week*, *The Blue Macushla* and *The Wake*. But it is never their main raison d'être. The specifying social particulars are only there to take us inside theatrical worlds, which are in the end imaginatively autonomous. And there is a whole other mode of his work in which he starts free from a localizing representational ground, in which he is more obviously explorer than excavator. It is to the plays in this other style that I want now to turn in the following chapters of my book.

CHAPTER 6
WORLDS OF THEIR OWN:
THE MORNING AFTER OPTIMISM,
THE SANCTUARY LAMP

It is a measure of just how ambitious a dramatist the young Murphy was that, after the production of *Whistle* and the drafting of *Crucial Week*, he embarked on *The Morning After Optimism* as his third full-length play in October 1962. He had achieved great theatrical success with his fiercely realistic rendering of the emigrant Irish family in Coventry. *Crucial Week*, though written in a very different style, was of a piece with *Whistle* insofar as it brought to life the stifling conditions of the Irish provincial town that drives the 'fooleen' John Joe to the point of emigration. *Optimism*, however, was something totally different. Here there was no recognizable social space but a fairy-tale forest in which appear, improbably, a prostitute and a pimp speaking a grotesque argot of their own, neither identifiably Irish or English, meeting surreal versions of themselves in the superclean Edmund and Anastasia who seem to have wandered in from some other play. Bringing a social-political lens to bear on *Optimism*, Fintan O'Toole places it with *Whistle* and *Crucial Week* as a trilogy concerned with the modernizing state of Ireland in 1960s when the early post-Independence dreams of a Golden Age had failed to materialize, leaving behind a 'morning after' dregs of disillusionment.[1] But it is equally possible for Alexandra Poulain to relate *Optimism* to much later plays, *The Sanctuary Lamp*, *The Gigli Concert*, *Too Late for Logic*, detecting in all of them comparable mythic rituals of initiation.[2]

Many of Murphy's plays represent situations shaped by their moments in Irish history. In *Famine*, most obviously, he sought to imagine the master-tragedy of the nineteenth century and its long consequences into the modern period. Again and again, he has returned to the 1950s and 1960s, the period of his adolescence and young manhood, but there are also plays like *Conversations* that catch the mood of the 1970s, *The Blue Macushla* or *The Wake* speaking to the conditions of their later periods. From as early in his career as *Optimism*, however, he looked to create other sorts of theatrical spaces in which time and history were no more than incidental.

So, for example, *The Sanctuary Lamp* is set in 'a church in a city' (*Plays*, 3, [98]). We can conjecture that the city is somewhere in England, the church is definitely Catholic, but we do not need to know more than that. The concentration is entirely on what this place means or does not mean to the three characters who stray into it. In *The Gigli Concert* we are certainly in Ireland, where JPW King is an expatriate Englishman, and the otherwise never named Irish Man sounds very much like a 1980s Irish property developer. But it is a locked-in drama in which nothing matters beyond the interaction of the three characters and the voice of Gigli that soars above them. The time and place of *Bailegangaire* is quite definitely given: '1984, the kitchen of a thatched house'.[3] But the contemporaneity of the 1980s social exterior, in which the local Japanese factory is under threat of closure, only emphasizes the time warp of the interior in which Mommo retells her story of long ago. And it is in some non-specifiable folkloric other time that the laughing competition actually dramatized in *A Thief of a Christmas* takes place.[4]

Though *Whistle* could be categorized as a classic naturalistic tragedy, the inevitable catastrophe precipitated by the interplay of specific social and psychological conditions, Murphy has never tied himself to naturalism, always varying the theatrical style to the subject from the freehand expressionism of *Crucial Week* through the Brechtian alienation of *Famine* to the staged film noir of *The Blue Macushla*. Several of his plays, however, are based on genres which are more radically non-representational. *Optimism* is a dystopian fairy tale in which the 'happy ending' comes with a double murder. The films of Fellini were among the imaginative sources for the poetic collage that is *The Sanctuary Lamp*. Myths underpin *The Gigli Concert* (Faust) and *Too Late for Logic* (Orpheus and Eurydice), and both plays depend on music as much as dialogue and action. The folk tale that Mommo so endlessly recites in her high shanachie style in *Bailegangaire* is a play within a nested set of plays receding back to *Thief* and *Brigit*, the oral narrative an embroidery upon stories that are themselves in mythic mode. The chapters that follow in this book are concerned with this mythifying dimension of Murphy's theatre, beginning with *Optimism* and *Sanctuary Lamp*.

Astray in the forest

It has long been a commonplace of Beckett scholarship that the genesis of his texts involved a process of 'vaguening', the removal of specifying details that linked the plays to an extra-theatrical real world.[5] With Murphy a comparable genetic development might be defined as simplification and excision. So, for example, in drafting *The Sanctuary Lamp*, he wrote whole episodes dramatizing the backstories of the three central characters before confining them to the one night in the church together.[6] Similarly, at an early stage of planning *The Morning after Optimism*, there was to be a scene in which the innocent Edmund character in search of his brother meets up in a pub with an Aristocrat, a Politician, a Cynic and a Philosopher, all of whom advance their different points of view and were designed to provide a choric commentary on the main action. For the same pub scene, he even considered an encounter with 'God who is in his working clothes, looking like a plumber in a boiler suit'.[7] These plans never made it into the first drafts of the play, but they are characteristic of the wildness of Murphy's writing imagination that needs to be pruned back to the theatrically viable.

This is more striking because, by Murphy's own account, the kernel of the play was there from the start, in James's story from Scene Five, beginning 'Once upon a time there was a boy, as there was always and as there always will be, and he was given a dream, his life' (*Plays*, 3, 43). It was this that dictated the style of the fairy tale: 'I wrote that speech first however sketchily and the play moved back from that and on to the conclusion' (Interview, p. 179).[8] The story tells of the several mutually supporting illusions of childhood sponsored by all the different authority figures, and the rewards on offer. 'His mother told him do not be naughty, who would be naughty, no one is naughty. And there would be a lovely girl for him one day, and she would have blue eyes and golden hair.' It was same with the teachers who were 'saintly men and could answer all his questions. They told him of the good laws, and how bad laws could not work because they were bad.' The church reinforced the message: 'And the church told him of God, kind God and guardian angels. And how everyone is made just like God – even the little boy himself was. There was a devil but he was not alive; he was dead really. And the kindest stork you ever saw with a great red beak would take care of any works and pomps.'

The fable ends with an image of balloons:

> everyone gave the little boy balloons, the most expensive balloons, already inflated, yellow, green, blue and red, the very best of colours, and they floated above him, nodding and bobbing, and lifting his feet clear off the ground so that he never had to walk a step anywhere. Until one day, one of them burst, and it was the beautiful blue one.

And he was not prepared for this. So, one day, he walked away into the forest forever.

(*Plays*, 3, 43–4)

Coded into the little satiric story was Murphy's own loss of his devout childhood faith, and the alienation of his move to London. 'I had no contact, immediate contact with my family. … The world I knew for twenty-seven years was suddenly gone. … The knowns were gone' (Interview, p. 179). But the 'optimism' here retrospectively conjured up went well beyond the personal, and the hung-over 'morning after' yielded the deeply rancorous hate-filled disillusionment that we see in the character of James. From the initial conception of the play, it was a quest narrative, the quest by the idealistic young Edmund for his long-lost older brother. And as much as Edmund yearns to find James, James as desperately does not want to be found by his innocent alter ego. In the naming of Edmund there may be a wry allusion to Shakespeare's brothers in *King Lear*. Murphy's Edmund, like Shakespeare's, is the younger illegitimate half-brother, but he plays the Edgar-like part of continuing to believe against all the odds in a providential sense of things, while it is the legitimate older brother James, in the Shakespearean Edgar's position, who defies all conventional faith. James and Edmund are the first of the sets of doubles who appear so often through Murphy's work: Francisco and Harry in *Sanctuary Lamp*, Tom and Michael in *Conversations*. The one torments the other with the 'tyranny of the idealised self';[9] the anti-idealist insists the more vehemently on a principled cynicism. James insists that 'he's a volunteer for dirty deeds, that he's mightily proud of getting worse, that he aims to hit rock-bottom, for his basis' (*Plays*, 3, 49).

From the beginning, *Optimism* was conceived as a four-hander. Where James was matched with his younger romantic half-brother Edmund, his partner the ageing Rosie had a female counterpart in the beautiful young orphan girl, initially called Juliana. The action consisted in an elaborate dance of cross-loving. James is entranced with the loveliness of Juliana, so unexpectedly encountered in the forest, and when he is unsuccessful in his wooing, he threatens to rape her. She is rescued from this horror by her destined hero Edmund, only to be separated from him and rescued once again. Rosie in her turn falls for Edmund and is repulsed by him. The rejected lovers pool their resentment and plan a murderous revenge but in the event are unable to carry out their intentions. The two couples part awkwardly but amicably, Juliana even giving James a farewell kiss, Rosie doing the same for Edmund. The disillusioned children of experience have definitively parted from their innocent earlier selves and must make do with one another.[10] It was this version which Murphy thought was going to be produced in London in 1963,[11] and which Cyril Cusack in a letter of 1964 said he preferred 'to any other modern play I have seen or read'.[12] However, through the 1960s it continued to await production, and it was only after the successful Abbey staging of *Famine* in 1968 and *Crucial Week* in 1969 that *Optimism* finally reached the theatre in the heavily revised text subsequently published.[13]

In rewriting the play, Murphy very much heightened the surreal incongruity of James and Rosie's appearance in the forest. Just who they are and what they have done previously was left unclear in the early versions; in an interim revision, Murphy considered making James a bank manager, disillusioned with success, Rosie his wife, who diagnoses his problem as 'weltzschmerz [*sic*]' and quotes Nietzsche on the death of God.[14] As finally reimagined James becomes unequivocally 'a ponce (pimp) temporarily retired', Rosie, 'a whore, his girl friend' (*Plays*, 3, [2]). The archaism of the figure of Anastasia (as she is renamed) is enhanced by giving her an urn, which she carries above her head like a figure of a water-carrier from some ancient frieze.[15] As a pointed contrast, Rosie lugs in a bottle-gas cylinder to equip the cabin, which she has improbably located in the woods; in the earlier drafts she and James talked of taking a room in a nearby town, not liking the look of the forest.[16]

James, in particular, was made into a much more bizarre figure. He is 'middle-aged and neurotic. His spivish dress is exaggerated: short-backed jacket, dickie-bow, crepe-soled shoes; a moustache.' At first entry, when 'he races across the stage to check the opposite direction for a pursuer': 'His running and posing are stylised: running at breakneck speed, or trotting daintily, feigning cockiness; posing, taking stances as if to say his body is a dangerous weapon; at other times his stance wilting pathetically' (*Plays*, 3, 5).

Almost all the reviewers of the first production commented on Colin Blakely's superb realization of this role, acting 'partly like a startled hare and partly like a tragic clown from an unwritten work by Samuel Beckett'.[17] The contrast could not be greater with Edmund when he finally appears: 'He is a handsome, confident young man in his early twenties. He is very innocent, romantic and charming. He wears a Robin Hood hat with a feather, an antique military tunic; jeans, high boots, a sword and a water-flask at his side' (*Plays*, 3, 20). The composite costume suggests the constructedness of the character, pieced together from a jumble of diverse storybook images. But to James (who in earlier versions had immediately recognized him as

Edmund), he is the terrifyingly unknown 'Feathers', his relentless pursuer whom he must escape at all costs.

When staged in 1971, *Optimism* was subtitled 'Grief'. Though the death of the mother of James and Edmund was a central motif in the initial conception of the play – it is to convey his mother's death-bed forgiveness of James that Edmund so desperately needs to find his brother – in the final text mourning is violently resisted. 'Nickerdehpazzee!', shouts James with that Tuam nonsense word for 'nonsense', used so often by Murphy:[18] 'Dead hand so mottled, brown so worn with care! I'll nail you witch! I'll nail you!' Seesawing between resentment and remorse, rather like Stephen Dedalus in *Ulysses*, James mocks conventional pieties by satiric quotations from poems of sentimental mother worship: 'God gave me a wonderful mammy, her memory will never grow old' (*Plays*, 3, 53).[19] He is haunted by 'that night rambling corpse of a mammy', but declares that 'I'll lay that dead witch sleeping' (*Plays*, 3, 11). Alexandra Poulain teases out the multiple meanings compacted in this last strange sentence. It suggests, 'the raw impulse of Oedipal love ("I'll lay her"), the rage of the abandoned child ("I'll slay her") and the possibility of the mourning process ("I'll lay her on her death bed, and hopefully I'll find sleep again")'.[20] The memory of the dead mother is the witch that must be slain, along with the dragon, 'that feathered bastard shadowing me' (*Plays*, 3, 11), his younger brother shining with hope and belief. The 'grief' of the play is not mourning for the mother but the wrenching need to have done with the past altogether. 'What is the past?' asks James. 'A fairy-tale', answers Rosie (*Plays*, 3, 42).

The most radical change to the original play was the introduction of the double murder. In the early version Edmund and Juliana literally ride off into the sunset as a happily married couple, and James and Rosie are left sadly to recognize that this sort of happiness is not for them. Instead of this anticlimactic coda, the final text yields a brilliantly satisfying theatrical conclusion. The ludicrously abortive sword fight between Edmund and James comes to an end, when James pretends to be unable to kill his brother even though he has him at his mercy. This is the anagnorisis Edmund has been waiting for, and he 'comes to James' and 'embraces him':

> **Edmund**   Now I know who you are.
> *Still embracing,* **James** *withdraws his knife from under his coat, and as he stabs* **Edmund** *in the back –*
> **James**   Now you can be sure of it.
>
> (*Plays*, 3, 95)

This is followed up by Rosie's killing of Anastasia just offstage. The weeping of the pair is combined with a sense of satisfied accomplishment:

Rosie   We done it, James.
James   We did.
Rosie   … What have we done?
James   … We'll see.
Rosie   … It's nice to cry, James.
James   … Don't be fooled by it, Rosie.
Rosie   … You can't trust it, James.
James   … We might be laughing in a minute.
They exit crying.

(Plays, 3, 96)

It is the perfect ending for the play. The ideal superego figures have been brutally dispatched and the antiphonal responses of the pair suggest a new reciprocity of feeling. Yet the mixture of emotions, the broken ellipses, indicate a recognition that there can never be a stable and definitive change of condition, that the renunciation of the tyranny of the idealized self does not yield some automatically enduring maturity.

One of Murphy's extraordinary achievements in *Optimism* was to find a new language for James and Rosie. While there are occasional Irish usages here and there, it is a regionally neutral English speech. As with Murphy's other pimps, James's dialogue is expressive of a hate-filled contempt for the female bodies he exploits, the girls 'dressed up in puppy-fat'. 'It would suit me to see them all as ugly as porridge. … Hairy faces and turkeys' craws … Mouths like torn pockets' (*Plays*, 3, 6–7). Rosie, for her part, builds into her private cabaret for James's entertainment a line weirdly expressive of her trade in non-procreative sex: 'My brains are danced on like grapes to make abortions' (*Plays*, 3, 8). They each are given moments of epiphany in which they glimpse alternative lives. In James's case it is a dream of lost beauty, soon to be apparently realized in the vision of Anastasia:

Once I saw a girl, her back, in headscarf and raincoat, once. I just passed by, I didn't see her face, in my blue motorcar, and turned left for Eros and the statue of Liberty, and became ponce in the graveyard. She may have been Miss Right, she certainly was Miss Possible, cause my hidden, real, beautiful self manifested itself in a twinge … .

(Plays, 3, 12)

With its shorthand gestures this effectively parodies clichés of the life-transforming vision of romance, and the road not taken. Rosie's is a more poignant realization of her situation, estranged from an ordinary continuum of life and death. She recounts it 'absently' to James: 'Once, in the dark, with a client, in that boxy room, in the silence, for a moment, a child cried from the heights of the floor above. … And from the depths of the floor below, from the basement, for a moment, the shuffling of that blind old man stopped' (*Plays*, 3, 70).

James and Rosie are urban creatures, ludicrously out of place in the strange space rendered impressionistically in Bronwen Casson's design for the first production with 'wreath-like forests rising forever like straw against a murky blue-green mystery with a cottage at once rustic and brassy set in the middle'.[21] James makes short work of Rosie's attempt nostalgically to recall a time when she was intimate with nature:

Rosie   I feel so guilty, once upon a time I knew the name of every single bird.
James   But could you recognise them?
Rosie   I could.
James   Well, it would suit me if someone came along and stabbed the lot of them.

(*Plays*, 3, 9)

However, the only bird we hear in the forest is the sinister sounding crow. In James's fable, 'the kindest stork you ever saw with a great red beak' is the bird that brings babies in the childhood myth of reproduction. The antithetical opposite is the terrifying crow of mortality who is the uncharacteristic subject of Edmund's nightmare. The crow alights from a tree and perches on his breast: 'The cakéd offal on his beak was grey, and then he ope'd it up to show the stiffened corpse of maggot for a tongue. … And then he pecked' (*Plays*, 3, 41–2). This is typical of Edmund's style in its use of pseudo-poetic language ('cakéd', 'ope'd'), uncharacteristic in its temporary lapse from his relentless romantic idealism. It is as though in assigning him this speech, Murphy sought to give Edmund language of a piece with the play's overall imagery of fairy-tale horror.

The power of this speech, however, only highlights the main weakness of the play, which is to find a satisfactory idiom for Edmund and Anastasia. There is satiric amusement in their adoption of every possible cardboard cutout attitude, as when Edmund refuses to kiss Rosie's hand: 'Believe you must. … That fidelity's single breach. … Would me impossible make for Anastasia.' 'My platonic poxy hand, for little Jesus' sake' is Rosie's exasperated response (*Plays*, 3, 29). Sexuality, so sordidly prominent in the dialogue of James and Rosie, is wrapped up by Edmund in attitudinizing euphemisms. He, like Don Ottavio in *Don Giovanni* listening to Donna Anna's account of Giovanni's attempted rape, is anxious to make sure that James did not succeed:

Anastasia   We struggled.
Edmund   He did not – ?
Anastasia   No.
Edmund   Twas good, twas good, indeed, for I've been told that in the woe of such an act, the brightest gold of female spirit turns to brass contaminate.

(*Plays*, 3, 23)

It is of course essential to the design of the play that Edmund and Anastasia should be fairy-tale figures, unreal constructs, but it is difficult to make something theatrically alive out of the inert compound of cliché and corn that constitute their speech. *Optimism* is a remarkable experiment in a dissident dramatic fable, and one can see why its first director Hugh Hunt called it 'a breakthrough in modern playwriting'.[22] But Murphy was to find in his later play *The Sanctuary Lamp* a more organic, less surreal form to express his drama of alienated isolation. One dimension to the psychopathology of disillusionment dramatized in *Optimism* was the spiritual homelessness experienced by former believers like Murphy himself in a post-Christian secular society. This was to be the central theme of *The Sanctuary Lamp*.

Holed up in the church

As with most of Murphy's plays, there was a variety of intellectual and imaginative prompts for *The Sanctuary Lamp*, including the reading of William James's *Varieties of Religious Experience*.[23] He himself picked out two that triggered the play out of the 'pool of mood and feeling': seeing a television documentary on Jack Doyle and hearing Father Peyton interviewed on radio.[24] Jack Doyle was an Irish heavyweight boxer-turned-Hollywood actor and singer whose playboy life and multiple affairs had earned him the nickname of 'the Gorgeous Gael'.[25] He was on the slide by the time Murphy met him in a Notting Hill pub in London in the 1960s. 'Doyle's slightly military and upper-class

British affectations of voice, his faded celebrity propped up by assumed images of dignity stayed in Murphy's mind and became part of Harry.[26] Father Patrick Peyton was an Irish priest who worked in the United States and pioneered the institution of the family Rosary with the slogan, 'The family that prays together, stays together.[27] On a radio interview that Murphy heard, Peyton

> talked about his going to California as a fourteen- or fifteen-year-old where he was given the job of locking up the church at night. … And before locking the door he would take a last peep in at the light, the sanctuary lamp. When I heard this, something went 'ping!' inside me. Now I know that this moment was the triggering action for a play waiting to be written.[28]

I have suggested elsewhere that there may have been another element that went into the making of *The Sanctuary Lamp*.[29] Federico Fellini's 1954 film *Las Strada* features a circus strongman, a tightrope walker, and their rivalry over a waif-like, mentally handicapped young woman. Different as the story arc is in Fellini, that configuration of characters, however unconsciously registered, seems likely to have provided the basis for the three figures in Murphy's play.

Even by Murphy's standards, the pathway from these suggestions to the final dramatic form was a tortuous one. Among his notes there is a self-mocking reference to his 'Tom Tolstoy' impulse to write a 'a 700 or 800 page work … the whole history of man in terms of the feeling of isolation.[30] An initial scenario for the play, when he had decided in favour of dramatic form, started in the circus featuring the contortionist Olga and the dwarf Sam as well as strong man Harry and juggler Francisco, and a pub scene with Maudie's grandparents Stella and Ted, in which Maudie is brutally beaten by her grandfather, then rescued by Harry. At one stage Murphy started 'to look for a myth a biblical take: Samson, Gideon, Parsifal.[31] With the last of these, he got as far as an alignment of his characters with those in Wagner's opera: Harry as Amfortas, the appointed keeper of the Holy Grail who has been wounded by the evil magician Klingsor (Francisco), Maudie playing the part of Kundry, Klingsor's enforced agent redeemed in the last act by Parsifal. Parsifal was the Young Priest, who appeared in the first staged and published version of the play.[32] However, he decided the mythic analogue was wrong for *The Sanctuary Lamp*, 'a play of our time.[33] The crucial stage came with the decision to focus just on the three central figures: 'So who are my characters? Harry, Francisco and Maudie are making all the running and are reproducing this world pain, this condition of man.'[34] With that, all the introductory scenes in the circus and pub, all the additional characters, Olga, Sam, Stella and Ted, were omitted.

Still in the first staged and published version of the play, there were three initial scenes of exposition which were later cut.[35] A wordless prologue showed Harry 'dancing. His movements are imitative of a child's and vaguely balletic.'[36] In the second scene, in which Francisco and Maudie are also introduced, Harry is busking outside the church. The third scene featured a Mass conducted by Monsignor, with a sermon by the Young Priest and the obstreperously disruptive behaviour of Francisco that results in his being turned out by one of the congregation. It was only in Scene Four that the action moved inside the church, with Monsignor offering Harry the post of clerk and keeper of the sanctuary lamp as in the final revised text. The context for the original *Sanctuary Lamp*, the 'play of our time' in 1975, was the situation of the Catholic Church in the wake of the Second Vatican Council (1962–5). Murphy had some first-hand experience of this in his two-year period as a lay member of International Commission of English in the Liturgy, set up in 1963 to find forms for the Mass in the vernacular, a key part of the strategy of Vatican II to make the church more generally accessible. The Young Priest, with his guitar and his sermon that begins with a tasteless joke about St Joseph shooting the Holy Spirit as 'a matter of honour', was very much a lampoon of the would-be populist clergy of the time.[37] It was this scene, together with the more violent blasphemies of Francisco, which provoked the controversy over the play's first staging.

The Sanctuary Lamp was certainly strong stuff for Dublin in 1975. Audience members walked out before the interval, there were phone calls of complaint to the Abbey Theatre, and a letter to the *Irish Independent* voiced the 'strongest possible abhorrence' at the play's 'insult to the Mass.'[38] Some of the critics reacted more in sorrow than in anger, seeing the play as 'a depressing example of the failure of a gently [*sic*], likeable and singularly gifted person to use his God-given talent constructively.'[39] There were objections to the 'guitar strumming priest' and to Francisco's 'anti-clerical sermonising', 'which can only be described as pulpit pornography.'[40] But even at this first production there were those who defended the play as 'powerfully moving, tragically revealing.'[41] And despite the fact that it was 'likely the most anti-clerical play ever staged by Ireland's national theatre', David Nowlan for the *Irish Times* concluded that '"The Sanctuary Lamp" seemed, to this reviewer at least, a profoundly religious play.'[42] The controversy died down, the play was successfully revived at the Abbey the following year and, even more remarkably, in 1977 it was staged by Murphy's own old amateur theatre group, the Tuam Theatre Guild, and it won multiple awards at the Galway Drama Festival.[43] Even in Ireland by the 1970s times were a changing.

The 1984 revision of the play (produced in the Abbey in 1985) by cutting the opening scenes removed much of the localizing context that had helped to cause the controversy. In that first production, Murphy said, 'It was set in a Dublin church, and the actors played it in Irish accents.' However, he denied that the setting was necessarily Dublin: 'I simply say it's a city.'[44] With the supernumeraries like the Young Priest and the specimen members of the congregation gone, it was possible to concentrate on the remaining four characters, of whom only Francisco is identifiably Irish. The 'church in a city' (*Plays*, 3, [98]), which is all that is specified in the text, becomes merely an undefined space of refuge for Harry and Maudie. With the unity of place and time that this gives, the play gains in power and resonance.[45] Bronwen Casson's set for the 1975 production allowed an audience to see a Mass in action in a more or less realized church.[46] Monica Frawley's design for the 2009 b*spoke production instead strongly featured the 'great columns to dwarf the human form' (*Plays*, 3, 101) and the sanctuary lamp itself as theatrical metonyms.

It is of the essence of the play that this is a more or less abandoned space, no longer really a functioning institution. Even the Monsignor wanders up and down reading Herman Hesse, at least semi-detached from his own church. Harry is a down-and-out, a 'half-lapsed Jew' (*Plays*, 3, 141), a most unlikely keeper of the sanctuary lamp. Maudie is a stowaway, using the confessional box to sleep in, having run away from her abusive grandparents. Francisco, brought up by the Jesuits, is a knowing, deliberate blasphemer when he uses the altar wine for tipple, ascends the pulpit and denounces the priesthood in scurrilous terms. But Harry and Maudie are asylum-seekers in a strange territory, defamiliarizing the church by their very ignorance of its practices and beliefs, knowing only that it is somehow supposed to be a sacred space.

The play begins and ends with Harry's characteristic 'Y'know!', a verbal tic apparently picked up from Murphy's memory of Jack Doyle. Each of the other two central characters has an equivalent expression. 'Do you know "dreaming"?' (*Plays*, 3, 117), asks Maudie, or 'Do you know "lamp-posts"?' (*Plays*, 3, 119). With Francisco it is 'Know what I mean?' (*Plays*, 3, 133). With such recurrent tags, they gesture towards the individual worlds in which they are locked, reaching out ineffectually towards the possibility of shared knowledge. Communication can never be more than partial, not only because so much of the story each has to tell is incommunicable, but because each speaks in such a distinctively different language. Yet the play's drama consists in the meeting of the three in the temporary space of the church and the way that meeting, in all its fractious dissonance, achieves some sort of solace for all of them.

Even in the first scene, Harry and Monsignor are inclined to talk past one another. Harry tries to explain about 'this compulsion to do this – terrible thing. Y'know?' The Monsignor naturally thinks is it good that he did not do it, but Harry says 'No'. 'The compulsion is there to go and do it now. And a feeling of wrongdoing because I haven't gone back to do it. A terrible deed! So what am I to do?' (*Plays*, 102–3). It is the struggle of conscience with honour: the ethical imperative against murdering Francisco and his wife Olga who have cuckolded him, and the sense that he has betrayed his masculinity in *not* having murdered them. But, as obscurely voiced here by Harry, it is understandable that the Monsignor has no advice to offer. It is only when Harry is left alone with the sanctuary lamp that he can begin fully to express himself in the long address to the lamp, which is one of the most extraordinary speeches in Murphy's work. It cannot be quoted in full but demands analysis in some detail.

Though without any understanding of the exact significance of the sanctuary lamp, Harry feels uneasy in its presence, conscious that he should not be dossing in the church: 'Why do you resent me?' he demands; 'I have every right to be here!', he proclaims defiantly, having been hired as the keeper of the light. He proposes a bargain: 'Supposing in exchange for the accommodation I engage to make good conversation – break the back of the night for you? (*To himself.*) Alleviate the holy loneliness.' By degrees, his story is told in the jerky fragments that characterize Harry's speech throughout: 'You know Francisco? Juggler actually. Well, he was my friend, I took him in. Then he usurped, sneaked my wife. And now he lives – my greatest friend! – quite openly with her. And we had brought a child into the world' (*Plays*, 3, 109). Much later, he tells the lamp about Olga: 'You know Olga? Wife actually, Olga. Well she was very lonely. And she seemed – y'know? Superior? … And I was one of the best sports, so we became married. And we had Teresa.' It is memories of his child Teresa, of her dancing, of her appearing at his bedside in the early morning, of cuddling her under his jersey in a shower of rain, that remind him of what it was to be happy: 'You never feel your soul when you're happy' (*Plays*, 3, 110). And against that there was the terrible urge, as he lay in the bedroom he shared with his daughter, to get up and kill his wife and her lover in the next door room, which he just resisted: 'I do not want to be like them. I believe in life!' Casually, ambiguously – it is not even clear that it is Teresa he is talking about – he tells of the event that precipitated his current state: 'And then of course she died. But very interesting – I was very surprised – all I could do was say what does it matter, and left.' (*Plays*, 3, 111). The speech culminates in a vehement prayer: 'Oh, Lord of Death, I cannot forget! Oh Lord of Death, don't let me forget! Oh Lord of Death, stretch forth your mighty arms, therefore! Stir, move, rouse yourself to strengthen me and I'll punish them properly this time!' (*Plays*, 3, 112). Whatever god may be addressed here, it is certainly not the Prince of Peace whose presence is symbolized in the sanctuary lamp, but Harry is incapable of registering such theological niceties.

He hears a noise in the church, gets his penknife out thinking it is Francisco and his prayers have been answered, but it is Maudie that he sees, Maudie who has a prior claim on overnighting in the church: 'I was here first' (*Plays*, 3, 112). There is a wonderfully comic deflation in their contemplation of the statue:

Harry That's Jesus … Do you adore him?
Maudie (*looks at him*) Do you?
Harry No. Y'know?
Maudie Neither do I.
Harry I've great respect for him, mind you. … A very high regard. A veritable giant of a man, if you want my opinion, but between one thing and another, his sense is gone a little dim.

(*Plays*, 3, 113–4)

In the traditional image of the Holy Family, Harry's sympathies are with St Joseph, a cuckold like himself. Maudie, however, believes that Jesus brings the 'forgiveness' that she feels she needs.

Maudie's story is all the more moving for the ingenuous simplicity with which she tells it. We hear of her appallingly brutal grandparents, with whom she lives, whose treatment of her was realized in earlier drafts of the play, and who dismiss her visions of her dead mother as 'dreaming'.

Maudie Well, grandad heard and said I were a whore's melt. And gran said I were a millstone. (*She smiles at* **Harry**).
Note: To **Maudie**, *this story is essentially one of personal triumph.*

(*Plays*, 3, 118)

Maudie's English seems to be that of the Midlands – the dialect 'were' for 'was' – but her grandfather is given the (to her incomprehensible) Irish term of abuse: 'whore's melt' means 'whore's bastard'.[47] Through her self-estranged self-narration, the details come through all too vividly, making Harry so uncomfortable he does not want to listen: the young girl, left alone at home by her grandparents; shinning up lamp posts for the amusement of the local children; the 'older boys' who call her out; the unwanted pregnancy and the lost baby Stephen. It is from the nuns who attend her in hospital after her delivery that she learns about 'forgiveness', which she hopes will bring alleviation from the haunting of her dead child and the guilt she has been made to feel without understanding.

Harry and Maudie find comfort in one another's company. In spite of a return visit from Monsignor who effectively dismisses his newly hired 'clerk', Harry still hopes to set up a domestic arrangement with Maudie in the church, when the first act ends with the appearance of Francisco. Francisco is described as 'Irish, self-destructive, usually considered a blackguard, but there are reasons for his behaviour'. The reasons soon become apparent in his aggressive attack on the religion in which he has been raised – no polite deference to Jesus as 'a veritable giant of a man here'.

> God made the world, right? and fair play to him. What has he done since? Tell me. Right, I'll tell you. Evaporated himself. When they painted his toe-nails and turned him into a church he lost his ambition, gave up learning, stagnated for a while, then gave up even that, said fuck it, forget it, and became a vague pain in his own and everybody's arse.
>
> (*Plays*, 3, 128)

Francisco is like a less abstract version of the all-devouring James in *Optimism*, more specific in that his background in Irish Catholicism sets him off against the non-believers Harry and Maudie. To Maudie he is at first completely unintelligible. In response to his initial 'Know what I mean? (*Maudie's face is blank*)', and with his onslaught against the Creator, she only 'laughs at the four letter words' (*Plays*, 3, 128).

The play's second act is built around the rivalry between Harry and Francisco for Maudie, replicating their rivalry over Olga. For Harry she is a surrogate daughter, a substitute for the dead Teresa, and he treats her protectively, offering her food, shelter, kindness. From the beginning, Francisco moves in on her, offering her a drink from the bottle of altar wine, inviting her back to share his lodgings in Paxton St, asking her bluntly about her relationship with Harry: 'Do you do the trick for him?' (*Plays*, 3, 130). Maudie does not even understand what he means. It is noticeable that where Harry always calls her 'Maudie', Francisco, like the 'older boys' of her remembered story, sexualizes her by naming her as an adult 'Maud' (*Plays*, 3, 134). When Harry returns with fish and chips, he tries to maintain the illusion of a polite shared meal between himself and Maudie, 'who, he feels, is giving too much attention to Francisco' (*Plays*, 3, 135). Harry, conscious that he is once again losing out to the predatory Francisco, is driven to boasting about his own early and glamorous conquests: 'Remember the movie queen, Maria del Nostro? I had her. ... I'd just like you all to know that. The ladies always came after me. For sex, actually. Very enjoyable' (*Plays*, 3, 137).[48] The struggle between the two men develops into a macho confrontation in which Maudie is little more than a passive onlooker or prize to be won.

Harry moves into the attack, beats Francisco and threatens him with his knife. But Francisco manages to get himself into the church pulpit where he is unassailable, and has a means of distracting Harry with the account of the 'last engagement' of the freelance entertainment group made up of himself, Olga and Sam – the engagement at which Harry failed to show, absconding as an act of revenge. The 'story of the critic's ball' is an extended set piece which loses nothing in the telling by Francisco. It is a striking exposé of the decadence of the rich people who hire the entertainers, in this case 'a mighty man who writes only for the most important papers and who even has his own television show'. Again, it may be that Fellini is in the background, the party scenes of films like *La Dolce Vita* suggestive of a perverse, sleazily permissive modernity. There is a satiric contempt for the partygoers: 'people there from all nations. The mandatory one black was there of course, T.V. personalities, people from the press, jilly-journalists ... talking about appliances, perversions, performances, their faces sexually awake as currant buns' (*Plays*, 3, 147). The voyeurism of this crowd delighting in the freak floor show is represented by Francisco with a sort of exhilarated disgust. But at the same time the story highlights the degradation of the performance and the performers, Olga not only stripping but being tacitly offered for sex afterwards, a routine that went badly wrong on this occasion leading to a fight and the physical ejection of the entertainers, leaving them screaming for their money on the wrong side of the door. Harry sees this as a punishment of them for having betrayed him, but Francisco taunts him with his own complicity: 'Everyone to blame but you, Har?' (*Plays*, 3, 146). Harry has claimed the high moral ground throughout as the deceived husband and friend, but it is he who has arranged such 'work', he who has allowed his wife to be so exploited.

Enraged by Francisco's jeers, Harry rushes at the pulpit and lifts it aloft with the juggler in it.[49] Lifting the pulpit is the challenge Harry has set himself earlier in the play and failed. He is here, very obviously, the Samson figure that Murphy had considered as one of his biblical archetypes, the strong man whose strength has returned. The analogy between Samson bringing down the temple of the Philistines and Harry lifting the pulpit, overturning the confessional, however, is not an exact one. It is Francisco, with his blistering anti-sermon, that is the real iconoclast, shattering the false and ungodly church and its priests. 'Hopping on their rubber-soled formulas and equations. Selling their product: Jesus. Weaving their theological cobwebs, doing their theological sums! Black on the outside but, underneath, their bodies swathed in bandages – bandages steeped in ointments, preservatives and holy oils! – Half mummified torsos like great thick bandaged pricks!' (*Plays*, 3, 154).

In its attack on the abstruse dogmas of Catholicism, its materialism and its fetishization of the bodies of dead saints, this could be seen as a sort of rogue Protestantism. The millennial optimism of Martin Luther King is invoked for the peroration with the imagination of a Last Judgement in which the sinners are saved, the pious priests are damned:

I have a dream, I have a dream! The day is coming, the second coming, the final judgment, the not too distant future, before that simple light of man: when Jesus, Man, total man, will call to his side the goats – 'Come ye blessed!' Yea, call to his side all those rakish, dissolute, suicidal, fornicating goats, taken in adultery and what-have-you. And proclaim to the coonics, blush for shame, you blackguards, be off with you, you wretches, depart from me ye cursed complicated affliction.

(*Plays*, 3, 155)

Francisco comes down from the pulpit, offers himself to Harry's knife, who cannot finally bring himself to take revenge. In the play's final scene a sort of peace is made in a shared mourning for Olga who, it is revealed, has died of an overdose two days after the 'critic's ball'. Maudie, who appears to have found her forgiveness, settles down to sleep in the horizontal confession box, resolving to return to her grandparents in the morning. The two men are left to swap their heterodox visions of the afterlife. For Harry the image is one of silhouettes:

> The soul – y'know? – like a silhouette. And when you die it moves out into … slow-moving mists of time and space. Awake in oblivion actually. And it moves out from the world to take its place in the silent outer wall of eternity. … And if a hole comes in one of the silhouettes already in that wall, a new one is called for, and implanted on the damaged one. And whose silhouette is the new one? The father's. The father of the damaged one. Or the mother's, sometimes. Or a brother's, or a sweetheart's. Loved ones.
>
> (*Plays*, 3, 158–9)

For Francisco, bliss is instead imagined as Limbo, the place for all the babies that escaped baptism, and thus the whole apparatus of salvation and damnation. 'Oh but Limbo, Har, Limbo! With just enough light rain to keep the place lush green, the sunshine and red flowers, and the thousands and thousands of other fat babies sitting under the trees, gurgling and laughing and eating bananas' (*Plays*, 3, 160).

One reviewer saw Francisco as the play's authorial spokesman: 'In the end Tom Murphy, like Francisco, emerges as a believer but unhappy with the post-Conciliar Catholic Church.'[50] Some of the anger in Francisco's denunciation of the church is certainly Murphy's own, like the disillusionment of James in *Optimism* with his burst balloons. But the playwright has moved beyond this sort of emotional recoil in *Sanctuary Lamp* and is closer to the visionary humanism of Harry than to Francisco's violent anticlericalism. In his only published poem, 'Lullaby', written as he explains as a sort of 'doodle' at the time of *Sanctuary Lamp*, he contrasts the 'angry mountains' of his 'Catholic childhood', with 'the poor evaporated God' who has become – Harry's image – 'but a sad, slow-moving mist / Now in the vacuum of space.'[51] The key insight for him in the triggering moment of Father Peyton's anecdote was the sanctuary lamp as 'a symbol of hope to the spirit of man. It was man who lit that lamp.'[52] The play dismantles the church, reveals it as an irrelevant obsolete institution, a disused space; the sanctuary lamp, however, remains as an image of transcendence, man's capacity for redemption through forgiveness in a de-deified Christianity.

Murphy works typically with the intensity of extreme situations, characters in the grip of anguish and despair. He has often commented on how he likes to work in 'broad strokes'.[53] Ironic, glancing indirection and innuendo are not for him: 'I wanted violence on the stage, immediate, direct, as against the Pinter sort of bollocks writing – "Pass the salt, dahling," which means "I hate your guts, I want to kill you."'[54] Though he found extreme enough situations, plenty of direct violence in plays such as *Whistle*, *Famine* or *The Blue Macushla*, it is understandable that he sought out also more stylized dramatic forms, bolder, less representational modes to realize this dimension of his theatrical imagination. The fairy tale-turned nightmare of *Optimism* allowed him to reach down to psychological archetypes and mythic matrices. The ill-assorted trio of marginal figures who come together in the half-light of the church in *Sanctuary Lamp* stand in for a whole post-Christian world. In each play the background music is evocative – the 'Symphonie Fantastique' of Berlioz in *Optimism*, Tchaikovsky's 'Sleeping Beauty' in *Sanctuary Lamp*. In *Too Late for Logic*, and most extraordinarily in *The Gigli Concert*, he was to experiment with making music integral to his theatre, the operatic voice counterpointing and contrasting the spoken dialogue as a measure of meaning beyond words and human action.

CHAPTER 7
WORDS AND MUSIC: *TOO LATE FOR LOGIC, THE GIGLI CONCERT*

Irish Man   ... Like, you can talk forever, but singing. Singing, d'yeh know? The only possible way to tell people.
JPW   What?
Irish Man (*shrugs, he does not know*) ... Who you are? ...

(*Plays*, 3, 179)

Murphy has always made music work for him throughout his plays. The 'Symphonie Fantastique' introduced and bridged the scenes of *The Morning After Optimism*, emphasizing its dream-like atmosphere. The sheer range and eclecticism of the playwright's knowledge of popular music, from sentimental Victorian party pieces to Gershwin, is apparent in the sing-song of *The Wake*. He often picks the song to suit the character, as when Harry in *The Sanctuary Lamp*, relentlessly cheerful against all the odds, sings snatches of the upbeat 'When the Red, Red Robin Comes Bob, Bobbin' Along', while Maudie is given Kris Kristofferson's plangent song of parting, 'For the Good Times'. However, operatic music has always had a special importance for Murphy. A boy chorister who grew up into an adult with a fine tenor voice, he has frequently admitted to envying professional singers. In the early 1970s, he confessed, 'I had an unbearable envy of singers. I thought it was the only possible thing to do in life; it was the only possible way to express yourself.'[1] In two plays of the 1980s, *The Gigli Concert* and *Too Late for Logic*, he made this extraordinary expressiveness of the operatic voice central to the drama, endowing the Irish Man in *Gigli* with his own desperate desire to sing.

Here, as so often, the similarities and differences with Murphy's contemporary Brian Friel are significant. For Friel, as for Murphy, music was always a key component in theatre. In *Philadelphia Here I Come!* (1964), Private Gar in melancholy mood indulges himself with listening to a Mendelssohn violin concerto, then tries to buck himself up with traditional Irish *ceilidh* music. Chopin's piano music is threaded through *Aristocrats*

(1979), the cultured atmosphere of the O'Donnells typified in the game where Casimir has to identify which piece his sister Claire is playing. In *Wonderful Tennessee* (1993) Friel has one character express himself entirely through music. The gifted accordionist George is dying of throat cancer and cannot speak, but the melodies he plays punctuate and give point to the action. Still more daringly in *Performances* (2003) Friel has an onstage string quartet perform parts of the 'Intimate Letters', Janáček's series of string quartets, to illustrate an argument staged between the dead composer and a graduate student Anezka. Anezka insists on her thesis – as graduate students will – that the 'Intimate Letters' were directly inspired by Janáček's late love affair with Kamilla Stősslová, while the composer himself makes light of the notion. It turns into a debate on words and music, with Janáček insisting on the superiority of his own medium: 'The people who huckster in words merely report on feeling. We *speak* feeling.'[2]

Friel, like Murphy, here affirms the superiority of music; writers, by comparison with composers, merely 'huckster' in words, the contemptuous verb suggesting a cheap trading in emotion as against the direct voicing of music – 'the only possible way to express yourself'. But, though Friel assigns Janáček all the winning lines in *Performances*, he allows Anezka a compellingly articulated counterargument on the basis of the composer's passionate letters to Stősslová. For all of the downgrading of language in this play, Friel's characters rarely lack fluency. The tongue-tied Gar Public is given his fast-talking Private alter ego to speak those thoughts Public cannot utter. Michael in the final lines of *Dancing at Lughnasa* speaks of 'dancing as if language no longer existed because words were no longer necessary', but it is in a hypnotically lyrical monologue that he evokes such a state beyond words.[3] By contrast, the Irish Man in the passage quoted above 'does not know' what singing can tell people: 'who you are?' he hazards uncertainly. In Murphy, as Friel's Janáček claims, music does indeed '*speak* feeling', but it is a feeling that is inexpressible by any other means. The drama lies in the gap between the transcendent harmony of the singing voice and the halting inadequacy of the characters' attempts to say what they feel.

In Murphy's plays operatic arias in all their perfect beauty sing out above the broken mess of unspeakable human lives. But it also takes the playwright below such surface chaos to the mythical structures adumbrated in the music. The legend of Faust underpins *Gigli* as the Orpheus and Eurydice story echoes through *Logic*. *Gigli*, staged in 1983, set the pattern for the later play, and many of the reviewers of *Logic* placed it as the complementary counterpart to *Gigli*. *Gigli* had been uncertainly received at first, before going on to establish itself as one of Murphy's most original and achieved plays. The admiring reviews of *Logic* were in part a tribute to the way in which the 1983 play had educated audiences to understand what Murphy was doing with the interplay of dialogue and music. However, the plays are actually quite different, and some part of that difference comes from the much more structurally integral position of music and myth in *Gigli*. An examination of the several diverse elements that came together in the evolution of *Logic* may help to illuminate the distinctive unity of its predecessor.

To be or not to be

Murphy never finds writing plays easy, but *Logic* was harder than most. This was no doubt in part because of the painful autobiographical situation it incorporated: the playwright, like the central character Christopher, had separated from his wife and children in order to give himself space for his work. It also had to do with the sheer intractable variety of the materials with which he struggled. The several components that were eventually to come together in *Logic* can be seen in the first ideas and sketches for the play, jotted down in a workbook started in February 1987.[4] The earliest scenario, headed 'Trying to give up Drink', was a four-hander involving a central character Tom, his son Bernard, his much younger lover Jean and his brother-in-law Jimmy. Tom and Bernard, who have an uneasy relationship, nonetheless have to cooperate in trying to prevent Jimmy, who is 'undergoing ridiculous grief', from committing suicide. Another scenario, entitled 'Revenge', relates to a long resented schoolboy injury that has one character Michael wanting to kill the bullying schoolmate, a desire to be taken over by another, one Christopher who is something like his double: 'Michael is possibly Christopher's "mask-let-down."'[5] A third sketch has Christopher, this time with his young wife's brother, going in search of a supposedly suicidal Michael, finding himself embroiled in a messy pub scene presided over by the kindly hostess who becomes Monica in the final play. The feature that comes out most clearly in this version is Christopher's resentment at always having to act to support and help others, being treated as an all-purpose father confessor.

At some point in the process, Murphy decided that the play should have a stylized setting to suggest 'that vast space, desolate; the conscious mind asleep, the unconscious troubled, trying for the solution to a problem of grave significance' and toyed with ideas of how that might be staged.[6] Finally, almost a year into the process of composition, in a draft called 'Trying to give up Smoking', Christopher has become a philosophy lecturer who is giving a lecture on Schopenhauer.[7] What is striking about this genetic sequence is that two of the most important elements, the framing flashback that has Christopher relive the events that lead up to his decision to kill himself (or not), and the musical continuum of operatic arias, do not emerge until very late on in the play's development.[8] It is worth looking at the way in which the separate imaginative strands feature in the play and the extent to which they are held together in its eventual structure.

The uneasy relationship between Tom and Bernard in the initial sketch for 'Trying to give up Drink' developed into the complex emotional dynamics between Christopher and his two children, son Jack and daughter Petra, in the finished play. Again it is likely that there were real-life prompts here. Murphy tells how the title for the play was gifted to him by Bennan, the eldest of his three children. The occasion was a dispute between Murphy and Bennan in a hotel in Chicago in April 1988: 'There was drink taken, and a discussion had moved to argument and was heading for something worse. But just as there was about to be open confrontation, Bennan declared, "Ah, it's too late for logic."'[9] The row was defused and Murphy had the perfect title for his play. Whatever the origins, the play dramatizes an edgy interplay of feelings that almost any parent of teenage children will recognize. Jack is described as having 'a close bond with Christopher, though the slow, single nod of the head, that he is given to, doesn't necessarily mean that he agrees'. By contrast, Jack's sixteen-year-old younger sister, Petra, 'resents Christopher's giving so much attention to Jack to her exclusion. … She is capable of great tenderness and great rage: a child-woman' (*Plays*, 5, 7).

Jack has dropped out of college after two terms, and the disappointed academic Christopher cannot help reproaching him for that. This goads Jack into accusing Christopher of having used his work as a pretext for walking out on his family, pretending that decision was by mutual consent: 'The reprehensible thing … is not that you walked out or that you deny it but that you did it to bury your head deeper in a book' (*Plays*, 5, 39). It is a standard father-son face-off, but as there is a basic sympathy between them they are capable of talking through their differences. Petra is angrier, not only because she takes her mother's side more fiercely than Jack – 'She's been fighting Mum's battle,' Jack explains to his father (*Plays*, 5, 38) – but because she feels Christopher is so little aware of her. Furious with him for ignoring the crisis brought about by the death of his sister-in-law Cornelia, and his brother Michael's threats of suicide, she can yet swing round to generous appreciation when Christopher helps them to find Michael. But that 'generosity is repulsed' (*Plays*, 5, 17), her efforts to reach out to her father make no impression. She tries to get Christopher to listen, to comprehend the disasters afflicting her contemporaries – suicides, unwanted pregnancies, abortions. The climax is her speech of anguished protest at her father's egotistical failure to notice her: 'Did I get pregnant, did I commit suicide, did I have to go away to have an abortion? Did I get my Junior Cert, will I get my Leaving – Does any of it matter – Does anything matter to you but *you*?' (*Plays*, 5, 46). As passionately played by Michèle Forbes in the part, this speech produced a spontaneous round of applause from the audience in the first production.[10] Both Jack and Petra dramatize the consequences of Christopher's flight from responsibility, and Petra in particular his masculine insensitivity to the women around him.

One of the most peculiar scenes in the play, which seems least related to the rest of the action, is that in which Christopher threatens to shoot Wally Peters in revenge for an episode of schoolboy bullying from many years before, while his wife Maud watches, listening to an operatic aria.[11] Yet this featured from an early point in the imaginative conception of the play in the scenario entitled 'Revenge'. In fact, the story of the man who dreams of taking revenge on the boy who tortured him in school every day for three months for an imagined slight appeared already in a draft of *Gigli*.[12] What makes the episode significant in the play is the element of transference. The desire to kill Wally is originally Michael's. When the search party of Christopher, Jack and Petra manage to track down the supposedly suicidal Michael, they find he is not threatening to shoot himself but Wally Peters. Though Christopher, when first told this, cannot even remember who Wally is, he takes on Michael's murderous mission along with the gun that has been removed from him. Michael and Christopher are even more intimately bound together than Murphy's other doubles: they are brothers who have married two sisters, Patricia and Cornelia. The mutual antagonism between them does not stop Christopher being drawn into Michael's emotional position, even to the point of adopting his mad fantasy of violence.

The search for Michael was to take Christopher and his children to a pub scene presided over by the proprietor Monica, who is described with a sort of affectionate appreciation that might suggest a real-life original: 'She's about forty; a laughing, welcoming woman (ideally, big; generous as she is large). She is remarkably, innocently forthright; and with a capacity to alternate seamlessly from celebration to concern. It's difficult not to respond to her warmth' (*Plays*, 5, 18).

In spite of this benevolent presence, the scene unravels into a chaos of confusion, cross-purposes and bristling, aimless aggression. Two extra characters, Geoffrey and Tony, Michael's drinking companions of the day, stray by and a fight starts up. As Colm Tóibín put it, commenting on the first production, Murphy 'writes drunken scenes better than anyone else'.[13] But the scene is designed to illustrate also the way Christopher gets entangled in the sort of situations he is trying to avoid. He is the man to go to when advice is needed, as in the case of Monica's son Young Dennis – a character who appeared in the original production though subsequently cut – who has met a 'blank wall' in his studies: 'we were thinking', says Monica, 'if he had someone like you to sit down with him for half an hour' (*Plays*, 5, 23). Whether reasonably or not, Christopher feels that everyone's problems are heaped on his head.

The non-sequiturs of the action, the swirl of peripheral characters, are justified insofar as this is the representation of a 'conscious mind asleep', something like a Strindbergian dream play. An intellectual centre to this shape-shifting phantasmagoria is provided by the lecture on Schopenhauer that Christopher is trying to write. A historical background is provided as a preamble to the lecture, placing Schopenhauer's thought in the context of the period in which he lived after the French Revolution, after the defeat of Napoleon: 'Man had lost himself again. … So it became a time of demoralisation and debilitation reverie' (*Plays*, 5, 8). The onstage action of the play is made into a dramatization of the central ideas of *The World as Will and Idea*, summed up by José Lanters as follows: 'For human beings, the will to live and to reproduce is a blind urge which represents a fundamental unrest and unhappiness, an endless craving and suffering, while the intellect serves the will but is also man's only hope of release from the will.'[14] Christopher, cloistering himself in his university rooms, seeking disengagement from his family, stands for the intellect, while Michael, who paws every woman in sight including his own niece Petra, and goes off with Jack's girlfriend Moreva at his dead wife's wake, stands for the sexual voracity of the will. However, the futility of Christopher's attempt to evade the consequences of his own will, in the form of his children and his estranged wife, is obvious from the start. It is hardly surprising when in the climactic Scene Six, the lecture, of which we have heard fragments on a tape-recorded rehearsal, turns into a nightmarish travesty of itself where Schopenhauer's philosophy is jumbled up with the lecturer's own problems. Given his pessimistic position, why did

Schopenhauer go on living? 'Why didn't he kill himself, instead of leaving it to me?' Christopher cries out (*Plays*, 5, 57).

The idea of having Christopher kill himself at the very beginning, with the rest of the action a flashback replay of the events leading up to that moment, came quite late in the development of the play. It is not until February 1989, two years into the process of composition, that a draft opens: 'A shot from a gun. The report reverberates and then becomes swallowed up in a cacophony of voices – like the barking of dogs just awakened. Something has gone wrong.'[15] It was a technique Murphy had used before in *The Blue Macushla*, which also starts with a pistol shot, rewinding the narrative to bring the audience through to the point where the shot is fired. It made perfect sense for *Logic*, with its theme of suicide, the principle of transference to the initially detached Christopher from the apparently despairing Michael, and the dream play form that had been planned from near the start. The various episodes, only partly logical, with characters who move in and out of the shadows, voices heard both live and recorded on tape and answerphone, become the projections of Christopher 'dreaming back'. Christopher was 'a ghost looking back at the last three days of his life, trying to find some logical reason for his suicide, trying to assure us and himself of his guiltlessness'. In the first production this was realized in Monica Frawley's design, 'a cloudscape which serves throughout for the locale for the action, which takes its movement from memory. For the opening moments, when this cloudscape is seen through billowing dry ice and rising gauze, the sense of suspension from quotidian existence is clearly established.' The outcome was a tragically belated learning process: 'Christopher's real failure was his refusal to trust in the love of those he loved most – Patricia, Petra, Jack. He killed himself because he failed to believe they could love him. By the end of the play, he can say, with all the poignancy of posthumous hindsight, "Now I know they do."'[16]

If the organizing principle of the suicide's retrospect on his life came late in the conception of the play, its musical infrastructure appeared still later. In most of the first drafts, the only music that featured was the 'Song to the Moon' from Dvořák's *Rusalka* played by Maud, herself an opera singer, in the scene between Christopher and Wally, and 'Down by the Sally Gardens' sung by Patricia and Petra at Cornelia's wake. In drafts dating from April to May 1989, Murphy introduced a whole series of arias, all to be taken from recordings by Maria Callas. Among those specified are 'J'ai perdu mon Eurydice' from Gluck's *Orphée et Eurydice*, 'Casta Diva' from Bellini's *Norma*, 'Porgi Amor' from Mozart's *Le Nozze di Figaro*, and the 'Ave Maria' from Verdi's *Otello*. The arias are used at the beginning of scenes and as bridges between one scene and another. They are all great soprano set pieces and have in common the yearning of the female voice for a state beyond their mortal predicament: the priestess Norma in 'Casta Diva' prays to the moon as the water sprite does in *Rusalka*; Mozart's neglected Countess asks Love for the restoration of her beloved – or for death; Desdemona's prayer to the Virgin in Verdi is sung shortly before Otello will enter to murder her. The music in this design expressed the transcendent female principle which Christopher in his narcissistic male obsessiveness neglected to his cost.

However, according to the director Patrick Mason, in rehearsals it was felt that using this range of arias did not really work: 'it all became too like *Gigli*' so only the 'Song to the Moon' and 'J'ai perdu mon Eurydice' were retained, the Gluck being used as leitmotif, different parts of it returning throughout the play. Mason adds that this 'seemed appropriate, given the action of the play is a sort reverse Orpheus story – dead husband tries to contact living wife to discover why he's dead, and if she can do anything about it.'[17] In the text, Murphy emphasizes this mythological underlay by turning Monica's pub into a Gothic-styled nightclub called the Abbey – surely an in-house joke there – with loud music and red lighting: 'Christopher is like a man entering a trap – hell: the red light – but can do nothing about it' (*Plays*, 5, 17). The Orpheus and Eurydice story plays about the action in complex ways. It is Cornelia, Michael's wife, who has died; however, Christopher's initially reluctant quest is not to bring her back from the dead but to find her husband who is apparently contemplating joining her in death. At the same time, Patricia's desperate calls for help, heard on the answerphone, sound like a disembodied voice from beyond, and Christopher by the end is in some sort trying to make contact again with his estranged wife. In all of this, the operatic music makes for a complex gender play because of the convention that has the male role of Orpheus sung by a mezzo-soprano. 'J'ai perdu mon Eurydice' is thus at once Christopher lamenting the loss of Patricia/Cornelia, and the female voice of all the women whom men such as Christopher and Michael have failed adequately to value. The poignancy is in the two-way sense of bereavement.

The play was extremely well received as a 'major new play' in 'a superb production'.[18] Yet Murphy evidently remained dissatisfied with it and made radical changes to the text for publication in 1990. It is normal practice for the playwright to revise his texts at each theatrical revival but quite unusual for him to rewrite a script on the occasion of its going to print. In a draft letter to Martin Fahy, the Abbey Theatre general manager, sending him the 'penultimate draft' of the play, Murphy had said, 'I would like more of an up-beat ending but the animal will not yield further to me right now.'[19] In the first production such an upbeat ending had not emerged: it was still the story of Christopher's suicide and his posthumous efforts to understand the reasons for his action from the space identified as Limbo, with extra-dramatic comments addressed to the audience at the end of each scene.[20] In the 1990 Methuen text this was changed. The gunshot heard at the start of the play, which appeared to be the sound of Christopher killing himself, is now given a different explanation: 'Throws the gun away: it fires on impact with the floor: he hardly reacts, if at all: he is lighting the cigarette.' What follows is a wry joke, given that Christopher has been trying to give up smoking – he holds an unlit cigarette right through the action. Instead of suicide, 'After long abstinence, he rejoined the persecuted minority of smokers, in slow death.' In this version, the play ends with Schopenhauer's little parable from *Parerga and Paralipomena*: the porcupines, who huddle together for warmth, move away because of the prickling, and find at last 'a moderate distance from one another at which they could survive best … .'[21] Christopher's discovery of the mutual love between himself and his family, which in the first production had come as a tragically belated understanding after death, is turned into a resigned acceptance of the need for an accommodation between deep attachment and its accompanying frictions.

José Lanters, in her thoughtful and illuminating article on the play, sees this changed ending as a transformational coup de théâtre: 'Magic, including Murphy's brand of theatrical magic, is necessarily devoid of logic and dependent upon faith and the absence of rational thought; such magic, created entirely in the here-and-now of the staged moment, occurs when Christopher, in the final instances of *Too Late for Logic*, re-casts the moment of his death, and lives.'[22] She compares it to the magical ending of *Gigli*. But the whole action of *Gigli* moves towards its extraordinary and triumphant conclusion. The rewritten ending of *Logic* appears instead as at best a bitter-sweet coda to the play, even perhaps something of a mere theatrical sleight of hand. The audience is fooled into thinking Christopher has killed himself, but he has not after all. That seems to destroy the rationale of the increasingly desperate protagonist reliving the action that led him to suicide. If Christopher is not in fact dead, what has the whole action been about?

This is a play that seems to illustrate the risks involved in Murphy's 'adventure' method of playwriting. He works with a whole series of imaginative suggestions, trusting the creative process to allow him to find a theatrical shape for them. In the case of *Logic* it was to be music and the relived life of the suicide that were to provide the integrating structure for the action. By making the single Gluck aria the dominant leitmotif, the play became a version of the Orpheus myth. Yet seeing *Logic* as a 'sort of reverse Orpheus story' leaves a lot unaccounted for: Christopher's difficult relationship with his children, the episode with Wally, the vividly rendered semi-satiric wake scene. The play overflows the constraints of the mythic archetype. The uncertainty over whether Christopher does or does not die at the end is suggestive of a lack of conviction by Murphy that he has found the right dramatic form for his materials. By contrast, what is so striking about *Gigli* is the achieved structure, in which music and language, myth and ordinary reality, are so strikingly integrated.

Myth, music, magic

'I want to write a play about a man who would love to be a great tenor rather than anything else,' Murphy wrote in an early workbook for *Gigli*.[23] This, from the playwright who confessed to his intolerable envy of tenors, makes clear the autobiographical dimension to the text. The Irish Man's fixation on the Italian tenor was the author's own. 'I was obsessive in listening to Gigli,' Murphy has said. 'You want to listen to him or you want to sing like him' (Interview, p. 185). Murphy too, like Irish Man in the play, had been seeking professional help, not from a quack dynamatologist like JPW but from his friend, the psychiatrist Ivor Browne;[24] in the first versions of the play it is a conventional psychiatrist that Man consults. JPW in an early draft remarks: 'I was 25 before I had my first drink – alcohol,' adding 'I've been making up for lost time.'[25] Murphy too was a total abstainer up to the same age, and like his fictional counterpart he indulged fairly heavily after that. By contrast with *Logic*, however, a formal vehicle for this personal material was discovered very early on. In the first workbook for *Gigli*, already, there are notes on versions of the Faust legend, both Goethe's two-part masterpiece and Marlowe's *Dr Faustus*. The urgent desire to sing like Gigli made the operatic arias integral to the design from the very beginning. Though the drafting of *Gigli*, like most of Murphy's plays, involved a process of trial and error with much cutting away of material finally considered extraneous, the ground plan of the Faustian pact, the mad obsession with singing like Gigli and the psychological magic by which that might be achieved, were foundational.

Goethe's *Faust* is one of the play's intertexts down to JPW's last line as he leaves Gigli to 'sing on forever' on his record player set to endless repeat:

'mankind still has a delicate ear' (*Plays*, 3, 240),[26] while earlier in this same scene he quoted from Marlowe: 'This night I'll conjure' (*Plays*, 3, 238).[27] Irony, however, plays about the use of such quotations. Unlike Marlowe's hero, JPW will 'conjure' but will not die damned as a result. The spectacle of Gigli singing to the 'pigsty' of JPW's abandoned bedsit-cum-office is a very far cry from the persistent romantic idealism of Goethe's Faust. And so it is with Murphy's counterparts to the figures in the Faust story. Helen appears in Marlowe as the ultimate illusion of Faustus's magic, saluted as 'the face that launched a thousand ships', but whose lips in making his 'soul immortal with a kiss' ironically doom him to damnation.[28] In *Faust* Part II, Goethe devotes the whole of Act 3 to the relationship of Faust to Helena. At one point, the Spartan queen laments the destructiveness of her beauty:

> Alas, what cruel fate
> I suffer, everywhere so to confound
> the hearts of men that they will neither spare
> themselves nor anything we venerate.[29]

In *Gigli*, JPW's Helen is an apparently modest suburban housewife, conjured up not by magic but by illegal number tapping on a disconnected telephone. When JPW assures her of his love, she exclaims like her namesake: 'What fate is following me that wreaks havoc in men's hearts, they lose all care for themselves, their jobs, their everything' (*Plays*, 5, 206-7). The cynical Irish Man, however, can see instantly through this mock ingénue pose: 'Oh she was leading you a merry dance,' he says, with a cynical chuckle (*Plays*, 5, 207). In Goethe Faust and Helena have a child, the golden Euphorion whose Icarus-like spirit drives him to attempt a disastrous flight above some cliffs. As he falls to his death, his voice is heard 'from the depths'. 'Mother, don't leave me here, /down in the darkness, alone!'[30] JPW, anything but a golden boy, as he struggles for life after his drink- and drug-induced 'performance' as Gigli, similarly exclaims, 'Mama? Mama? Do not leave me in the dark' (*Plays*, 3, 239). JPW, however, does not go down into the abyss like Euphorion.

Perhaps Murphy's most iconoclastic recasting of Goethe comes with the character of Margarete or Gretchen. The seduction of Gretchen, aided and abetted by the evil Mephistopheles, is Faust's most heinous crime in Part I. She becomes pregnant, kills her baby, is tried and condemned for the murder. In spite of Faust's remorseful attempts to save her, she is executed in the tragic conclusion to the play. Mona in Murphy is designed to be Gretchen's counterpart and antitype. 'Who picked up whom', wonders JPW

of their first encounter, 'that evening in the supermarket?' (*Plays*, 3, 193).
Mona makes no bones of the fact that it was she who seduced him away
from four years of chastity, vowed for the sake of his teasingly unresponsive
Helen. Mona had a child as an unmarried teenager and deeply regrets having
been forced to give him away for adoption. She indulges in promiscuous
sex with JPW and others in the hope of conceiving again, a hope doomed
by her approaching death from cancer. *Faust* Part II ends with a Chorus
of repentant women led by the apotheosized Gretchen who guarantee the
magician's salvation on the basis of the principle that 'Woman, eternally, /
Shows us the way'.[31] Mona faces death completely unrepentant, but she too
is in some sense JPW's saviour insofar as he realizes too late the value of her
mortal physical love. Murphy deliberately subverts Goethe's conventionally
patriarchal imagination of gender relations.

In the relationship between JPW and Irish Man, Murphy radically
reworks the Faustian pact. On the face of it at the beginning, it is Irish Man
who could be identified as Faust coming to JPW looking for the magical
powers to sing like Gigli. JPW, with his absurd theories of 'dynamatology'
illustrated on a chart, spins out a patter like the conjuring invocations of the
magical adept: 'Circles within circles, concentric and eccentric, squiggles,
swirls of objects, and at the bottom, this dark area here, sediment: despair'
(*Plays*, 3, 198). JPW's quack strategies for 'possibilising the quiet power of the
possible within you' satirize conventional psychotherapy by equating it with
magic (*Plays*, 5, 199). Yet from the very start of the play there is an affinity
between patient and analyst, glimpsed in the despairing line each one utters
independently: 'Christ, how I am going to get through today?' (*Plays*, 3, 166,
173). These are two men at rock bottom, one as much in need of help as the
other. And insofar as they do stand in for Faust and Mephistopheles, they
switch positions. In a distorted version of the principle of analysand-analyst
transference, it is JPW who takes on Irish Man's obsession with the need to
sing like Gigli. In trying to help Irish Man, JPW declares 'I even learned the
baritone role of the duet on that thing – and I am the tenor!' (*Plays*, 3, 228).
It is indeed JPW who goes on magically to 'sing' the tenor part in Donizetti's
Lucia in the climactic final scene, when the tempting Mephistopheles/Irish
Man has withdrawn from the action.

The one explicit reference to the Faust legend in the play comes in Scene
Four when Irish Man insists that JPW listen to Gigli sing on the new record
player he has brought along for the purpose. The aria he chooses is 'Dai
campi, dai prati' from *Mefistofele*, Arrigo Boito's version of Goethe's play,
much less well known than Gounod's earlier *Faust*. It comes early in the

opera when the still innocent Faust, who has not yet met Mephistopheles, sings of the peace and calm he feels returning from the fields and meadows. JPW, picking up the record sleeve, comments: "'Mefistofele': ah yes, he *is* the devil' (*Plays*, 3, 201) – he senses that the singing of Gigli is the obsessive temptation for him it proves to be. It is an important moment in the play. It is the only time when the source of an aria is actually identified, but it is also the point at which the music becomes a part of the action itself. Through the first three scenes the audience has heard parts of Meyerbeer's 'O Paradiso' but only as a background theme tune coming from outside the drama. Now, with the Gigli aria played on stage and JPW's comments on it, the status of the music is changed. The difference was underlined in the Gate production of 2015. 'O Paradiso' in the opening scenes came audibly from amplifiers either side of the proscenium. From the time when Irish Man brings on his record player, the source of the music shifted to the stage itself.

What distinguishes the theatrical use of operatic music from instrumental is that it is itself theatrical, the lyrics contributing to the dramatic situation from which it is taken. So, for instance, an operatically knowledgeable audience member listening to 'O Paradiso' over the play's opening might be aware of the context from which the aria is taken: at this point in Meyerbeer's *L'Africaine* Vasco da Gama wonders at the idyllic beauty of the African island which he is seeing for the first time. What could be more ironic than this explorer's salute to the brave new world of the sixteenth-century European discoveries sounding out over JPW's appallingly sordid living quarters? The significance of the original context of the aria we hear is much clearer with JPW's final 'singing' of Donizetti's 'Tu che a Dio spiegasti l'ali'. In *Lucia di Lammermoor* this is Edgardo's last aria, as he prepares to kill himself and join Lucia in heaven. Murphy specifies that this should be Gigli's solo recording, in place of the version played earlier in which the voices of Manfredo and the chorus are heard seeking to dissuade Edgardo from suicide. JPW left alone is lamenting his lost love Mona, but he, unlike Edgardo, will not die.

Elsewhere in the play, Murphy aligns the action directly with the music. So, in Scene Eight, as Mona exits and JPW is left unable to express his feelings for her directly, the voice of Gigli takes over from that of soprano Elizabeth Rethberg in a recording of the trio 'Tu sol quest anima' from Verdi's *Attila*, and the entrance of Irish Man is timed with the bass solo (*Plays*, 3, 235). But more often the music does not relate directly to the dramatic action; rather it is left to make its own impact by free association. Irish Man says that singing is 'the only possible way to tell people … who you are'. However, it is exactly the individuality of individuals and their situation that music does not voice. The point is made at the opening of Scene Eight as Mona and JPW lie on the bed listening to Gigli singing 'Caro mio ben' and 'Amarilli'. These are not dramatic arias from nineteenth-century opera like so many of the other tracks heard in the play. They are comparatively simple seventeenth-century songs, with lyrical melodies. 'What's he singing, what's he saying now?' asks Mona.

> **JPW**   You don't have to know, whatever you like.
> **Mona**   Beloved.
> **JPW**   If you like.
> **Mona**   That everything ends.

These are indeed love songs but neither of them is concerned with the mortality that brings love to an end, the feeling of Mona facing death at this point. Instead they inspire the nearest JPW is capable of coming to an expression of his love for her: 'That you are now breathing, now, this moment … alive in Time at the same time as I … and that I can only hold my breath at the thought' (*Plays*, 3, 231). The very hesitancy and brokenness of the expression is the more poignant contrasted with the beautiful fluency of the two songs.

And yet JPW's lines are recycled. Earlier, in Scene Four, telling Irish Man about his love for Helen, he had reported his words to her: 'how remarkable, you and I alive in Time at the same time' (*Plays*, 3, 207). The transfer of the line from Helen to Mona marks the change in JPW's affections. But throughout the play identities, life-narratives, are thus transferable: the men switch roles, Faust becoming Mephistopheles, Mephistopheles Faust. The non-individual expressiveness of music facilitates this sort of shifting status of the persona. So, Irish Man, when asked about his life by JPW, channels the autobiography of Gigli in a sort of verbal karaoke: 'I was born with a voice and little else.' An audience seeing the play for a first time may be as baffled as JPW is by the mismatch between the story he tells and the so visibly and audibly Irish Man who is standing on stage:

> **JPW**   Where was this?
> **Irish Man**   Recanati.
> **JPW**   Recan?
> **Irish Man**   Ati.
> **JPW**   What county is that in?
> **Irish Man**   Recanati is in Italy.

(Plays, 3, 176)

All the details here and in what follows are taken directly from Gigli's
Memoirs: the cobbler father, the dramatic approach from the people of
Macerata to the boy to play the soprano lead in *Angelica's Elopement*, the
surprising agreement of his elder brother Abramo to allow him to go, his
astonishing success.[32] Irish Man may not be able to sing like Gigli, but he can
inhabit the singer's life story.

The Irish Man's childhood experience will reappear in different forms
later in the play, Abramo transmuting into the all too plausibly brutal Mick,
viciously abusive to his younger siblings, but then again into a saintly version
of this same older brother. Even more significant, though, is his return to
the Gigli *Memoirs* with the story of Ida, the telephonist with whom he fell
in love. Separated when he was doing his military service, he returned to
find her dying in hospital of a broken heart; she had promised her family
to have nothing more to do with him.[33] Again taken all but word for word
from the *Memoirs*, it is played out to the accompaniment of Gigli singing
Toselli's 'Serenade'. The stage direction specifies that 'his Ida story concludes
with the conclusion' of the song 'if possible' (*Plays*, 3, 210). It is possible,
and the 2015 Gate production was one of the extraordinary theatrical
effects, the telling of the story by Denis Conway as Irish Man keeping exact
pace with the saccharine sound of the violin-backed song of love and loss.
JPW is brutally dismissive of this piece of sentimental fantasy, prescribing
whorehouses where Irish Man can relieve his sexual needs. When Irish Man
points out, 'Don't yeh see: the similarities between your story and mine?' the
dynamatologist is indignant: 'My story is about a real live living person, your
story is bullshit' (*Plays*, 3, 210). Yet we can see that JPW's fixation on Helen is
no less 'bullshit' than Gigli's Ida story as enacted by Irish Man to the strains
of Toselli. Both are the escapist fictions of men who substitute narratives of
unrequited love for any capacity to connect with actual women.

Irish Man is so obsessed with the vocal expressiveness of Gigli, so
passionately wants to be able to sing like him, because this stands at the
extreme opposite of his own incapacity to communicate with anyone. 'I've
come to a standstill,' he tells JPW at their first encounter. 'I was never a great
one to talk much. Now I'd prefer to walk a mile in the other direction than say
how yeh or fuck yeh to anyone' (*Plays*, 3, 173). His predicament is appallingly
illustrated in his account of his late-night dialogue with his concerned wife.
When she turns to go up to bed, her efforts to distract her husband from his
obsessive listening to his record having gone nowhere, 'she said I love you so
much. And I said I love you too … but not out loud.' Instead, 'It came out. My
roar. Fuck you, fuck you … fuck you' (*Plays*, 3, 185). It is the exact same blocked

capacity that afflicts JPW at Mona's exit, when he shouts after her: 'I love! I love you! Fuck you! I love! Fuck you! I love! – I love! Fuck you – fuck you! I love ... ' (*Plays*, 3, 235). One of the most affecting scenes in the play is the Irish Man's wordless aria of anger and grief in Scene Five: 'A few whimpers escape ... fixed, rooted in his position, he starts to shout, savage, inarticulate roars of impotent hatred at the doorway ... developing into sobs which he cannot stop. ... He is on his hands and knees. Terrible dry sobbing, and rhythmic, as if from the bowels of the earth' (*Plays*, 3, 218).[34]

It is to cross the vast abyss from such locked-down emotions to the beautiful fluency of Gigli's singing that magic is needed. 'You are going to ask me what is magic. In a nutshell, the rearrangement and redirection of the orbits and trajectories of dynamatological whirlings, i.e., simply new mind over old matter' (*Plays*, 3, 238). This 'dynamatology', the magic that Murphy invented for the play, is a pseudo-science, a psychological alchemy, even a theology of sorts. Murphy's friend, the philosopher Richard Kearney, explains how the word was coined. The effort to sing like Gigli was an aspiration 'to come into contact with [one's] inner potential'. The term to convey the meaning of this '"logic of the dynamizing potential"' was *dynamatology*', derived from 'the Greek *dynamis*, meaning potentiality or potency'.[35] What in Kearney becomes a serious book-length study of 'the God who may be' in Murphy's play is JPW's hilarious monologue at the end of Scene Four, expatiating on the theory that 'God created the world in order to create himself'. He interrogates God's enigmatic pronouncement, 'I am who am,' in response to Moses' question as to His name in Exodus. God, JPW declares, 'got it wrong'.

> Because what does it mean, 'I am who am'? It means this is me and that's that. This is me and I am stuck with it. You see? Limiting. What God should have been saying, of course, was 'I am who may be'. Which is a different thing, which makes sense – both for us and for God – which means, I am the possible, or, if you prefer, I am the impossible.
>
> (*Plays*, 3, 211)

JPW is given the task of reaching up to that impossible potential in Irish Man's desire to sing like Gigli, and to achieve it he looks to psychology.

JPW engages in psychological research in the effort to find a means to make the singing happen. In Scene Seven, when Irish Man is already moving back towards 'normality', renouncing his obsession, JPW indignantly displays the array of books that he has filched on his patient's behalf: 'Here, these are yours. Kierkegaard, you read it, make sense of it, stolen out of the South Side Library. Here, Jung, Freud, Otto Rank, Ernest Becker, Stanislas Grof, anonymous donations to your cause' (*Plays*, 3, 225). In fact, most of Murphy's own knowledge of these authors came from Ernest Becker's 1973 Pulitzer Prize-winning work *The Denial of Death*.

Becker was a controversial academic psychologist whose book was an overview of various psychoanalytic thinkers, to illustrate its master thesis that the denial of mortality underlies the 'heroism' of human life. Murphy took detailed notes on *The Denial of Death*, paying particular attention to Kierkegaard, whom Becker treats as a psychoanalytic thinker *avant la lettre*. According to Becker, Kierkegaard maintains that man lives in a state of denial because he has the capacity for imagining infinite possibility but realizes the limitation of his bodily mortality. The defence mechanism against this, which Kierkegaard calls 'shut-upness', but psychoanalysts would term 'repression', is the lie of character that enables man to live in the world subjecting himself to its norms and fears. 'Philistinism tranquilises itself in the trivial.'[36] The passage which Murphy noted down and incorporated into the play was Kierkegaard's threefold division of psychological types, the first two corresponding to the 'psychotic syndromes of schizophrenia and depression':

> For with the audacity of despair that man soared aloft who ran wild with possibility; but crushed down by despair that man strains himself against existence to whom everything has become necessary. But philistinism spiritlessly celebrates its triumph ... imagines itself to be the master, does not take note that precisely thereby it has taken itself captive to be the slave of spiritlessness and to be the most pitiful of all things.[37]

It is in these terms of Kierkegaard that JPW characterizes the impact of Irish Man upon him: 'You came in that door with the audacity of despair, wild with the idea of wanting to soar, and I was the most pitiful of spiritless things' (*Plays*, 3, 238). JPW warns the 'cured' Irish Man who, it is revealed, suffers from recurrent bouts of depression: 'You have taken yourself captive again, but dread still lies nesting' (*Plays*, 3, 237).

For Kierkegaard, the acceptance of dread leads to faith. JPW instead takes over the Irish Man's audacity of despair and prepares himself to sing like Gigli. When, echoing Marlowe's Faustus, he resolves, 'This night I'll conjure' (*Plays*, 3, 238), it is to the infernal powers that he looks for his magic. Rejecting heaven and earth, he addresses his words 'to the floor': 'You, down there! Assist please' (*Plays*, 3, 239). However, the most immediate assistance comes from drink and drugs. With swigs from a vodka bottle he washes down his squares of bread and jam, each adorned with a Mandrax pill. Mandrax was a real drug, a brand name for methaqualone, prescribed as a sleeping pill for the likes of Irish Man, but withdrawn from the market in the 1980s, as JPW remarks, because of its addictive and hypnotic properties: 'People in America jumping out of windows on wings of Mandrax' (*Plays*, 3, 175). Irish Man, however, has saved up a stock of the pills, and this is the 'trump card' that he carries in his pocket, which JPW for much of the play believes is a gun. Having come through his breakdown, the Irish Man can dump the container of Mandrax in JPW's waste-paper basket, no longer needing to contemplate suicide. In downing large numbers of these pills with quantities of vodka, JPW's attempt to sing like Gigli looks to be suicidal.

Murphy, in fact, in the earliest draft of the play did have him die after his performance.[38] Instead, in the final text, JPW not only succeeds in 'singing' Gigli's solo version of the aria from *Lucia* but survives in spite of the overdosing. This Faust is not dragged down to hell, but, after a blackout in which he calls out the words of the doomed Euphorion, he staggers to his feet and manages to exit, leaving Gigli, on the record player's automatic repeat, to sing on for ever. It is a triumphant affirmation of the magic of theatre itself. Of course, everyone in the audience knows that the actor on stage is not actually singing the aria but is miming to the recorded voice of the Italian tenor. This is a very special case of the willing suspension of disbelief that makes theatre possible. It is the logical outcome of the narrative drive that starts with the Irish Man's yearning to sing like Gigli, now transferred to his supposed therapist. It is the final expression of the expressiveness of music, so far beyond anything the words of the characters can utter. And it allows JPW a sort of liberation that Irish Man, once again having taken himself captive, will never achieve.

In draft dialogue for the play's opening scene, Murphy initially placed it in a contemporary present: the central character, watching television, comments on 'Charlie' Haughey and 'Dessie' O'Malley, key political figures in the early 1980s.[39] The unnamed Irish Man, as the character eventually became, is an immediately recognizable type of the time, the self-proclaimed self-made man, the 'operator' who has built a thousand houses. 'Them houses', he tells JPW, 'were built out of facts: corruption, brutality, backhanding, fronthanding, backstabbing, lump labour and a bit of technology' (*Plays*, 3, 172–3). In the original production, where Kate Flynn played Mona with a Northern Irish accent, it was even possible to see something like a national allegory in the script. It has been suggested that 'the exchanges between J.P.W. and Beniamino [*sic*] can be interpreted as emblems of the age-old conflict between England and Ireland – with the Northern Mona as a sort of neglected go-between: the woman victimized by the male-dominated struggle for power'. But Richard Kearney, who makes this suggestion, points out that 'one of the most conspicuous features of Murphy's work is its ability to transcend, while reflecting, its local setting'.[40] Though the Irishness of the Irish Man and JPW's Englishness are significant features of the interaction between them, the local setting scarcely features in a play locked into the one room, which might be anywhere. It is as little a play about 1980s Ireland as *Optimism* or *Sanctuary Lamp* were plays about the 1970s when they were first staged. The psychological struggles of the two men both suffering from extreme despair are counterpointed by the hauntingly disembodied voice of Gigli, which takes an audience into some transcendent space beyond any empirical reality.

Within that configuration, the part of Mona is a difficult one, with very limited stage time and relatively few lines, in a play dominated by the two male characters each with a titanic role. Murphy did even write a radio version of the play leaving Mona out altogether.[41] Her marginalized status is of course a key part of the meaning of the drama. It is because JPW is so taken up with his fantasy of Helen, then by his fascination with the Irish Man's obsessions, that he fails to notice Mona and the love she has to offer. This was made most movingly apparent in Monica Frawley's design for the 1991 Abbey revival of the play, 'a studio attic with its end wall of glass'.[42] The glass allowed the audience to see Mona (Ingrid Craigie) standing outside beating at the locked door, calling 'Jimmy? … Jimmy?' at the end of Scene Four. We learn later that at this point she urgently needs to tell JPW of her cancer diagnosis, but he is too drunk, both literally and metaphorically, even to hear her cries. Murphy here, as in *Logic*, exposes the narcissistic self-preoccupation of the men who are unable to go out to the love and tenderness of their women. Christopher ignores the poignant phone messages of his deserted wife Patricia, repulses the overtures of his teenage daughter Petra, just as JPW can come to appreciate Mona only too late. 'The purpose of women is to teach men how to live,' declared Murphy in an interview at the time of the premiere of *Logic*,[43] but they do not succeed in his plays because they are talked down, drowned out by the insistent voices of the male characters. The only theatrical solution to this gender skewing was to make a woman character the central figure, as in *Alice Trilogy*, or to keep men off the stage altogether as in *Bailegangaire*.

CHAPTER 8
THE LIVES OF WOMEN: *ALICE TRILOGY,*
THE MOMMO PLAYS

The action of a Murphy play is most often worked out within a restricted time period. The tension within the family in *Whistle* builds to its inevitably tragic conclusion over just two days. The grocer's assistant, John Joe, must make his decision to go or to stay over a crucial week. Urgency is added to *Gigli* by the six daily sessions with the dynamatologist that Irish Man has paid for: 'Tomorrow we start transcending a few things,' declares JPW at the close of Scene Five, 'Tuesday you sing' (*Plays*, 3, 220). In *Logic*, the seeming suicide Christopher relives the days that led him up to the moment of the pistol shot. In *The White House* Murphy experimented with after and before scenes in the same location ten years apart, but was not satisfied with the result. Instead, he recast the text as a single act in which the night's drinking of the group in the pub is played almost in real theatrical time, the chiming of the two clocks outside marking the passage of the hours. All of these plays are dominated by men, and the crises in their lives. Their ennui, their anguish, their despair is dramatized in violent action or voiced in torrents of words. The women in the plays are abused (Betty in *Whistle*), sidelined (Peggy in *Conversations*, Mona in *Gigli*) or just ignored (Petra and Patricia in *Logic*). Their presence, marginal though it may be, is crucial to the meaning of the play, as in the climactic moment of *Conversations* when Peggy sings. But the plays are not centrally about the lives of the women characters. To dramatize such lives, which so frequently featured prolonged inaction, situations of chronic abuse or neglect, Murphy had to discover other theatrical forms offering longer perspectives rather than the compressed confrontations of his men.

Both *Alice Trilogy* and the collection which finally appeared as *The Mommo Plays* have complex genetic histories. *Alice* had its origins in what was imagined as a sequence of prose fiction: 'I planned seven short stories which would cohere in women's names: Alice was one, and Vera was another' (Interview, p. 187). The first of these from November 1990 was the story given the provisional title 'In the Apiary' or 'The Famous Grouse'.[1] The central character speaks of herself in the third person and is never named, but this is evidently the Alice story and contains the substance of what, as 'In the Apiary', was to become the first part of *Alice*. The Vera story took off and went on to become the novel *The Seduction of Morality* and subsequently *The Wake*. But Murphy refers to having written 'something else' between (Interview, p. 187) and this appears to have been the story entitled 'Stella', which was to be recast as 'At the Airport', the third part of *Alice*. As in the play, a woman whose grown-up son has died in an accident waits, numb with grief, in an airport restaurant, only to have the otherwise entirely silent waitress, Stella, tell her a more terrible story of a baby she had fostered who has just been murdered by his mentally ill mother. There is no indication that the central figure is Alice; the title indicates that it is the unexpected intervention of Stella that is to be the crux of the tale. In 1994, Murphy recast the 'Apiary' story as a 'one-act play for two young women', [2] a dialogue between Alice and Image, the reflection of herself in a mirror, as though a literalization of her namesake in *Through the Looking Glass*.[3] Eventually, Murphy was to write 'By the Gasworks Wall' as a middle section of *Alice* linking the earlier 'In the Apiary' with 'At the Airport', making all three episodes in Alice's life.

What were to become the *Mommo Plays* had if anything an even more complicated textual history. In March 1981 Murphy drafted what he intended to be two complementary television scripts, *Brigit* and *The Contest*.[4] *Brigit* is the story of Seamus O'Toole and his wife – named only as Woman in the text – who look after their three young grandchildren; Seamus is an amateur sculptor commissioned by the nuns to create a statue of St Brigit out of bog oak, who is so outraged by their request for him to cover up the finished wood with paint that he threatens to burn it. *The Contest* is the story of the laughing competition in which Seamus engages against the Bochtán champion Costello and, as in *Thief of a Christmas* and *Bailegangaire*, with fatal consequences for Costello. However, at this stage the couple returns to find all three of their grandchildren safe – Tom does not suffer the fatal accident he does in *Bailegangaire*. *Brigit* was eventually made as a television play by RTÉ in 1988 and at some point in time Murphy prepared an outline for three TV plays, including *Brigit*, *The Challenge* (a retitled version of *The Contest*) and *Mommo*, a reworking of *Bailegangaire*.[5] *Bailegangaire* itself apparently began as a story written by Murphy as a Christmas present for his children, but it outgrew its origins and developed into a stage play. But that in turn generated another play, *A Thief of a Christmas*, written for the Abbey, as *Bailegangaire* was written for Druid; it was the actuality of how

'Bailegangaire came by its appellation' of which its companion play was the story. Eventually, in 2014, *Brigit*, the television script, was revised for the stage and produced by Druid in a double bill with *Bailegangaire*.

There is nothing unusual in Murphy experimenting with the same material in different media. Many of his plays were television or films scripts first, and many others that started in the theatre were rewritten for television or radio. What is striking in the case of the two texts under consideration in this chapter is the way the successive reconfigurations made possible the dramatic representation of a span of time and its consequences for the women characters. Women's experience was at the centre of the original planned set of stories that mutated into *Alice*, which became three episodes in a single life. But both *Brigit* and *The Contest* were male dominated. One is concerned with the sculptor Seamus's imagination of the figure of Brigit, the other the macho competition between the two laughing champions, with Seamus's wife playing a very marginal role. *Bailegangaire*, however, in filtering those events through the senile memory of the storytelling Mommo and making manifest the remaining trauma in the characters of her adult granddaughters, changed the focus of the whole. The two essays by Alexandra Poulain and Lucy McDiarmid, in Chapter 9, illuminate the astonishingly rich text of *Bailegangaire* in very different ways. What I want to do here is to look at how the play draws upon and resonates with its two companion pieces and to compare that with the effect of *Alice*.

Innerworlds

In a draft of the one-act play 'In the Apiary', Murphy thought of ending the play with Glenn Campbell's 1968 song 'Dream of an Everyday Housewife', heard from down below the attic where Alice sits drinking her coffee laced with whisky.[6] One can see why the lyrics might have been apposite:

She looks in the mirror and stares at the wrinkles
That weren't there yesterday
And thinks of the young man that she almost married
What would he think if he saw her this way?[7]

The play literally featured Alice's dialogue with her mirror image, and 'By the Gasworks Wall' was to dramatize her encounter with a 'young man that she almost married'. Alice's situation is less banal than that in the song, but she is indeed something like an everyday housewife. In this she is unlike any earlier women featured in Murphy's drama, so frequently marginalized, beaten or exploited by the men in their lives. By contrast Alice is in comfortable circumstances. 'What's the complaint?' she asks her alter ego Al, enumerating all the things she has to be grateful for: 'This is a nice area, this is a nice house. … And the children are all healthy, thank God, thank God.' She is, she concludes, 'well off, up and down' (*Plays*, 5, 309). Alice, like Nora Helmer in *A Doll's House*, is married to a banker, but, unlike Nora, she has no illusions about her husband. He is kind and decent and dully conventional but 'he's not the sharpest knife in the drawer' (*Plays*, 5, 315). There will be no occasion for the sort of dramatically disillusioning revelation that precipitates Nora's departure from her doll's house home and marriage.

Alice's psychological state is an internalized one, not caused by any immediate circumstances of her life. Notes that Murphy made at the time of drafting the play 'In the Apiary' in 1994 suggest what he wanted to dramatize in the play. His concern was with a 'problem that has no name', a 'passion for unlived life'. Alice's situation illustrates the effect of 'patriarchal mandates: how they can lead to a woman's self-hatred for her own being … and can operate with lethal intent on her creativity'.[8] To express such an introjection of mental attitudes, it was necessary to find a way to represent the interior life: hence the dialogue of Alice with what in earlier drafts was her Image, stepped out of the mirror, and eventually became her interlocutor Al.[9] There are many other doubles in Murphy's work – James and Edmund in *Optimism*, Harry and Francisco in *Sanctuary Lamp*, the 'twins' Michael and Tom in *Conversations* – but they are all men and they represent polar opposites, the incurable idealist against the naysayer, the romantic against the cynic. Alice and Al speak from within a single person, their dialogue dramatizing an endogenous despair.

In the internal debate Murphy found a means of expressing Alice's mental anguish, and in the cramped roof space with its 'few objects of broken furniture' he found the appropriate theatrical space to house it (*Plays*, 5, 299). Alice, of course, is not a madwoman in the attic like Bertha Rochester in *Jane Eyre*. She is not mad, she insists, as she takes her Valium:

Al   It's just that she's upset.

Alice   At the *moment* she's upset. …

Al   And it's just that she cannot think what it is exactly is upsetting her at the moment.

(*Plays*, 5, 301)

Alice has not been confined to the attic by a tyrannical husband; on the contrary, she seeks it out as a refuge from 'down below', her everyday housewife's life represented by 'the thump-thump, thump-thump of a washing machine engaging with the sounds of a radio' (*Plays*, 5, 299). It is a sanctuary of escape, like the pills she pops or the Famous Grouse whisky with which she laces her coffee. Yet it figures simultaneously her trapped state of confinement, which has its analogue in the aviary where her husband keeps his budgies. The somewhat obscure significance of the play's title *In the Apiary* is brought out in one of the drafts, in which her alternative self was still Image:

> **Alice** I know that it is an aviary.
> **Image** But ask her – go on ask her – and she'll tell you
> **Alice** I prefer to call it an apiary
> **Image** She calls things what she likes
> **Alice** I call things what I like
> **Image** Her mind, her life.
> **Alice** *My* mind, *my* life.[10]

The only freedom available to Alice is the freedom knowingly to create her own misapplied vocabulary.

'By the Gasworks Wall' is the only part of *Alice* where Alice is given an external interlocutor through most of the text. This is Alice ten years on from the first part, no longer, we have to assume, so dependent on drugs and alcohol. She had a drink problem, she confesses to Jimmy, 'until I was brought to my senses with a bump' by a car crash (*Plays*, 5, 331). The ending of 'In the Apiary', as she sets out to pick up the children from school having topped up her cup of coffee several times with Famous Grouse, suggests this might have been the occasion of the accident. She has pulled back from the state of despair in which she contemplated killing herself and her children:

> **Alice** Drowning … We get into the car, drive the ten miles to the docks, and over the edge.
> **Al.** With the children?
> **Alice.** Oh I couldn't leave them behind … my beautiful children …
> (*Plays*, 5, 316).[11]

But her life as the well-to-do wife of Bill the successful banker is hardly more satisfying, with book club every other Thursday morning and creative writing on Tuesday evenings: 'If I hear another woman reading out her piece about remembering watching Daddy shaving when she was a little girl, I'll shoot myself – with a razor' (*Plays*, 5, 331). In this situation, on a whim, she writes to Jimmy, her boyfriend in the long ago when they were both young, not believing for a moment that he, now a well-known television personality, will respond. But he does.

Their meeting takes place 'by the gasworks wall', a sort of no man's land in an unidentifiable town. Murphy takes an impish pleasure in appropriating Salford, the 'Dirty Old Town' of Ewan McColl's lyric – 'I met my love by the gasworks wall' – and grafting it on to his native Tuam. Tuam too had its nineteenth-century gasworks, though hardly on the scale of the industrial Salford, and the 'sounds off' of 'a cattle mart in session' (*Plays*, 5, 323) hardly suggest an urban landscape. When Jimmy tells Alice that he left his taxi in 'the Square', telling the 'driver to have a meal in the hotel' (*Plays*, 5, 341), anyone from Tuam would have recognized the town's central meeting place, only ever known as the Square, and the hotel as the Imperial, setting for *The Wake*. The panopticon atmosphere of the town is emphasized by the inquisitive Bundler who twice passes by. A 'known newsmonger', like Mullins in *Crucial Week*, he is imagined by Alice passing on the word of her encounter with Jimmy: 'Jesus, d'ye know who I seen just now down the Lane in the dark with a stranger?' (*Plays*, 5, 335). Still, for the duration of the play, the Lane by the gasworks for Alice and Jimmy is a nowhere place in a time warp back to their youth and the path not taken.

There is a good deal of awkward reminiscing about their innocent romance of twenty-one years before, before they start to talk about their current lives. Unlike in 'In the Apiary', where Alice denies that she is mad, here she responds to Jimmy's confession – 'Sometimes I think I'm going crazy' – with an emphatic counter-declaration: 'I don't think I'm *going* crazy, I think I *am* crazy. Well, a little stocktaking of how things are up here (*in her head*) and all the evidence is there to prove it: *I'm crazy*.' But then, looking about at her supposedly 'normal' fellow townspeople, she is led to wonder 'if sanity after all is only another form of insanity' (*Plays*, 5, 338). By this time, in fact, she is trying to humour Jimmy and talk him out of what she has discovered is a much more extreme form of mental disorder than the one she is experiencing. Reaching out to Jimmy was merely a diversion for her, a way of relieving the stifling monotony of her ordinary life. He, however, it turns out, has taken it with a dangerous degree of seriousness.

'It isn't possible for you to be seventeen again,' he admits to Alice, 'for me to be twenty-three, but it's possible – it *is* possible – to backtrack to see if those emotions that were authentic then can be rediscovered' (*Plays*, 5, 339–40). This is like Michael in *Conversations* trying to time travel back to the White House pub atmosphere of the 1960s. But in the case of Jimmy what emerges is something more like full-blown paranoia. 'Anger: discovering that one's friends are false, fair-weather friends, who … express admiration for me and my work, to my face, but who really hold me cheap and want to see my humiliation' (*Plays*, 5, 340). He is far enough gone to imagine that a renewed relationship with Alice, a return to the past, will allow him to escape from all that. And when Alice, ever so gently tries to talk him down from this state, she becomes another one of his persecutors: 'Are you enjoying your triumph? … How much, to what degree, do you enjoy belittling me?' (*Plays*, 5, 343). He even threatens to murder her: 'Fear of consequences is not stopping me. I could kill you right now? I could? I could?' To which Alice can only reply, 'You could, Jimmy, but you won't' (*Plays*, 5, 344). *Alice Trilogy* is concerned with a deeply painful female alienation, but one that is in the end grounded in some sort of grasp on reality. The meeting with Jimmy in 'By the Gasworks Wall' enables Alice to say that it is time that she 'got my head down from up there and accepted my – limitations' (*Plays*, 5, 342). With the more florid forms of delusion of a man like Jimmy no such acceptance is possible.

The scenic progress of *Alice* is from inner to outer. 'In the Apiary' is a closed interior, the attic or roof space housing the private dialogue of self with self. At the edges of the dark lane of 'By the Gasworks Wall' is the surrounding town, with its monitoring representative in the passing Bundler. Exasperated by his snooping presence, Alice throws back into the darkness specimen examples of the Bundler's sort of talk: '(*She's animated, angry, the frustrations of her innerworld making her move about and pitch the next mimicry at the town, as in defiance.*) "Goodnight to ye!" – "How are ye!" – "Some fuckin' hurlers them Cork boyos"!' (*Plays*, 5, 335).

In 'At the Airport', Alice is in that most heterogeneous of social spaces, an airport restaurant with miscellaneous movement all round her. And where her distress in the earlier parts of the sequence is internally grounded, here she has suffered the most terrible of blows from the world without, the death of her beloved son William, already picked out from among her three children as 'sweet, sweet William' in 'In the Apiary' (*Plays*, 5, 319). Murphy suggests a degree of stylization in the staging, which 'can be put down to the idea that we are encountering this place through **Alice**'s odd mental state' (*Plays*, 5, 348). That state is registered in the third-person form with which she observes her own situation and its surrounding circumstances as though beside herself in shock. 'Looking at it rationally the worst has happened. The worst? Has it? And it is conceivable that her heart is breaking. Is it?' (*Plays*, 5, 348).

The horror of what she is experiencing is made the more acute because of the ordinariness of what she observes. Her husband Bill – it is the only time we actually see him in the sequence – continues placidly to eat the meal they have ordered. She can only look on with a degree of estrangement that disables her from accepting anyone or anything for what it is. 'She looks across the table at her husband who is eating a. Who looks across the table? She looks across the table. Who? She-she-her-she, this woman, me, looks across the table at that man, her husband, who is eating a meal of fish and chips in the manner of someone performing a duty and who is he, she wonders.' She reflects that Bill 'keeps the world at bay' by finishing anything he starts, in a way that is characteristic of his gender. 'He sees himself as some kind of stoic. Men, a lot of them, are like that. Whereas, emotionality, they believe, would you believe in this post-post-feminist day and age, emotionality is women's territory.' The irony of it 'would make a person smile, almost. It would nearly make a person cry' (*Plays*, 5, 350). But the inability to cry, the failure of the heart to break, is the real agony. Life 'is tediously suffocating and stubbornly bearable' (*Plays*, 5, 352).

The behaviour and attitudes of husband and wife are replicated in the Waiter and Waitress who hover about them in the restaurant. The Waiter 'seems a jolly sort – and would become jollier given the chance' (*Plays*, 5, 347). His upbeat, reassuring mantra is 'Alright, alright, everything alright?' (*Plays*, 5, 354). By contrast, the Waitress moves, silently, almost automaton-like, to fulfil her orders, otherwise standing at her station 'tray clapped under her arm' (*Plays*, 5, 348). This makes more surprising and more devastating the moment, when Bill has gone to make arrangements for receiving the coffin, where she sits down beside Alice and speaks:

> Missus? … I have to tell someone. My daughter-in-law, a lovely woman, had a baby fourteen months ago. She rejected the baby, a lovely woman, she couldn't help it. So my husband and myself took the baby and kept him for over a year. I wouldn't ever run down anybody's child but that baby was the best, we loved him as much if not more than any of our own. More than words can say. We gave him back last Thursday. She killed him two days ago. I had to tell someone.
>
> (*Plays*, 5, 361)

And this heart-stopping story from a complete stranger releases Alice's frozen grief, allows her to feel for others as never before.

It makes for a moving conclusion to the play, Alice's access of love for her dead son and his girlfriend, for her husband, and for the waitress Stella, as she 'clings to her for a moment in sympathy and in gratitude for releasing this power within her' (*Plays*, 5, 362). *Alice* affords the opportunity for a great starring role for the protagonist, played in the original London production by Juliet Stevenson, and in Dublin by Jane Brennan. But there are some problems with the play. One is simply structural. So, for example, it requires the casting of a woman actor for the part of the Waitress to appear only in the final section, and with just one speech, which is nonetheless vital to the success of the whole play. This encounter fitted perfectly as the unexpected narrative twist of the original short story, but in terms of the normal demands of theatre it seems unbalanced and unprepared. The adaptation from story form causes other difficulties as well. The internal dialogue of 'In the Apiary' provides its own drama, and the third-person monologue of 'At the Airport' is an appropriate way of voicing Alice's alienated state of grief. But overall it creates a fairly static sequence. In *Bailegangaire* Murphy found a brilliantly innovative way of adapting narrative to theatrical ends, rendering the lives of the three women characters in a powerfully dynamic form.

Telling their story

Alice represented the span of a woman's life by dramatizing three discrete episodes. Sketched in also was the backstory of Alice's parents: the unhappy relationship of a socially ambitious mother who pushed her to marry a banker and a metalworker father who 'looked at other women and … drank' (*Plays*, 5, 317). Though it is never stressed, Alice is obviously conditioned by that background, resentful of her mother, drinking like her dead father. By contrast with the thirty years covered in *Alice Trilogy*, the action of *Bailegangaire* takes place in a single evening. The Sunday Concert on the radio marks the passing of time, as the chiming of the clocks does in *Conversations*. And yet Murphy contrives within that one night to render not only the life of Mommo and that of her two granddaughters Mary and Dolly but the history of the family, even of the nation. The missing generation between the three women, the strange absence of Mommo's children, Mary and Dolly's parents, is explained in the course of the story of the laughing contest, in which their deaths are among the 'misfortunes' that provided the occasion for laughter. Looming in the mists of Mommo's confused consciousness also is the figure of her father, gnomic philosopher with a 'big stick' to beat off Mommo's suitors as a young girl (*Mommo Plays*, 71). With the device of the endlessly repeated folktale, Murphy found a non-representational form unlike the psychological realism of *Alice*, which allowed him to suggest the deepest levels of historical trauma out of which the unhappy family emerged. *Bailegangaire* can stand alone theatrically as an extraordinarily achieved play. But it has an extra resonance when considered with its two companion texts, *Brigit* and *Thief*, and it is worth looking at how those two were developed in order to appreciate how they interact with *Bailegangaire*.

Brigit had a double source, as Shaun Richards points out, 'a story from Murphy's childhood involving his father, who had been short-changed for work he had done for the church and boycotted Mass in retaliation and another from the nineteen seventies and the experience of a friend, a painter, who furnished a parish with a statue'.[12] In putting the two together, Murphy made Seamus O'Toole a man doubly disgruntled, not only having been cheated of his rightful pay but having had his best creation insulted by the request that the bog oak so essential to the conception of the statue of St Brigid be garishly painted over. In this version, the Woman – which is the only name she is given in the drafted television screenplay – has a fairly conventional role. She secretly disobeys her husband by sneaking the young grandchildren off to Mass by the back door; normally submissive, she fires up against Seamus when she thinks he has been having an affair with a neighbour – he in fact only wants to use the neighbour's face as a model for the statue. But she is otherwise simply a hard-working wife and grandmother.

In revising the television play for the theatre, Murphy gave the figure of the saint a whole new dimension by stressing her pagan origins, the fertility goddess Brigit who preceded the venerated St Brigid. And Mommo (as she is now styled) is the source for this information. The feast day of St Brigid, Mommo tells the family, is

first of February, first of Spring, and in the old, olden days, the first of Spring was called Imbolg. Imbolg, in the belly. New life, the days getting longer, new life from the earth, fertility: sheep, cows, the fields, mothers. 'The eternal cycle': my father had it all. The mind of that man! She was a goddess before she was a Christian saint, but as my father said, much as the standing of a saint is, 'I am not sure they were right to drop her from the footing of a goddess.'

(*Mommo Plays*, 24)

This establishes Mommo as the inheritor of traditional lore from her father, but it also makes her collaborator, almost co-creator of the statue with Séamus.[13] The oak is sacred to Brigit, as Mommo reminds her grandchildren, making the desire of the nuns to paint over the bog oak of the statue a more obvious symbol of the Christian appropriation of the pagan. This gives an extra depth to Mommo's final plea to Séamus to spare the statue which he is threatening to burn: 'Give it to me, Séamus. Don't burn it. I'm Brigit too, though so long it's been since anyone called me by first name, I've near forgot it myself' (*Mommo Plays*, 51). It is the intended moment of rapprochement between the couple, the wife's appeal to the husband to turn his attention from the inanimate image to the flesh and blood companion he has so little regarded. But in the context of the revised stage play, Mommo appears also in some sort as an avatar of the pre-Christian Brigit.

The story of the laughing contest was told as something that actually happened in a little village near Tuam around the turn of the century.[14] In its first version as the draft television play 'The Contest', it was paired with 'Brigit' as a planned diptych to be entitled *Fatalism*. Murphy yoked the two together by making O'Toole the sculptor and the challenger in the laughing competition, the events of 'The Contest' happening a few months after those in 'Brigit'.[15] The 'fatalism' of the title was that of Seamus. When he decides to take on the commission for the statue, the direction reads: 'Seamus has risen, he has decided to do the job: he stands there for a few moments, the fatalistic streak in his nature telling him that it is not going to work out well.'[16] This is taken up again in 'The Contest', with the comment on the character: 'Experience has taught him to guard his optimism. He distrusts life – there is a streak of fatalism about him. But there is also a defiance and a refusal to submit.'[17] It is this impulse of defiance that leads him to challenge Costello to the laughing contest. When, in this draft, the couple arrives home to see their grandchildren safely waiting for them, 'Seamus glances at the sky: in this briefest of gestures his acknowledgment of Providence.'[18] He acknowledges Providence because his challenge to fate has not resulted in the punishment he might have expected.

In writing *Bailegangaire* and subsequently *Thief*, Murphy radically altered his conception of the drama, transforming the Woman/Stranger's Wife from a more or less passive onlooker in the contest to a crucially responsible agent. In what appears to be the first extant version of *Bailegangaire*, Mommo's story is told straight through to the end; though Mary and Dolly are present, they are not really integrated into the text, and do not interrupt the storytelling.

Here it is Seamus who makes the decision to continue with the challenge when it seems about to be called off:

> And then he sat beside her to start consider his answer and the things in his head that were vexing him for years. And the church owed him money! and – oh-ho – owes it to him still – Och-ha! Till he came to the consideration he'd renege nothing no longer, and with a set of his jaw didn't he rise to his feet indicating for all twas a challenge was in it.[19]

It is very striking to compare this with the final text of *Bailegangaire* where the anger and the fierce exclamations have been transferred to Mommo:

> Costello could decree. All others could decree. But what about the things had been vexin' *her* for years? No, a woman isn't stick or stone. The forty years an' more in the one bed together (and) he to rise in the mornin' (and) not to give her a glance. An' so long it had been he had called her by first name, she'd near forgot it herself. Brigit … Hah? … An' so she thought he hated her an' maybe he did, like everything else … An' (*Her head comes up, eyes fierce.*) 'Yis, yis-yis, he's challe'gin' ye, he is!' She gave it to the Bocháns. And to her husband returning? – maybe he would recant, but she'd renege matters no longer. 'Hona ho gus hah-haa!'
>
> (*Mommo Plays*, 97)

Similarly, it is Mommo who makes the ultimately fatal decision that the winner will be the one who laughs last – in the first version this was also Seamus's proposal – and she who proposes the topic of 'misfortunes' to 'keep them laughing near for ever' (*Mommo Plays*, 116). With these changes, Murphy made *Bailegangaire* a play about the frustrations of Mommo's woman's life, her bitterness, her trauma and guilt as the survivor Poulain shows her to be in the chapter that follows.

Mommo is literally the central character of the play, sitting up in the double bed in 'the central room of the traditional three-roomed thatched house' (*Mommo Plays*, 55). But in his invention of the theatrical device of Mommo's 'unfinished symphony', the ceaseless repetition by the senile old woman of her never-ended story, Murphy contrived to make the characters of Mary and Dolly equal sharers in the drama. At the play's opening, we are bound to feel for the predicament of Mary, locked in with the endlessly recycled story of her recalcitrant grandmother who (perhaps wilfully) refuses to recognize her but treats her as a suspect paid carer. Mary's sense of trapped loneliness can only heighten the tension with her sister Dolly who drops in only when she feels like it. The opposition between them goes back to childhood stereotyping, where Mary the eldest was 'the clever one', while Dolly was 'like a film-star and she was grandad's favourite' (*Mommo Plays*, 121). In the paired production by Druid of *Brigit* with *Bailegangaire*, it was heartbreaking to see the children in the first play – Dolly as grandad's favourite, indeed, listening to his commentary as he carved the statue – and to see their grim afterlives.

Mary, the 'clever one', used her education to take off to England where she trained for a highly successful career as a nurse. Dolly feels that she 'had it easy'. But Mary protests that 'no one who came out of this – house – had it easy' (*Mommo Plays*, 104). She is like so many of Murphy's deracinated emigrés who can find satisfaction neither at home nor abroad. In fact, 'home' is exactly what she has returned to seek, and what makes the hostility and non-recognition by Mommo so peculiarly painful. She can only keep going by ceaseless housework, but she 'is near breaking point' (*Mommo Plays*, 55). The film star-like child Dolly at thirty-nine is 'dolled up in gaudy, rural fashion' (*Mommo Plays*, 61), engaging in promiscuous sex as a gesture of contempt for the men she uses. She is a grass widow, sustained by remittances from her husband Stephen, who returns home at Christmas when he beats her up for her infidelities. Her passionate denunciation of her husband and his abuse of her is one of the most terrifying speeches in the play (*Mommo Plays*, 105–6). For both Mary and Dolly this one evening is a crisis point in their lives. Mary feels she has to decide whether to stay or leave again; the pregnant Dolly fears that her husband may kill her when he sees this visible proof of her unfaithfulness.

The action of *Bailegangaire* is very precisely dated in 1984, the year of the play's composition. Mary and Dolly live in that contemporary present, sketched in with news of the local Japanese-owned computer plant threatened with closure. The 1980s was indeed a time of economic recession for an only partially modernized Ireland. McDiarmid, in the conclusion to her essay in the next chapter, shows how this was also a period of emerging consciousness of the plight of Irish women like Mary and Dolly, lives that Murphy himself, writing in 1984, felt no one was watching, in exact antithesis to the Big Brother dystopia of Orwell's novel. Notionally, it is possible to date precisely when the laughing contest took place from the relative ages of Mary and Dolly: in *Bailegangaire* Mary is forty-one, Dolly thirty-nine, while in *Brigit* their ages are given as twelve and nine (*Mommo Plays*, 55, 61, 4) – so there is almost exactly thirty years between the two plays. In fact, in one draft of *Bailegangaire*, we can see Murphy working out a precise chronology for the story, with dates of birth for Mary, Dolly and Tom, and for the principal events in their lives.[20] But he abandoned this sort of historical precision and allowed the archaism of the folk tale to blur the period of its events. The play operates a sort of double time scheme, the dated present of 1984 against an indefinite past receding into oral folk memory.

The disjunction of these two was represented scenically in the original production by the 'kitchen of a thatched house … stylised to avoid cliché' as required by the stage direction (*Mommo Plays*, 54), backed by a 'crude electricity pole'.[21] This is replicated, when the play begins, by the split-level drama of Mommo's shanachie storytelling, bizarre and obscure as it is, and the painfully familiar life of her carer Mary. Audience attention is divided between what must be an initially all but incomprehensible narrative and the immediate experience of the granddaughters. The connection between the two is made glancingly for the first time when Mary, breaking the 'frame' of the story in McDiarmid's terms, responds to Mommo's question about the Stranger's Wife:

Mommo   And how many children had she bore herself?
Mary   Eight?
Mommo   And what happened to them?
Mary   Nine? Ten?
Mommo   Hah?
Mary   What happened to us all?

(Mommo Plays, 60)

That switch from the 'them' of Mommo's narrative to Mary's 'us' makes of the non-denumerable offspring of the unnamed stranger's wife the actual family of the characters we see on stage.

In 'At the Airport' in *Alice*, Murphy used a third-person narrative to register the alienated consciousness of the speaker. Similarly, in the story of the laughing contest Mommo never owns to her identity or that of her husband – they are never anything but the stranger and the stranger's wife. But this disavowal of the first person, as with Mouth in Beckett's *Not I*, originates in a much deeper level of trauma than that of Alice, Mommo's guilty sense of responsibility for her part in the laughing contest with its terrible outcome, and, further back than that, the accusation of her mistreatment of her own children: 'Them (that) weren't drowned or died they said she drove away' (*Mommo Plays*, 60). Yet the style of the narrative makes this seem, as it were natural, personal experience displaced into a folklorized story told with its own highly ornamented vocabulary and rhythms: 'It was a bad year for the crops, a good one for mushrooms and the contrary and adverse connection between these two is always the case' (*Mommo Plays*, 57). The third person adopted here is in fact ironically an inversion of the normal convention of the Irish folk tale, which is usually told in the first person as an incident that was actually witnessed by the storyteller.[22] But it allows an audience to escape into the strangeness of the story, borne along by the sheer richness and wonder of it in spite of its obscurity. It is only as the play develops that the parallel tracks of the story and the drama of the present begin to come together in the shared lives of the three women and the family's history.

At first, Mommo's story is no more than background noise, intolerable to Mary who has to live with it day in, day out, to Dolly a meaningless 'harping on misery' (*Mommo Plays*, 64). The two women know the story off by heart so that Dolly can supply a casual prompt 'Good man, Josie!' for the next phrase in Mommo's recitation (*Mommo Plays*, 66). And when Mommo falls asleep, Mary 'idly at first' can take up the narrative: 'Now as all do know the world over ...' (*Mommo Plays*, 80). This is the beginning of the 'turn-taking' as McDiarmid calls it, by which Mommo and Mary share the story. Initially, Mary has tried to stop the storytelling which drives her distracted; suddenly an earlier line of Dolly comes back to her: 'Why doesn't she finish it and have done with it' (*Mommo Plays*, 83). This is the beginning of a new momentum in the play, the urge towards completion, a conclusion that may begin some sort of closure not only to the story itself but to the history of the whole family and what it represents.

Mary first decides that 'we'll do it together' (*Mommo Plays*, 83), but Mommo will not cooperate: with her usual hostile resistance to anything coming from Mary, she 'lapses into silence, she grows drowsy, or feigns drowsiness' (*Mommo Plays*, 84). So Mary resolves, 'I won't just help you, I'll do it for you.' As she starts to take up the story, she even 'corrects' her more educated speech to reproduce exactly Mommo's own style: 'Now John Mahony. (*She corrects her pronunciation.*) Now John *Mah'ny*'. The ventriloquizing of Mommo is a fine technical opportunity for the actor playing Mary, but it also allows an audience to listen to the story without interruption and begin to take a new sort of interest in it. Among Mary's self-corrections is the identification of the challenger in the laughing competition: 'An' says Grandad. An' says the stranger' (*Mommo Plays*, 85).

This momentarily breaks Mommo's deliberately sustained anonymizing of the characters in the story and bridges the gap between the long-ago folk tale and the people on stage in the theatrical present.

Because the play operates on a split level, and the never-finished, always repeated story is on a loop, as it were, it can be faded back into the background, as it is for the conclusion of Act 1 and the opening of Act 2, which are concentrated on the relationship of Dolly and Mary. There is a temporary reconciliation in their stand-off as Mary breaks down in tears and is comforted by Dolly, while Mommo can be heard telling the last section of the story told previously by Mary. Act 1 has revealed the misery of Mary's situation, in her isolation, facing Mommo's daily hostility, paralysed in an inability to decide whether to leave or stay. Act 2 brings vividly before us the horror of Dolly's life, as lone parent for most of the year, brutalized by her husband on his annual visits home. It is little wonder she exclaims, 'Jesus, how I hate him! Jesus, how I hate them! Men!' (*Mommo Plays*, 106). But in spite of Dolly's best efforts to soften Mary up to be receptive to her 'proposition', that she should take on the new baby as her own, thus shielding Dolly from her husband's violent revenge on her, Mary is now concentrated on the finishing of the story: 'A laughing competition there *will* be!' (*Mommo Plays*, 91). And that completion is to fill in the gaps in the family history, to give a sense of the haunted house in which the action takes place, and bring the two strands of the play into convergence, the outer frame of the drama meeting the inner frame of the story, as McDiarmid points out.

In *Brigit* there is no indication of why the elderly grandparents should be the carers for their three grandchildren. In *Bailegangaire*, when Mary, the older sister, asks Dolly 'do you remember Daddy?' the only response is 'well, the photographs. (*They look about at the photographs on the wall.*) Aul' brown ghosts' (*Mommo Plays*, 65–6). We hear more of that lost generation of Mommo's children in her contributions to the theme of 'misfortunes' when the story of the laughing competition rises to its height. 'Her Pat was her eldest, died of consumption, had his pick of the girls an' married the widdy again' all her wishes,' and the sequel in which she forced her younger son Willie to fight Pat to stop him taking two sheep that belonged to him away from the family home. When Willie objected, '"Is it goin' fighting me own brother?" ... she told him a brother was one thing, but she was his mother, an' them were her orders to give Pat the high road, and no sheep, one, two or three were leavin' the yard' (*Mommo Plays*, 117). She continues on with the 'rollcalling of the dead' to renewed gales of laughter: 'An' for the sake of an auld ewe stuck in the flood was how she lost two of the others, Jimmy and Michael. … An' the nice wife was near her time, which one of them left behind him?' Mary supplies the identification, 'Daddy'. 'Died tryin' to give birth to the fourth was to be in it. An' she herself left with the care of three small childre waitin' (*Mommo Plays*, 118). In *Riders to the Sea*, Maurya's recitation of the names of her dead sons is a tragic threnody. In the grotesque context of the laughing contest, Mommo's equivalent recollection is a mixture of defiant exorcism and guilty confession.[23]

This backstory of Mommo's children, of the family conditions that shaped the experience of Mary and Dolly, shows us the deformations of a deprived culture of poverty. It is not only that a sheep stuck in the flood is worth the risk of two men's lives, but the harsh conditions of subsistence make any piece of property the occasion for violent conflict where matriarchal authority is at stake. The laughter at misfortunes that Mommo initiates opens up the whole Bochtán community to a collective chorus of similar disasters – and we need to remind ourselves that the very name 'Bochtán' means a 'poor person'.[24]

> And it started up again with the subject of potatoes, the damnable
>   crop was in that year.
> 'Wet an' wat'rey?' says the stranger.
> 'Wet an' wat'rey,' laughing Costello.
> 'Heh heh heh, but not blighted?'
> 'No ho ho, ho ho ho, but scabby and small.'
> 'Sour an' soapy – Heh heh heh.'
> 'Yis – ho ho,' says the hero. 'Hard to wash, ladies, hard to boil, ladies?'
> 'An' the divil t'ate – Heh heh heh!'

While a failed potato crop in an Irish context necessarily recalls the great famine of the nineteenth century, it is specified here that the potatoes were not blighted. It is the more commonplace agricultural catastrophes that are chronicled here: the hay 'rotted', the 'bita oats' 'lodged in the field', 'the cow that just died, an' the man that was in it lost both arms to the thresher' (*Mommo Plays*, 117). The glimpse that Mommo gives us of the Bochtán villagers – 'the wretched and neglected, dilapidated an' forlorn, the forgotten an' despairing, ragged and dirty, eyes big as saucers' (*Mommo Plays*, 118) – is amplified in *Thief* into a full-stage picture. The direction at the opening of Act 2 of *Thief* evokes those who have entered the pub to watch the contest:

> Those who have arrived in the last two hours are shaped and formed by poverty and hardship. Rags of clothing, deformities. But they are individual in themselves. If there is a beautiful young woman present; she, too, looks freakish because of her very beauty. The sounds of sheep, goats, sea-birds can be heard in their speech, and laughter.
>
> (*Mommo Plays*, 163)

This is a vision of rural Ireland reaching back beyond any identifiable period in the past.

As Mommo's narrative gathers pace in Act 2, Mary's sense of urgency that it should be brought to a conclusion is conveyed to the audience. We want quite simply to know how it ends. But there is a sense, also, that its completion may bring the resolution of the emotional impasses from which all three women separately suffer, and a reconfiguration of the granddaughters' modern present with the sundered past of Mommo's folk tale. We inch towards it with a part of the story Mary and Dolly have never heard before, Mommo's revelation of her motives in forcing the laughing contest to continue, quoted above: 'But what about the things had been vexin' *her* for years?' (*Mommo Plays*, 97). This disclosure of the aggression born of long years of an inert marriage, however, is followed up later by an extraordinary vignette of togetherness in the midst of the laughing crowd: 'An' then, like a girl, smiled at her husband, an' his smile back so shy, like the boy he was in youth. An' the moment was for them alone. Unaware of all cares, unaware of all others' (*Mommo Plays*, 115). There is a glimpse here of the tenderness of which the couple are capable even as they are trapped in the consequences of their long silence.

One of the major blockages of the dramatic situation through much of *Bailegangaire* is Mommo's refusal to recognize Mary – if indeed it is deliberate – and her refusal to cooperate with her. Mommo is prepared to embrace and welcome Dolly, and Mary continues to be treated as the home help, addressed suspiciously as 'Miss'. Some signs of a thaw come in Act 2 when those roles are reversed. 'Who was that woman?' Mommo enquires about Dolly who has just left temporarily, and she seems close to recognition when she asks Mary 'Who are you?' (*Mommo Plays*, 112). That actual recognition, however, can only come after the story has been finished, Mommo telling out her part to the conclusion of the laughing contest with the death of Costello and the beating up of the victorious 'stranger', Mary relating the terrible sequel with Tom's accidental death by burning. Mommo finally takes ownership of her story by at last naming the 'stranger' who died of his injuries just days after the episode at Bochtán/Bailegangaire: 'Poor Séamus'. And this then precipitates the long-withheld acknowledgement of Mary: 'And sure a tear isn't such a bad thing, Mary, and haven't we everything we need here, the two of us' (*Mommo Plays*, 122).

Poulain writes tellingly of the conclusion:

> By the end of the play, once the story has been completed and past tragedies remembered, Mommo intones a familiar prayer: 'To thee do we cry – Yes? Poor banished children of Eve' (*Mommo Plays*, 122). The simple words create a new community of 'children', Mommo, Mary and Dolly, huddling in bed together and united in their renewed capacity to feel both grief and hopefulness
>
> (Poulain, p. 208)

It might be added that the recitation of the *Salve Regina* prayer at this point is the more poignant as it recalls the nightly ritual led by Mommo with the three young children in *Brigit*. Mommo's delusion that she is telling her 'nice story' to her 'fondlings' sitting at the foot of her bed has been one of the most terrible signs of her senile regression. It is anything but a nice story, and the two surviving children are the deeply troubled all but middle-aged women we see before us on stage. To tell the carnivalesque tale of the laughing contest through to the end is to traverse again a history of poverty, the miseries and horrors of a family and a people, the desolate legacy it has left for the survivors. But in Mary's last words there is an acceptance both of the past and the present, which enables some sort of future: 'To conclude. It's a strange old place alright, in whatever wisdom He has to have made it this way. But in whatever wisdom there is, in the year 1984, it was decided to give that – fambly … of strangers another chance, and a brand new baby to gladden their home' (*Mommo Plays*, 122).

McDiarmid rightly points to the way in which this resolution of *Bailegangaire* is achieved by 'a circle of female interdependence' (McDiarmid, p. 198), as against *Thief* where male competitiveness cannot be stopped once it is launched. *Alice* comparably ends with an image of two women embracing, allowing for a form of emotional release in shared grief. What differentiates *Alice* from *Bailegangaire* is the greater groundedness of the latter. In seeking to render the internal life of his protagonist Alice, Murphy deliberately relegated to an unmarked periphery the social world in which she is embedded. The concentration is on the introjected constrictions of her gendered self rather than a drama of interactive relatedness. That means that the encounter with Stella at the conclusion of the last part of the play, affecting as it is in the theatre, comes out of nowhere. It is completely unexpected as the intervention of an unknown stranger. The ending of *Bailegangaire*, by contrast, has been hard earned by the women in the play: the hostility and aggression between Mommo and Mary, Mary and Dolly, have to be worked through; the deaths of Tom and Séamus, and her responsibility for them, which have kept Mommo from finishing the story, have to be finally accepted; the fiercely derisive, all but blasphemous laughter at misfortunes in the remembered tale has to be replaced by the capacity for tears; a folkloric past, narrated in a richly ornate idiom, must be connected to a drab modern present.

Seeing *Bailegangaire* produced with its 'prequel' *Brigit* in 2014 made for a theatrically illuminating companionship. When in *Bailegangaire* Mommo growls out 'the church-owed-him money. Oh, the church is slow to pay out, but if you're givin', there's nothin' like money to make the church fervent' (*Mommo Plays*, 84), it appears to be an entirely random remark; but *Brigit* starts with that grievance, and shows us Séamus and Father Kilgariff going over once again the disputed pound he was never paid. 'The cursèd paraffin', Mommo cries out in horror as Mary lights the candle at the start of *Bailegangaire* (*Mommo Plays*, 56). She is thinking of the death of Tom, which will only be revealed at the very end of the play. In the staging of *Brigit* we saw the open fire blaze up as Séamus prepared to burn the rejected statue of Brigit. For the set of *Bailegangaire*, that open fire was replaced by a stove, a plausible piece of modernization of the cottage, which had the effect of making it that bit more cheerless. Still, when Mary gestures towards the stove telling of the accident of how 'Tom had got the paraffin and, not the careful way Grandad did it, shhtiolled it on the embers, and the sudden blaze came out on top of him' (*Mommo Plays*, 121), the afterimage of the blazing fire from the previous play was before us. The absent presence of Tom and Séamus as they appeared in *Brigit* haunted *Bailegangaire* played as its sequel. There has never been a comparable double staging of *Bailegangaire* with *Thief*; there are logistical problems making such a production difficult, not least the need to employ some thirty or forty extras to throng the pub with laughers in *Thief*. Still, it would be magnificent to be able to see the two together, the chamber music of the one play rescored for full orchestra in the other. *Bailegangaire* on its own is one of Murphy's great achievements, but it takes on an added dimension, gains in richness and complexity as the last part of the triptych made up by the three *Mommo Plays*, as it represents the three women characters living out the legacy of the family's past history.

CHAPTER 9
CRITICAL PERSPECTIVES

INTERVIEW WITH TOM MURPHY[1]

NG: I'm interested in how your sense of family was affected by your own experience as the youngest of ten children, with your siblings and your father all disappearing off to England. Did your father go for a while and then come back, or was he gone more or less permanently?

TM: It wasn't seasonal work: I was either eight or nine, when my father emigrated, and I was twenty-seven when he came home – in fact, he died shortly after coming back to Ireland. He was away apart from a week or two weeks' holidays each year. It was a short sojourn he would have at home, generally at New Year. His suitcase, which was made of timber, had tea and tyres for bicycles in it, and, the most wonderful thing, he had a string bag, with a hundred, two hundred, three hundred threepenny bits. He would have one for me, one for my sister, and perhaps one for my brother who was about six years older than me – that was pirate's swag! And he brought me a bicycle – a post office bicycle. It was the equivalent of a tank! With the rest of the family gone, eventually it was just myself and my mother. And by the time I was grown up, my mother had claimed me. It was a common enough thing, I presume, the affection and the love bypassing the husband on to a son.

NG: What did being an altar boy mean to you? Was that a standard thing to do for boys of your age?

TM: I think I was exceptionally pious. One year I managed to serve Mass every morning during Lent, weekdays and Saturdays. I think I swallowed it hook, line and sinker like Harry in *A Whistle in the Dark*. He wanted to be a priest. Nearly everyone wanted to be a priest.

NG: Did you ever think you had a vocation?

TM: I did. And I was so earnest about it that I noticed that the recruiting officer, the priest who came along maybe twice a year, singled me out. I wanted to be a mission priest and I chose my mission field early enough: England, a pagan country. I asked my mother to let me go, and she said, 'You're too young.' I was thirteen.

NG: And did you continue to be so devout?

TM: I was twenty-five before I started to drink alcoholic drink. My eldest brother, I prayed and prayed so hard for him. He was, perhaps, eighteen or nineteen years older than me, and he was divorced, and this meant he was banished.

NG: From the family or from the Church?

TM: Excommunicated from the Church. But it caused my mother untold pain. And I believe one of my sisters rooted out the photographs of him and burned them!

NG: What about your schooling? You give a very vivid picture of the sadism of the teacher Harry recalls in *Whistle*. Were you okay in school?

TM: I was. I was fairly bright, and I was, to a degree, cunning, so I escaped most of the brutality, but my heart sank into my boots going through the gateway. Out of a class of forty-two, thirty or thirty-five would be waiting around the room at ten o'clock – school started at half nine – waiting to be beaten. And of those forty-two, just five of us got through the Intermediate Certificate, so the standard of teaching must have been abysmal.

NG: But the transfer to the Technical School got you out of the Christian Brothers?

TM: Yes, it was a bright school with lay teachers. Rather than pupils seeing the day's disaster on the master's face, you could see that the masters could see the previous night's disaster on the pupil's face.

NG: People might be surprised that you took the route you did after school: apprentice in the factory as a fitter-welder and then metalwork teaching. When you were working in the factory, did you see yourself going on there or were you already thinking of yourself as a writer or something different from where you were?

TM: You took what you could get, and I remember the brother next to me, a carpenter, said, 'You're fixed for life' when I got the apprenticeship in the sugar factory. The first year in the factory was very exciting. I was earning two guineas a week.

NG: Wealth!

TM: Yes, yes! But I was very unhappy in my second year. I had no feel for it, and therefore I left it. I saw this ad in a paper for metalwork teachers to train, and I replied, had a couple of interviews, and I got it! There would have been some sense in it had I become a woodwork teacher, but I hate machines.

NG: So, coming to Dublin to train, aged?

TM: Twenty.

NG: Must have been a big change.

TM: Yes, but it was wonderful. Four pound ten a week: a big jump up. It meant you could go twice to the cinema on Saturday or Sunday, and then to a dance. I saw [John Murphy's] *The Country Boy* at the Abbey, then playing at the Queen's, and I think this is a fulcrum on which modern Irish theatre turned. *The Country Boy* is written all over Friel's *Philadelphia*, even if Friel was too good a writer to have a kiss-and-make-up ending. The emigrant who comes back from America with his comrade is a failure, and that fascinated me too, and may have contributed to *Grocer's Assistant*.

NG: So, acting. When did that start?

TM: I was a member of the Tuam Little Theatre Guild at sixteen when I was still at school. To show how serious the Theatre Guild was, at sixteen I was playing Daniel Burke [in Synge's *The Shadow of the Glen*]. I was directed to get up out of the bed and hit the table with the stick. In the Tech, we did *Teach na mBocht*, [Lady Gregory's] *The Workhouse Ward,* and I got a medal as the best actor in the festival of the school.

NG: So you were playing one of the old men in the bed in *The Workhouse Ward*?

TM: Yes. I specialized in old men in beds! When I was teaching in Mountbellew, I was involved in the Theatre Guild again. We did Ugo Betti, *The Burnt Flowerbed* and John Drinkwater, *X = O* and a couple of [M.J.] Molloy plays like *The King of Friday's Men* and *Tomorrow Never Comes* [by Louis d'Alton]. Father O'Brien, who was also known as P.V., exposed us to not the usual fare that amateurs would be doing. I read *Death of a Salesman*, and I know I read *Camino Real*. I wouldn't hazard a guess as to what that is about now, but I remember discussing it – too big a word – with Father O'Brien, saying it was better than *Streetcar* and *Cat on a Hot Tin Roof*.

NG: So he must have been an unusual priest?

TM: Yes. He had a nigh-perfect voice. It wasn't the voice beautiful, it was clipped but not in British officer way: he must have done voice production.

NG: How soon did you know you wanted to write for the theatre yourself?

TM: I don't know. I thought the writing bug happened when [Noel] O'Donoghue said 'Why don't we write a play?' which resulted in *On the Outside*, but now in retrospect it was probably on the cards from much earlier.

NG: *On the Outside* obviously did very well for you: amateur production in Cork and then a broadcast on RTÉ. And *Whistle in the Dark* the following year won the manuscript award in the amateur drama festival, leading on eventually to its production in London. Tell me about the origins of *Whistle*. How long did it take you to write the play? Was it knocking around as an idea for a while?

TM: I remember finishing the second act, which, with the first act, came to all of twenty pages of a school book; I threw it into a corner and a month or two went by. Obviously my subconscious was working on it, because I think I wrote the third act in a night. It goes through my mind occasionally because it took me two years to write *Famine*, and I ask myself, 'How could I do *Whistle in the Dark* in a matter of months and have it impeccably constructed?'

NG: The production of *Whistle* led on to your moving to London. What was the sequence of events there?

TM: The first night happened in September 1961, and I resigned from teaching the following February. I'm not proud of leaving the school in midterm, but there was a bit of pressure from London. The film rights were sold, and there was a pressure on me to get over there and write the screenplay. And I'd fallen in love with Mary, whom I later married.

NG: Were you involved in the rehearsals of *Whistle in the Dark*?

TM: I know I was because we were rehearsing in Stratford East and, coming home to London, we had an accident and the director Edward Burnham injured his back.

NG: That fixes your memory of being involved in rehearsals. And this would have been your first experience of professional theatre rehearsals?

TM: Yes.

NG: Was it anything of a revelation to you at that stage? Did you feel that this was something new? You had obviously done a lot of amateur acting yourself and knew about putting on plays and so on.

TM: I think it sort of washed off my back. The experience of London was such a jump. Paradoxically, I was a high jumper.

NG: You were talking about the various things that decided you to make the move to London: your personal relationship and a script for a film of the play.

TM: I sold the film rights. I disappeared for a day and when I came back to my social base which was the Queen's Elm pub, people began to applaud me, and I was in the dark. I hadn't seen the headline in the *Evening News*, 'His Play Sells for £154,000.' Robin Fox the producer and Michael Craig the principal actor were trying to get me all day to let me know this was a PR job because six or eight grand was what I actually got for the film rights.

NG: There was also a possibility at this time of your writing about the Congo?

TM: Yes. A regiment from the Curragh was going to the Congo, and the Head of Drama at the BBC had some sort of notion that it would make a documentary play, and we had certainly one meeting about it. I think what scotched it fortunately was that the Irish Government or the Irish Army wouldn't take responsibility for me. So I could be dead if it went ahead because I was not streetwise or junglewise.

NG: You did quite a lot of work for television in your time in London. How did that come about?

TM: I had a meeting with John Elliot, a producer at the BBC, and told him I had two ideas, one called *Veronica*, and one called *The Fooleen*. And Elliot said to me, why don't you do the two of them? Obviously, I was delighted, even though my instinct is for the stage and the feedback I get is always from stage. But it was money, and it gave me the opportunity to work with Herbert Wise, a fairly famous television director, with Jim MacTaggart who was possibly the best director I ever worked with, and with John McGrath of 7:84, who became a friend for life. This was part of my apprenticeship: I was pleased to get the work. Nobody was knocking down my doors to do stage plays of mine, even though Oscar Lewenstein had taken an option on *The Fooleen* and Michael Craig took an option on *The Morning After Optimism*.

NG: So for you it was a source of regular income?

TM: Well, I got 925 pounds sterling for *The Patriot Game*. That was good money in 1964 or 1965. When I was a young teacher at the end of the 1950s into the 1960s, I had just under 500 a year. And I was smoking, running a car, and playing poker – badly.

NG: After *Whistle*, when you moved into an experimental mode with a play such as *The Fooleen*, which was to become *A Crucial Week in the Life of a Grocer's Assistant*, were you aware that yours was an expressionist style?

TM: I was doing my own thing under the direction of the plays. As I said long ago, the subject of the play dictates its style. In the case of *Grocer's Assistant*, I had a principal character who was silent so I had to come up with a convention that allowed him to talk. *Optimism* started from the line 'Once upon a time there was a boy, as there was always and there always will be.' That dictated the style of the fairy tale; I wrote that speech first however sketchily and the play moved back from that and on to the conclusion. And the speech in its mood of disillusionment was fairly subjective. I had no immediate contact with my family, mother and father particularly. The world I knew for twenty-seven years was suddenly gone and I think I was a bit frightened. The knowns were gone. But I had a good time writing *Optimism* – I was experimenting with language, having flexed my poetic muscles in *Crucial Week*. The most interesting question I've ever been asked is 'where does the amazing language come from?' I had escaped the sugar factory, my family, teaching, and I think retrospectively something was growing inside. I was looking for myself and I felt that I had the freedom to do anything I liked. I was the last of ten children and I tried to walk like my brothers, I invested in them the repository of all knowledge.

NG: So there was a sense of getting out from under that family position, always being junior to the others, contributing to the extraordinary exhilaration in being able to write in the way you were writing then. You have talked about how much going to the theatre in London at the time meant to you. How often did you go and what sort of range of things did you see?

TM: Well, I saw a lot of plays. My mother-in-law was a woman who had a background in theatre. She lived in Spain and she came over for a month every year and my wife would accompany her to Chichester, Guildford and the West End. I might have had fifteen magical evenings, a few hundred good evenings, a lot of rubbish. Of the fifteen magical nights I've forgotten all but a few. I saw *The Persians* in the Peter Daubeny World Theatre Season – I was goggle-eyed by that: just a messenger coming in and telling the story, but the sweep it had ... . A few years later I saw *Hedda Gabler* directed by Ingmar Bergman and I didn't like it; it was stylized, on set everything was crimson. When she burns the script in a scarlet stove, she burned her hand. I thought 'for fuck's sake, you cannot burn your hand on such a thing'. *Oh What a Lovely War*, that was very exciting. I was gobsmacked by *Six Characters in Search of an Author*, with Barbara Jefford and Michael Hordern. That was tremendous stuff that fed my spirit and let me know that all was not naturalism.

NG: In your own work in the London period *Famine* is the other big play. You've talked about how the Woodham-Smith book *The Great Hunger* struck you and you felt somebody was going to write a play about this. But it's a very intractable subject, isn't it?

TM: Yes, and modestly I waited for two years thinking there would be a rash of such plays. In early concept I was starting in Derry and was going to Cobh but that didn't work out. So I kept narrowing it down till I came to a single village Glanconnor. I think I was very influenced by Brecht – Brecht was the flavour of the 1960s. *Baal* with Peter O'Toole – I was bored at that – but the director Bill Gaskill was never better than with *The Good Woman of Szechwan*.

NG: So, Brecht was in the atmosphere. Theatre Workshop that staged *Whistle* very much used a style derived from Brecht. But essentially you were working with the material in Woodham-Smith and you found the shape by concentrating in on the village. But presumably you must have been aware that this was your first time to take on the history of Ireland. You weren't daunted by that prospect or did you see it as a challenge?

TM: Well, the research took me a year and I could be still researching it now because research perpetuates itself to stop getting on with the writing. I know I had the play written in 1967 because I submitted it to the Irish Life Play competition, but they made no award that year because no script came up to the standard. I am bitter about this because 500 quid would have meant a lot.

NG: And in fact it was the following year that Tomás Mac Anna put it on in the Peacock. Had you had previous connections with Mac Anna?

TM: No. From what I remember, none whatsoever. He was very kind to me and he was in love with Brecht.

NG: So he saw this as a script with the kind of style he wanted to bring to it as director?

TM: Yes, he did a couple of Brechts at the Abbey or the Peacock.

NG: Did you come back for the production?

TM: I came back for a number of rehearsals because I remember incidents during rehearsals. Niall Tóibín made a backhanded compliment to me: 'He knows what he wants.' From early on, punctuation was important to rhythm rather than planing against the grain or swimming against the tide. 'Get up off your knees, you gadahan': Mac Anna took that literally, that the gadahan had to be kneeling, which is understandable but –

NG: – not the way you work. It would seem that your coming back with *Famine, Crucial Week*, and then *Morning after Optimism* was a sort of return in triumph, the local boy whom the Abbey turned down. But maybe that's a misreading of it?

TM: I think it is. I had to wait seven years for my next play to be staged after *Whistle*, so I was grateful, not triumphant when Mac Anna decided to do *Famine*.

NG: It's such an epic play: what was it like in the very small restricted space of the Peacock?

TM: Well, it moved up into the Abbey. Niall Toíbín, though not a famine figure, was good in the part, and I was delighted with Geoff Golden's looks who replaced him because he was a fine figure of a man, and more suitably accoutred to play the lead. Toíbín had played Brendan Behan and I kept sort of seeing Behan as John Connor.

NG: Do you remember much of the production of *Crucial Week*? McCann by all accounts was already quite something as an actor?

TM: He was wonderful – such a presence on the stage.

NG: I hadn't realized Alan Simpson directed it.

TM: Yes. And he did a terrific job. It was quite stylized. Brian Collins designed the set and it was like a melodeon, the street. Alan got Mairin O'Sullivan [as Mother] to talk at double speed for long speeches. There were a great bunch of people – Des Cave, Seamus Newham. It was very successful: they brought it back in 1970.

NG: Then there was *Morning after Optimism* with Colin Blakely. He played James presumably in *Optimism* and it would have been a part to suit him, I guess?

TM: Blakely was dynamic in his acting – Olivier apparently said Blakely was the best actor in the world. He came to play the part because he decided to spend a year in Ireland for tax reasons: I don't think we'd ever have got him otherwise. He had a flat in Dun Laoghaire and we became fast friends, lying on the floor drunk, or half drunk, listening to tenors. Blakely was having lessons from Veronica Dunne and his mother had sung with Heddle Nash who was a famous English tenor. That was ten years before I wrote *The Gigli Concert*, but I may have been thinking of the play already.

NG: *The White House* was obviously not a play that in the end you felt happy with: you have never published it, and rewrote it as *Conversations*. What was going on there?

TM: David Storey had written the play where the riggers put up a tent –

NG: – it's called *The Contractor* –

TM: Yes. I was taken by that notion; I saw the cast decorating the White House pub. Then I had a friend who used to mimic Kennedy down to the stabbing finger, he was a good man for the arts and inspiring people. It was done on RTÉ with both parts and Tony Doyle – the lovely Tony – almost made it work, playing JJ in 'Speeches on a Farewell'.

NG: You were on the Board of the Abbey for a term? Did that give you another point of view on the theatre?

TM: I was on the Board for eleven years – three as an observer. It was boring being on the Board. I was given a headline in *Variety*, the trade paper: 'Youth makes the Board of the Abbey.' I was thirty-seven. Fifteen or twenty minutes were spent discussing gout and rheumatism.

NG: *The Sanctuary Lamp*: you set it in a city, but you don't say where it is. It more or less has to be England, doesn't it?

TM: I felt it probably is London: Harry was always meant to be a Jew but an English Jew of mid-European extraction. But the first time it was done here, it was all Irish, including Harry.

NG: Presumably, though, you wanted them in a space that isn't anywhere in particular: it's not in Kilburn.

TM: I think there were thousands of other things to resolve. I set it in a circus, the wings of a circus: desultory applause and Harry comes in dressed as Batman and little Sam was Robin. The Irishman Francisco was the villain and Olga was the heroine who had to be rescued. I remember one of the lines. They cartwheel on and Sam the dwarf takes off his mask and says 'What a poxy fucking act I end up with.' And a row broke out and Harry gives a punch to the other three, including Olga. Then the next scene was in the park. Harry befriends a down-and-out sleeping rough and starts talking to him. And the down-and-out waits until Harry is asleep and gives him a kicking. And the next scene is a pub and Maudie's grandfather and grandmother were it in it. The priority was not to state which city it was set in.

NG: So it's marginal spaces, spaces on the edge of other things that you're looking for rather than, this is in such and such a community, this is in such and such a place. The play stirred up controversy: you were accused of anticlericalism.

TM: Yes. I think now it was retaliatory. The one true Church which I grew up in and the hypocrisy of the Church – I have a go at Catholicism in several plays, but when I found the setting was in a church it begged for a commentary.

NG: Francisco's 'sermon' is indeed hard-hitting stuff.

TM: Yes. I was involved in the Church, as you probably know: ICEL – International Committee on English in the Liturgy. We were an advisory committee to bishops. The first meeting I had with the Committee was in London, then Washington, Toronto: a great way to see the world.

NG: Were there other writers involved?

TM: No. I took over from [the Shakespearean scholar] G. B. Harrison. There was one other layman who was a Londoner and the others were clerics – DDs.

NG: Do you know who recommended you, why you were picked?

TM: They had a meeting in Dublin and they went to the Abbey and the *Grocer's Assistant* was on, which is mildly anticlerical, so they invited me. I replied, in case they were expecting more of me, that I wouldn't wish my Catholic background on anyone. I got a typewritten letter back, asking me to come to the next meeting which was in London, and a letter enclosed which roughly said we all have had our problems. So I went.

NG: How long were you involved, Tom?

TM: Two years.

NG: Quite a lot of time.

TM: Six meetings, seven meetings, but I felt it wasn't right to be fashioning prayers for others –

NG: – that you didn't want to say yourself –

TM: Yes. And I had enough of it.

NG: Well, it's another unusual dimension to the life of a writer. *The Blue Macushla* – where did that come from, film noir style?

TM: I took time off because I didn't want to let myself in for an experience like *The Sanctuary Lamp*. We had 17 acres in Rathfarnham and a few years after I moved up there, I sought out 1930s, 1940s, early 1950s films. I wanted to wean myself back to writing and I thought of putting a live movie on the stage.

NG: You didn't have *The Blue Dahlia* especially in mind, did you?

TM: No. But Alan Ladd, James Cagney and Pat O'Brien…

NG: I was away from Ireland through the 1970s, so *The Gigli Concert* was the first play of yours I saw on stage. I was just blown away by it. Do you think Patrick Mason brought a special quality to the direction?

TM: I think so: style. I had an input to it but I respected him. I was at most of the rehearsals and he listened to me.

NG: The music: was it an obsession of your own?

TM: Yes. I was always interested in music and I thought I was a tenor, but I envied singers so strongly that I couldn't bear to listen to them. 'The only possible way to tell people who you are' – that line comes from myself. I was obsessive in listening to Gigli. You want to listen to him or you want to sing like him. I had to be familiar with the music so I could choose.

NG: Because the individual arias are important for the particular moments.

TM: I think it was the second time out with Patrick again and he said to me or I said to him, 'I'm getting very cheesed off with "O Paradiso!"' He said I agree, but there was no way we could change it.

NG: I wanted to talk to you about the work with Druid and Garry Hynes. You started off with them in 1983: Did you know their work before that?

TM: No. I knew of them through Mick Lally who was a friend.

NG: So, did she contact you?

TM: Yes. I had an office, a work place in the Appian Way; she visited that place one day and declared abruptly 'I want you to be writer in residence.' And I agreed very readily, but I said that residence was out of the question, so we came up with 'writer in association'.

NG: So no way were you going to move to Galway?

TM: No, no. Perhaps I would liked to, but I had a bit of a farm in the foot hills in Rathfarnham, and I had three young children.

NG: There was quite a bit of talk in the press about the Galway writer returning to his roots. Did you feel that way at all? Was there the sense of the connection because they were Galway based?

TM: I don't think I consciously thought of it, but I was made conscious of it. Marie [Mullen], Sean [McGinley], Ray McBride and Maeliosa [Stafford] were all part of the West coast.

NG: I was very struck by how much you were doing in that 1984–5 period, rewriting *The White House* as *Conversations* and then the two big plays, *Thief of a Christmas* and *Bailegangaire*. You were busy that time.

TM: *The White House* was done in 1971 and 'Conversations' always worked: audiences were flying when they came out of that part of the double bill. I reversed the order and 'Conversations' won again. I took the play out every few years to see what I could do with it to make it entirely successful. When I took it out in 1983 the thought struck me, do I need 'Speeches of a Farewell', and that was bingo in my mind.

NG: So you didn't substantially alter the original 'Conversations' or did you expand it?

TM: I expanded it by an odd line here and there which I thought would reinforce the play. I decided JJ would be a potent presence by his absence.

NG: I loved that production so much and I still remember those voices. It seemed to me that a part of why it worked so well was that those actors were so used to playing together. It is very important in that play to get the rhythm correct, isn't it?

TM: Garry rehearsed them a hundred times, a thousand times, on a single section.

NG: The twin plays, *Bailegangaire* and *Thief of a Christmas*, were you writing them at the same time?

TM: No. *Bailegangaire* was written first for my children – hence Bailegangaire. I was thinking what title would fascinate them – Puddle-beyond-the-Marsh. But when it came to five thousand words and it was only starting, I said to myself, 'sorry, children, Dinky toys again, this year'. I was trying to make up for the selfishness all writers have.

NG: And *Thief*?

TM: The Abbey offered me an adaptation of [Charles Kickham's novel *Knocknagow* or] *The Homes of Tipperary* – Matt the Thrasher is the hero.

It's considered a minor Irish classic, but it took me a month to read the first fourteen pages. Then I came up with the notion of writing a play about the actuality of *Bailegangaire* and Tomás Mac Anna bought that idea.

NG: You talked to me about cutting *Bailegangaire* substantially at a very late stage. Did you know you were going to have to cut it?

TM: No. I had gone as far as I could with writing it, and Garry did not want me anywhere near the rehearsal room in Galway. However, I came down to the first dress rehearsal. It went up on time, but it was ten o'clock when they ended the first act. And Garry said, 'I'll have to let them go home.' I was staying in the Great Southern and about twelve I went to bed; I had the script and I started to cut reams out of it. I stopped about six and I had a few hours for sleep, because I knew that Druid wouldn't open until half nine, and I walked up there and I said 'these are the cuts.'

NG: It must have been difficult for Siobhán McKenna playing Mommo to take that on board, with that enormous long part.

TM: Siobhán was a terrific professional. I went to see her when she was already in her costume and she was glued to the script, walking up and down the dressing room. She didn't hear me come in, but she came abreast of me and she said 'They're great cuts.' I get emotional every time I think of that.

NG: *The Seduction of Morality*: why did you decide to write a novel, or was that something you had been thinking about for a while?

TM: I had had a psychological block about prose, but I thought I'd give prose a whirl. I planned seven short stories which would cohere in women's names: Alice was one, and Vera was another. And I wrote Alice and something else. Vera took off – not a rare occurrence – so I went with it. I thought there was a play in there, but I said that's mental suicide you're trying to commit: keep on with the story in prose. I think it took me three years to write it, waiting for another year for it to be published. So I then set about making it into the play, *The Wake*.

NG: *The House* goes back to the 1950s: was there a particular reason for your going back to that period?

TM: That had its first outing as a film – I think I called it The Golondrina, Christy was in it. I met a bulky American on my way back from New York. 'I'm George.' 'I'm Tom.' 'What do you do, Tom? I'm an attorney.' I said, 'I'm a writer.' 'You're a writer: do you want a plot?' He said he was from Boston and he arrived at work and a friend of his was sitting on the steps to his office. And the friend said to him you have to help me, I'm in trouble with my wife. I was out with a lady last night and, if my wife gets wind of that, my marriage folds. So, George said he arranged for the friend to be locked up. And he said, 'Tom, if that friend of mine had committed a murder, he had a perfect alibi.' I cursed George because I was trying to fit the story into the plot of my play and it wasn't organically evolving. I had terrible problems with that.

NG: So the gift of the plot was not such a great gift after all – a poisoned chalice. The big Abbey retrospective of your work in 2001, apart from your own production of *Bailegangaire*, which I remember very fondly, were there other productions in that season which you thought really stood out?

TM: I was pleased with Gerry Stembridge's take on *Optimism* because I never thought of it like that. I thought Stephen Brennan and Frank McCusker were particularly good [in *The Sanctuary Lamp*] – Frank with the beard looked like Jesus.

NG: Final question about *Alice Trilogy* in London and Dublin: did you feel you had a different atmosphere?

TM: The Irish audience responded more because they knew me and they knew the actors. I directed the Dublin production myself but I'm grateful to [Ian] Rickson because I think he is a terrific director and I learned so much from his production in London.

NG: You revise the text of your plays for each revival, don't you?

TM: Yes. That is my usual form: my last will and testament on the plays. I'm meeting the director of the current production of *Gigli* later today, and I was thinking cutting can be a disease. I was thinking of the cross-fade of the sextet from *Lucia* and *Caro Mio Ben* and Mona says 'you could go away for a year with that thing switched on and when you came back it would still be playing'. To which JPW says 'Yeh' – he's thinking about Helen. And I had cut this, and I want to reinstate it tonight.

MISFORTUNES: *A THIEF OF A CHRISTMAS*
AND *BAILEGANGAIRE*
Lucy McDiarmid

Bernard O' Donoghue's poem 'Concordiam in Populo' lists the 'prodigious events' that happened in Cullen, Co Cork, at the time of his father's funeral in 1962: 'neighbours who hadn't talked / For twenty years … Cooperated', and

> Husbands who'd not addressed a civil word
> To wives for even longer referred to them
> By Christian name in everybody's hearing:
> *Lizzie* or *Julanne* or *Nora May*.

It was, the poem says,

> . . . just as Kate had told us once
> How she crept into bed when the thunder seemed
> To throw giant wooden boxes at the house,
> Beside the husband that she hadn't spoken to
> Since the first month after their sorry wedding.[2]

No such prodigious events happen in the lives of Brigit and Séamus O'Toole, whose marriage is central to the narrative of the three *Mommo Plays*. 'I'm Brigit too', she says at the end of *Brigit*, 'though so long it's been since anyone called me by first name, I've near forgot it myself.'[3] There's a moment towards the end of *A Thief of a Christmas* when the 'Stranger' (Séamus) comes over to his wife (aka Brigit, Mommo) smiling, and as they laugh together, '*Tears brim to her eyes*,' and she introduces the subject of their marriage into the conversation: 'I see the animals in the field look more fondly on each other than we do,' and a few lines later, 'She embraces him.'[4] But that moment is an anomaly, and as the much older Mommo in *Bailegangaire* remembers her late husband, he might have been one of O'Donoghue's neighbours in Cullen: 'The forty years an' more in the one bed together an' he to rise in the mornin' (and) not to give her a glance. An' so long it had been he had called her by first name, she'd near forgot it herself' (*Plays*, 2, 140).

The marriage of the O'Tooles does not change significantly in the time covered by the trilogy, though we do hear Mommo sigh 'Poor Séamus' at the end of *Bailegangaire* (*Plays*, 2, 169). The years of frustrating silence, in which verbal exchange is thwarted in the marital relationship, feature only glancingly in the two major plays, *Thief of a Christmas* and *Bailegangaire*. However, the plays are structured by and focus on rituals of oral performance. These rituals require expressiveness of a kind on the parts of those who perform them and gradually provoke verbal responses from the other characters. The 'topic' of both performances is the enumeration of 'misfortunes', the word Mommo introduces into the dialogue: for different purposes and in different styles, the two oral performances prompt those who listen to join in the direct expression of misfortunes. The laughing competition in *Thief* and the storytelling in *Bailegangaire* create framed experiences within the outer theatrical frame.[5]

Because breaking the inner frame and merging its content with that of the outer frame's narrative is the central action in both plays, and because a play is itself a framed experience, it is useful to consider *Thief* and *Bailegangaire* in terms of the ideas in Erving Goffman's *Frame Analysis: An Essay on the Organization of Experience*. For an unframed experience, Goffman introduces the word 'strip', which means 'any arbitrary slice or cut from the stream of ongoing activity'. It refers to 'any raw batch of occurrences … that one wants to draw attention to as a starting point for analysis'. A 'frame' is the definition of a situation based on 'principles of organization which govern events … and our subjective involvement in them'.[6] A framed experience forms a definable segment within a strip of action, such as attendance at a theatrical performance, a visit to a doctor's office, a holiday, an academic lecture or the telling of a joke. Any such experience may be understood in terms of frame analysis. A frame is 'broken' when an 'occurrence' happens that 'cannot be effectively ignored and to which the frame cannot be applied', such as when an actor faints in the middle of a play, or a fire alarm goes off in the middle of a lecture, or someone telling a joke gets a coughing fit before the punch line. Goffman uses the word 'rim' to define the 'points at which the internal activity leaves off and the external activity takes over – the rim of the frame itself'.[7] This concept helps to characterize the relation between the oral performances in the two Murphy plays and the 'strip' of activity within which they occur. Every framed experience, even Mommo's long, repetitive, unending story, is 'anchored' or bound to a strip of activity, 'embedded in ongoing reality',[8] just as that reality itself exists within a theatrical frame anchored by curtains, applause and architectural means in the world of its audience.

A Thief of a Christmas

The laughing competition that is the oral performance in *Thief* resembles other Irish verbal forms that are ritualized witty and belligerent exchanges. The argument between Oisín and St Patrick, found in some versions of the *Agallamh na Seanórach* (Colloquy of the Ancients), in Lady Gregory's translation and at the end of Yeats's *Wanderings of Oisin*, may be one of the earliest. The Irish tradition of invective forms part of this genre too, as when Gregory's St Patrick tells his opponent, 'Stop your talk, you withered, witless old man.'[9] The *Iomarbháibh na bhFileadh* (Contention of the Bards), a learned seventeenth-century controversy among the poets of Ireland, is a more elaborate and extended debate, and the *agallamh beirte* (conversation of two people), with its quick banter on naughty subjects or sacred ones, remains a competitive genre among Irish speakers today.[10]

Thief's competition has some of the characteristics of an athletic contest also, because loud and prolonged laughing requires physical strength. It is that aspect that kills the large Costello, who collapses and dies after his exertions. The physicality of the talent required – both the danger of exhaustion and the sense of threat, as two male rivals circle one another – gives an edge to the belligerence, which seems a distinctly Irish aspect. In recent years, laughing competitions have been held in Thailand, Japan, Canada, the United Kingdom, the Czech Republic, France, Austria, Slovenia and the United States (though not in Ireland). As they appear in online videos, these contests do not require verbal challenges, and in *Thief* it is the verbal component that licenses the direct voicing of aggression, that in fact allows the laughing competition to become a collective expression of defiance and desperation as well as of anger.[11]

The laughing competition is understood by its participants, the audience and the sponsor (John Mahony, the publican) as a genre or form of sport with distinct rules that must be enunciated and accepted by all; as, in Goffman's term, an event with a frame, set off from an outer 'strip' of activity. Just as in *The Quiet Man* Michaeleen Óg Flynn has to shout 'Marquis of Queensbury rules' as Sean Thornton and Will Danaher begin to fight, so here the regulations are made clear. The space is cleared: 'clear back off the floor' (*Plays*, 2, 207), Costello shouts to the others in the pub, as he accepts the Stranger's implicit challenge to see who is the 'better laugher' (*Plays*, 2, 202). The cleared space in which they fight is an 'arena' (*Plays*, 2, 238). The way that it is 'indisputably decided who is the winner' must be determined. The Stranger's wife decides: 'He who laughs last' (*Plays*, 2, 225). Costello asks for 'the topic to launch us' (*Plays*, 2, 214) and – also as the fight in *The Quiet Man* begins – everyone in the audience, excited and expectant at the beginning of a fray, bets frantically, and Rose Mahony records all the bets. And in both cases, 'the drinks are on the house'.

The apparent mutual respect of the participants, expressed in a mix of banter and belligerence, is also similar: 'It's been a pleasure beatin' you,' Danaher says to Thornton, and 'Your widow, me sister ... She could've done a lot worse.'

> The **Stranger** *gets his whiskey and raises his glass to* **Costello**.

Costello   An' to you an' yours again! – Wo-ho-ho!
Stranger   Heh-heh-heh, an' if mine ever come across you and yours --
Costello   I hope they'll do as much for them –
Stranger]
Costello]   As you and yours did for me an' mine!
They laugh together. Others laughing.

(Plays, 2, 218)

The verbal wit is an important component of the struggle because it triggers the laughter. Hence Costello's mockery of the 'gallant John Mahony', his former rival for the buxom Rose, and of Mahony's attempt at a romantic courtship: 'There's shtars (*stars*) up that side, he said, an' there's shtars up that side!' (*Plays*, 2, 217).

Even before the laughing competition starts, the locals are ready for performances of various kinds: musicians arrive, Josie does his party piece (Ride-the-blind-donkey), Bina begins 'Swanee River', and Costello tells jokes – 'The Dutch has taken Holland!' (*Plays*, 2, 180) – and quotes Shakespeare – 'The bright day is done ... and we are for the dark' (*Plays*, 2, 191) – a quotation probably inspired by the imminent arrival of a character called Anthony. All of these are typical of an ordinary evening in a lively village pub, though the number of inconclusive beginnings suggests a pervasive malaise. In the informal atmosphere of a session, frame-breaking is almost a standard part of the frame; that is, the interaction of the audience with the performers is an accepted and expected part of the performance itself. This casual frame-breaking attaches to the laughing competition also, as when Costello sets up the joke about the man 'driving the one auld sheep' and turning to the others, asks, 'What did Peadar say?' Then 'several voices' give the punch line: 'It's very hard to bring one of them together!'(*Plays*, 2, 216). As the local champion, Costello is used to such exchanges with his neighbours, who know all the auld stories; the Stranger's communication outside the formal frame of the competition is only with his wife.

With the betting and the witty exchanges, the non-participants in the laughing competition are already more than audience, but when Costello begins to understand the 'topic' of the competition – 'I understand yeh now, ma'am – misfortunes' (*Plays*, 2, 231) – the role of those outside the 'arena' becomes more participatory, and the frame of the competition disappears, although no one present calls attention to the changed situation. The collective enumeration of misfortunes builds from humour to hysteria; as Nicholas Grene puts it, 'The pent-up frustrated energies of the group spiral out of control.'[12] Bina's contribution that the potatoes are 'the divil to ate' leads to laughter, but the mention of the 'dead', and of the most painful and personal misfortunes, transforms the nature of the laughter. The laugh-lines have gone way beyond auld sheep and rotted potatoes:

> **Costello**   An' the dead – Wo-ho-ho! – An' the dead, ma'am? Me father, is it, you're referring to? Sure, he killed himself, sure: drowned himself in the barrel at the gable-end of the house. 'Twas a difficult feat?
> **Stranger**   Heh-heh-heh-heh-heh-heh-heh!
> **Costello**   Wo-ho-ho-ho-ho …! An' yourself, ma'am?
> **Stranger's Wife**   Hih-hih-hih – I had nine sons –
> **Stranger**   Heh-heh-heh-heh-heh-heh-heh!
>
> (*Plays*, 2, 232)

Costello's invitation to the Stranger's Wife to contribute her misfortunes indicates that the laughing competition has become more than a sport. Soon the formal turn-taking becomes a collective yell:

> **Others**   Those lost to America!
> Arms lost to the thresher!
> Suicide an' bad weather!
> Blighted crops!
> Bad harvests!
> Bad markets!
> How to keep the one foot in front of the other!
>
> (*Plays*, 2, 235–6)

The laughing competition has become, in Grene's words, 'a ritual exorcism of defiance and despair',[13] but it is a failed exorcism, because the power of the psychic demons becomes stronger. After Costello dies, or seems to, the original frame is gone; the group of neighbours becomes a mob and attacks the Stranger, and then, as the stage direction says, 'Mayhem breaks loose' (*Plays*, 2, 240).

The conflict of a cultural controversy, a more sedate form of verbal belligerence than this laughing competition, may be resolved (if it is at all) by bluff and bravado, by performative skills and improvisational flair.[14] But no resolution is possible in *Thief*. The feelings associated with the misfortunes themselves break through the formal structure of their enumeration. The ludic element has vanished, and there are no more jokes about single sheep or courtships. The entire pub becomes the 'arena' in which there is a direct expression of misfortunes. This is no longer entertainment: it is a direct encounter with the misery from which the original performances, music, song and Ride-the-blind-donkey, might have provided distraction. No resolution is possible, because all the people (no longer two rivals and an audience) are poor and suffering and will remain so; the *Maragadh Mór* (the Christmas market), and much else, has failed them.

Bailegangaire

In *Bailegangaire*, Mommo's story of the 'misfortunes' of years back (the laughing competition and the subsequent deaths of her grandson Tom and husband Séamus) is the oral performance that establishes the inner frame within the outer frame of the play. Because the 'nice story' is, in Mommo's mind, a bedtime story for her grandchildren, its imagined context is about thirty years earlier. The surviving grandchildren, Mary and Dolly, are adults who have heard the story begin many times and never reach its tragic conclusion. The play takes place in the same 'three-roomed thatched house' where they grew up (*Plays*, 2, 91).

The relation between the inner frame of oral performance, the story, and the outer frame of the play differs from that of *Thief*. Mommo's story is almost, but not quite, coextensive with the play. Because in the first lines of the script – 'Scoth caoc! Shkoth! … Dirty aul' things about the place … And for all they lay!' – Mommo is talking to 'imagined hens', she is not telling her story. She exists in the frame of the play as a 'senile' old woman eating in bed. In her next few lines, the notion of another frame, that of her story, is introduced gradually. First (looking towards the 'imagined children at the foot of the bed'), she utters the earliest suggestion of a story, the 'rim', in Goffman's term, of the frame by which the inner activity is connected to outer ones: 'Let ye be settling now, my fondlings, and I'll be giving ye a nice story again tonight when I finish this. For isn't it a good one?' (*Plays*, 2, 91). Then Mommo clears her narrative space by alluding dismissively to Mary, who is making tea: 'An' no one will stop me! Tellin' my nice story.' Having thus established a frame for 'tellin'' by differentiating it from the outer frame in which Mary exists, she begins; or, as the stage direction says, she '*Reverts to herself*': 'Yis, how the place called Bochtán and its *graund* (*grand*) inhabitants – came by its new appellation, Bailegangaire, the place without laughter' (*Plays*, 2, 92).

No sooner is the story's frame constructed than it is broken, as it is regularly throughout the play by Mary, by Dolly, and by Mommo herself. Having announced her topic, the origin of the 'appellation', Mommo at once breaks her own frame by asking Mary 'What time is it?' (*Plays*, 2, 92). Because Mommo is senile, and because, as Murphy says, when she tells the story she 'reverts to herself', *Bailegangaire* can be understood, to use Grene's phrase, as 'a split-level drama' existing in a single theatrical frame, in which a senile woman moves in and out of relationship with the other characters. But Mommo's 'nice story' constructs a powerful line of action within its frame; as Grene says, it is characterized, as all stories are, by an 'urge toward narrative closure'.[15] So strong is that drive towards closure that soon Mary begins moving into and out of the frame with Mommo, helping her – and compelling her – to tell the story. The final lines of the play merge the two frames, as Mary, who at that point has taken over the telling entirely, wraps the facts of the present into the story's frame.

The inner frame is created not only by phrases (such as 'An' no one will stop me! Tellin' my nice story') that suggest a 'rim' but by a stylistic distinction. The art of the story's language distinguishes it from the thoughtful, more educated language of Mary – 'Because I don't want to wait till midnight, or one or two or three o'clock in the morning, for more of your – unfinished symphony' (*Plays*, 2, 122) – and from Dolly's vulgar register – 'that other lean and lanky bastard' (*Plays*, 2, 107). Mommo speaks in two idioms, a mix of Irish words ('bonavs', 'cráite') with the Latinate 'specialist style' of the *seanchaí* (words like 'appellation', 'over-enlargement', 'felicitations', 'protraction', and 'the contrary and adverse connection') when she is in the story's inner frame, and vernacular language when she is speaking in the play's outer frame, 'What's birthdays to do with us?' (*Plays*, 2, 93). When

Mary joins Mommo within the story, she, too, speaks in its elaborate style, because she is echoing the words Mommo has been using night after night: 'the road to Bochtán, though of circularity, was another means home' (*Plays*, 2, 98). Although Dolly must also have heard the same words when she was taking care of Mommo, she never repeats the fancier phrases; she sticks with the shorter, more informal ones such as 'Good man Josie' or 'Then the root in the arse' (*Plays*, 2, 105, 100).

Mary's ability to reproduce long portions of the story in Mommo's high register and Dolly's ability to echo the lower one indicate that the ritualized oral performance in *Bailegangaire* is enacted by collaboration and not, as it is in *Thief*, competition. The collaboration is hard won; Mommo initially resists Mary's intervention in the story. At first she thinks of Mary as an obstacle: 'An' no one will stop me! Tellin' my nice story.' When Mary says, 'Please stop,' Mommo defiantly says, 'to *continue*' (*Plays*, 2, 98). Mary's comments remain outside the frame. When Mommo asks, in story mode, 'and how many children had she bore herself?' and then 'And what happened to them?' Mary sighs in response, 'What happened us all?' (*Plays*, 2, 97). So long as they are in different frames, Mommo is rude to Mary, rejecting the birthday cake and Mary's ministrations, and making clear her preference for Dolly. 'Who is that woman?' Mommo asks Dolly, hugging her warmly in bed and indicating Mary who 'stands by, isolated' (*Plays*, 2, 110). At that rejection, Mary leaves the room and returns with her suitcase packed, ready to leave the house.

After Dolly goes out temporarily, Mary tests whether Mommo has truly gone to sleep by reciting the next line of the story: '"Now as all do know the world over"?'[16] The script has inverted commas around that clause to indicate that Mary is not telling but quoting the story; that is, she is not inside the frame. And it is that provisional quotation that enacts the transition to full recital mode. Mary engages in some stage business with the radio, the light and the candles, but the next words she says are part of the story, speaking it '*Idly at first*': 'Now as all do know the world over. … Now as all do know. … Now as all do know the world over the custom when entering the house of another is to invoke our Maker's benediction on all present.'[17] Now there are no inverted commas around the words of the story, because Mary is no longer using the words to test Mommo; she is in the story's frame with her.

As Mommo awakens, Mary picks up the story where she herself left off: 'The customary salutation was given' (*Plays*, 2, 123). Although Mommo has slept through a passage, she joins in at Mary's place in the story. As they begin their combined effort, Mommo occasionally wants to evade the traumas of the story and go back to sleep. Gradually, however, Mommo accepts Mary's contributions, and they tell the story in a kind of turn-taking.

> **Mary**   And then, without fuss, the man indicated a seat in the most private corner.
> **Mommo**   An' they were wrongin' them there again! So they wor.
> **Mary**   They were.
> **Mommo**   They wor. The whispers bein' exchanged were *not* of malevolent disposition. Yis! – to be sure! – that woman! – Maybe! – had a distracted look to her. Hadn't she reason?
> **Mary**   The Bochtáns gawpin' at them.[18]
> **Mommo**   They knew no better.
> **Mary**   Where would they learn it?
>
> (*Plays*, 2, 123–4)

While advancing the story, Mary's contributions also show sympathy to Mommo, as she affirms that the Stranger and his wife were wronged by the Bochtáns.

The new energy Mary devotes to the story transfers to her relationship with Dolly. Before that decision, she calls attention to Dolly's pregnancy ('Why don't you take off your coat?') and critiques her promiscuity: 'You're disgusting' (*Plays*, 2, 112). Mary also describes herself as a sexual rival: 'Your husband wined, dined and bedded me! Stephen? *Your* Stephen? It was *me* he wanted! But I told him: "Keep off! Stop following me!" That's why he took you!'[19] Dolly leaves soon after that to have sex with a man whose identity is never mentioned. By the time she returns, however, Mary and Mommo have already worked out a provisional rhythm of narrative turn-taking. Having discovered a way to adapt to Mommo's story, Mary now begins to enter Dolly's life 'story'. With what the stage direction calls 'A gesture of invitation', she says to Dolly, 'You need to talk to someone' (*Plays*, 2, 129). By the end of the first act, they are crying in sympathy and embracing one another.

The narrative of the outer frame requires collaboration too: 'Oh the saga will go on', Dolly says, echoing the end of Mary's sentence, 'to make *sure* the saga goes on' (*Plays*, 2, 147). In the second act, Mary insists that Dolly finish *her* story: 'Why can't you ever finish a subject or talk straight?' (*Plays*, 2, 142). Mary's persistence is successful with Dolly also; soon Dolly is asking

Mary to enter into her story by accepting the 'brand new' baby that is on the way. By her willingness to take the baby, Mary is collaborating with Dolly in another way, a favour for which Dolly will support her financially.

The resolution of the play, its impasses surmounted in large part through Mary's determination, evolves from a circle of female interdependence. Even the terminally ill old woman whom Mary nursed in the English hospital participates in this circle, an interdependence audible in the way they all echo one another. The woman's remark to Mary – 'You're going to be alright, Mary' – was a '*promised* blessing' (*Plays*, 2, 160), and it's one that Mary repeats to Dolly a few minutes later, at the end of the play: 'You're going to be alright, Dolly.' And just as she took care of the patient, she takes care of Dolly, saying next, 'Roll in under the blanket' (*Plays*, 2, 167).

In *Thief,* the distinction between inner and outer frames, the laughing competition and the activities in the pub, dissolves as the audience of Bochtáns join in enumerating the misfortunes, the 'topic' that was supposed to 'launch' the two rivals. The competition has consequences in the world outside it when the Bochtáns turn on the Stranger, that decent man and his decent wife. In *Bailegangaire*, the frame of the story is broken repeatedly, and the captive audience, the granddaughters, move back and forth between the story and the 'saga' of their own lives, as Mommo does also, though less frequently. But in the final moments of the play, as Mary takes over the narration altogether, the inner frame of the story expands to include the outer frame of the play.

The merging of the content of both frames is as gradual as the initial creation of the frame of the story. Mary begins the final, saddest part in the third-person mode that Mommo has used. Like the Bochtáns, she joins in the enumeration of misfortunes that now becomes a direct expression of sorrow: 'The three small children were waiting for their gran and their grandad to come home.' In this sentence, 'grandad' transforms from the character in the story to the grandfather Mary remembers. In the most recent edition of the play, the text marks that shift by using an upper case G for Grandad later in the speech:

Mary Two mornings later, and he had only just put the kettle on the hook, didn't Grandad, the stranger, go down too, slow in a swoon... Mommo?[20]

Mommo's response sounds like an acknowledgement of fact rather than a line in the story: 'It got him at last.' The passage that follows exists in the new, merged frame, as the past of the story moves into the present of the family, what's left of them:

Mary   Will you take your pills now?
Mommo   The yellow ones.
Mary   Yes.
Mommo   Poor Séamus.

(Plays, 2, 169)

In her next lines, Mommo speaks as if the story she was telling her fondlings has now come to its conclusion; she begins the prayer *Salve Regina* that, as the play *Brigit* shows, was the prayer she said with her three grandchildren when they went to bed: 'To thee do we send up our sighs.' But when she finishes the prayer, she says to the adult Mary, 'And sure a tear isn't such a bad thing, Mary, and haven't we everything we need here, the two of us.' And the adult Mary, herself with 'tears of gratitude', answers in the same frame of the present moment, 'Oh we have, Mommo' (*Plays*, 2, 169–70).

Now apparently loved and accepted, Mary joins Dolly in the bed with Mommo. Concluding the story that Mommo began, Mary in her final lines echoes both Mommo's fancy diction and Dolly's vernacular 'brand new baby'. Mary's use of the third person suggests that although the two frames are now one, the play has been wrapped into the story's frame. This rhetorical move is almost the opposite of a *plaudite,* because the drama the audience has been watching is now inside the story Mommo has been telling. Mary's emotion, however, as well as Dolly's phrase, anchors the event described, the coming of the 'brand new baby', in the outer frame of dramatic action:

Mary   … To conclude. It's a strange old place, alright, in whatever wisdom He has to have made it this way. But in whatever wisdom there is, in the year 1984, it was decided to give that – fambly … of strangers another chance, and a brand new baby to gladden their home.

(Plays, 2, 170)

To conclude

In a conversation with Nicholas Grene, Tom Murphy said that the characters in *Bailegangaire* led lives that 'no one is watching'.[21] But 'in the year 1984', to quote Mary, a lot of writers and filmmakers were watching rural Irish women and unmarried pregnant women. Had Irish women's pregnancies ever been watched so closely before? In the previous year, 1983, an amendment protecting the life of the foetus was added to the Irish Constitution. Margot Harkin of Derry Film and Video set *Hush-a-bye Baby* (1989), a film about a pregnant fifteen-year-old in Derry, in 1984. Harkin was, she has said, inspired by the Kerry Babies case (April 1984) and the death of Ann Lovett (January 1984), both events mentioned in the film and alluded to in *Bailegangaire*.[22] Soon after *Hush-a-bye Baby* was screened, Paula Meehan's poem 'The Statue of the Virgin at Granard Speaks', also inspired by the death of Ann Lovett, was published.[23] Pat Murphy's film *Anne Devlin* (1984) was made for 'the women forgotten by history'.[24] Bob Quinn's film *Budawanny* (1987) features a priest who impregnates his young housekeeper. Placed within the historical context of Irish women's history, *Bailegangaire* marks a moment when women like Dolly were becoming the focus of national attention and beginning to protest to a national audience. Although the real-life counterparts of the sad and witty eccentrics of *Thief* may have drawn less attention than those of the strong women of *Bailegangaire*, the rural poor were remembered and studied in the early 1990s when the 150th anniversary of the Great Famine was commemorated.

Inspired by these national misfortunes, *Thief and Bailegangaire* may be understood in terms of the representation of emotions. To a large extent, emotions function differently in the two plays. In *Thief* the inner frame of the laughing contest, itself male dominated and competitive, releases the uncontrollable grief of the community in a voicing of misfortunes that breaks that frame irreparably, whereas in *Bailegangaire,* after the irregular breaking of the frame of Mommo's story by her granddaughters' conversation and her own naps, the story, guided by Mary and told by herself and Mommo, allows for a deliberate confrontation and cathartic release of emotion. The story's frame becomes the outer frame of the drama. But in their different ways, both the laughing contest with its catalogues of misfortunes and deaths – 'I had nine sons' (*Plays*, 2, 232) – as well as the story that Mommo tells, function as a kind of keen: 'Maybe she's crying now,' Mary says (*Plays*, 2, 143). What frame analysis shows is the way the oral performances in the two plays begin as indirect modes of expressiveness but ultimately become more directly expressive. Awareness of the frames makes it possible to recognize the way feelings break through them. The complex patterns of frame-breaking in *Thief* and *Bailegangaire* show emotions withheld and expressed, conveyed in performances and in conversation, present in hysterical laughter and in the tear that 'isn't such a bad thing'. The end of *Bailegangaire* names directly what it means to catalogue misfortunes, 'Mourning and weeping in this valley of tears' (*Plays*, 2, 169).

ABOUT SURVIVAL: READING MURPHY WITH LYOTARD
Alexandra Poulain

Bailegangaire is arguably Tom Murphy's most quintessentially Irish play, and has consistently been read as a comment on Irish history and culture. The language of the play (a play which centrally reflects on the power of language and replaces conventional action with the collaborative act of storytelling) combines the sophisticated, orotund prose of the *seanchaí* with the more prosaic, contemporary yet recognizably Irish English of 1980s rural Ireland. As Nicholas Grene has shown, the play parodies some of the most influential plays in the Irish theatrical canon – Synge's *Riders to the Sea*, Yeats's *Cathleen ni Houlihan* and Beckett's *Not I*[25] – and thus asks to be read in that context, as a critical engagement with the aesthetic and ideological assumptions which uphold this tradition. Commentators have emphasized the play's complex cultural politics, with Mommo both a figure of the Irish nation's potentially crippling obsession with past stories and a reminder of the necessity to accommodate the past in the face of the widely accepted ideology of progress and modernization at all cost. [26] While *Bailegangaire* is widely regarded as one of the most important Irish plays, there have been relatively few productions outside of Ireland, and fewer translations into foreign languages.[27] However, I wish to argue that the play is also relevant in other contexts, and in particular that it speaks forcefully to contemporary preoccupations about the nature of survival – about what it means to survive disaster, and what responsibilities it entails. Reading *Bailegangaire* with Jean-François Lyotard's 1988 text 'Survivant',[28] I will suggest that *Bailegangaire* harbours two antagonistic conceptions of survival: one melancholic, which conceives of survival as the aberrant prolonging of a life which one recognizes as merely the deferral of death; the other more productive, whereby survival is construed as the childish ability to pretend, in the face of ineluctable death, that life is worth living after all, so that a tradition can be passed on.

The issue of survival is at the core of *Bailegangaire*, which borrows its structure from the tradition of folk tales. As Fintan O'Toole writes, 'Mommo and her story belong to this pre-literate world, a world full of widows and orphans, sudden deaths, cruel diseases that cannot be overcome, a vicious struggle for survival.'[29] O'Toole's comment captures the sense of pervasive danger to which 'the stranger and his wife' (like all the characters in the story) are exposed, and to which the stranger ultimately succumbs. What O'Toole's reading tends to downplay, however, is the cost of survival, the agony of having to keep going after the loss of one's loved ones, and the guilt born of such a situation. The culminating moment in the laughing contest occurs when Mommo makes her own contribution to the topic of misfortunes, 'rollcalling the dead'[30] to keep the champions laughing.

> **Mommo**   Her Pat was her eldest, died of consumption. … An' for the sake of an auld ewe stuck in the flood was how she lost two of the others, Jimmy and Michael. …An' the nice wife was near her time, which one of them left behind him?
> **Mary**   Daddy.
> **Mommo**   Died tryin' to give birth to the fourth was to be in it. An' she herself left with the care of three small childre waitin' … And Willie too, her pet, went foreign after the others. An' *did* she drive them all away? Never ever to be heard of, ever again. Save Willie, aged thirty-four, in Louisaville Kentucky, died, peritonitis.
>
> (*Mommo Plays*, 117–18)

That Mary and Dolly, Mommo's granddaughters, take turns caring for Mommo and are cast, reluctantly, as the recipients of her story, points out the structural anomaly on which the dramatic situation rests: the fact that the generation of their parents and uncles has been wiped out, so that Mommo is the aberrant survivor of her own children, as well as of her husband and grandson Tom. The guilt she registers, here and elsewhere, reads as survivor's guilt, the horror of finding oneself incomprehensibly alive when one feels, irrationally, that according to the natural order of things, one ought to be dead. Lyotard's insights can help us to make sense of the play's probing of this state of survival.

Lyotard starts with what he calls a commonplace: if survival is about the deferral of death, then it follows that the surviving entity is implicated in a temporal relationship with its own beginning and end, with the enigma of its own non-being. Lyotard sees two ways of philosophically accounting for this state of survival. For Hegel, the mind is only alive insofar as it has died to what it was: at any moment in the present, it is conscious of no longer being what it was in the past, so that it can no longer speak of the entity that it was in the first person: 'I can only speak of myself as *it, then*, in the third person' (*Lectures d'enfance*, 60). In the process, what is lost is the dimension of presence: what existed as contingency, possibility, in the past is now bound by necessity. Accounting for one's past life, one hands down a story of oneself, creating a *tradition* which is always also a betrayal ('*trahison*') of the past: 'The betrayal of the living ("vivant") is inherent in the tradition conveyed by the survivor ("survivant"). The witness is always a bad witness, a traitor. But at least, he testifies' (*Lectures d'enfance*, 62). According to this conception, which in fact runs throughout the tradition of western philosophy, the experience of life as survival is essentially one of loss, of the melancholic loss of the irretrievable presence of the past.

It is easy to see how strongly *Bailegangaire* resonates with this description of survival. As a survivor, Mommo's sole activity in the present is the crafting of a narrative with which she hands down both the cultural tradition of the *seanchaí*, and the family history, 'the saga' as Mary and Dolly call it in derision. Being now dead to who she was in the past, she is bound to tell her story in the third person, further distancing herself from her former self by foreclosing the use of her own name, using instead the periphrasis 'the stranger's wife'. The endlessly repeated narrative, which Mary and Dolly have heard so often that they know it off by heart, creates an immutable version of tradition which admits of no variation but must be repeated word for word, night after night:

> **Mommo** [about Josie]   An' the threadbare fashion'ry, not a top-coat to him, the shirt neck open.
> **Mary** (*to herself*)   Not a gansey.
> **Mommo**   Nor a gansey.
> **Mary**   *Nor* a gansey.
>
> (*Mommo Plays*, 74)

It is precisely this exclusion of contingency, of creative innovation (at least until the final moments of the play), which makes chillingly obvious the extent to which the narrative, exhilarating and beautifully crafted though it may be, constitutes a betrayal of the past, of the pure, exuberant possibility which the laughing contest constituted.

Lyotard reading Hegel is talking about life in general – the life of the Hegelian subject, of the mind – as a modality of survival. Murphy's play creates a specific context for Mommo's grieving for the past, and her turning of past presence into tradition, into a narrative in which each event, each sentence is bound to the next by the law of necessity. Mommo is a survivor in the ordinary sense of the word, in the sense that she has survived the deaths of all her children against generational logic, and the even more traumatic deaths of Séamus and Tom. Yet I want to suggest that Mommo's plight speaks to us so vividly because at one level it tells us of our own plight, as human subjects who are at all times aware of living under a suspended sentence. Perhaps what we recognize in Mommo's situation is her effort to keep at bay thoughts of the terrible events of the past, which constitute her as a survivor and thus tell her insistently, beyond the agonizing grief of loss, of her own mortality. While Mommo's narrative ostentatiously serves to enshrine the events of the past in a traditional narrative, the deferral of its catastrophic conclusion really ensures that tradition has safely coalesced into endless repetition of the same, and serves to preclude her confrontation with the ineluctability of annihilation.

This first, melancholic conception of survival as the awareness that we are living under a suspended death sentence can be reversed, Lyotard argues, if we take into consideration not annihilation, but the other enigmatic relationship between the mind and non-being, that of apparition. Where melancholy focuses on the imminence of death, a counter-nihilistic stance is possible, which takes the form of a 'timid question: if the truth is that there is really nothing, why it is that there seems to be something? Or: why does truth lie, why is death deferred by birth and life?' (*Lectures d'enfance*, 64). To ask this question is to retain the child-like faculty of pretending, against the certainty that we are bound for annihilation, that an event, a beginning, is possible after all. 'Childhood is the state of the soul inhabited by something to which no answer is ever brought; whatever it undertakes, it is led by an arrogant faithfulness to this unknown host by which it is held hostage' (*Lectures d'enfance*, 66). Childhood, Lyotard continues, is about honouring a debt to life; it is about making life fruitful, not in order that we can enjoy it, but in order that we can pass it on as tradition. To survive, in this other sense, is to preserve the child in our adult selves, in spite of our knowledge of the ineluctability of death.

Lyotard then turns to Hannah Arendt, and quotes her reading in *The Human Condition* of the fact of nativity, 'the birth of new men' and the capacity for new beginnings that it restores: 'It is this faith in and hope for the world that found perhaps its most glorious and most succinct expression in the few words with which the Gospels announced their "glad tidings": "A child has been born unto us."'[31] Lyotard comments:

The greatness of Christ, compared to any tradition, Roman, Eastern or Jewish, is that he teaches, in word and deed, that the Son of Man has the faculty to forgive offences. What offends is always simply what is as having-been. The miracle of Christ is that he produces an event in the order of necessity. The glad tidings, which tell us that a child has been born unto us, is the birth of birth itself, and the fact that the offence of being here, in the world of beings, can be forgiven.

(Lectures d'enfance, 71)

At one level, Mommo's story of Bailegangaire is about the celebration, and eventual suppression, of childhood. The laughing contest, where 'misfortunes' are offered for general hilarity and exorcized, is described as a ritual of defiance, a fierce rejection of the order of necessity:

Mommo The nicest night ever, that's what I'm sayin'. And all of them present, their heads threwn back abandoned in festivities of guffaws: the wretched and neglected, dilapidated an' forlorn, the forgotten an' despairing, ragged an' dirty, eyes big as saucers ridiculing an' defying of their lot on earth below – Glintin' their defiance of Him – their defiance an' rejection, inviting of what else might come or *care* to come! – driving bellows of refusal at the sky through the roof. Hona ho gus hah-haa!

(Mommo Plays, 118)

Laughing in the face of fate, ridiculing the force of determinism which keeps them tethered to their miserable condition is a way of claiming the value of their lives in spite of all, of being faithful to a 'debt to life'. In *A Thief of a Christmas*, the play which stages the events that constitute Mommo's story in *Bailegangaire*, the contest even culminates with the prospect of an actual 'new beginning' for the whole community. The play is a travesty of the Passion of Christ interpreted in economic terms. When the stranger challenges the local champion, claiming that 'I'm a better laugher than your Costello' (*Mommo Plays*, 85, 149), the publican John Mahony, to whom most of the community is indebted, chooses to back him, while most of the community support Costello and wage their last resources against the gombeen man, who enters the wagers into his 'holy book', the register of the debts owing to him. When Costello collapses at the end of the night, granting the stranger victory (the winner being 'he who laughs last' [*Mommo Plays*, 116, 173]), Mahony insists that 'the book h-has to stand' (*Mommo Plays*, 185), and the bets are not cancelled, notwithstanding Costello's death. But when Costello resurrects briefly after the stranger's brutal eviction and issues a final laugh, thus winning the competition, the villagers merely repeat John's verdict – 'the book stands' (*Mommo Plays*, 187) – and are freed from their debts. A 'somewhat grotesque Christ',[32] Costello dies and comes to life to offer economic, rather than spiritual, redemption to the Bochtáns, effectively bringing about a new beginning. Yet the spirit of childhood embodied by the Christ-like laughing champion is crushed when Mahony bans laughter from Bochtán at the end of the play, returning the community to silent resignation: 'k-cause if I ever hear as much as a-a – (*giggle*) – in here ever again, I'll – I'll – I'll!' (*Mommo Plays*, 188). The association of laughter with childhood is made explicit at the end of *Bailegangaire*, after Mary and Mommo have completed the story together:

> **Mary**   They don't laugh there anymore.
> **Mommo**   Save the childre, until they arrive at the age of reason. Now! Bochtán for ever is Bailegangaire.
>
> (*Mommo Plays*, 120)

In Mommo's extremely sophisticated, highly *literate* (*pace* O'Toole) prose, the phonetically transcribed laughs rupture the order of language; they do not signify, they are the other of 'reason', this *infantia* (from in-fans, a child who cannot yet speak) which haunts discourse: 'A childhood which is not an age of life and which does not pass.'[33] Banning laughter is a way of quashing this haunting *infantia*, of containing the community's capacity to wonder and question, to take life seriously and make new beginnings.

While Mommo's story traces the bleak suppression of the spirit of childhood and the turning of Bochtán into Bailegangaire, its purpose in the present of the play is to delay, indeed to suppress, her realization of the death of a real child, her grandson Tom who was burnt in a paraffin fire on the night of the events of the laughing contest. Reperforming the laughing contest as a one-woman show every night, Mommo literally removes herself onto the alternative stage of Bochtán and escapes the fated space of the house where the tragedy took place some thirty years ago. By an ironic twist, however, the denial of Tom's death has resulted in the suppression of *infantia* from her world, turning her and Mary's lives into a succession of empty routines and precluding the possibility of new beginnings: 'I can't do anything the way things are,' Mary complains to Dolly (*Mommo Plays*, 91). When Mommo begins the story in Mary's presence, she ignores her but addresses instead imaginary children: 'Let ye be settling now, my fondlings, and I'll be giving ye a nice story again tonight when I finish this. An' ye'll be goin' to sleep' (*Mommo Plays*, 55). The gap between Mommo's real onstage audience – the adult Mary, whom she blanks out – and her imagined audience – presumably the 'three little children' who were waiting for her return home on the night of the events, including the ten-year-old Mary – makes poignantly palpable the *absence* of children, and turns Mommo's performance into a melancholic, ever-repeated invocation of past presence. Mommo herself supplements this absence by stepping into the role of the child, whimpering for her father's return, suspiciously reviewing the sweets Dolly has brought her ('Do I like them ones?'; *Mommo Plays*, 67), and letting Mary attend to all her bodily needs. Yet she is a grotesque, senile version of a child, vulnerable and dependent like a child but locked in a set of routines, emotionally and cognitively removed from the present situation and incapable of confronting 'the enigma of non-being'.

The movement of the play, however, reverses that of the narrative, and restores *infantia* in Mommo and her granddaughters' lives. By forcing Mommo to finish the story, Mary makes a bid in favour of life, and refuses to be locked into the order of necessity which the immutable, ever-repeated tale so forcefully performs. Collaborating in the performance, and finishing the tale in Mommo's style, but in her own words and from her point of view, she effectively participates in the creation of the family tradition, testifying to what was for the benefit of future generations. Reading Arendt's *The Crisis in Culture*, Lyotard points out the ambivalence of tradition. A rich tradition, he argues, can bring an excess of certainty to the children who are born into it, who then 'may lose even the sense of non-being, so confident are they that they are inscribed in a continuity which straddles deaths and births' (*Lectures d'enfance*, 76). Tradition then congeals into the mere survival of what is already there, 'a death imposed on the improbability of the incipient'. And yet, even in such a rich, authorized tradition, 'the enigma of something to which this tradition can bring no answer must continue to inhabit the mind in secret, the question "why me?", the enigma of the singularity of birth, which is unshareable, like that of death'. But such an enigma can only present itself through tradition, insofar as I can only learn of my birth and death from stories: 'My birth told by others, and my death told to me in the stories of the deaths of others, my own stories and the stories of others' (*Lectures d'enfance*, 65). Reviving a dead tradition, Mary embraces 'the improbability of the incipient' and produces a new ending which will tell Dolly's baby of the deaths of its kinfolks, and of its own birth.

Dolly's unplanned, unwanted baby is the literal embodiment of this 'new beginning', the objective correlative of Mary's creative contribution to the story. While Mommo's narrative (as indeed *A Thief of a Christmas*, as the title indicates) addresses Christmas derisively, culminating with the banning of laughter and the suppression of *infantia*, in the present of the play the Christmas motif is travestied but not invalidated. The scene in which Dolly puts her 'proposition' to Mary, offering her share of the house and other material goods if Mary will take on Dolly's illegitimate baby as her own is a parodic Annunciation, with Dolly cast as an improbable Gabriel, the bringer of 'glad tidings', announcing the arrival of a 'brand new' child (*Mommo Plays*, 101) whose father's identity is a matter of speculation ('I have my suspicions,' Dolly remarks [*Mommo Plays*, 103]). Nevertheless the new baby's imminent birth raises urgent issues and asks that imaginative measures be taken, rupturing the deadly chain of daily repetition; symbolically, it reinscribes the possibility of new beginnings and restores *infantia*. By the end of the play, once the story has been completed and past tragedies remembered, Mommo intones a familiar prayer: 'To thee do we cry – Yes? Poor banished children of Eve' (*Mommo Plays*, 122) The simple words create a new community of 'children', Mommo, Mary and Dolly, huddling in bed together and united in their renewed capacity to feel both grief and hopefulness. They have become 'survivors' in Lyotard's second, positive sense, laughing and grieving children, hostages to the unspeaking enigma of their births and deaths, preservers of a living tradition which they will pass on to the next generation because they choose to honour a debt to life.

Murphy's *Bailegangaire*, like most of his dramatic oeuvre, speaks to us beyond the boundaries of Ireland precisely because it reflects so lucidly and honestly on specific traditions, on the value and potential dangers of these traditions, and on the need to keep them alive, rather than enshrined in immutable forms. *Bailegangaire* balances out two modalities of survival, one a melancholic contemplation of past presence, the other a child-like commitment to attend to life, *as if* it really mattered – and takes a firm stance in favour of the latter.

CONCLUSION

Stage directions in Murphy have a distinctive character. His is not the discursive analysis of Ibsen or Shaw, the subtextual notation of Chekhov, nor yet the precise, laconic signs of Beckett or Pinter. He writes rather a freehand of the theatrical imagination that mediates between study and stage. Sometimes there is a suggestive sketch of a scene and atmosphere, as in the opening of *The Sanctuary Lamp*: 'A church. Late afternoon light filtering through a stained-glass window – the window depicting the Holy Family; great columns to dwarf the human form … ' But he goes on to note: 'Other features as required, as benefits director/designer's ideas' (*Plays*, 3, 101). There are poetically suggestive vignettes as with the last line of *Conversations on a Homecoming*: '**Anne** continues in the window as at the beginning of the play, smiling her gentle hope out at the night' (*Plays*, 2, 87). Often, though, we are given only glancing impressions of a character, as with the description of Mary at the beginning of *Bailegangaire*: 'A "private" person, an intelligent, sensitive woman, a trier, but one who is possibly near breaking point. It is lovely when she laughs' (*Plays*, 2, 91). The 'possibly' is typical of Murphy's tentativeness, his reluctance to claim complete certainty in relation to the details of his work.

In early worksheets, there are often fuller outlines of the characters – Dada in *A Whistle in the Dark*, JJ in *The White House*. One of the excitements for me in writing this book has been the exploration of the voluminous body of archival materials that lie below the published plays. With a playwright who believes in the 'adventure method' of playwriting, following his trail is itself an adventure. It has been fascinating to discover the range of prompts that produced the work, and in particular the eclecticism of the reading involved. Murphy may study William James for one play, Jacques Lacan for another, biographies of John F. Kennedy, the novels of William Carleton or an economic history of Irish brewing. He is a diligent researcher, taking detailed notes in his clear well-formed handwriting – a gift for someone researching his researches. But the reading is all completely assimilated into the imaginative texture of the plays, often detectable only in a single phrase or idea. The discarded offcuts of the drafts help us to understand the shape of the finished text, though with Murphy the shape is never finished. The chisel is taken out again for each revival. Murphy's plays are emphatically scripts to be realized in the rehearsal room and the theatre, and in recognition of that fact I have tried as much as possible through this book to illustrate their dramatic effect, drawing on my own experience of seeing them in production and on the traces of performance in theatre reviews, and video recordings where these exist.

Though relatively rarely directly autobiographical, much of Murphy's work is in the deepest sense personal. If his plays constitute 'an inner history of Ireland', as Fintan O'Toole claims,[1] it has been because that inner history has been felt as his own. He went out to the imaginative exploration of the nineteenth-century famine, that most unimaginable of subjects, as he understood it to be the trauma that created the Ireland of his own times in all its deformations: a cowed people dominated by a tyrannic church and a brutal, class-ridden system of education; gender dynamics distorted by patriarchy and sexual repression; the mean materialism generated by the hungry pursuit of property; and the aping of America by a nation without adequate national self-esteem. A playwright who disavows any political intention has nevertheless created a powerful vision of a small postcolonial country struggling to come to terms with modernity.

That disavowal of political intent, however, is not just disingenuous. Politics are never Murphy's primary concern. He starts always from situations of emotional and psychological extremity, dead-end states, feelings of anguish and frustration. In many cases these arise out of the conditions of Irish life, but such conditions in themselves do not constitute the essence of the drama. In working through the horror and anguish that afflict his characters, the theatre itself becomes its own psychic space. The dramatic action in Murphy moves from blocked and tortured self-imprisonment to some sort of clarification: clarification and resolution for the characters in plays such as *The Sanctuary Lamp* or *Bailegangaire*, or the tragic clarification that is for the audience alone in *Whistle in the Dark* and *The House*. This is what gives Murphy's plays their formal purpose and design, often underpinned by the matrix of myth. And it is the reason why mere representation – the life-like rendering of this or that social situation – is never enough for him. He needs the full range of theatrical materials available, sight and sound, music and song, storytelling and the rhythms of non-communicating language, to say what only the live theatre can say. This is not a writer who just happens to write plays; this is a playwright, a theatre maker, for whom the stage is the sole viable means of expression.

NOTES

Preface

1. See, for instance, 'Tom Murphy Talking', *Education Times*, 27 November 1975.

Chapter 1

1. All dates are of first production unless otherwise stated.
2. See Nicholas Grene, 'An Interview with Garry Hynes', *Irish University Review*, 45.1 (2015), pp. 117–25 [120].
3. Fintan O'Toole, *Tom Murphy: the Politics of Magic*, rev. edn (Dublin: New Island Books; London: Nick Hern Books, 1994 [1987]), p. 19.
4. Tom Murphy, *Plays: Three* (London: Methuen Drama, 1994), p. 98. This six-volume edition of Murphy's plays (Methuen Drama, 1992–2010) is the one used throughout this book, except where otherwise stated, and will be cited parenthetically in the text.
5. Brian Friel, 'Exiles', programme note for *The Blue Macushla*, Abbey Theatre, 1980.
6. One notebook from 1959 in the Trinity College Library collection of Murphy papers suggests that he did attempt to gather ideas for a collection of short stories, but significantly one of them 'The Iron Men', was the germ for *A Whistle in the Dark*, and the notebook already contains a sketch for how the story might be dramatized: MS 11115/4/4. Future references to manuscript material are all to the Trinity collection, unless otherwise stated. It is not possible to give a precise location for all quotations, but folio numbers are given for those manuscripts that have been foliated, and page numbers in cases where Murphy himself has numbered his manuscripts.
7. Personal interview, 11 November 2014. Tom Murphy generously granted me four extended interviews about his life and work over the period November 2014 to December 2015. An edited version of this material is used in the 'Critical Perspectives' chapter of the book, and I have given parenthetical references to quotations taken from this text.
8. Deirdre Purcell, 'Into the Dark', *Sunday Tribune*, 19 October 1986.
9. For all Murphy's dislike of his schooling with the Christian Brothers, the poetry he learned off by heart from Patrick J. Kennedy's prescribed anthology,

Intermediate Poetry (Dublin: Gill and Sons, [1942]), reappears in many of his plays, and his set Shakespeare play, *Henry IV, Part 1*, has a similar intertextual presence.

10. *The Fly Sham* was screened on BBC TV on 19 May 1963: see http://www.imdb.com/title/tt1385025/ (accessed 26 October 2015). None of Murphy's television plays has been published, but there are drafts of *The Fly Sham* in the Trinity Library collection: MS 11115/2/1/1-4.

11. *A Young Man in Trouble* was screened by Thames Television on 6 July 1970: see http://www.imdb.com/title/tt0890150/ (accessed 26 October 2015). There are drafts of the script at MS 11115/2/5/1-4. *On the Inside*, first staged in 1974, was published with *On the Outside* (Dublin: Gallery Press, 1976).

12. See Gerald Whelan with Carolyn Swift, *Spiked: Church-State Intrigue and* The Rose Tattoo (Dublin: New Island, 2002).

13. Anthony Roche, 'Thomas Murphy: An Irish Playwright Stretches Out', *Santa Barbara News and Reviews*, 23 April 1980.

14. Murphy, 'Preface', *On the Outside/On the Inside*, p. 9.

15. Ibid.

16. This is as Murphy remembered it, but a TS draft of *On the Outside* is given as 'a one-act play by Dionysus': see MS 11115/1/2/11.

17. O'Toole, *Tom Murphy*, 43. For the origin of the word 'sham', see Bernard Share, *Slanguage: A Dictionary of Irish Slang and Colloquial English in Ireland* (Dublin: Gill and Macmillan, 1997).

18. See particularly O'Toole, *Tom Murphy*, pp. 11–12.

19. MS 11115/2/2/1b. The play was transmitted on the BBC on 17 November 1963, directed by Herbert Wise.

20. *A Crucial Week in the Life of a Grocer's Assistant* was screened as the BBC Wednesday Play on 4 February 1967, directed by James MacTaggart, who Murphy thought 'was possibly the best director I ever worked with' (Interview, p. 178).

21. *Snakes and Reptiles* was transmitted in colour on BBC2 as 'Thirty Minute Theatre' on 14 February 1968, directed by David Andrews.

22. Gus Smith, 'Murphy: "I'll be back"', *Sunday Independent*, 3 March 1963.

23. John Boland, 'Back to Broad Strokes', *Hibernia*, 6 March 1980.

24. Raymond Deane, 'The Tyranny of the Idealised Self', *In Dublin*, 23 September 1983.

25. *A Crucial Week*, then called *The Fooleen*, was written in 1962, *Philadelphia* in 1963, but neither playwright would have been aware of the other's work at that point.

26. See Mária Kurdi, 'An Interview with Tom Murphy', *Irish Studies Review*, 12.2 (2004), pp. 223–40. Murphy has often used this phrase in relation to his own work; it appears to derive from the psychiatric theory of Karen Horney.

27. *The Orphans* was published both as a 'Drama Supplement' to the *Journal of Irish Literature*, III:3 (1974) and as a separate volume by Proscenium Press, Newark, Delaware in the same year. Murphy was very unhappy with the play and has never republished it or sanctioned a revival.

28. O'Toole, *Tom Murphy*, 54.

29. Desmond Rushe, 'Profound Approach in New Famine Play', *Irish Independent*, 27 March 1968.

30. Sean Page, 'A triumph at the Peacock', *Sunday Press*, 24 March 1968.

31. Henry Kelly, 'Applause for Play by Thomas Murphy', *Irish Times*, 22 March 1968.

32. Page, 'A triumph'.

33. Maureen O'Farrell, 'A Play of Truth and Laughter', *Evening Press*, 11 November 1969.

34. Gus Smith, 'Abbey Fantasy', *Sunday Independent*, 21 March 1971.

35. J[ohn] B[arber], 'Regression into jaded whimsy', *Daily Telegraph*, 16 March 1971.

36. Mel Gussow, '"Morning After" Set in Irish Whimsy', *New York Times*, 28 June 1974.

37. Maureen O'Farrell, 'Great Theatre! A great play?', *Evening Press*, 16 March 1971.

38. Pearse Hutchison, 'Murphy's best play to date', *Irish Press*, 16 March 1971; Noreen Dowling, 'A new play of immense power', *Cork Examiner*, 17 March 1971; David Nowlan, 'Impressive Revival at Abbey', *Irish Times*, 15 July 1971.

39. Page, 'A triumph'.

40. See O'Toole, *Tom Murphy*, 169.

41. See MS 11115/6/2/9.

42. See Shelley Troupe, 'From Druid/Murphy to *DruidMurphy*', in Nicholas Grene and Chris Morash (eds), *Oxford Handbook of Modern Irish Theatre* (Oxford: Oxford University Press, 2016), pp. 404–21.

43. See 'Playwrights in Profile: Tom Murphy', *Drama on One*, RTÉ Radio 1, transmitted 18 March 2007. http://www.rte.ie/drama/radio/player.html?clipId=3494807, quoted in ibid., p. 408.

44. The title 'Writer in Association' was chosen because Murphy refused to contemplate 'Writer in Residence', being unwilling to move to Galway.

45. Fintan O'Toole, 'Down among the gombeens', *Sunday Tribune*, 21 April 1985.

46. Fintan O'Toole, 'The Old Woman's Brood', *Sunday Tribune*, 8 December 1985.

47. Michael Sheridan, '"Homecoming" triumph for Galway's Druid', *Irish Press*, 18 April 1985.

48. Fintan O'Toole, 'The Playboy meets Gary Cooper', *Sunday Tribune*, 5 January 1986.

Notes

49. Seamus Phelan, 'Druid production of Murphy play acclaimed in Sydney', *Irish Times*, 9 January 1987.

50. Mel Gussow, 'Stage: "Homecoming": from Ireland', *New York Times*, 29 July 1986.

51. Irene Backalenich, '"Conversations" bespeaks sharp realism, richness with a "seedy, lived-in" set', *The Advocate*, 26 July 1986.

52. Mick Barnes, 'A festival night of pure Irish magic', *Sun Herald*, 11 January 1987.

53. Kevin O'Connor, on 'Morning Ireland', RTÉ, Radio 1, 7 October 1986.

54. David Nowlan, '"A Whistle in the Dark" at the Abbey', *Irish Times*, 7 October 1986.

55. John Finegan, 'Revived play a winner', *Evening Herald*, 2 September 1988.

56. Anthony Roche, *Contemporary Irish Drama*, 2nd edn (Basingstoke: Palgrave Macmillan, 2009), p. 97.

57. David Burke, *Druid: The First Ten Years* (Galway: Druid Performing Arts and Galway Arts Festival, 1985), p. 37.

58. Alannah Hopkin, 'The Dublin Theatre Festival', *Financial Times*, 9 October 1993.

59. Paul Taylor, '*Famine*', *The Independent*, 9 October 1993.

60. John Peter, *Sunday Times*, 10 October 1993, Michael Coveney, *Observer*, 10 October 1993.

61. Grene, 'An Interview with Garry Hynes', pp. 120–1.

62. Ibid., p. 120.

63. Charles Isherwood, 'Raw Wit of the Irish Soul, Fed by Hope and Fear', *New York Times*, 10 July 2012.

64. Joe Dziemianowicz, 'DruidMurphy puts three plays by Irish writer Tom Murphy at center stage', *Daily News*, 10 July 2012.

65. See, for example, Enda Walsh, 'In Conversation: Joe Dowling and Enda Walsh', https://www.youtube.com/watch?v=BCJdK-U1Q-4&list=RDBCJdK-U1Q-4#t=86 (accessed 1 December 2015).

66. For details, see Nicholas Grene, 'Tom Murphy: Playwright Adventurer', in W. E. Vaughan (ed.), *The Old Library Trinity College Dublin 1712-2012* (Dublin: Four Courts, 2013), pp. 380–3.

67. 'Tom Murphy in conversation with Michael Billington', in Nicholas Grene (ed.), *Talking about Tom Murphy* (Dublin: Carysfort Press, 2002), p. 95.

68. Colm Tóibín, 'Murphy's dark vision', *Sunday Independent*, 5 January 1986.

69. Michael Ross, 'An Interview with Tom Murphy', *St Stephens*, 4.1 (December 1986), p. 22.

70. J. M. Synge, 'Preface to *The Playboy of the Western World*', in Ann Saddlemyer (ed.), *Collected Works*, IV, *Plays*, Book II (London: Oxford University Press, 1968), p. 54.

71. Colm Tóibín, 'Interview with Tom Murphy', *BOMB*, 120 (Summer 2012), p. 45.

72. Ross, 'Interview', p. 23.

73. John Waters, 'Wounded Lion: Tom Murphy's Archaeology of Darkness', *Magill*, September 1988.

74. *Young Man in Trouble* or *What is this thing called Love?*, MS 11115/2/5/1, p. 1.

75. *Snakes and Reptiles*, MS 11115/2/4/1, p. 20.

76. Ibid., p. 41.

77. For the film script drafts, see MS 11115/2/25.

78. O'Toole, *Tom Murphy*, p. 230.

79. Tom Murphy, *The Mommo Plays: Brigit, Bailegangaire, A Thief of a Christmas* (London: Bloomsbury, 2014).

80. To take just a few examples, there was the Red Rex production of *The Blue Macushla* in 1983, which did much to redeem the reputation of the play after its unsuccessful premiere at the Abbey, *Alice Trilogy* given its first staging by the Royal Court in 2005, with Juliet Stevenson in the lead, and the fine touring production of *The Sanctuary Lamp* by b*spoke, directed by Murphy himself, in 2009.

Chapter 2

1. Ciaran Carty, 'Getting out of his own sex', *Sunday Independent*, 14 April 1985.

2. Murphy quoted in Gloria Cole, 'Irish Playwright Tells his Own Story', *Fairpress*, 17 March 1976.

3. Fintan O'Toole, *Tom Murphy: The Politics of Magic*, rev. edn (Dublin: New Island Books; London: Nick Hern Books, 1994), pp. 37–8.

4. Aidan Arrowsmith, 'Gender, Violence and Identity in *A Whistle in the Dark*', in Christopher Murray (ed.), *'Alive in Time': The Enduring Drama of Tom Murphy* (Dublin: Carysfort, 2010), pp. 221–38 [226].

5. Claire Gleitman, 'Clever Blokes and Thick Lads: The Collapsing Tribe of Tom Murphy's *A Whistle in the Dark*', *Modern Drama*, 42.3 (1999), pp. 315–25 [318].

6. Lionel Pilkington, 'Response', in Nicholas Grene (ed.), *Talking about Tom Murphy* (Dublin: Carysfort, 2002), pp. 31–9 [39].

7. Murphy has always been scrupulous in acknowledging Noel O'Donoghue's co-authorship of the play. However, in the Trinity College Library collection all of the surviving manuscripts are in Murphy's hand, so it seems likely that, even if the work was jointly planned, the writing was Murphy's own. In what follows, I have treated it as primarily his work.

8. Tom Murphy, 'Preface', *On the Outside/On the Inside* (Dublin: Gallery Press, 1976), p. 9.

9. Anthony Roche, *Contemporary Irish Drama*, 2nd edn (London: Palgrave, 2009), p. 86.

10. http://www.irishstatutebook.ie/eli/1935/act/2/enacted/en/html (accessed 4 April 2016).

11. MS 11115/2/5. While this television play was not staged until 1969, as early as 1962 Murphy had apparently written a version of 'Young Man in Trouble' as a radio play to be broadcast by the BBC Third Programme: see G. S., '"Whistle in Dark" is Bound for Great White Way', *Sunday Independent*, 11 March 1962.

12. *On the Outside* was given its first professional production at the Project Arts Centre in September 1974, with Murphy making his directorial debut. It then went on to be staged together with the newly written *On the Inside* in the Peacock, before transferring to the Abbey main stage, in November 1974: see Murphy, *On the Outside/On the Inside*, pp. 9–11.

13. Murphy was reflecting his own experience here: 'We danced in ballrooms and, depending on the answer to "What do you do?" we fell in love' (*Plays*, 1, xii).

14. MS 11115/1/8/2.

15. In the worksheets for *Crucial Week*, there is evidence of an early draft divided into acts and scenes (MS 1115/1/5/2) and a full manuscript of the text in eleven scenes (MS 1115/1/5/3b), originally called *Happy the Man* – an ironic quotation from lines in Pope's 'Ode on Solitude' used as the play's epigraph – then entitled *The Fooleen*. There are several professionally typed versions of this text showing some signs of revision (MS 1115/1/5/4-7) before a completely new recast manuscript draft close to the play's final form (MS 1115/1/5/8).

16. Already before the opening of *Whistle* in September 1961, Murphy claimed to be 'half-way through' his next play, unidentified news cutting, MS 11115/6/2/3; the reverse of the final page of the MS 1115/1/5/3b draft is dated '12-2-1962 Tuam'. At one point in the draft Murphy used Hippisley, the name of his future wife Mary whom he had met in London in 1961, as the surname of one of John Joe's rivals, and initially John Joe was twenty-seven, Mona nineteen, the actual ages of Murphy and Mary Hippisley at this time.

17. MS 1115/1/5/3a.

18. MS 1115/1/5/3b.

19. *The Fooleen* survived as the play's title up to its first publication by Proscenium Press, in Dixon, California in 1968, and appears still as a bracketed subtitle in the 1978 Dublin Gallery Press edition of *A Crucial Week in the Life of a Grocer's Assistant*.

20. He is still only 29 in the 1968 and 1978 published texts but is 33 in *A Whistle in the Dark and Other Plays* (London: Methuen Drama, 1989), the text reissued as *Plays*, 4 in 1997.

21. MS 1115/1/5/3a.

22. Maureen O'Farrell, 'A Play of Truth and Laughter', *Evening Press*, 11 November 1969, John Finegan, 'Revived play a winner', *Evening Herald*, 2 September 1988.

23. See Tom Murphy, 'In Conversation with Michael Billington', in Grene, *Talking about Tom Murphy*, p. 98.

24. See Bernard F. Dukore, '"Violent Families": *A Whistle in the Dark* and *The Homecoming*', *Twentieth Century Literature*, 36.1 (1990), pp. 23–34. In a letter to Dukore, Pinter said that he was out of London when *Whistle* was staged and he had never read the play.

25. See Michael Billington, *The Life and Work of Harold Pinter* (London: Faber, 1966), p. 163.

26. Deirdre Purcell, 'Into the Dark', *Sunday Tribune*, 19 October 1986.

27. This opening scene, added to the play at the request of the director of the original London production, was cut by Murphy for the 2012 DruidMurphy production, beginning the play instead with the expository scene between Michael and Betty that follows: see Tom Murphy, *DruidMurphy: Conversations on a Homecoming, A Whistle in the Dark, Famine* (London: Methuen Drama, 2012), pp. 93–6.

28. Murphy, 'In Conversation', in Grene, *Talking About Tom Murphy*, p. 97.

29. As noted in the previous chapter, Murphy would have known *1 Henry IV* well as a prescribed text for the Intermediate Certificate examination and uses a recitation of Hal's monologue, 'I know you all and will a while uphold' (1.2.155ff) at the climax of *Conversations on a Homecoming*.

30. MS 11115/1/1/2.

31. Bernard O'Reilly, *True Men As We Need Them: A Book of Instruction for Men in the World* (New York: 1888).

32. W. A. Darlington, 'Play Ends as Scrimmage', *Daily Telegraph* [September 1961]. In this case and in other references taken from news cuttings in MS 1115/6/2/3, the date is not shown, but it is a review of the production at Theatre Royal, Stratford East, which opened on 11 September 1961.

33. Arrowsmith, 'Gender, Violence and Identity', in Murray, *Alive in Time*, p. 233.

34. Milton Shulman, 'Not exactly a great night for the Irish', *Evening Standard* [September 1961].

35. Felix Barker, 'It's the noisiest show in town' [*Evening News*, September 1961].

36. Kenneth Tynan, 'Wolves at the Door', *Observer*, 17 September 1961.

37. Alan Brien, 'The Adman Cometh', *Sunday Telegraph* [October 1961].

38. *Irish Times*, 12 March 1962.

39. J. J. F[inegan], *Evening Herald*, 13 March 1962.

40. M. O'S., 'Violence is my Villain', *Evening Press*, 10 March 1962.

41. John Lahr, 'On-stage', *Village Voice*, 13 November 1969.

Chapter 3

1. 'Full of sound and brewery, signifying nothing' was Seamus Kelly's dismissive comment, imitating the terrible punning of the play itself: 'New Tom Murphy Play at Pavilion', *Irish Times*, 10 November 1976.

2. MS 11115/1/11/6.

3. https://www.ucc.ie/celt/pearsefic.html (accessed 21 April 2016).

4. MS 11115/1/11/4. Thirty-three pages of these notes are taken from Patrick Lynch and John Vaizey, *Guinness's Brewery in the Irish Economy, 1759-1876* (Cambridge: Cambridge University Press, 1960), with a supplementary seven pages on the history of Guinness's English rivals Bass.

5. MS 11115/1/11/1.

6. Originally published in four volumes from 1929 to 1931, this became the standard textbook of Irish history through to the 1960s.

7. See R. F. Foster, *The Irish Story: Telling Tales and Making it Up in Ireland* (London: Allen Lane, 2001).

8. See http://www.decadeofcentenaries.com/ (accessed 16 May 2016).

9. Colin Murphy, *Inside the GPO* (Fishamble), *Sunder* (ANU), Emma Donoghue and others, *Signatories* (Verdant/UCD).

10. Jim Nolan, *Johnny I hardly Knew Ye* (Garter Lane, Waterford), *Maloney's Dream* (Branar).

11. I am most grateful to Philip Crawford for this information through a phone call on 31 May 2016.

12. MS 11115/2/10/1, p. 1.

13. W. B. Yeats, *Poems*, ed. Daniel Albright, rev. edn (London: Everyman, 1994), p. 228.

14. MS 11115/2/10/1, p. 21.

15. See Roisín Higgins, *Transforming 1916* (Cork: Cork University Press, 2012).

16. See Declan Kiberd, 'The Elephant of Revolutionary Forgetfulness', in Máirin Ni Donnchadha and Theo Dorgan (eds), *Revising the Rising* (Derry: Field Day, 1991), pp. 1–20.

17. MS 11115/1/20/1, p. 1.

18. The description here is based on the video recording held as part of the digitized Abbey archives in the Hardiman Library, NUI, Galway. I am very grateful to Barry Houlihan in helping me access this material.

19. Alexandra Poulain, 'Playing out the Rising: Sean O'Casey's *The Plough and the Stars* and Tom Murphy's *The Patriot Game*', *Études Anglaises*, 59.2 (2006), pp. 156–69.

20. Helen Lucy Burke, 'Murphy a clear winner in the 1916 Memorial Stakes', *Sunday Tribune*, 19 May 1991.

21. Patsy McGarry, 'Lively, theatrical and declamatory visions of 1916', *Irish Press*, 16 May 1991.

22. Treasa Brogan, 'Entranced and impressed by The Patriot Game', *Evening Press*, 16 May 1991.

23. Joyce McMillan, '*Pax/The Patriot Game*', *Guardian*, 24 September 1991.

24. Chris Morash, 'Sinking Down into the Dark: the Famine on Stage', *Bullán*, 3.1 (1997), pp. 75–86.

25. Margaret Kelleher, 'Irish Famine in Literature', in Cathal Póirtéir (ed.), *The Great Irish Famine* (Cork and Dublin: Mercier Press in association with Radio Telefís Éireann, 1995), pp. 232–47 [232].

26. The draft is headed 'Famine' and dated 22/6/65, MS 11115/1/3/1, ff. 85v-90v.

27. MS 11115/1/3/1.

28. MS 11115/1/3/1 ff. 1–13.

29. MS 11115/1/3/1 f. 114v..

30. MS 11115/1/3/1 f. 80r. In context, this is the vengeful statement of Sarah McGowan, daughter of the Black Prophet, thwarted in her love for Condy Dalton by the heroine Mave Sullivan. The actual lines read: 'This world, father, has nothing good or happy in it for me – now Ill be aiquil to it; if it gives me nothing good, it'll get nothing good out of me.' William Carleton, *The Black Prophet* (New York and London: Garland, 1979, [1847]), p. 234.

31. MS 11115/1/3/2.

32. These collections are now incorporated into the Department of Folklore of University College Dublin.

33. MS 11115/1/3/1, f. 75r. A variant of this appears in the archive of the Department of Folklore as 'Translation of an Irish caoine, sung by an old woman of Googan Barra, the source of the river Lee and taken by Thomas C Croker 1814'. It begins: 'Cold and silent is thy repose. Damp falls the dew of Heaven yet the sun shall bring joy and the mists of night shall pass away before his beams. But thy breast shall not vibrate with the pulse of light' (IFC1127:128–9). I am most grateful to Anna Bale of the Department of Folklore for supplying this information.

34. Cormac Ó Gráda, *Black '47 and Beyond: the Great Irish Famine in History, Economy and Memory* (Princeton: Princeton University Press, 1999), p. 46.

35. Vivian Mercier, 'Noisy Desperation: Murphy and the Book of Job', *Irish University Review*, 17.1 (1987), pp. 18–23.

36. Fintan O'Toole, 'Second Opinion: Down to Zero', *Irish Times*, 9 October 1993.

37. It also represents a more complex awareness of the context of the Famine than Woodham-Smith's *The Great Hunger*, often criticized for its personalized and judgemental narrative.

38. This, like all other information about *Famine* in this chapter, for which no other source is given, is taken from a personal interview with Tom Murphy, 23 August 2004.

39. Gerard Healy, *The Black Stranger* (Dublin: James Duffy, 1950), p. 24.

40. Ibid., p. 39.

41. Ibid., p. 52.

42. MS 11115/1/3/1, f. 106v.

43. Brian Friel, *Selected Plays* (London: Faber, 1984), p. 395.

44. Fintan O'Toole, *Tom Murphy: The Politics of Magic*, rev. edn (Dublin: New Island Books; London Nick Hern Books, 1994), p. 115.

Chapter 4

1. James Joyce, *Dubliners*, ed. Terence Brown (Harmondsworth: Penguin, 1992), p. 190.

2. Ryan Tubridy, *JFK in Ireland: Four Days that Changed a President* (London: Collins, 2010).

3. See http://cain.ulst.ac.uk/sutton/ (accessed 11 June 2016).

4. See, for instance, his interview with Michael Billington in Nicholas Grene (ed.), *Taking about Tom Murphy* (Dublin: Carysfort Press, 2001), pp. 101–3.

5. I am very grateful to Clement Grene for picking out these specific echoes in the play.

6. MS 11115/1/13/2.

7. MS 11115/1/13/1.

8. See Brian Hanley and Scott Millar, *The Lost Revolution: the Story of the Official IRA and the Workers' Party* (Harmondsworth: Penguin, 2009), pp. 154–5, and Liz Walsh, *The Last Beat: Gardaí Killed in the Line of Duty* (Dublin: Gill and Macmillan, 2001), pp. 1–22.

9. Originally called the Irish Republican Socialist Party, they came to use the name INLA from 1976: see Jack Holland and Henry McDonald, *INLA: Deadly Divisions* (Dublin: Torc, 1994).

10. MS 11115/1/13/1.

11. MS 11115/1/13/4.

12. MS 11115/1/13/8.

13. Michael Sheridan, 'Murphy play lost in mid-Atlantic', *Irish Press*, 7 March 1980.

14. For an evocation of the set and costumes, see John Finegan, 'Abbey joke is too long', *Evening Herald*, 7 March 1980.

15. Colm Cronin, 'B Movie Cutouts', *Hibernia*, 13 March 1980.

16. Kathy McArdle, '*The Blue Macushla*: Anatomy of a Failure', *Irish University Review*, 17.1 (1987), pp. 82–9 [88].

17. Alexandra Poulain, 'The Politics of Performance in *The Hostage* and *The Blue Macushla*', in Christopher Murray (ed.), '*Alive in Time*': *The Enduring Drama of Tom Murphy* (Dublin: Carysfort Press, 2010), pp. 123–36 [132].

18. Elgy Gillespie, interview with Tom Murphy, *Irish Times*, 8 March 1980.

19. McArdle, '*The Blue Macushla*', 83.

20. See David Nowlan, 'Theatre Festival First Nights: The Blue Macushla at the Mansion House', *Irish Times*, 28 September 1983.

21. MS 11115/1/7/17. In this plan for *The White House*, the successive parts were to be '*Conversations* (1971) *Attitudes* (1967)? *Images* (1963)'.

22. MS 11115/1/7/2.

23. Fintan O'Toole, *Tom Murphy: the Politics of Magic*, rev. edn (Dublin: New Island Books; London: Nick Hern Books, 1994), p. 143.

24. MS 11115/1/7/16.

25. MS 11115/1/7/3, p. 2.

26. MS 11115/1/7/2, p. 3.

27. MS 11115/1/7/17. This is a hardbound notebook labelled JFK on the outside, and it also contains notes taken from R.L. Bruckberger, *Images of America* and William Manchester, *The Death of a President*.

28. MS 11115/1/7/2, pp. 4, 13. For the original text of the inaugural. see http://www.jfklibrary.org/Asset-Viewer/BqXIEM9F4024ntFl7SVAjA.aspx (accessed 19 June 2016).

29. MS 11115/1/7/2, p. 22. The quotation is taken from a speech Kennedy delivered at the National Cultural Center in November 1962: http://www.presidency.ucsb.edu/ws/?pid=9033 (accessed 19 June 2016).

30. MS 11115/1/7/3, p. 36.

31. MS 11115/1/7/2, p. 3.

32. MS 11115/1/7/2, p. 33.

33. John Barber, 'Comic portrait of vegetating lives', *Daily Telegraph*, 21 March 1972.

34. Leslie Caplan, '"The White House" at Dublin Theatre Festival', *The Stage*, 30 March 1972.

35. Garry O'Connor, 'The White House', *Financial Times*, 23 March 1972.

36. There are texts of this television version from 1975, MS 11115/2/7.

37. MS 11115/1/7/6.

38. Junior here misquotes the refrain, 'Flash, bam, alakazam', from the song 'Orange Coloured Sky'.

39. Television interview with Declan Kiberd, 11 November 1985, http://www.rte.ie/archives/2015/1110/740797-tom-murphy-and-druid/ (accessed 22 June 2016).

40. The line is adapted from Kennedy's tribute to Robert Frost in his remarks at Amherst College, October 1963, http://www.jfklibrary.org/Asset-Viewer/80308LXB5kOPFEJqkw5hlA.aspx (accessed 23 June 2016). The precise wording is 'When power leads man towards arrogance, poetry reminds him of his limitations'.

41. In the 2012 DruidMurphy production, Liam always sat at a separate table from the rest of the group.

42. MS 11115/1/7/1.

43. It is not immediately clear from *Conversations* that Anne is JJ's daughter by his first marriage, not the daughter of Missus, another reason for Michael's fixation with her.

44. MS 11115/1/7/28, f. 38v.

45. In drafts dated April 1984 for the Druid theatre production, Peggy sings 'Che faro senza Eurydice' in Italian (MS 11115/1/7/30-32). Perhaps Murphy realized that it might be a bit too demanding for the actor playing Peggy to be able to sing this hugely demanding mezzo–soprano aria from Gluck's *Orfeo ed Eurydice*.

46. David Nowlan, 'Small-town Ireland is theme of Abbey play', *Irish Times*, 21 March 1972.

Chapter 5

1. Mikhail Saltykov-Shchedrin, *The Golovlyov Family*, trans. Ronald Wilks (London: Penguin, 1988), p. 277.

2. Ibid., p. 280.

3. The properties named all have their counterparts in Murphy's home town of Tuam. The Imperial Hotel, the centre of the O'Tooles' intrigues, is now the Corralea Court, but was the Imperial for most of its history, standing as in the novel and play on the Square in the centre of the town. And there was an Odeon Cinema and a real Woolstore owned by the Browne family. While the ballroom was the Phoenix rather than the Shamrock, Murphy may have borrowed the name from the nineteenth-century Shamrock Bar: Riana O'Dwyer, personal email 13 July 2016. I am extremely grateful to Dr O'Dwyer for sharing her local knowledge of Tuam and Murphy's plays with me and giving me a very helpful tour of the town.

4. Tom Murphy, *The Seduction of Morality* (London: Little, Brown, 1994), p. 8.

5. Ibid., p. 37.

6. Ibid., p. 36.

7. There are drafts from October 1994: MS 11115/1/23/1.

8. MS 11115/1/23/10, a notebook in use in May 1995.

9. MS 11115/1/23/8.

10. MS 11115/1/23/18. Murphy erased some of this so it read merely, 'perhaps she has "betrayed" herself'.

11. I owe this insight into the emotional dynamics of fosterage within the family to Ella Daly, director of the Dublin Youth Theatre.

12. In *Seduction* the grandmother, Vera had been told, was born 'about a dozen years before the century' (Murphy, *Seduction*, p. 35). This is revised in *The Wake* to read 'about a half a dozen years after the century' (*Plays*, 5, 81).

13. Patsy McGarry, '100 died at Letterfrack school', *Irish Times*, 2 November 2002, http://www.irishtimes.com/news/100-died-at-letterfrack-school-say-brothers-1.1104242 (accessed 15 July 2016).

14. See http://www.childabusecommission.ie/rpt/pdfs/CICA-VOL1-08.PDF (accessed 15 July 2016).

15. Murphy, *Seduction*, pp. 206–14.

16. Murphy worked on the text extensively in 1994–5, before changing the title on a draft dating from January to March 1996: MS 11115/1/23/20.

17. MS 11115/1/23/5.

18. MS 11115/1/23/14, p. 77.

19. The poem was included in Patrick J. Kennedy's *Intermediate Poetry* (Dublin: Gill and Sons, [1942]), the prescribed text which Murphy, like all other students of his generation, would have had to study for the compulsory English examination at Intermediate Certificate. Memorization was a standard feature of teaching at the time, and Henry in the play (*Plays*, 5, 172) can even remember Kennedy's gloss on Mangan's use of the word 'Khan': 'a Turkish word meaning prince or chief. Mangan substitutes the spelling for the Irish Ceann', Kennedy, *Intermediate Poetry*, p. 217.

20. MS 11115/1/23/5, p. 1.

21. MS 11115/1/23/8.

22. Quoted by Ulf Dantanus, *Brian Friel: A Study* (London: Faber, 1988), p. 87.

23. MS 11115/2/25/1, p. 1.

24. Many of these features persisted into late drafts of the play written in 1998: see, for example, MS 11115/1/24/5, a draft from July 1998.

25. Several reviewers identified the town as Newcastle because of the reference at the auction to 'Woodlawn House in the townland of Newcastle' (*Plays*, 5, 260), but the local references all point to a Tuam location. See below for further details.

26. 'Irishmen of criminal tendencies invariably went to England and improved their criminal skills there, encouraged in this by the Irish police', quoted from *Irish Times*, 25 February 1963 in Tony Farmar, *Ordinary Lives: Three Generations of Irish Middle Class Experience 1907, 1932, 1963* (Dublin: Gill and Macmillan, 1991), p. 190.

27. John McGahern, 'The Fifties', programme note for Abbey production of *The House*, 2000, Abbey digital archive, Hardiman Library, NUI, Galway.

28. MS 11115/1/24/1.

29. Besides seeing the original production, I have had access to the archival recording held in the Abbey digital archive, Hardiman Library, NUIG on 18 July 2016.

30. In notes for the play, Murphy copied out Frank O'Connor's translation of a prayer attributed to St Manchán of Offaly: 'Grant me, sweet Christ, the grace to find / – Son of the living God – / A small hut in a lonesome spot / To make it my abode,' MS 11115/1/24/6a. The source in all probability was O'Connor's anthology of translations from the Irish, *Kings, Lords and Commons* (London: Macmillan, 1961).

31. MS 11115/1/24/3,7.

32. Personal email to the author, 13 July 2016. O'Dwyer goes on to explain the topography which Murphy evidently had in mind when imagining Susanne's murder: '[The house] was close to a bridge over the River Clare on the Ballygaddy Road, which was a popular bathing spot in the forties and fifties. By means of the Gardenfield avenue, you could access the river banks for courting and general wandering.' This is evidently also the Woodlawn to which Michael invites Anne for a walk in *Conversations*.

33. MS 11115/2/25/1, p. 2.

34. Michael Coveney, 'Chekhov's Irish Charm', *Daily Mail*, 21 April 2000.

35. See Ian Kilroy, 'Epistle in the Dark', *Magill*, May 2000.

36. Tom Murphy, *The Cherry Orchard* (London: Methuen Drama, 2004), pp. 5–6.

37. Where in many of the drafts of the film and the play, Christy is shown having to rob to get the cash, in the final text we are left to assume that he has simply enough savings to be able to afford it.

38. Murphy, *Cherry Orchard*, p. 60.

39. Jacques Lacan, Jacques-Alain Miller and James Hulbert, 'Desire and the Interpretation of Desire in Hamlet', *Yale French Studies*, No. 55/56, Literature and Psychoanalysis. The Question of Reading: Otherwise (1977), pp. 11–52 [15]. Murphy's notes are to be found in MS 11115/2/25/12.

40. Ibid., p. 36.

41. Elizabeth Wright, 'Modern psychoanalytic criticism', in Ann Jefferson, David Robey and David Forgacs (eds), *Modern Literary Theory: A Comparative Introduction* (London: Batsford, 1982), p. 121. (Murphy appears to have used a different edition of this work to judge by the page numbers he cites in his notebook: MS 11115/2/25/12.)

42. MS 11115/2/25/1, p. 18, MS 11115/1/24/6b.

43. MS 11115/1/24/7, p. 65.

44. Sophie Gorman, 'Ovation as old ground given new depth', *Irish Independent*, 13 April 2000.

45. Emer O'Kelly, 'A house of destruction and decay', *Sunday Independent*, 16 April 2000.

46. Fintan O'Toole, 'The house that Tom built', *Irish Times*, 12 April 2000.

47. Mic Moroney, 'Beneath the surface', *Guardian*, 18 April 2000.

Chapter 6

1. Fintan O'Toole, *Tom Murphy: the Politics of Magic*, rev. edn (Dublin: New Island; London: Nick Hern Books, 1994), pp. 94–111.

2. Alexandra Poulain, *Homo famelicus: le théâtre de Tom Murphy* (Caen: Presses Universitaires de Caen, 2008), pp. 69–127.

3. Tom Murphy, *The Mommo Plays* (London: Bloomsbury Methuen Drama, 2014), p. [54]. I have used this most recent edition for citations from *Brigit*, *Bailegangaire* and *A Thief of a Christmas* rather than the earlier *Plays* 2 edition.

4. The fact that Murphy specifies that the time of *Thief* is 'about 50 years ago' in the *Plays* 2 edition from 1993 and 'about 30 years ago' in the 2014 *Mommo Plays* only underlines the undecidable time period of this archaic action.

5. See Rosemary Pountney, *Theatre of Shadows: Samuel Beckett's Drama 1956–76* (Gerrards Cross: Colin Smythe; Totowa, NJ: Barnes and Noble, 1988), p. 149. The term 'vaguen' appears as a MS injunction by Beckett to himself on a draft of *Happy Days*. The process was first analysed in detail by S. E. Gontarski, *The Intent of Undoing in Samuel Beckett's Dramatic Texts* (Bloomington: Indiana University Press, 1985).

6. See MS 11115/1/10/2.

7. MS 11115/1/6/9. These early ideas for the play appear among notes dated 3 October 1963.

8. A version of the story was published just before the play opened at the Abbey with a prefatory note in which it is said that the play 'is based on this fairy-tale': Thomas Murphy, 'the morning after optimism', *Irish Press*, 13 March 1971.

9. Murphy declared that *Optimism* is about 'the tyranny of the idealised self. If one carries that "tyranny" through life, everything one does is a betrayal of what one thought the self to be', Mária Kurdi, 'An Interview with Tom Murphy', *Irish Studies Review*, 12.2 (2004), pp. 223–40 [238].

10. There are professionally prepared texts of this version of the play which appear to date from the period 1962–3 (MSS 11115/1/6/11-12).

11. See Gus Smith, 'Murphy: "I'll be back"', *Sunday Independent*, 3 March 1963.

12. Letter from Cyril Cusack to Tom Murphy, 9 August 1964, MS 11115/6/1/9.

13. The play was first published by Mercier Press in Cork in 1973, a text re-issued with – for Murphy – relatively few changes in *Plays*, 3.

Notes

14. This revision is in a notebook dated '26/7/66', MS 11115/1/6/8.

15. The cover image of the 1973 edition of the play strikingly renders the incongruity of the statuesque Eithne Dunne as Anastasia, her urn borne aloft, towering over the grotesque figure of James (Colin Blakely) beside her.

16. MS 11115/1/6/10.

17. Desmond Rushe, 'Delicious if grim comedy', *Irish Independent*, 15 March 1971.

18. According to Murphy, 'it's old Tuam slang … a colourful way of saying "knickers" – or nonsense!'. Email from Jane Brennan to author, 10 August 2016. The word is also used in *The Wake*.

19. The verses are adapted from Pat O'Reilly's 'A Wonderful Mother', http://archiver.rootsweb.ancestry.com/th/read/IrelandGenWeb/2006-01/1136880523 (accessed 18 August 2016).

20. Alexandra Poulain, 'Fable and vision: *The Morning After Optimism* and *The Sanctuary Lamp*', in Nicholas Grene (ed.), *Talking About Tom Murphy* (Dublin: Carysfort Press, 2002), pp. 41–6 [45].

21. David Nowlan, '"Morning After Optimism" at the Abbey', *Irish Times*, 16 March 1971. There are images of the set in MS 11115/1/6/10, which give a sense of this visual effect.

22. Quoted from Quidnunc, 'An Irishman's Diary', *Irish Times*, 12 March 1971, in Christopher Griffin, '"The Audacity of Despair": *The Morning After Optimism*', *Irish University Review*, 17.1 (1987), pp. 62–70 [63].

23. Marianne McDonald, 'Thomas Murphy's Interview', in *Ancient Sun, Modern Light* (New York: Columbia University Press, 1992), pp. 187–200 [185].

24. MS 11115/1/10/2, f. 5r.

25. Michael Taub, *Jack Doyle: The Gorgeous Gael* (Dublin: Lilliput, 2007 [1990]).

26. O'Toole, *Tom Murphy*, 186.

27. See http://www.museumsofmayo.com/peyton1.htm (accessed 1 September 2016).

28. Kurdi, 'An Interview with Tom Murphy', 236.

29. See my 'Tom Murphy and the Children of Loss', in Shaun Richards (ed.), *Cambridge Companion to Twentieth-Century Irish Drama* (Cambridge: Cambridge University Press, 2004), pp. 204–17 [210-11].

30. MS 11115/1/10/2, f. 6r. This sequence of notes seems to have been drafted retrospectively charting the development of the work, in response to a question as to how he went about writing a play.

31. MS 11115/1/10/2, f. 10r.

32. Ibid., f. 1r.

33. Ibid., f. 10r.

34. Ibid., f. 11r.

35. The play was first published as Thomas Murphy, *The Sanctuary Lamp* (Dublin: Poolbeg, 1976). A 'revision' was issued by Gallery Books in 1984, and this provided the basis for the *Plays*, 3 edition, used as the standard text in this chapter.

36. *Sanctuary Lamp* (1976), p. 7.

37. Ibid., p. 13.

38. Matt J. Doolan, 'An insult to the Mass', *Irish Independent*, 15 October 1975.

39. Desmond Rushe, 'Flashes of talent in a bleak wasteland', *Irish Independent*, 8 October 1975.

40. Michael Sheridan, 'Red light area in Sanctuary', *Irish Press*, 8 October 1975.

41. Gus Smith, 'Tom Murphy rocks "cradle of genius"', *Sunday Independent*, 12 October 1975.

42. David Nowlan, 'Tom Murphy's "The Sanctuary Lamp" at the Abbey', *Irish Times*, 8 October 1975.

43. 'Tuam group takes top awards', *Irish Independent*, 14 March 1977.

44. McDonald, 'Thomas Murphy's Interview', p. 199.

45. Harry White is unusual in preferring the original text to the 1984 revision: '*The Sanctuary Lamp*: An Assessment', *Irish University Review*, 17.1 (1987), pp. 71–81.

46. A still from that production shows the Monsignor sitting at the side altar, four rows of pews and a statue of Jesus: Ian R. Walsh, 'Directors and designers since 1960', in Nicholas Grene and Chris Morash (eds), *Oxford Handbook of Modern Irish Theatre* (Oxford: Oxford University Press, 2016), pp. 443–58 [450].

47. Bernard Share, *Slanguage* (Dublin: Gill and Macmillan, 1997).

48. It is likely that Murphy was here also drawing on memories of Jack Doyle. Apart from his marriage to Movita, the film star who subsequently married Marlon Brando, he was rumoured to have had many other high-profile Hollywood affairs: see Taub, *Jack Doyle*, pp. 350–2.

49. There is a dramatic image on the front cover of the play's first edition with Geoffrey Golden as Harry with the pulpit containing Francisco (John Kavanagh) hoisted above his head.

50. Smith, 'Tom Murphy rocks "cradle of genius"'.

51. Tom Murphy, 'Lullaby', in Gerald Dawe and Jonathan Williams (eds), *Krino: the Review. An Anthology of Modern Irish Writing* (Dubin: Lilliput, 1996), p. 75.

52. MS 11115/1/10/2, f. 5r.

53. '"Back to Broad Strokes" – John Boland talks to playwright Tom Murphy', *Hibernia*, 6 March 1980.

54. John Waters, 'Wounded Lion: Tom Murphy's Archaeology of Darkness', *Magill*, September 1988.

Chapter 7

1. Tom Murphy in conversation with Michael Billington, in Nicholas Grene (ed.), *Talking about Tom Murphy* (Dublin: Carysfort Press, 2002), p. 105.
2. Brian Friel, *Performances* (Oldcastle: Gallery Press, 2003), p. 31.
3. Brian Friel, *Dancing at Lughnasa* (London: Faber, 1990), p. 71.
4. MS 11115/1/19/1. Here, as often, Murphy used an old blank Dataday diary for an earlier year, in this case 1978, correcting the 1978 dates to 1987.
5. Ibid.
6. Ibid.
7. Ibid. There is an outline for this version dated 22 January 1988.
8. It is in a draft dated 1 February 1989 that the flashback is introduced, MS 11115/1/19/6, and music only becomes a prominent feature in the later draft in MS 11115/1/19/13, dated April to May 1989, just months before the play's premiere in October of that year.
9. Gerry Moriarty, 'Tom's last word on our dark forces', *Irish Press*, 7 October 1989.
10. Brian Brennan, 'Late Great Logic', *Sunday Independent*, 8 October 1989.
11. Michael Billington, long-term admirer of Murphy, picked this out as a 'particularly odd scene' reviewing a 2001 revival of the play at the Edinburgh Festival. 'Too Late for Logic', *Guardian*, 16 August 2001.
12. MS 11115/1/16/1.
13. Colm Tóibín, 'Murphy's Logic', *Sunday Independent*, 8 October 1989.
14. José Lanters, 'Schopenhauer with Hindsight: Tom Murphy's *Too Late for Logic*', *Hungarian Journal of English and American Studies*, 2.2 (1996), pp. 87–95 [88].
15. MS 11115/1/19/6. This draft of the opening scene is dated 1/2/89.
16. Quotations here are from Jennifer Johnston, Derek West and Richard Kearney, each of whom supplied views on the play in 'Too Late for Logic', *Theatre Ireland*, 21 (1989), pp. 50–6 [51, 55]: http://www.jstor.org.elib.tcd.ie/stable/25489481?seq=1#page_scan_tab_contents (accessed 3 October 2016).
17. Patrick Mason, personal email to author, 9 September 2016.
18. Jeremy Kingston, 'Too Late for Logic', *Times*, 5 October 1989.
19. MS 11115/1/19/13.
20. MS 11115/1/19/10.
21. Tom Murphy, *Too Late for Logic* (London: Methuen, 1990), p. 54.
22. Lanters, 'Schopenhauer with Hindsight', 94.
23. MS 11115/1/16/2, f. 6v.
24. Declan Kiberd, 'Theatre as Opera', in Eamonn Jordan (ed.), *Theatre Stuff: Critical Essays on Contemporary Irish Theatre* (Dublin: Carysfort Press, 2000), pp. 145–58 [152].

25. MS 11115/1/16/1.

26. Murphy had copied the lines from *Faust* in his workbook: 'Mankind has still a delicate ear / And pure words still inspire to noblest deeds.' MS 11115/1/16/1

27. The full line, spoken as Faustus first determines to pursue magic, is 'This night I'll conjure, though I die therefore', 1.1.159 [B-text], Christopher Marlowe, *Doctor Faustus*, ed. David Scott Kastan (New York, Norton: 2005).

28. Ibid, 5.1.93, 95.

29. Johann Wolfgang von Goethe, *Faust I & II*, ed. and trans. Stuart Atkins (Princeton and Oxford: Princeton University Press, 2014 [1984]), ll. 9247–50, p. 234.

30. Ibid., ll. 9905–6, p. 249.

31. Ibid., ll.12, 110–11, p. 305.

32. See Beniamino Gigli, *Memoirs*, trans. Darina Silone (London: Cassell, 1957), pp. 1, 22–6.

33. Ibid., pp. 39–41, 50–1.

34. In relation to this scene, John Devitt speaks tellingly about the heroic performance of Godfrey Quigley who created the part in 1983: John Devitt, Nicholas Grene and Chris Morash, *Shifting Scenes: Irish Theatre-Going 1955–1985* (Dublin: Carysfort Press, 2008), p. 70.

35. Richard Kearney, *The God Who May Be* (Bloomington: Indiana University Press, 2001), p. 6.

36. Quoted from Søren Kierkegaard, *The Sickness unto Death* in Ernest Becker, *The Denial of Death* (New York: Free Press, 1973), p. 74.

37. Ibid., p. 81.

38. MS 11115/1/16/1.

39. MS 11115/1/16/2, f. 1r.

40. Richard Kearney, 'Tom Murphy's Long Day's Journey into Night', in *Transitions: Narratives in Modern Irish Culture* (Manchester: Manchester University Press, 1988), p. 168.

41. There is a script of this version which was broadcast by BBC Northern Ireland in 1993 at MS 11115/1/16/19.

42. Helen Lucy Burke, 'Emperor with no clothes', *Sunday Tribune*, 24 March 1991.

43. Moriarty, 'Tom's last word on our dark forces'.

Chapter 8

1. MS 11115/4/8.

2. MS 11115/1/22/ 3. In MSS 11115/1/22, 4a, 4b, 5, one sheet of which is dated 19/9/94, we can see Murphy in the process of revising the original story as a play.

3. Peter James Harris offers a detailed analysis of the relationship between the finished *Alice* play and the Lewis Carroll books in '*Alice Trilogy*: Seen through the Looking-Glass of the London Critics', in Christopher Murray (ed.), *Alive in Time* (Dublin: Carysfort Press, 2010), pp. 189–201.

4. MS 11115/2/8/1-2.

5. MS 11115/2/8/8. Shaun Richards takes this undated outline to have been written before *Bailegangaire*, but it seems to me more probable that it was sketched after the play as an attempt to build the two earlier conceived plays into a trilogy with the *Bailegangaire* situation of Mommo's recollections as frame. See 'From *Brigit* to *Bailegangaire*: the Development of Tom Murphy's Mommo Trilogy', *Irish University Review*, 46.2 (2016), pp. 324–39. Fintan O'Toole also writes of a separate, earlier planned trilogy that would have consisted of *Brigit*, *The Challenge* and a quite separate play about a miraculous apparition of the Virgin near Tuam. Fintan O'Toole, *Tom Murphy: The Politics of Magic* (Dublin: New Island Books; London: Nick Hern Books, 1994 [1987]), p. 230. However, I have been unable to find any remaining evidence for this plan in the Murphy papers.

6. MS 11115/1/22/3.

7. https://play.google.com/music/preview/Tuuwoys52qzdec5ahhqec2 cs64u?lyrics=1&utm_source=google&utm_medium=search&utm_campaign=lyrics&pcampaignid=kp-songlyrics (accessed 22 November 2016).

8. MS 11115/1/22/3. I have been unable to locate the text which Murphy was reading here; there are notes on the animus and anima which suggest a feminist work of Jungian psychology.

9. Murphy had used a similar technique in a radio version of *Bailegangaire* broadcast by both RTÉ and BBC Northern Ireland in 1987. In this script, Mary is given an 'interior voice' which 'is not simply a train of thought or commentary; it is a quarrel going on with the self'. MS 11115/1/17/15.

10. MS 11115/1/22/ 8, p. 7.

11. This is what Caitriona, the comparably unhappy wife and mother in *The Seduction of Morality*, actually attempts (*Seduction*, 207).

12. Richards, 'From *Brigit* to *Bailegangaire*', 337. The painter was Tony O'Malley, and he was not himself the artist in the incident with the bog oak statue about which he told Murphy: personal interview with Tom Murphy, 11 November 2014.

13. In the revised theatrical form of the play, Séamus has the accent on his name unlike in earlier versions of the script.

14. O'Toole, *Tom Murphy*, p. 231.

15. MS 11115/2/8/1 contains drafts of the two screenplays.

16. Ibid.

17. Ibid.

18. Ibid.

19. MS 11115/1/17/13.

20. MS 11115/1/17/5.

21. Cathy Halloran, 'Latest Offering from Pen of Tom Murphy', *Connacht Sentinel*, 10 December 1985, quoted by Shelley Troupe, 'From Druid/Murphy to *DruidMurphy*', in Nicholas Grene and Chris Morash (eds), *Oxford Handbook of Modern Irish Theatre* (Oxford: Oxford University Press, 2016), pp. 404–21 [415].

22. See the comment by J. M. Synge, *The Aran Islands: Collected Works*, II: *Prose*, ed. Alan Price (London: Oxford University Press, 1966), p. 72.

23. I have elaborated on this comparison in *The Politics of Irish Drama* (Cambridge: Cambridge University Press, 1999), pp. 228–9.

24. Terence Patrick Dolan, *Dictionary of Hiberno-English*, 2nd edn (Dublin: Gill and Macmillan, 2006).

Chapter 9

1. This text is an edited compilation from four substantial interviews which I recorded between November 2014 and December 2015. I am most grateful to Tom Murphy for the generosity of his response.

2. Bernard O'Donoghue, 'Concordiam in Populo', *Outliving* (London: Chatto and Windus, 2003), p. 14.

3. Tom Murphy, *The Mommo Plays* (London: Bloomsbury Methuen Drama, 2014), p. 51.

4. Tom Murphy, *Plays: Two* (London: Methuen Drama, 1993), p. 228. In this essay, all quotations from *Bailegangaire* and *A Thief of a Christmas* are taken from this edition, and are cited parenthetically in the text, with a few exceptions where the most recently revised text in *The Mommo Plays* is used because of the significance of the variants introduced there.

5. Erving Goffman, *Frame Analysis: An Essay on the Organisation of Experience* (Cambridge, MA: Harvard University Press, 1974), pp. 124ff.

6. Ibid., pp. 10–11.

7. Ibid., p. 249.

8. Ibid., p. 250.

9. Lady Gregory, *Gods and Fighting Men* (Gerards Cross: Colin Smythe, 1976), p. 350.

10. See Lucy McDiarmid, *The Irish Art of Controversy* (Ithaca, NY: Cornell University Press, 2005), pp. 212–13, 226.

11. See for instance: https://www.youtube.com/watch?v=p9OFhs2wjQQ (accessed 21 October 2016). There are also contests defined by *resistance* to laughter, in which a winning contestant keeps a straight face longer.

Notes

12. Nicholas Grene, Introduction, Murphy, *Mommo Plays*, p. [ix].

13. Ibid.

14. McDiarmid, *The Irish Art of Controversy*, p. 7.

15. Nicholas Grene, *The Politics of Irish Drama* (Cambridge: Cambridge University Press, 1999), pp. 222, 227.

16. This nuance is added in the revised text, Murphy, *Mommo Plays*, 80.

17. Ibid.

18. The *Plays*, 2 text has 'The Bailegangaires gawpin' at them': in the *Mommo Plays* text this is corrected to 'the Bochtáns', no doubt because the village did not acquire its new 'appellation' until after that night.

19. Murphy, *Mommo Plays*, p. 74.

20. Ibid., p. 121.

21. Grene, *Politics of Irish Drama*, p. 219.

22. P. Murphy, '"*Hush-a-bye Baby*": An interview with Margo Harkin and Stephanie English', *Film Base News*, 16 (February to March 1990), pp. 8–10. For the connection of *Bailegangaire* with these events, see also Grene, *The Politics of Irish Drama*, p. 226.

23. Paula Meehan, 'The Statue of the Virgin at Granard Speaks', *The Man who was Marked by Winter* (Loughcrew, Co Meath: Gallery Press, 1991), pp. 40–2.

24. Ruth Barton, *Irish National Cinema* (London and New York: Routledge, 2004), p. 116.

25. Grene, *The Politics of Irish Drama*, pp. 219–41, and Nicholas Grene 'Talking, Singing, Storytelling. Tom Murphy's *After Tragedy*', *Colby Quarterly*, 27.4 (1991), pp. 210–24.

26. Shaun Richards, 'From *Brigit* to *Bailegangaire*: The Development of Tom Murphy's Mommo Trilogy', *Irish University Review*, 46.2 (2016), pp. 324–39.

27. Notable exceptions are Isabelle Famchon's 1993 French translation, Jan Hančil's 2000 Czech translation and Brazilian company Cia Ludens' 2014 adaptation of the diptych *A Thief of a Christmas/Bailegangaire* in Domingo Nunez' translation, which merged the two plays into one show set in a Brazilian context.

28. Jean-François Lyotard, 'Survivant', in *Lectures d'enfance* (Paris: Galilée, 1991). The text was initially delivered as a lecture at the Goethe Institute in 1988, in the context of a conference on Hannah Arendt's political thought. There is no published English translation, so all translations from this volume are mine, with references to the French text given parenthetically.

29. Fintan O'Toole, *Tom Murphy: The Politics of Magic* (Dublin: New Island Books; London: Nick Hern Books, 1994 [1987]), p. 242.

30. Tom Murphy, *Bailegangaire* in *The Mommo Plays* (London: Bloomsbury, 2014), p. 118. In this essay all further references from *Bailegangaire* and *A Thief of a Christmas* are to this edition and will be indicated parenthetically.

31. Hannah Arendt, *The Human Condition* (Chicago and London: University of Chicago Press, 1998 [1958]), p. 247. Though of course the words Arendt here quotes come from Isiaiah and not from the Gospels, because of Handel's *Messiah* they are so associated with the Christian revelation of the Nativity that the slip is understandable.

32. O'Toole, *The Politics of Magic*, p. 240.

33. Lyotard, 'Infantia' in *Lectures d'enfance*, p. 9.

Conclusion

1   Fintan O'Toole, *Tom Murphy: the Politics of Magic*, rev. ed. (Dublin: New Island Books; London: Nick Hern Books, 1994 [1987]), p. 19.

BIBLIOGRAPHY

Works by Murphy

After Tragedy: The Gigli Concert, Bailegangaire, Conversations on a Homecoming (London: Methuen, 1988).
Alice Trilogy (London: Methuen Drama, 2005).
Bailegangaire (Dublin: Gallery Press, 1986).
The Cherry Orchard (London: Methuen Drama, 2004).
Conversations on a Homecoming (Dublin: Gallery Press, 1986).
A Crucial Week in the Life of a Grocer's Assistant (Dublin: Gallery Press, 1978)
DruidMurphy: Conversations on a Homecoming, A Whistle in the Dark, Famine (London: Methuen Drama, 2012).
Famine (Dublin: Gallery Press, 1977).
The Fooleen (Dixon, CA: Proscenium Press, 1969).
The Gigli Concert (Dublin: Gallery Press, 1984).
The House (London: Methuen, 2000).
The Informer (Dublin: Carysfort, 2008).
The Last Days of a Reluctant Tyrant (London: Methuen Drama, 2009).
'Lullaby', in Gerald Dawe and Jonathan Williams (eds), *Krino: the Review. An Anthology of Modern Irish Writing* (Dubin: Lilliput, 1996), p. 75.
'The morning after optimism', *Irish Press*, 13 March 1971.
The Morning After Optimism (Cork: Mercier Press, 1973).
The Mommo Plays: Brigit, Bailegangaire, A Thief of a Christmas (London: Bloomsbury, 2014).
On the Outside/On the Inside (Dublin: Gallery Press, 1976).
The Orphans (Newark, Delaware: Proscenium Press, 1974).
Plays, 6 vols (London: Methuen Drama, 1992–2010).
The Sanctuary Lamp (Dublin: Poolbeg, 1976).
The Sanctuary Lamp (Dublin: Gallery Press, 1984)
The Seduction of Morality (London: Little, Brown, 1994).
She Stoops to Folly (London: Methuen Drama, 1996).
Too Late for Logic (London: Methuen, 1990).
The Wake (London: Methuen Drama, 1998).
A Whistle in the Dark and Other Plays (London: Methuen Drama, 1989).

Unpublished papers

The papers of Thomas Murphy, Trinity College Dublin Library: MS 11115.
https://manuscripts.catalogue.tcd.ie/CalmView/Record.aspx?src=CalmView.
Catalog&id=IE+TCD+MS+11115

Works on Murphy and related material

Arendt, Hannah, *The Human Condition* (Chicago and London: University of Chicago Press, 1998 [1958]).

Arrowsmith, Aidan, 'Gender, Violence and Identity in *A Whistle in the Dark*', in Christopher Murray (ed.), *'Alive in Time': The Enduring Drama of Tom Murphy* (Dublin: Carysfort, 2010), pp. 221–38.

Barton, Ruth, *Irish National Cinema* (London and New York: Routledge, 2004).

Becker, Ernest, *The Denial of Death* (New York: Free Press, 1973).

Billington, Michael, *The Life and Work of Harold Pinter* (London: Faber, 1966).

Burke, David, *Druid: The First Ten Years* (Galway : Druid Performing Arts and Galway Arts Festival , 1985).

Carleton, William, *The Black Prophet* (New York and London: Garland, 1979 [1847]).

Carty, James, *A Class-book of Irish History*, 4 vols. (London: 1929–31).

Dantanus, Ulf, *Brian Friel: A Study* (London: Faber, 1988).

Devitt, John, Nicholas Grene and Chris Morash, *Shifting Scenes: Irish Theatre-Going 1955–1985* (Dublin: Carysfort Press, 2008).

Dolan, Terence Patrick, *Dictionary of Hiberno-English*, 2nd edn (Dublin: Gill and Macmillan, 2006).

Dukore, Bernard F., '"Violent Families": A Whistle in the Dark and The Homecoming', *Twentieth Century Literature*, 36.1 (1990), pp. 23–34.

Farmar, Tony, *Ordinary Lives: Three Generations of Irish Middle Class Experience 1907, 1932, 1963* (Dublin: Gill and Macmillan, 1991).

Foster, R. F., *The Irish Story: Telling Tales and Making it Up in Ireland* (London: Allen Lane, 2001).

Friel, Brian, *Dancing at Lughnasa* (London: Faber, 1990).

Friel, Brian, 'Exiles', programme note for *The Blue Macushla*, Abbey Theatre, 1980.

Friel, Brian, *Performances* (Oldcastle: Gallery Press, 2003).

Friel, Brian, *Selected Plays* (London: Faber, 1984).

Gigli, Beniamino, *Memoirs*, trans. Darina Silone (London: Cassell, 1957).

Gleitman, Claire, 'Clever Blokes and Thick Lads: The Collapsing Tribe of Tom Murphy's *A Whistle in the Dark*', *Modern Drama*, 42.3 (1999), pp. 315–25.

Goethe, Johann Wolfgang von, *Faust I & II*, ed. and trans. Stuart Atkins (Princeton and Oxford: Princeton University Press, 2014 [1984]).

Goffman, Erving, *Frame Analysis: An Essay on the Organisation of Experience* (Cambridge, MA: Harvard University Press, 1974).

Gontarski, S.E., *The Intent of Undoing in Samuel Beckett's Dramatic Texts* (Bloomington: Indiana University Press, 1985).

Gregory, Lady, *Gods and Fighting Men* (Gerards Cross: Colin Smythe, 1976).

Grene, Nicholas, 'An Interview with Garry Hynes', *Irish University Review*, 45.1 (2015), pp. 117–25.

Grene, Nicholas, and Chris Morash (eds), *Oxford Handbook of Modern Irish Theatre* (Oxford: Oxford University Press, 2016).

Grene, Nicholas, *The Politics of Irish Drama* (Cambridge: Cambridge University Press, 1999).

Grene, Nicholas (ed.), *Talking about Tom Murphy* (Dublin: Carysfort Press, 2002).

Grene, Nicholas, 'Talking, Singing, Storytelling. Tom Murphy's *After Tragedy*', *Colby Quarterly*, 27.4 (1991), pp. 210–24.

Grene, Nicholas, 'Tom Murphy and the Children of Loss', in Shaun Richards (ed.), *Cambridge Companion to Twentieth-Century Irish Drama* (Cambridge: Cambridge University Press, 2004), pp. 204–17.

Grene, Nicholas, 'Tom Murphy: Playwright Adventurer', in W.E. Vaughan (ed.), *The Old Library Trinity College Dublin 1712–2012* (Dublin: Four Courts, 2013), pp. 377–88.

Griffin, Christopher, '"The Audacity of Despair": *The Morning After Optimism*', *Irish University Review*, 17.1 (1987), pp. 62–70.

Hanley, Brian, and Scott Millar, *The Lost Revolution: The Story of the Official IRA and the Workers' Party* (Harmondsworth: Penguin, 2009).

Harris, Peter James, '*Alice Trilogy*: Seen through the Looking-Glass of the London Critics', in Christopher Murray (ed.), *Alive in Time* (Dublin: Carysfort Press, 2010), pp. 189–201.

Healy, Gerard, *The Black Stranger* (Dublin: James Duffy, 1950).

Higgins, Roisín, *Transforming 1916* (Cork: Cork University Press, 2012).

Holland, Jack, and Henry McDonald, *INLA: Deadly Divisions* (Dublin: Torc, 1994).

Joyce, James, *Dubliners*, ed. Terence Brown (Harmondsworth: Penguin, 1992).

Kearney, Richard, *The God Who May Be* (Bloomington: Indiana University Press, 2001).

Kearney, Richard, *Transitions: Narratives in Modern Irish Culture* (Manchester: Manchester University Press, 1988).

Kelleher, Margaret, 'Irish Famine in Literature', in Cathal Póirtéir (ed.), *The Great Irish Famine* (Cork and Dublin: Mercier Press in association with Radio Telefís Éireann, 1995), pp. 232–47.

Kennedy, Patrick J. (ed.), *Intermediate Poetry* (Dublin: Gill and Sons, [1942]).

Kiberd, Declan, 'The Elephant of Revolutionary Forgetfulness', in Máirin Ni Donnchadha and Theo Dorgan (eds), *Revising the Rising* (Derry: Field Day, 1991), pp. 1–20.

Kiberd, Declan, 'Theatre as Opera', in Eamonn Jordan (ed.), *Theatre Stuff: Critical Essays on Contemporary Irish Theatre* (Dublin: Carysfort Press, 2000), pp. 145–58.

Lacan, Jacques, Jacques-Alain Miller and James Hulbert, 'Desire and the Interpretation of Desire in Hamlet', *Yale French Studies*, No. 55/56, Literature and Psychoanalysis. The Question of Reading: Otherwise (1977), pp. 11–52.

Lanters, José, 'Schopenhauer with Hindsight: Tom Murphy's *Too Late for Logic*', *Hungarian Journal of English and American Studies*, 2.2 (1996), pp. 87–95.

Lynch, Patrick, and John Vaizey, *Guinness's Brewery in the Irish Economy, 1759–1876* (Cambridge: Cambridge University Press, 1960).

Lyotard, Jean-François, *Lectures d'enfance* (Paris: Galilée, 1991).

McArdle, Kathy, '*The Blue Macushla*: Anatomy of a Failure', *Irish University Review*, 17.1 (1987), pp. 82–9.

McDiarmid, Lucy, *The Irish Art of Controversy* (Ithaca, NY: Cornell University Press, 2005).

Bibliography

McGahern, John, 'The Fifties', programme note for Abbey production of *The House*, 2000.

McGarry, Patsy, '100 died at Letterfrack school', *Irish Times*, 2 November 2002.

Marlowe, Christopher, *Doctor Faustus*, ed. David Scott Kastan (New York, Norton: 2005).

Meehan, Paula, *The Man who was Marked by Winter* (Loughcrew, Co Meath: Gallery Press, 1991).

Mercier, Vivian, 'Noisy Desperation: Murphy and the Book of Job', *Irish University Review*, 17.1 (1987), pp. 18–23.

Morash, Chris, 'Sinking Down into the Dark: The Famine on Stage', *Bullán*, 3.1 (1997), pp. 75–86.

Murphy, P., '"Hush-a-bye Baby": An Interview with Margo Harkin and Stephanie English', *Film Base News*, 16 (February to March 1990), pp. 8–10.

Murray, Christopher (ed.), *'Alive in Time': The Enduring Drama of Tom Murphy* (Dublin: Carysfort, 2010).

O'Connor, Frank, *Kings, Lords and Commons* (London: Macmillan, 1961).

O'Donoghue, Bernard, *Outliving* (London: Chatto and Windus, 2003).

Ó Gráda, Cormac, *Black '47 and Beyond: The Great Irish Famine in History, Economy and Memory* (Princeton: Princeton University Press, 1999).

O'Reilly, Bernard, *True Men As We Need Them: A Book of Instruction for Men in the World* (New York, 1888).

O'Toole, Fintan, *Tom Murphy: The Politics of Magic*, rev. edn (Dublin New Island Books; London: Nick Hern Books, 1994 [1987]).

Pilkington, Lionel, 'Response', in Nicholas Grene (ed.), *Talking about Tom Murphy* (Dublin: Carysfort, 2002), pp. 31–9.

Poulain, Alexandra, 'Fable and vision: *The Morning After Optimism* and *The Sanctuary Lamp*', in Nicholas Grene (ed.), *Talking About Tom Murphy* (Dublin: Carysfort Press, 2002), pp. 41–6.

Poulain, Alexandra, *Homo famelicus: le théâtre de Tom Murphy* (Caen: Presses Universitaires de Caen, 2008).

Poulain, Alexandra, 'Playing out the Rising: Sean O'Casey's *The Plough and the Stars* and Tom Murphy's *The Patriot Game*', *Études Anglaises*, 59.2 (2006), pp. 156–69.

Poulain, Alexandra, 'The Politics of Performance in *The Hostage* and *The Blue Macushla*', in Christopher Murray (ed.), *'Alive in Time': The Enduring Drama of Tom Murphy* (Dublin: Carysfort Press, 2010), pp. 123–36.

Pountney, Rosemary, *Theatre of Shadows: Samuel Beckett's Drama 1956–76* (Gerrards Cross: Colin Smythe; Totowa, NJ: Barnes and Noble, 1988) .

Richards, Shaun, 'From *Brigit* to *Bailegangaire*: The Development of Tom Murphy's Mommo Trilogy', *Irish University Review*, 46.2 (2016), pp. 324–39.

Roche, Anthony, *Contemporary Irish Drama*, 2nd edn (Palgrave Macmillan: Basingstoke, 2009).

Saltykov-Shchedrin, Mikhail, *The Golovlyov Family*, trans. Ronald Wilks (London: Penguin, 1988).

Share, Bernard, *Slanguage: A Dictionary of Irish Slang and Colloquial English in Ireland* (Dublin: Gill and Macmillan, 1997).

Synge, J. M., *Collected Works*, 4 vols., gen ed. Robin Skelton (London: Oxford University Press, 1962–8).

Taub, Michael, *Jack Doyle: The Gorgeous Gael* (Dublin: Lilliput, 2007 [1990]).

Troupe, Shelley, 'From Druid/Murphy to *DruidMurphy*', in Nicholas Grene and Chris Morash (eds), *Oxford Handbook of Modern Irish Theatre* (Oxford: Oxford University Press, 2016), pp. 404–21.

Tubridy, Ryan, *JFK in Ireland: Four Days that Changed a President* (London: Collins, 2010).

Walsh, Ian R., 'Directors and Designers since 1960', in Nicholas Grene and Chris Morash (eds), *Oxford Handbook of Modern Irish Theatre* (Oxford: Oxford University Press, 2016), pp. 443–58.

Walsh, Liz, *The Last Beat: Gardaí Killed in the Line of Duty* (Dublin: Gill and Macmillan, 2001).

Whelan, Gerald, with Carolyn Swift, *Spiked: Church-State Intrigue and The Rose Tattoo* (Dublin: New Island, 2002).

White, Harry, '*The Sanctuary Lamp*: An Assessment', *Irish University Review*, 17.1 (1987), pp. 71–81.

Wright, Elizabeth, 'Modern Psychoanalytic Criticism', in Ann Jefferson, David Robey and David Forgacs (eds), *Modern Literary Theory: A Comparative Introduction* (London: Batsford, 1982).

Yeats, W. B., *Poems*, ed. Daniel Albright, rev. edn (London: Everyman, 1994)

Theatre reviews and interviews

Backalenich, Irene, '"Conversations" bespeaks sharp realism, richness with a "seedy, lived-in" set', *The Advocate*, 26 July 1986.

B[arber], J[ohn], 'Regression into jaded whimsy', *Daily Telegraph*, 16 March 1971.

Barber, John, 'Comic portrait of vegetating lives', *Daily Telegraph*, 21 March 1972.

Barker, Felix, 'It's the noisiest show in town', [*Evening News*, September 1961].

Barnes, Mick, 'A festival night of pure Irish magic', *Sun Herald*, 11 January 1987.

Billington, Michael, 'Too Late for Logic', *Guardian*, 16 August 2001.

Boland, John, 'Back to Broad Strokes', *Hibernia*, 6 March 1980.

Brennan, Brian, 'Late Great Logic', *Sunday Independent*, 8 October 1989.

Brien, Alan, 'The Adman Cometh', *Sunday Telegraph*, [October 1961].

Brogan, Treasa, 'Entranced and impressed by The Patriot Game', *Evening Press*, 16 May 1991.

Burke, Helen Lucy, 'Emperor with no clothes', *Sunday Tribune*, 24 March 1991.

Burke, Helen Lucy, 'Murphy a clear winner in the 1916 Memorial Stakes', *Sunday Tribune*, 19 May 1991.

Caplan, Leslie, '"The White House" at Dublin Theatre Festival', *The Stage*, 30 March 1972.

Carty, Ciaran, 'Getting out of his own sex', *Sunday Independent*, 14 April 1985.

Cole, Gloria, 'Irish Playwright Tells his Own Story', *Fairpress*, 17 March 1976.

Coveney, Michael, *Observer*, 10 October 1993.

Bibliography

Coveney, Michael, 'Chekhov's Irish Charm', *Daily Mail*, 21 April 2000.

Cronin, Colm, 'B Movie Cutouts', *Hibernia*, 13 March 1980.

Darlington, W. A., 'Play Ends as Scrimmage', *Daily Telegraph*, [September 1961]

Deane, Raymond, 'The Tyranny of the Idealised Self', *In Dublin*, 23 September 1983.

Doolan, Matt J., 'An insult to the Mass', *Irish Independent*, 15 October 1975.

Dowling, Noreen, 'A new play of immense power', *Cork Examiner*, 17 March 1971.

Dziemianowicz, Joe, 'DruidMurphy puts three plays by Irish writer Tom Murphy at center stage', *Daily News*, 10 July 2012.

F[inegan], J. J., *Evening Herald*, 13 March 1962.

Finegan, John, 'Abbey joke is too long', *Evening Herald*, 7 March 1980.

Finegan, John, 'Revived play a winner', *Evening Herald*, 2 September 1988.

G. S., '"Whistle in Dark" is Bound for Great White Way', *Sunday Independent*, 11 March 1962.

Gillespie, Elgy, interview with Tom Murphy, *Irish Times*, 8 March 1980.

Gorman, Sophie, 'Ovation as old ground given new depth', *Irish Independent*, 13 April 2000.

Gussow, Mel, '"Morning After" Set in Irish Whimsy', *New York Times*, 28 June 1974.

Gussow, Mel, 'Stage: "Homecoming": from Ireland', *New York Times*, 29 July 1986.

Hopkin, Alannah, 'The Dublin Theatre Festival', *Financial Times*, 9 October 1993.

Hutchison, Pearse, 'Murphy's best play to date', *Irish Press*, 16 March 1971.

Isherwood, Charles, 'Raw Wit of the Irish Soul, Fed by Hope and Fear', *New York Times*, 10 July 2012.

Johnston, Jennifer, Derek West and Richard Kearney, 'Too Late for Logic', *Theatre Ireland*, 21 (1989), pp. 50–6.

Kelly, Henry, 'Applause for Play by Thomas Murphy', *Irish Times*, 22 March 1968.

Kelly, Seamus, 'New Tom Murphy Play at Pavilion', *Irish Times*, 10 November 1976.

Kilroy, Ian, 'Epistle in the Dark', *Magill*, May 2000.

Kingston, Jeremy, 'Too Late for Logic', *Times*, 5 October 1989.

Kurdi, Mária, 'An Interview with Tom Murphy', *Irish Studies Review*, 12.2 (2004), pp. 223–40.

Lahr, John, 'On-stage', *Village Voice*, 13 November 1969.

M. O'S., 'Violence is my Villain', *Evening Press*, 10 March 1962.

McDonald, Marianne, 'Thomas Murphy's Interview', in *Ancient Sun, Modern Light* (New York: Columbia University Press, 1992), pp. 187–200.

McGarry, Patsy, 'Lively, theatrical and declamatory visions of 1916', *Irish Press*, 16 May 1991.

McMillan, Joyce, '*Pax/The Patriot Game*', *Guardian*, 24 September 1991.

Moriarty, Gerry, 'Tom's last word on our dark forces', *Irish Press*, 7 October 1989.

Moroney, Mic, 'Beneath the surface', *Guardian*, 18 April 2000.

Murphy, Tom, 'In Conversation with Michael Billington', in Nicholas Grene (ed.), *Talking about Tom Murphy* (Dublin: Carysfort Press, 2002), pp. 91–112.

Murphy, Tom, Television interview with Declan Kiberd, 11 November 1985, http://www.rte.ie/archives/2015/1110/740797-tom-murphy-and-druid/.

Nowlan, David, 'Impressive Revival at Abbey', *Irish Times*, 15 July 1971.

Nowlan, David, '"Morning After Optimism" at the Abbey', *Irish Times*, 16 March 1971.

Nowlan, David, 'Small-town Ireland is theme of Abbey play', *Irish Times*, 21 March 1972.

Nowlan, David, 'Theatre Festival First Nights: The Blue Macushla at the Mansion House', *Irish Times*, 28 September 1983.

Nowlan, David, 'Tom Murphy's "The Sanctuary Lamp" at the Abbey', *Irish Times*, 8 October 1975.

Nowlan, David, '"A Whistle in the Dark" at the Abbey', *Irish Times*, 7 October 1986.

O'Connor, Garry, 'The White House', *Financial Times*, 23 March 1972.

O'Connor, Kevin, on 'Morning Ireland', RTÉ, Radio 1, 7 October 1986.

O'Farrell, Maureen, 'Great Theatre! A great play?', *Evening Press*, 16 March 1971.

O'Farrell, Maureen, 'A Play of Truth and Laughter', *Evening Press*, 11 November 1969.

O'Kelly, Emer, 'A house of destruction and decay', *Sunday Independent*, 16 April 2000.

O'Toole, Fintan, 'Down among the gombeens', *Sunday Tribune*, 21 April 1985.

O'Toole, Fintan, 'The house that Tom built', *Irish Times*, 12 April 2000.

O'Toole, Fintan, 'The Old Woman's Brood', *Sunday Tribune*, 8 December 1985.

O'Toole, Fintan, 'The Playboy meets Gary Cooper', *Sunday Tribune*, 5 January 1986.

O'Toole, Fintan, 'Second Opinion: Down to Zero', *Irish Times*, 9 October 1993.

Page, Sean, 'A triumph at the Peacock', *Sunday Press*, 24 March 1968.

Peter, John, *Sunday Times*, 10 October 1993.

Phelan, Seamus, 'Druid production of Murphy play acclaimed in Sydney', *Irish Times*, 9 January 1987.

Purcell, Deirdre, 'Into the Dark', *Sunday Tribune*, 19 October 1986.

Roche, Anthony, 'Thomas Murphy: An Irish Playwright Stretches Out', *Santa Barbara News and Reviews*, 23 April 1980.

Ross, Michael, 'An Interview with Tom Murphy', *St Stephens*, 4.1 (December 1986).

Rushe, Desmond, 'Delicious if grim comedy', *Irish Independent*, 15 March 1971.

Rushe, Desmond, 'Flashes of talent in a bleak wasteland', *Irish Independent*, 8 October 1975.

Rushe, Desmond, 'Profound Approach in New Famine Play', *Irish Independent*, 27 March 1968.

Sheridan, Michael, '"Homecoming" triumph for Galway's Druid', *Irish Press*, 18 April 1985.

Sheridan, Michael, 'Murphy play lost in mid-Atlantic', *Irish Press*, 7 March 1980.

Sheridan, Michael, 'Red light area in Sanctuary', *Irish Press*, 8 October 1975.

Shulman, Milton, 'Not exactly a great night for the Irish', *Evening Standard*, [September 1961].

Smith, Gus, 'Abbey Fantasy', *Sunday Independent*, 21 March 1971.

Smith, Gus, 'Murphy: "I'll be back"', *Sunday Independent*, 3 March 1963.

Smith, Gus, 'Tom Murphy rocks "cradle of genius"', *Sunday Independent*, 12 October 1975.

Taylor, Paul, 'Famine', *The Independent*, 9 October 1993.

Bibliography

Tóibín, Colm, 'Interview with Tom Murphy', *BOMB*, 120 (Summer 2012).

Tóibín, Colm, 'Murphy's dark vision', *Sunday Independent*, 5 January 1986.

Tóibín, Colm, 'Murphy's Logic', *Sunday Independent*, 8 October 1989.

'Tom Murphy Talking', *Education Times*, 27 November 1975.

'Tuam group takes top awards', *Irish Independent*, 14 March 1977.

Walsh, Enda, 'In Conversation: Joe Dowling and Enda Walsh', https://www.youtube.com/watch?v=BCJdK-U1Q-4&list=RDBCJdK-U1Q-4#t=86.

Waters, John, 'Wounded Lion: Tom Murphy's Archaeology of Darkness', *Magill*, September 1988.

NOTES ON CONTRIBUTORS

Lucy McDiarmid is Marie Frazee-Baldassarre Professor of English at Montclair State University. The recipient of fellowships from the Guggenheim Foundation, the Cullman Center for Scholars and Writers at the New York Public Library, and the National Endowment for the Humanities, she is the author or editor of eight books. Her scholarly interest in cultural politics, especially quirky, colourful, suggestive episodes, is exemplified by *Poets and the Peacock Dinner* (2014; paperback 2016) as well as by *The Irish Art of Controversy* (2005). She is also a former president of the American Conference for Irish Studies. Her most recent book, *At Home in the Revolution: what women said and did in 1916*, was Foreword Reviews' 2015 Indiefab bronze winner for the history book of the year. Her current project is a book on twenty-first-century Irish poetry.

Alexandra Poulain is Professor of Postcolonial Literature and Theatre at the University of Paris 3 – Sorbonne Nouvelle. She is the author of *Homo famelicus: le théâtre de Tom Murphy* (2008) and Endgame *ou le théâtre mis en pièces* (2009, co-authored with Elisabeth Angel-Perez). She has edited and co-edited several volumes on theatre, including *Hunger on the Stage* (2007, with Elisabeth Angel-Perez), *Passions du corps dans les dramaturgies contemporaines* (2010), *Tombeau pour Samuel Beckett* (2015, with Elisabeth Angel-Perez), a special issue on W. B. Yeats of *Études anglaises* (68-4: 2015) and *Animals on the Stage* (*Sillages critiques* 20: 2016, with Elisabeth Angel-Perez) and has published extensively on modern Irish theatre from the Irish Literary Revival to the present day. Her new book *Irish Drama, Modernity and the Passion Play* (2017) looks at rewritings of the Passion narrative as a modality of political resistance in Irish plays from Synge to the present day.

INDEX

Index

Index

Index

Index